GW00739010

Meg Cabot is the autho[...]ful *The Princess Diaries*[...] copies sold around the [...] the US and UK best-s[...] won several awards. Two movies based on the series have been massively popular throughout the world.

Meg is also the author of the best-selling *All American Girl, Teen Idol, Nicola and the Viscount, Victoria and the Rogue* and *The Mediator* series as well as several other books for teenagers and adults. She lives in Florida with her husband and one-eyed cat, Henrietta, and says she is still waiting for her real parents, the king and queen, to restore her to her rightful throne.

Visit Meg Cabot's website at www.megcabot.co.uk

Also by Meg Cabot

The Princess Diaries
The Princess Diaries: Take Two
The Princess Diaries: Third Time Lucky
The Princess Diaries: Mia Goes Fourth
The Princess Diaries: Give Me Five
The Princess Diaries: Sixsational

The Princess Diaries Guide to Life
The Princess Diaries Princess Files
The Princess Diaries Guide to Christmas

All American Girl
All American Girl: Ready or Not

Teen Idol

Nicola and the Viscount
Victoria and the Rogue

The Mediator: Love You to Death
The Mediator: High Stakes
The Mediator: Mean Spirits
The Mediator: Young Blood
The Mediator: Grave Doubts

Look out for

The Princess Diaries: Seventh Heaven
The Mediator: Heaven Sent
Avalon High

For older readers

The Guy Next Door
Boy Meets Girl
Every Boy's Got One

The PRINCESS DIARIES

Books 1 & 2

Meg Cabot

MACMILLAN

First published 2000 as *The Princess Diaries* and *The Princess Diaries: Take Two*
by HarperCollins Children's Books, USA

This edition published 2005 by Macmillan Children's Books
a division of Macmillan Publishers Limited
20 New Wharf Road, London N1 9RR
Basingstoke and Oxford
www.panmacmillan.com

Associated companies throughout the world

ISBN 0 330 44018 7

1 3 5 7 9 8 6 4 2

A CIP catalogue record for this book is available from
the British Library.

Typeset by Intype Libra Ltd
Printed and bound in Great Britain by Mackays of Chatham plc, Chatham, Kent

The author wishes to express her gratitude to the people who contributed in so many ways to the creation and publication of these books: Beth Ader, Jennifer Brown, Barbara Cabot, Sarah Davies, Laura Langlie, Abigail McAden, David Walton and, most especially, Benjamin Egnatz.

The
PRINCESS
DIARIES

'Whatever comes,' she said, 'cannot alter one thing. If I am a princess in rags and tatters, I can be a princess inside. It would be easy to be a princess if I were dressed in cloth of gold, but it is a great deal more of a triumph to be one all the time when no one knows it.'

A Little Princess
Frances Hodgson Burnett

Tuesday, September 23

Sometimes it seems like all I ever do is lie.

My mom thinks I'm repressing my feelings about this. I say to her, 'No, Mom, I'm not. I think it's really neat. As long as you're happy, I'm happy.'

Mom says, 'I don't think you're being honest with me.'

Then she hands me this book. She tells me she wants me to write down my feelings in this book, since, she says, I obviously don't feel I can talk about them with her.

She wants me to write down my feelings? OK, I'll write down my feelings:

I CAN'T BELIEVE SHE'S DOING THIS TO ME!

Like everybody doesn't *already* think I'm a freak. I'm practically the biggest freak in the entire school. I mean, let's face it: I'm five foot nine, flat-chested, and a freshman. How much *more* of a freak could I be?

If people at school find out about this, I'm dead. That's it. Dead.

Oh, God, if you really do exist, please don't let them find out about this.

There are four million people in Manhattan, right? That makes about two million of them guys. So out of TWO MILLION guys, she has to go out with Mr Gianini. She can't go out with some guy I don't know. She can't go out with some guy she met at D'Agostino's or wherever. Oh, no.

She has to go out with my Algebra teacher.

Thanks, Mom. Thanks a whole lot.

Wednesday, September 24, Fifth Period

Lilly's like, 'Mr Gianini's cool.'

Yeah, right. He's cool if you're Lilly Moscovitz. He's cool if you're good at Algebra, like Lilly Moscovitz. He's not so cool if you're flunking Algebra, like me.

He's not so cool if he makes you stay after school EVERY SINGLE SOLITARY DAY from 2:30 to 3:30 to practise the FOIL method when you could be hanging out with all your friends. He's not so cool if he calls your mother in for a parent/teacher conference to talk about how you're flunking Algebra, then ASKS HER OUT.

And he's not so cool if he's sticking his tongue in your mom's mouth.

Not that I've actually seen them do this. They haven't even been on their first date yet. And I don't think my mom would let a guy put his tongue in her mouth on the first date.

At least, I hope not.

I saw Josh Richter stick his tongue in Lana Weinberger's mouth last week. I had this totally close-up view of it, since they were leaning up against Josh's locker, which is right next to mine. It kind of grossed me out.

Though I can't say I'd mind if Josh Richter kissed *me* like that. The other day Lilly and I were at Bigelow's picking up some alpha hydroxy for Lilly's mom, and I noticed Josh waiting at the check-out counter. He saw me and he actually sort of smiled and said, 'Hey.'

He was buying Drakkar Noir, a men's cologne. I got a free sample of it from the salesgirl. Now I can smell Josh whenever I want to, in the privacy of my own home.

Lilly says Josh's synapses were probably misfiring that day, due to heatstroke or something. She said he probably thought I looked familiar, but couldn't place my face without the cement block walls of Albert Einstein High behind me. Why else, she asked, would the most popular senior in high school say hey to me, Mia Thermopolis, a lowly freshman?

But I know it wasn't heatstroke. The truth is, when he's away from Lana and all his jock friends, Josh is a totally different person. The kind of person who doesn't care if a girl is flat-chested or wears size eight shoes. The kind of person who can see beyond all that, into the depths of a girl's soul. I know because when I looked into his eyes that day at Bigelow's, I saw the deeply sensitive person inside him, struggling to get out.

Lilly says I have an overactive imagination and a pathological need to invent drama in my life. She says the fact that I'm so upset about my mom and Mr G is a classic example.

'If you're that upset about it, just *tell* your mom,' Lilly says. '*Tell* her you don't want her going out with him. I don't understand you, Mia. You're always going around, lying about how you feel. Why don't you just assert yourself for a change? Your feelings have worth, you know.'

Oh, right. Like I'm going to bum my mom out like that. She's so totally happy about this date, it's enough to make me want to throw up. She goes around *cooking* all the time. I'm not even kidding. She made pasta for the first time last night in, like, months. I had already opened the Suzie's Chinese take-out menu, and she says, 'Oh, no cold sesame noodles tonight, honey. I made pasta.'

Pasta! My mom made *pasta*!

She even observed my rights as a vegetarian and didn't put any meatballs in the sauce.

I don't understand any of this.

Things To Do:

1. Buy cat litter.
2. Finish FOIL worksheet for Mr G.
3. Stop telling Lilly everything.
4. Go to Pearl Paint: get soft lead pencils, spray mount, canvas stretchers (for Mom).
5. World Civ. report on Iceland (5 pages, double space).
6. Stop thinking so much about Josh Richter.
7. Drop off laundry.
8. October rent (make sure Mom has deposited Dad's cheque!!!).
9. Be more assertive.
10. Measure chest.

Thursday, September 25

In Algebra today all I could think about was how Mr Gianini might put his tongue in my mom's mouth tomorrow night during their date. I just sat there, staring at him. He asked me a really easy question – I swear, he saves all the easy ones for me, like he doesn't want me to feel left out, or something – and I totally didn't even hear it. I was like, 'What?'

Then Lana Weinberger made that sound she always makes and leaned over to me so that all her blonde hair swished onto my desk. I got hit by this giant wave of perfume, and then Lana hissed in this really mean voice:

'FREAK.'

Only she said it like it had more than one syllable. Like it was spelled FUR-REEK.

How come nice people like Princess Diana get killed in car wrecks, but mean people like Lana never do? I don't understand what Josh Richter sees in her. I mean, yeah, she's pretty. But she's so *mean*. Doesn't he *notice*?

Maybe Lana is nice to Josh, though. *I'd* sure be nice to Josh. He is totally the best-looking boy in Albert Einstein High School. A lot of the boys look totally geeky in our school's uniform, which for boys is grey trousers, white shirt, and black sweater, long-sleeved or vest. Not Josh, though. He looks like a model in his uniform. I am not kidding.

Anyway. Today I noticed that Mr Gianini's nostrils stick out A LOT. Why would you want to go out with a guy whose nostrils stick out so much? I asked Lilly this at lunch and she said, 'I've never noticed his nostrils before. Are you gonna eat that dumpling?'

Lilly says I need to stop obsessing. She says I'm taking my anxiety over the fact that this is only our first month in high school and I already have an F in something, and

5

transferring it to anxiety about Mr Gianini and my mom. She says this is called displacement.

It sort of sucks when your best friend's parents are psychoanalysts.

Today after school the Drs Moscovitz were totally trying to analyse me. I mean, Lilly and I were just sitting there playing Boggle. And every five minutes it was like, 'Girls, do you want some Snapple? Girls, there's a very interesting squid documentary on the Discovery channel. And by the way, Mia, how do you feel about your mother starting to date your Algebra teacher?'

I said, 'I feel fine about it.'

Why can't I be more assertive?

But what if Lilly's parents run into my mom at Jefferson Market, or something? If I told them the truth, they'd *definitely* tell her. I don't want my mom to know how weird I feel about this, not when she's so happy about it.

The worst part was that Lilly's older brother Michael overheard the whole thing. He immediately started laughing his head off, even though I don't see anything funny about it.

He went, '*Your* mom is dating Frank Gianini? Ha! Ha! Ha!'

So great. Now Lilly's brother Michael knows.

So then I had to start begging him not to tell anybody. He's in 5th period Gifted and Talented class with me and Lilly, which is the biggest joke of a class, because Mrs Hill, who's in charge of the G & T programme at Albert Einstein's, doesn't care what we do, as long as we don't make too much noise. She hates it when she has to come out of the teachers' lounge, which is right across the hall from the G & T room, to yell at us.

Anyway, Michael is supposed to use 5th period to work on his online webzine, *Crackhead*. I'm supposed to use it for catching up on my Algebra homework.

6

But anyway, Mrs Hill never checks to see what we're doing in G & T, which is probably good, since mostly what we're all doing is figuring out ways to lock the new Russian kid, who's supposedly this musical genius, in the supply closet, so we don't have to listen to any more Stravinsky on his stupid violin.

But don't think that just because Michael and I are united in our front against Boris Pelkowski and his violin that he'd keep quiet about my mom and Mr G.

What Michael kept saying was, 'What'll you do for me, huh, Thermopolis? What'll you do for me?'

But there's nothing I can do for Michael Moscovitz. I can't offer to do his homework, or anything. Michael is a senior (just like Josh Richter). Michael has gotten all straight A's his entire life (just like Josh Richter). Michael will probably go to Yale or Harvard next year (just like Josh Richter).

What could *I* do for someone like that?

Not that Michael's perfect, or anything. Unlike Josh Richter, Michael is not on the crew team. Michael isn't even on the debate team. Michael does not believe in organized sports, or organized religion, or organized anything, for that matter. Instead, Michael spends almost all of his time in his room. I once asked Lilly what he does in there, and she said she and her parents employ a 'don't ask, don't tell' policy with Michael: They won't ask if he won't tell.

I bet he's in there making a bomb. Maybe he'll blow up Albert Einstein High School as a senior prank.

Occasionally Michael comes out of his room and makes sarcastic comments. Sometimes when he does this he is not wearing a shirt. Even though he does not believe in organized sports, I have noticed that Michael has a really nice chest. His stomach muscles are extremely well-defined.

I have never mentioned this to Lilly.

Anyway, I guess Michael got tired of me offering to do stuff like walk his sheltie, Pavlov, and take his mom's empty Tab cans back to Gristedes for the deposit money, which is his weekly chore. Because in the end, Michael just said, in this disgusted voice, 'Forget it, OK, Thermopolis?' and went back into his room.

I asked Lilly why he was so mad, and she said because he'd been sexually harassing me, but I didn't notice.

How embarrassing! Supposing Josh Richter starts sexually harassing me some day (I wish) and I don't notice? God, I'm so stupid sometimes.

Anyway, Lilly said not to worry about Michael telling his friends at school about my mom and Mr G, since Michael has no friends. Then Lilly wanted to know why I cared about Mr Gianini's nostrils sticking out so much, since I'm not the one who has to look at them, my mom is.

And I said, Excuse me, I have to look at them from 9:55 to 10:55 and from 2:30 to 3:30 EVERY SINGLE DAY, except Saturdays and Sundays and national holidays and the summer. If I don't flunk, that is, and have to go to summer school.

And if they get married, then I'll have to look at them EVERY SINGLE DAY, SEVEN DAYS A WEEK, MAJOR HOLIDAYS INCLUDED.

Define set: collection of objects element or member; belongs to a set

A = (Gilligan, Skipper, Mary Ann)
rule specifies each element

A = (x:x is one of the castaways on Gilligan's Island)

8

Friday, September 26

Lilly Moscovitz's List of Hottest Guys

(compiled during World Civ., with commentary by Mia Thermopolis)

1. *Josh Richter* (agree – six feet of unadulterated hotness. Blond hair, often falling into his clear blue eyes, and that sweet, sleepy smile. Only drawback: he has the bad taste to date Lana Weinberger.)
2. *Boris Pelkowski* (strongly disagree. Just because he played his stupid violin at Carnegie Hall when he was twelve does not make him hot. Plus he tucks his school sweater into his trousers, instead of wearing it out, like a normal person.)
3. *Pierce Brosnan, best James Bond ever* (disagree – I liked Timothy Dalton better.)
4. *Daniel Day Lewis in* Last of the Mohicans (agree – Stay alive, no matter what occurs.)
5. *Prince William of England* (duh)
6. *Leonardo in* Titanic (As if! That is so 1998.)
7. *Mr Wheeton, the crew coach* (hot, but taken. Seen opening the door to the teachers' lounge for Mademoiselle Klein.)
8. *That guy in that jeans ad on that giant billboard in Times Square* (totally agree. Who IS that guy? They should give him his own TV series.)
9. *Dr Quinn, Medicine Woman's boyfriend* (whatever happened to him? He was hot!)
10. *Joshua Bell, the violinist* (totally agree. It would be so cool to date a musician – just not Boris Pelkowski.)

Later on Friday

I was measuring my chest and totally not thinking about the fact that my mom was out with my Algebra teacher when my dad called. I don't know why, but I lied and told him Mom was at her studio. Which is so weird, because obviously, Dad knows Mom dates. But for some reason, I just couldn't tell him about Mr Gianini.

This afternoon during my mandatory review session with Mr Gianini I was sitting there practising the FOIL method (first, outside, inside, last; first, outside, inside, last – Oh my God, when am I ever going to have to actually use the FOIL method in real life? WHEN???) and all of a sudden Mr Gianini said, 'Mia, I hope you don't feel, well, uncomfortable about my seeing your mother socially.'

Only for some reason for a second I thought he said SEXUALLY, not socially. And then I could feel my face getting totally hot. I mean like BURNING. And I said, 'Oh, no, Mr Gianini, it doesn't bother me at all.'

And Mr Gianini said, 'Because if it bothers you, we can talk about it.'

I guess he must have figured out I was lying, since my face was so red.

But all I said was, 'Really, it doesn't bother me. I mean, it bothers me a LITTLE, but really, I'm fine with it. I mean, it's just a date, right? Why get upset about one measly date?'

That was when Mr Gianini said, 'Well, Mia, I don't know if it's going to be one measly date. I really like your mother.'

And then, I don't even know how, but all of a sudden I heard myself saying, 'Well, you better. Because if you do anything to make her cry, I'll kick your butt.'

Oh my God! I can't even believe I said the word butt to a teacher! My face got even REDDER after that, which I wouldn't have thought possible. Why is it that the only time I can tell the truth is when it's guaranteed to get me into trouble?

But I guess I *am* feeling sort of weird about the whole thing. Maybe Lilly's parents were right.

Mr Gianini, though, was totally cool. He smiled in this funny way and said, 'I have no intention of making your mother cry, but if I ever do, you have my permission to kick my butt.'

So that was OK, sort of.

Anyway, Dad sounded really weird on the phone. But then again, he always does. Transatlantic phone calls suck because I can hear the ocean swishing around in the background and it makes me all nervous, like the fish are listening, or something. Plus Dad didn't even want to talk to me. He wanted to talk to Mom. I suppose somebody died, and he wants Mom to break it to me gently.

Maybe it was Grandmere. Hmmm . . .

My breasts have grown exactly *none* since last summer. Mom was totally wrong. I did *not* have a growth spurt when I turned fourteen, like she did. I will probably *never* have a growth spurt, at least not on my chest. I only have growth spurts UP, not OUT. I am now the tallest girl in my class.

Now if anybody asks me to the Cultural Diversity Dance next month (yeah, right) I won't be able to wear a strapless dress, because there isn't anything on my chest to hold it up.

Saturday, September 27

I was asleep when my mom got home from her date last night (I stayed up as late as I could, because I wanted to know what happened, but I guess all that measuring wore me out), so I didn't get to ask her how it went until this morning when I went out into the kitchen to feed Fat Louie. Mom was up already, which was weird, because usually she sleeps later than me, and *I'm* a teenager, *I'm* supposed to be the one sleeping all the time.

But Mom's been depressed ever since her last boyfriend turned out to be a Republican.

Anyway, she was in there, humming in a happy way and making pancakes. I nearly died of shock to see her actually cooking something so early in the morning, let alone something vegetarian.

Of course she had a fabulous time. They went to dinner at Monte's (not too shabby, Mr G!) and then walked around the West Village and went to some bar and sat outside in the back garden until nearly two in the morning, just talking. I kind of tried to find out if there'd been any kissing, particularly of the tongue-in-mouth variety, but my mom just smiled and looked all embarrassed.

OK. Gross.

They're going out again this week.

I guess I don't mind, if it makes her this happy.

Today Lilly is shooting a spoof of the movie *The Blair Witch Project* for her TV show, *Lilly Tells It Like It Is*. *The Blair Witch Project* is about some kids who go out into the woods to find a witch, and end up disappearing. All that's found of them is film footage and some piles of sticks. Only instead of *The Blair Witch Project*, Lilly's version is called *The Green Witch Project*. Lilly intends to take a hand-held camera down to

Washington Square Park and film the tourists who come up to us and ask if we know how to get to Green Witch Village (it's actually Greenwich Village – you're not supposed to pronounce the *w* in Greenwich. But people from out of town always say it wrong).

Anyway, as tourists come up and ask us which way to Green Witch Village, we are supposed to start screaming and run away in terror. All that will be left of us by the end, Lilly says, is a little pile of Metrocards. Lilly says after the show is aired, no one will ever think of Metrocards the same way.

I said it was too bad we don't have a real witch. I thought we could get Lana Weinberger to play her, but Lilly said that would be typecasting. Plus then we'd have to put up with Lana all day, and nobody would want that. Like she'd even show up, considering how she thinks we're the most unpopular girls in the whole school. She probably wouldn't want to tarnish her reputation by being seen with us.

Then again, she's so vain, she'd probably jump at the chance to be on TV, even if it *is* only a public access channel.

After filming was over for the day, we saw the Blind Guy crossing Bleecker. He had a new victim, this totally innocent German tourist who had no idea that the nice blind man she was helping to cross the street was going to feel her up as soon as they got to the other side, then pretend like he hadn't done it on purpose.

Just my luck, the only guy who's ever felt me up (not that there's anything to feel) was BLIND.

Lilly says she's going to report the Blind Guy to the 6th Precinct. Like they would care. They've got more important things to worry about. Like catching murderers.

13

Things To Do:

1. Get cat litter.
2. Make sure Mom sent out rent cheque.
3. Stop lying.
4. Proposal for English paper.
5. Pick up laundry.
6. Stop thinking about Josh Richter.

Sunday, September 28

My dad called again today, and this time, Mom really *was* at her studio, so I didn't feel so bad about lying last night, and not telling him about Mr Gianini. He sounded all weird on the phone again so finally I was like, 'Dad, is Grandmere dead?' and he got all startled and said, 'No, Mia, why would you think that?'

And I told him it was because he sounded so weird, and he was all, 'I don't sound weird,' which was a lie, because he DID sound weird. But I decided to let it drop and I talked to him about Iceland, because we're studying Iceland in World Civ. Iceland has the world's highest literacy rate, because there's nothing to do there but read. They also have these natural hot springs, and everybody goes swimming in them. Once, the opera came to Iceland, and every show was sold out and something like 98 per cent of the population attended. Everybody knew all the words to the opera and went around singing it all day.

I would like to live in Iceland some day. It sounds like a fun place. Much more fun than Manhattan, where people sometimes spit at you for no reason.

But Dad didn't seem all that impressed by Iceland. I suppose by comparison, Iceland does make every other country look sucky. The country Dad lives in is pretty small, though. I would think if the opera went there, about 80 per cent of the population would attend, which would certainly be something to be proud of.

I only shared this information with him because he is a politician, and I thought it might give him some ideas about how to make things better in Genovia, where he lives. But I guess Genovia doesn't need to be better. Genovia's number one import is tourists. I know this because I had to do a fact sheet on every country in Europe in the seventh grade, and Genovia was right up there with Disneyland as far as income from the tourist trade is concerned. That's probably why people in Genovia don't have to pay taxes: the government already has enough money. This is called a principality. The only other one is Monaco. My dad says we have a lot of cousins in Monaco, but so far I haven't met any of them, not even at Grandmere's.

I suggested to Dad that next summer, instead of spending it with him and Grandmere at Grandmere's chateau in France, we go to Iceland. We'd have to leave Grandmere at Miragnac, of course. She'd hate Iceland. She hates any place where you can't order up a decent Sidecar, which is her favourite drink, twenty-four hours a day.

All Dad said was, 'We'll talk about that some other time,' and hung up.

Mom is so right about him.

Absolute value: the distance that a given number is from zero on a number line . . . always a positive

Monday, September 29, G & T

Today I watched Mr Gianini very closely for signs that he might not have had as good a time on his date with my mom as my mom did. He seemed to be in a really good mood, though. During class, while we were working on the quadratic formula (what happened to FOIL? I was just starting to get the hang of it, and all of a sudden there's some NEW thing: No *wonder* I'm flunking), he asked if anybody had gone out for a part in the fall musical, *My Fair Lady*.

Then later he said, in the way he does when he gets excited about something, 'You know who would be a good Eliza Dolittle? Mia, I think you would.'

I thought I would totally die. I know Mr Gianini was only trying to be nice – I mean, he is dating my mom, after all – but he was SO far off: first of all, because of course they already held auditions, and even if I could've gone out for a part (which I couldn't, because I'm flunking Algebra, hello, Mr Gianini, remember?) I NEVER would've gotten one, let alone the LEAD. I can't sing. I can barely even *talk*.

Even Lana Weinberger, who always got the lead in junior high, didn't get the lead. It went to some senior girl. Lana plays a maid, a spectator at the Ascot Races, and a Cockney hooker. Lilly is House Manager. Her job is to flick the lights on and off at the end of intermission.

I was so freaked out by what Mr Gianini said, I couldn't even *say* anything. I just sat there and felt myself turning all red. Maybe that was why later, when Lilly and I went by my locker at lunch, Lana, who was there waiting for Josh, was all, 'Oh, hello, *Amelia*,' in her snottiest voice, even though nobody has called me Amelia (except Grandmere) since kindergarten, when I asked everybody not to.

Then, as I bent over to get my money out of my

17

backpack, Lana must have got a good look down my blouse, because all of a sudden she goes, 'Oh, how sweet. I see we still can't fit into a bra. Might I suggest Band-Aids?'

I would have hauled off and slugged her – well, probably not: the Drs Moscovitz say I have issues about confrontation – if Josh Richter hadn't walked up AT THAT VERY MOMENT. I knew he totally heard, but all he said was, 'Can I get by here?' to Lilly, since she was blocking his path to his locker.

I was ready to go slinking down to the cafeteria and forget the whole thing – God, that's all I need, my lack of chest pointed out *right in front* of Josh Richter! – but Lilly couldn't leave well enough alone. She got all red in the face and said to Lana, 'Why don't you do us all a favour and go curl up some place and die, Weinberger?'

Well, nobody tells Lana Weinberger to go curl up some place and die. I mean, nobody. Not if they don't want their name written up all over the walls of the Girls' Room. Not that this would be such a heinous thing – I mean, no boys are going to see it in the Girls' Room – but I sort of like keeping my name off walls, for the most part.

But Lilly doesn't care about things like that. I mean, she's short and sort of round and kind of resembles a pug, but she totally doesn't care how she looks. I mean, she has her own TV show, and guys call in all the time and say how ugly they think she is, and ask her to lift her shirt up (*she* isn't flat-chested. She wears a C-cup already) and she just laughs and laughs.

Lilly isn't afraid of anything.

So when Lana Weinberger started in on her for telling her to curl up and die, Lilly just blinked up at her and was like, 'Bite me.'

The whole thing would have escalated into this giant girl

fight – Lilly has seen every single episode of *Xena, Warrior Princess*, and can kick-box like nobody's business – if Josh Richter hadn't slammed his locker door closed and said, 'I'm outta here,' in a disgusted voice. That was when Lana just dropped it like a hot potato and scooted after him, going, 'Josh, wait up. Wait up, Josh!'

Lilly and I just stood there looking at each other like we couldn't believe it. I still can't. Who *are* these people, and why do I have to be incarcerated with them on a daily basis?

Homework:

Algebra: Problems 1–12, pg. 79
English: Proposal
World Civ.: questions at end of Chapter 4
G & T: none
French: use avoir in neg. sentence, rd. lessons one to three, pas de plus
Biology: none

B = (x:x is an integer)
D = (2,3,4)
4ED
5ED
E = (x:x is an integer greater than 4 but less than 258)

Tuesday, September 30

Something really weird just happened. I got home from school, and my mom was there (she's usually at her studio all day during the week). She had this funny look on her face, and then she went, 'I have to talk to you.'

She wasn't humming any more, and she hadn't cooked anything, so I knew it was serious.

I was kind of hoping Grandmere was dead, but I knew it had to be much worse than that, and I was worried something had happened to Fat Louie, like he'd swallowed another sock. The last time he did that, the vet charged us $1,000 to remove the sock from his small intestines, and he walked around with a funny look on his face for about a month.

Fat Louie, I mean. Not the vet.

But it turned it wasn't about my cat, it was about my dad. The reason my dad kept on calling was because he wanted to tell us that he just found out, because of his cancer, that he can't have any more kids.

Cancer is a scary thing. Fortunately, the kind of cancer my dad had was pretty curable. They just had to cut off the cancerous part, and then he had to have chemo, and after a year, so far, the cancer hasn't come back.

Unfortunately, the part they had to cut off was . . .

Ew, I don't even like writing it.

His *testicle*.

GROSS!

It turns out that when they cut off one of your testicles, and then give you chemo, you have, like, a really strong chance of becoming sterile. Which is what my dad just found out he is.

Mom says he's really bummed out. She says we have to be

very understanding of him right now, because men have needs, and one of them is the need to feel progenitively omnipotent.

What I don't get is, what's the big deal? What does he need more kids for? He already has me! Sure, I only see him summers and at Christmastime, but that's enough, right? I mean, he's pretty busy, running Genovia. It's no joke, trying to make a whole country, even one that's only a mile long, run smoothly. The only other things he has time for besides me are his girlfriends. He's always got some new girlfriend slinking around. He brings them with him when we go to Grandmere's place in France in the summer. They always drool all over the pools and the stables and the waterfall and the twenty-seven bedrooms and the ballroom and the vineyard and the farm and the airstrip.

And then he dumps them a week later.

I didn't know he wanted to *marry* one of them, and have kids.

I mean, he never married my mom. My mom says that's because at the time, she rejected the bourgeois mores of a society that didn't even accept women as equals to men and refused to recognize her rights as an individual.

I kind of always thought that maybe my dad just never asked her.

Anyway, my mom says Dad is flying here to New York tomorrow to talk to me about this. I don't know *why*. I mean, it doesn't have anything to do with *me*. But when I went to my mom, 'Why does Dad have to fly all the way over here to talk to me about how he can't have kids?' she got this funny look on her face, and started to say something, and then she stopped.

Then she just said, 'You'll have to ask your father.'

This is bad. My mom only says 'Ask your father' when I

21

want to know something she doesn't feel like telling me, like why people sometimes kill their own babies and how come Americans eat so much red meat and read so much less than the people of Iceland.

Note to self: Look up the words *progenitive*, *omnipotent*, and *mores*

distributive law
5x + 5y-5
5(x + y-1)

Distribute WHAT??? <u>FIND OUT BEFORE QUIZ!!!</u>

Wednesday, October 1

My dad's here. Well, not here in the loft. He's staying at the Plaza, as usual. I'm supposed to go see him tomorrow, after he's 'rested'. My dad rests a lot, now that he's had cancer. He stopped playing polo too. But I think that's because one time a horse stepped on him.

Anyway, I hate the Plaza. Last time my dad stayed there, they wouldn't let me in to see him because I was wearing shorts. The lady who owns the place was there, they said, and she doesn't like to see people in cut-offs in the lobby of her fancy hotel. I had to call my dad from a house phone, and ask him to bring down a pair of trousers. He just told me to put the concierge on the phone, and the next thing you know, everybody was apologizing to me like crazy. They gave me this big basket filled with fruit and chocolate. It was cool. I didn't want the fruit, though, so I gave it to a homeless man I saw on the subway on my way back down to the Village. I don't think the homeless man wanted the fruit either, since he threw it all in the gutter, and just kept the basket to use as a hat.

I told Lilly about what my dad said, about not being able to have kids, and she said that was very telling. She said it revealed that my dad still has unresolved issues with his parents, and I said, 'Well, duh. Grandmere is a *huge* pain in the ass.'

Lilly said she couldn't comment on the veracity of that statement, since she'd never met my grandmother. I've been asking if I could invite Lilly to Miragnac for, like, years, but Grandmere always says no. She says young people give her migraines.

Lilly says maybe my dad is afraid of losing his youth, which many men equate with losing their virility. I really

23

think they should move Lilly up a grade, but she says she likes being a freshman. She says this way, she has four whole years to make observations on the adolescent condition in post-Cold War America.

The 3rd power of x is called cube of x – negative numbers have no sq root

Starting today I will:

1. Be nice to everyone, whether I like him/her or not.
2. Stop lying all the time about my feelings.
3. Stop forgetting my Algebra notebook.
4. Keep my comments to myself.
5. Stop writing my Algebra notes in my journal.

Notes from G & T

Lilly – I can't stand this. When is she going to go back to the teachers' lounge?

> *Maybe never. I heard they were shampooing the carpet today. God, he is so CUTE.*

Who's cute?

> *BORIS!*

He isn't cute. He's gross. Look what he did to his sweater. Why does he DO that?

> *You're so narrow-minded.*

I am NOT narrow-minded. But someone should tell him that in America, we don't tuck in our sweaters.

> *Well, maybe in Russia they do.*

But this isn't Russia. Also, someone should tell him to learn a new song. If I have to hear that requiem for dead King Whoever *one* more time . . .

> *You're just jealous, because Boris is a musical
> genius, and you're flunking Algebra.*

Lilly, just because I am flunking Algebra does NOT mean
I'm stupid.

> *OK, OK. What is wrong with you today?*

NOTHING!!!!!

slope: slope of a line denoted m is m = $\frac{y2-y1}{x2-x1}$

Find equation of line with slope = 2

Find the degree of slope to Mr G's nostrils

Thursday, October 2,
Ladies' Room at the Plaza Hotel

Well.

I guess now I know why my dad is so concerned about not being able to have more kids.

BECAUSE HE'S A PRINCE!!!

Geez! How long did they think they could keep something like *that* from me?

Although, come to think of it, they managed for a pretty long time. I mean, I've BEEN to Genovia. Miragnac, where I go every summer, and also most Christmases, is the name of my grandmother's house in France. It is actually on the border of France, right near Genovia, which is between France and Italy. I've been going to Miragnac ever since I was born. Never with my mother, though. Only with my dad. My mom and dad have never lived together. Unlike a lot of kids I know, who sit around wishing their parents would get back together after they get divorced, I'm perfectly happy with this arrangement. My parents broke up before I was ever born, although they have always been pretty friendly to one another. Except when my dad is being moody, that is, or my mom is being a flake, which she can be, sometimes. Things would majorly suck, I think, if they lived together.

Anyway, Genovia is where my grandmother takes me to shop for clothes at the end of every summer, when she's sick of looking at my overalls. But nobody ever mentioned anything about my dad being a PRINCE.

Come to think of it, I did that fact sheet on Genovia two years ago, and I copied down the name of the royal family, which is Renaldo. But even then I didn't connect it with my *dad*. I mean, I know his name is Phillipe Renaldo. But the name of the Prince of Genovia was listed in the encyclopedia I used as Artur Christoff Phillipe Gerard Grimaldi Renaldo.

And that picture of him must have been totally old. Dad hasn't had any hair since before I was born (so when he had chemo, you couldn't even tell, since he was practically bald anyway). The picture of the Prince of Genovia showed someone with A LOT of hair, sideburns, and a moustache too.

I guess I can see now how Mom might have gone for him, back when she was in college. He was something of a hottie.

But a PRINCE? Of a whole COUNTRY? I mean, I knew he was in politics, and of course I knew he had money – how many kids at my school have summer homes in France? Martha's Vineyard, maybe, but not *France* – but a PRINCE?

So what I want to know is, if my dad's a prince, how come I have to learn Algebra?

I mean, seriously.

I don't think it was such a good idea for Dad to tell me he was a prince in the Palm Court at the Plaza. First of all, we almost had a repeat performance of the shorts incident: the doorman wouldn't even let me in at first. He said, 'No minors unaccompanied by an adult', which totally blows that whole *Home Alone II* movie, right?

And I was all, 'But I'm supposed to meet my dad—'

'No minors,' the doorman said again, 'unaccompanied by an adult.'

This seemed totally unfair. I wasn't even wearing shorts. I was wearing my uniform from Albert Einstein's. I mean, pleated skirt, knee socks, the whole thing. OK, maybe I was

27

wearing Doc Martens, but come on! I practically WAS that kid Eloise, and she supposedly ruled the Plaza.

Finally, after standing there for, like, half an hour, saying, 'But my dad . . . but my dad . . . but my dad . . .' the concierge came over and asked, 'Just who *is* your father, young lady?'

As soon as I said his name, they let me in. I realize now that's because even THEY knew he was a prince. But his own daughter, his own daughter nobody tells!

Dad was waiting at a table. High tea at the Plaza is supposed to be this very big deal. You should *see* all the German tourists snapping pictures of themselves eating chocolate chip scones. Anyway, I used to get a kick out of it when I was a little girl, and since my dad refuses to believe fourteen is not little any more, we still meet there when he's in town. Oh, we go other places too. Like we always go to see *Beauty and the Beast*, my all-time favourite Broadway musical, I don't care what Lilly says about Walt Disney and his misogynistic undertones. I've seen it seven times.

So has my dad. His favourite part is when the dancing forks come out.

Anyway, we're sitting there drinking tea and he starts telling me in this very serious voice that he's the Prince of Genovia, and then this terrible thing happens:

I get the hiccups.

This only happens when I drink something hot and then eat bread. I don't know why. It had never happened at the Plaza before, but all of a sudden, my dad is like, 'Mia, I want you to know the truth. I think you're old enough now, and the fact is, now that I can't have any more children, this will have a tremendous impact on your life, and it's only fair I tell you. I am the Prince of Genovia.'

And I was all, 'Really, Dad?' *Hiccup*.

'Your mother has always felt very strongly that there wasn't any reason for you to know, and I agreed with her. I had a very . . . well, *unsatisfactory* childhood—'

He's not kidding. Life with Grandmere couldn't have been any *picque-nicque. Hiccup.*

'I agreed with your mother that a palace is no place to raise a child.' Then he started muttering to himself, which he always does whenever I tell him I'm a vegetarian, or the subject of Mom comes up. 'Of course, at the time I didn't think she intended to raise you in a *bohemian artist's loft* in *Greenwich Village*, but I will admit that it doesn't seem to have done you any harm. In fact, I think growing up in New York City instilled you with a healthy amount of scepticism about the human race at large—'

Hiccup. And he had never even *met* Lana Weinberger.

'—which is something I didn't gain until college, and I believe is partly responsible for the fact that I have such a difficult time establishing close interpersonal relationships with women . . .'

Hiccup.

'What I'm trying to say is, your mother and I thought by not telling you, we were doing you a favour. The fact was, we never envisioned that an occasion might arise in which you might succeed to the throne. I was only twenty-five when you were born. I felt certain I would meet another woman, marry her, and have more children. But now, unfortunately, that will never be. So, the fact is, you, Mia, are the heir to the throne of Genovia.'

I hiccuped again. This was getting embarrassing. These weren't little lady-like hiccups, either. They were huge, and made my whole body go sproinging up out of my chair, like I was some kind of five-foot-nine frog. They were loud too. I mean *really* loud. The German tourists kept looking over, all giggly and stuff. I knew what my dad was saying was super-serious, but I couldn't help it, I just kept hiccuping! I tried holding my breath and counting to thirty – I only got to ten before I hiccuped again. I put a sugar cube on my tongue and let it dissolve. No go. I even tried to scare myself, thinking about my mom and Mr Gianini French kissing – even *that* didn't work.

Finally, my dad was like, 'Mia? Mia, are you listening? Have you heard a word I said?'

I said, 'Dad, can I be excused for a minute?'

He looked sort of pained, like his stomach hurt him, and he slumped back in his chair in this defeated way, but he said, 'Go ahead', and gave me five dollars to give to the washroom attendant, which I of course put in my pocket. Five bucks for the washroom attendant! Geez, my whole allowance is ten bucks a week!

I don't know if you've ever been to the Ladies' Room at the Plaza, but it's like totally the nicest one in Manhattan. It's all pink and there are mirrors and little couches everywhere, in case you look at yourself and feel the urge to faint from your beauty or something. Anyway, I banged in there, hiccuping like a maniac, and all these women in these fancy hairdos looked up, annoyed at the interruption. I guess I made them mess up their lip-liner, or something.

I went into one of the stalls, each of which, besides a toilet, has its own private sink with a huge mirror and a dressing table, with a little stool with tassels hanging off it. I sat on the stool and concentrated on not hiccuping any more. Instead, I concentrated on what my dad had said:

He's the Prince of Genovia.

A lot of things are beginning to make sense now. Like how when I fly to France, I just walk onto the plane from the terminal, but when I get there, I'm escorted off the plane before everyone else and get taken away by limo to meet my dad at Miragnac.

I always thought that was because he had Frequent Flyer privileges.

I guess it's because he's a prince.

And then there's that fact that whenever Grandmere takes me shopping in Genovia, she always takes me either before the stores are officially open, or after they are officially closed. She calls ahead to ensure we will be let in, and no one has ever said no. In Manhattan, if my mother had tried to do this, the clerks at the Gap would have fallen over from laughing so hard.

And when I'm at Miragnac, I notice that we never go out to eat anywhere. We always have our meals there, or sometimes we go to the neighbouring chateau, Mirabeau, which is owned by these nasty British people who have a lot of snotty kids who say things like, 'That's rot', to one another. One of the younger girls, Nicole, is sort of my friend, but then one night she told me this story about how she was Frenching a boy and I didn't know what Frenching was. I was only eleven at the time, which is no excuse, because so was she. I just thought Frenching was some weird British thing, like toad-in-the-hole, or air raids, or something. So then I mentioned it at the dinner table in front of Nicole's parents, and after that, all those kids stopped talking to me.

I wonder if the Brits know that my dad is the Prince of Genovia. I bet they do. God, they must have thought I was mentally retarded, or something.

Most people have never heard of Genovia. I know when we had to do our fact sheets, none of the other kids ever had. Neither had my mother, she says, before she met my dad. Nobody famous ever came from there. Nobody who was born there ever invented anything, or wrote anything, or became a movie star. A lot of Genovians, like my grandpa, fought against the Nazis in World War II, but other than that, they aren't really known for anything.

Still, people who *have* heard of Genovia like to go there, because it's so beautiful. It's very sunny nearly all the time, with the snow-capped Alps in the background, and the crystal blue Mediterranean in front of it. It has a lot of hills, some of which are as steep as the ones in San Francisco, and most of which have olive trees growing on them. The main export of Genovia, I remember from my fact sheet, is olive oil, the really expensive kind my mom says only to use for salad dressing.

There's a palace there too. It's kind of famous because they filmed a movie there, once, a movie about the three Musketeers. I've never been inside, but we've driven by it before, me and Grandmere. It's got all these turrets and flying buttresses and stuff.

Funny how Grandmere never mentioned having *lived* there all those times we drove past it.

My hiccups are gone. I think it's safe to go back to the Palm Court.

I'm going to give the washroom attendant a dollar, even though she didn't attend me.

Hey, I can afford it: my dad's a prince!

Later on Thursday, Penguin House,
Central Park Zoo

I'm so freaked out I can barely write, plus people keep bumping my elbow, and it's dark in here, but whatever. I have to get this down exactly the way it happened. Otherwise, when I wake up tomorrow, I might think it was just a nightmare.

But it wasn't a nightmare. It was REAL.

I'm not going to tell anybody, not even Lilly. Lilly would NOT understand. NOBODY would understand. Because nobody I know has ever been in this situation before. Nobody ever went to bed one night as one person, and then woke up the next morning to find out that she was some-body completely different.

When I got back to our table after hiccuping in the Ladies' Room at the Plaza, I saw that the German tourists had been replaced by some Japanese tourists. This was an improvement. They were much quieter. My dad was on his mobile phone when I sat back down. He was talking to my mom, I realized right away. He had on the expression he only wears when he is talking to her. He was saying, 'Yes, I told her. No, she doesn't seem upset.' He looked at me. 'Are you upset?'

I said, 'No', because I wasn't upset – not THEN.

He said, into the phone, 'She says no.' He listened for a minute, then he looked at me again. 'Do you want your mother to come up here and help to explain things?'

I shook my head. 'No. She has to finish that mixed media piece for the Kelly Tate gallery. They want it by next Tuesday.'

My dad repeated this to my mom. I heard her grumble

back. She is always very grumbly when I remind her that she has paintings due by a certain time. My mom likes to work when the muses move her. Since my dad pays most of our bills, this is not usually a problem, but it is not a very responsible way for an adult to behave, even if she is an artist. I swear, if I ever met my mom's muses, I'd give 'em such swift kicks in the toga, they wouldn't know what hit them.

Finally my dad hung up and then he looked at me. 'Better?' he asked.

So I guess he had noticed the hiccups after all. 'Better,' I said.

'Do you really understand what I'm telling you, Mia?'

I nodded. 'You are the Prince of Genovia.'

'Yes . . .' he said, like there was more.

I didn't know what else to say. So I tried, 'Grandpere was the Prince of Genovia before you?'

He said, 'Yes . . .'

'So Grandmere is . . . what?'

'The Dowager Princess.'

I winced. Ew. That explained a whole lot about Grandmere.

Dad could tell he had me stumped. He kept on looking at me all hopeful-like. Finally, after I tried just smiling at him innocently for a while, and that didn't work, I slumped over and said, 'OK. What?'

He looked disappointed. 'Mia, don't you know?'

I had my head on the table. You aren't supposed to do that at the Plaza, but I hadn't noticed Ivana Trump looking our way. 'No . . .' I said. 'I guess not. Know what?'

'You're not Mia Thermopolis any more, honey,' he said. Because I was born out of wedlock, and my mom doesn't believe in what she calls the cult of the patriarchy, she gave me her last name, instead of my dad's.

34

I raised my head at that. 'I'm not?' I said, blinking a few times. 'Then who am I?'

And he went, kind of sadly, 'You're Amelia Mignonette Grimaldi Thermopolis Renaldo, Princess of Genovia.'

OK.

WHAT? A PRINCESS?? ME???

Yeah. Right.

This is how NOT a princess I am. I am so NOT a princess that when my dad started telling me that I was one, I totally started crying. I could see my reflection in this big gold mirror across the room, and my face had gotten all splotchy, like it does in PE whenever we play dodge ball and I get hit. I looked at my face in that big mirror and I was like, *This* is the face of a princess?

You should see what I look like. You never saw anyone who looked LESS like a princess than I do. I mean, I have really bad hair, that isn't curly or straight, it's sort of triangular, so I have to wear it really short or I look like a Yield sign. And it isn't blonde or brunette, it's in the middle, the sort of colour they call mouse brown, or dishwater blonde. Attractive, huh? And I have a really big mouth and no breasts and feet that look like skis. Lilly says my only attractive feature is my eyes, which are grey, but right then they were all squinty and red-looking, since I was trying not to cry.

I mean, princesses don't cry, right?

Then my dad reached out and started patting my hand. OK, I love my dad, but he just has no clue. He kept saying how sorry he was. I couldn't say anything in reply, because I was afraid if I talked I'd cry harder. He kept on saying how it wasn't that bad, that I'd like living at the palace in Genovia with him, and that I could come back to visit my little friends as often as I wanted.

35

That's when I lost it.

Not only am I a princess, but I have to MOVE???

I stopped crying almost right away. Because then I got mad. Really mad. I don't get mad all that often, because of my fear of confrontation and all, but when I *do* get mad, look out.

'I am NOT moving to Genovia,' I said, in this really loud voice. I know it was loud, because all the Japanese tourists turned around and looked at me, and then started whispering to one another.

My dad looked kind of shocked. The last time I yelled at him had been years ago, when he agreed with Grandmere that I ought to eat some foie gras. I don't care if it *is* a delicacy in France: I'm not eating anything that once walked around and quacked.

'But, Mia,' my dad said, in his Now-Let's-Be-Reasonable voice. 'I thought you understood—'

'All I understand,' I said, 'is that you *lied* to me my whole life. Why should I come live with *you?*'

I realize this was a completely *Party of Five* kind of thing to say, and I'm sorry to say that I followed it up with some pretty *Party of Five* kind of behaviour. I stood up real fast, knocking my big gold chair over, and rushed out of there, nearly bowling over the snobby doorman.

I think my dad tried to chase me, but I can run pretty fast when I want to. Mr Wheeton is always trying to get me to go out for track, but that's, like, such a joke, because I hate running for no reason. A letter on a stupid jacket is no reason to run, as far as I'm concerned.

Anyway, I ran down the street, past the stupid touristy horse and carriages, past the big fountain with the gold statues in it, past all the traffic outside of FAO Schwartz, right into Central Park, where it was getting kind of dark and cold and spooky and stuff, but I didn't care. Nobody was going to attack me, because I was this five-foot-nine girl running in combat boots, with a big backpack with bumper stickers on it that said stuff like *Support Greenpeace* and *I Brake For Animals*. Nobody messes with a girl in combat boots, particularly when she's also a vegetarian.

After a while I got tired of running, and then I tried to figure out where I could go, since I wasn't ready to go home yet. I knew I couldn't go to Lilly's. She is vehemently opposed to any form of government that is not by the people, exercised either directly or through elected representatives. She's always said that when sovereignty is vested in a single person whose right to rule is hereditary, the principles of social equality and respect for the individual within a community are irrevocably lost. This is why today, real power has passed from reigning monarchs to constitutional assemblies, making royals such as Queen Elizabeth mere symbols of national unity.

At least, that's what she said in her oral report in World Civ. the other day.

And I guess I kind of agree with Lilly, especially when you consider the whole part about how we as a country struggled for independence from the yoke of servitude to our British oppressors – but my dad isn't like that. Yeah, he plays polo and all, but he would never dream of subjecting anyone to taxation without representation.

Still, I was pretty sure the fact that the people of Genovia don't have to pay taxes wasn't going to make any difference to Lilly.

I knew the first thing my dad would do was call Mom, and she'd be all worried. I hate making my mom worry. Even though she can be very irresponsible at times, it's only with things like bills and the groceries. She's never irresponsible

37

about *me*. Like, I have friends whose parents don't even remember sometimes to give them subway fare. I have friends who tell their parents they're going to So-and-So's apartment, and then instead they go out drinking, and their parents never find out, because they don't even check with the other kid's parents.

My mom's not like that. She ALWAYS checks.

So I knew it wasn't fair to run off like that, and make her worry. I didn't care much then about what my dad thought. I was pretty much hating him by then. But I just had to be alone for a little while. I mean, it takes some getting used to, finding out you're a princess. I guess some girls might like it, but not me. I've never been good at girly stuff, you know, like putting on make-up and wearing pantyhose and stuff. I mean, I can *do* it, if I have to, but I'd rather not.

Much rather not.

Anyway, I don't know how, but my feet sort of knew where they were going, and before I knew it, I was at the zoo.

I love the Central Park Zoo. I always have, since I was a little kid. It's way better than the Bronx Zoo, because it's really small and cosy, and the animals are much friendlier, especially the seals and the polar bears. I love polar bears. At the Central Park Zoo, they have this one polar bear, and all he does all day long is the backstroke. I swear! He was on the news once, because this animal psychologist was worried he was under too much stress. It must suck to have people looking at you all day. But then they bought him some toys, and after that, he was all right. He just kicks back in his enclosure – they don't have cages at the Central Park Zoo, they have enclosures – and watches you watching him. Sometimes he holds a ball while he does it. I love that bear.

So after I forked over a couple of dollars to get in – that's the other good thing about the zoo: it's cheap – I paid a little call on the polar bear. He appeared to be doing fine. Much better than I was, at the moment. I mean, *his* dad hadn't told him he was the heir to the throne of anywhere. I wondered where that polar bear had come from. I hoped he was from Iceland.

After a while it got too crowded at the polar bear enclosure, so then I went into the penguin house. It smells kind of bad in here, but it's fun. There are these windows that look underwater, so you can see the penguins swimming around, sliding on the rocks and having a good penguin time. Little kids put their hands on the glass, and when a penguin swims towards them, they start screaming. It totally cracks me up. There's a bench you can sit on too, and that's where I'm sitting now, writing this. You get used to the smell after a while. I guess you can get used to anything.

Oh my God, I can't believe I just wrote that! I will NEVER get used to being Princess Amelia Renaldo! I don't even know who that is! It sounds like the name of some stupid line of make-up, or of somebody from a Disney movie who's been missing and just recovered her memory, or something.

What am I going to do? I CAN'T move to Genovia, I just CAN'T!! Who would look after Fat Louie? My mom can't. She forgets to feed *herself*, let alone a *CAT*.

I'm sure they won't let me have a cat in the palace. At least, not a cat like Louie, who weighs twenty-five pounds and eats socks. He'd scare all the ladies-in-waiting.

Oh, God. *What am I going to do?*

If Lana Weinberger finds out about this, I'm dead.

Even later on Thursday

Of course, I couldn't hide out in the penguin house for ever. Eventually, they flicked the lights, and said the zoo was closing. I put my journal away and filed out with everybody else. I grabbed a downtown bus and went home, where I was sure I was going to get it BIG-TIME from my mom.

What I didn't count on was getting it from BOTH my parents at the same time. This was a first.

'Where have you been, young lady?' my mom wanted to know. She was sitting at the kitchen table with my dad, the telephone between them.

My dad said, at the exact same time, 'We were worried sick!'

I thought I was in for the grounding of a lifetime, but all they wanted to know was whether I was all right. I assured them that I was, and apologized for going all Jennifer Love Hewitt on them. I just needed to be alone, I said.

I was really worried they'd start in on me, but they totally didn't. My mom did try to make me eat some Ramen, but I wouldn't, because it was beef-flavoured. And then my dad offered to send his driver to Nobu to pick up some blackened sea bass, but I was like, 'Really, Dad, I just want to go to bed.' Then my mom started feeling my head and stuff, thinking I was sick. This nearly made me start crying again. I guess my dad recognized my expression from the Plaza, since all of a sudden he was like, 'Helen, just leave her alone.'

To my surprise, she did. And so I went into my bathroom and closed the door and took a long, hot bath, then got into my favourite pyjamas, the cool red flannel ones, found Fat Louie where he was trying to hide under the futon couch (he doesn't like my dad so much), and went to bed.

Before I fell asleep, I could hear my dad talking to my mom in the kitchen for a long, long time. His voice was rumbly, like thunder. It sort of reminded me of Captain Picard's voice, on *Star Trek: The Next Generation*.

My dad actually has a lot in common with Captain Picard. You know, he's white and bald and has to rule over a small populace.

Except that Captain Picard always makes everything OK by the end of the episode, and I sincerely doubt everything will be OK for me.

Friday, October 3 – Homeroom

Today when I woke up, the pigeons that live on the fire escape outside my window were cooing away (Fat Louie was on the windowsill – well, as much of him that could fit on the windowsill, anyway – watching them), and the sun was shining, and I actually got up on time, and didn't hit the snooze button seven-thousand times. I took a shower and didn't cut my legs shaving them, found a fairly unwrinkled blouse at the bottom of my closet, and even got my hair to look sort of halfway passable. I was in a good mood. It was *Friday*. Friday is my favourite day, besides Saturday and Sunday. Fridays always mean two days – two glorious, relaxing days – of NO Algebra are coming my way.

And then I walked out into the kitchen, and there was all this pink light coming down through the skylight right on my mom, who was wearing her best kimono and making French toast using Egg Beaters instead of real eggs, even though I'm no longer ovo-lacto since I realized eggs aren't fertilized so they could never have been baby chicks anyway.

And I was all set to thank her for thinking of me, and then I heard this rustle.

And there was my DAD sitting at the dining room table (well, really it's just a table, since we don't have a dining room, but whatever), reading The *New York Times* and wearing a suit.

A *suit*. At seven o'clock in the morning.

And then I remembered. I couldn't believe I'd forgotten it:

I'm a *princess*.

Oh my God. Everything good about my day just went right out the window after that.

As soon as he saw me, my dad was all, 'Ah, Mia.'

I knew I was in for it. He only says *Ah, Mia* when he's about to give me a big lecture.

He folded his paper all carefully and laid it down. My dad always folds papers carefully, making the edges all neat. My mom never does this. She usually crumples the pages up and leaves them, out of order, on the futon couch, or next to the toilet. This kind of thing drives my father insane and is probably the real reason why they never got married.

My mom, I saw, had set the table with our best K-Mart plates, the ones with the blue stripes on them, and the green plastic cactus-shaped margarita glasses from Ikea. She had even put a bunch of fake sunflowers in the middle of the table in a yellow vase. She had done all that to cheer me up, I know, and she'd probably gotten up really early to do it too. But instead of cheering me up, it just made me sadder.

Because I bet they don't use green plastic cactus-shaped margarita glasses for breakfast at the palace in Genovia.

'We need to talk, Mia,' my dad said. This is how his worst lectures always start. Except this time, he looked at me kind of funny before he started. 'What's wrong with your hair?'

I put my hand up to my head. 'Why?' I thought my hair looked good, for a change.

'Nothing is wrong with her hair, Phillipe,' my mom said. She usually tries to ward off my dad's lectures, if she can. 'Come and sit down, Mia, and have some breakfast. I even heated up the syrup for the French toast, the way you like it.'

I appreciated this gesture on my mom's part. I really did. But I was *not* going to sit down and talk about my future in Genovia. I mean, come on. So I was all, 'Uh, I'd love to, really, but I gotta go. I have a test in World Civ. today, and I promised Lilly I'd meet her to go over our notes together—'

43

'*Sit down.*'

Boy, my dad can really sound like a starship captain in the Federation when he wants to.

I sat. My mom shovelled some French toast on my plate. I poured syrup over it and took a bite, just to be polite. It tasted like cardboard.

'Mia,' my mom said. She was still trying to ward off my dad's lecture. 'I know how upset you must be about all of this. But really, it isn't as bad as you're making it out to be.'

Oh, right. All of a sudden you tell me I'm a princess, and I'm supposed to be happy about it?

'I mean,' my mom went on, 'most girls would probably be delighted to find out their father is a prince!'

No girls I know. Actually, that's not true. Lana Weinberger would probably *love* to be a princess. In fact, she already thinks she is one.

'Just think of all the lovely things you could have if you went to live in Genovia.' My mom's face totally lit up as she started listing the lovely things I could have if I went to live in Genovia, but her voice sounded strange, as if she were playing a mom on TV or something. 'Like a car! You know how impractical it is to have a car here in the city. But in Genovia, when you turn sixteen, I'm sure Dad will buy you a—'

I pointed out that there are enough problems with pollution in Europe without my contributing to it. Diesel emissions are one of the largest contributors to the destruction of the ozone layer.

'But you've always wanted a horse, haven't you? Well, in Genovia, you could have one. A nice grey one, with spots on its back—'

That hurt.

'Mom,' I said, my eyes all filling up with tears. I

completely couldn't help it. Suddenly, I was bawling all over again. 'What are you *doing?* Do you *want* me to go live with Dad? Is that it? Are you tired of me, or something? Do you want me to go live with Dad so you and Mr Gianini can . . . can . . .'

I couldn't go on, because I started crying so hard. But by then my mom was crying too. She jumped up out of her chair and came around the end of the table and started hugging me, saying, 'Oh, no, honey! How could you think something like that?' She had stopped sounding like a TV mom. 'I just want what's best for you!'

'As do I,' my dad said, looking annoyed. He had folded his arms across his chest and was leaning back in his chair, watching us in an irritated way.

'Well, what's best for me is to stay right here and finish high school,' I told him. 'And then I'm going to join Greenpeace and help save the whales.'

My dad looked even *more* irritated at that. 'You are *not* joining Greenpeace,' he said.

'I am too,' I said. It was totally hard to talk, because I was crying and all, but I told him, 'I'm going to go Iceland to save the baby seals too.'

'You most certainly are not.' My dad didn't just look annoyed. Now he looked mad. 'You are going to go to college. Vassar, I think. Maybe Sarah Lawrence.'

That made me cry even more.

But before I could say anything, my mom held up a hand and was like, 'Phillipe, don't. We aren't accomplishing anything here. Mia has to get to school, anyway. She's already late—'

I started looking around for my backpack and coat real fast. 'Yeah,' I said. 'I gotta renew my Metro card.'

My dad made this weird French noise he makes

sometimes. It's halfway between a snort and sigh. It kind of sounds like, *Pfuit!* Then he said, 'Lars will drive you.'

I told my dad that this was unnecessary, since I meet Lilly at Astor Place every day, where we catch the uptown 6 train together.

'Lars can pick up your little friend too.'

I looked at my mom. She was looking at my dad. Lars is my dad's driver. He goes everywhere my dad goes. For as long as I've known my dad – OK, my whole life – he's always had a driver, usually a big beefy guy who used to work for the president of Israel, or somebody like that.

Now that I think about it, of course I realize these guys aren't really drivers at all, but bodyguards.

Duh.

OK, so the last thing I wanted was for my dad's body-guard to drive me to school. How would I ever explain it to Lilly? *Oh, don't mind him, Lilly. He's just my dad's chauffeur.* Yeah, right. The only person at Albert Einstein High School who gets dropped off by a chauffeur is this totally rich Saudi Arabian girl named Tina Hakim Baba whose dad owns some big oil company, and everybody makes fun of her because her parents are all worried she'll get kidnapped between 75th and Madison, where our school is, and 75th and Fifth, where she lives. She even has a bodyguard who follows her around from class to class and talks on a walkie-talkie to the chauf-feur. This seems a little extreme, if you ask me.

But Dad was totally rigid on the driver thing. It's like now that I'm an official princess, there's all this concern for my welfare. Yesterday, when I was Mia Thermopolis, it was per-fectly OK for me to ride the subway. Today, now that I'm Princess Amelia, forget it.

Well, whatever. It didn't seem worth arguing over. I mean, there are way worse things I have to worry about.

Like which country am I going to be living in in the near future.

As I was leaving – my dad made Lars come up to the loft to walk me down to the car. It was totally embarrassing – I overheard my dad say to my mom, 'All right, Helen. Who's this Gianini fellow Mia was talking about?'

Oops.

ab = a + b
solve for b
ab-b = a
b(a–1) = a
b = a
    a–1

More Friday, Algebra

Lilly could tell right away something was up.

Oh, she swallowed the whole story I fed her about Lars: 'Oh, my dad's in town, and he's got this driver, and you know . . .'

But I couldn't tell her about the princess thing. I mean, all I kept thinking about was how disgusted Lilly sounded during that part in her oral report when she mentioned how Christian monarchs used to consider themselves appointed agents of divine will and thus were responsible not to the people they governed but to God alone, even though my dad hardly ever even goes to church, except when Grandmere makes him.

Lilly believed me about Lars, but she was still all over me with the crying thing. She was like, 'Why are your eyes so red and squinty? You've been crying. Why were you crying? Did something happen? What happened? Did you get another F in something?'

I just shrugged and tried to look out the passenger window at the uninspiring view of the East Village crack-houses, which we had to drive by to get to the FDR. 'It's nothing,' I said. 'PMS.'

'It is not PMS. You had your period last week. I remember because you borrowed a pad from me after PE, and then you ate two whole packs of Yodels at lunch.' Sometimes I wish Lilly's memory wasn't so good. 'So spill. Did Louie eat another sock?'

First of all, it was, like, totally embarrassing to discuss my menstrual cycle in front of my dad's bodyguard. I mean, Lars was kind of a hottie. He was concentrating really hard on driving though, and I don't know if he could hear us in the front seat, but it was embarrassing, just the same.

'It's nothing,' I whispered. 'Just my dad. *You know.*'

'Oh,' Lilly said, in her normal voice. Have I mentioned that Lilly's normal voice is really loud? 'You mean the infertility thing? Is he still bummed out about that? Gawd, does *he* ever need to self-actualize.'

Lilly then went on to describe something she called the Jungian tree of self-actualization. She says my dad is way on the bottom branches, and he won't be able to reach the top of the thing until he accepts himself as he is and stops obsessing over his inability to sire more offspring.

I guess that's part of my problem. I'm way at the bottom of the self-actualization tree. Like, underneath the roots of it, practically.

But now that I'm sitting here in Algebra, things don't seem so bad, really. I mean, I thought about it all through Homeroom, and I finally realized something:

They can't *make* me be princess.

They really can't. I mean, this is America, for crying out loud. Here, you can be anything you want to be. At least, that's what Mrs Holland was always telling us last year, when we studied US History. So, if I can be whatever I want to be, I can *not* be a princess. Nobody can *make* me be a princess, not even my dad, if I don't want to be one.

Right?

So when I get home tonight, I'll just tell my dad thanks, but no thanks. I'll just be plain old Mia for now.

Geez. Mr Gianini just called on me, and I totally had no idea what he was talking about, because of course I was writing in this book instead of paying attention. My face feels like it's on fire. Lana is laughing her head off, of course. She is such a cow.

What does he keep picking on *me* for, anyway? He should know by now that I don't know the quadratic formula from a hole in the ground. He's only picking on me because of my mom. He wants to make it look as if he's treating me the same as everybody else in the class.

Well, I'm *not* the same as everybody else in the class.

What do I need to know Algebra for, anyway? They don't use Algebra in Greenpeace.

And you can bet you don't need it if you're a princess. So however things turn out, I'm covered.

Cool.

$$\text{solve } x = a + aby \text{ for } y$$
$$x - a + aby$$
$$\frac{x - a}{ab} + \frac{aby}{ab}$$
$$y + \frac{x - a}{ab}$$

Really late on Friday,
Lilly Moscovitz's bedroom

OK, so I blew off Mr Gianini's help session after school. I *know* I shouldn't have. Believe me, Lilly let me know I shouldn't have. I know he has these help sessions just for people like me, who are flunking. I know he does it in his own spare time, and doesn't even get paid overtime for it or anything. But if I won't ever need Algebra in any foreseeable future career, why do I need to go?

I asked Lilly if it would be OK if I spent the night at her house tonight and she said only if I promised to stop acting like such a head case.

I promised, even though I don't think I'm acting like a head case.

But when I called my mom from the payphone outside school to ask her if it was OK if I stayed overnight at the Moscovitzes, she was all, 'Um, actually, Mia, your father was really hoping that when you got home tonight, we could have another talk.'

Oh, great.

I told my mom that although there was nothing I wanted to do more than have another talk, I was very concerned about Lilly, whose stalker was recently released from Bellevue again. Ever since Lilly started her cable access TV show, this guy named Norman has been calling in, asking her to take off her shoes. According to the Drs Moscovitz, Norman is a fetishist. His fixation is feet, in particular Lilly's feet. He sends stuff to her care of the show, CDs and stuffed animals and things like that, and writes that there'll be more where that came from, if Lilly would just take her shoes off on air. So what Lilly does is, she takes her shoes off, all right, but then she throws a blanket over her legs and kicks her feet around under it and goes, 'Look, Norman, you freak! I took my shoes off! Thanks for the CDs, sucker!'

This angered Norman so much that he started wandering around the Village, looking for Lilly. Everyone knows Lilly lives in the Village, since we filmed a very popular episode where Lilly borrowed the pricing gun from Grand Union and stood on the corner of Bleecker and La Guardia and told all the European tourists wandering around NoHo that if they wore a Grand Union price sticker on their foreheads, they could get a free latte from Dean & DeLuca (a surprising amount of them believed her).

Anyway, one day a few weeks ago, Norman the foot fetishist found us in the park, and started chasing us around, waving twenty dollar bills and trying to get us to take off our shoes. This was very entertaining, and hardly scary at all, especially because we just ran right up to the command post on Washington Square South and Thompson Street, where the 6th Precinct has been parking this enormous trailer so they can secretly spy on the drug dealers. We told the police that this weird guy was trying to assault us, and you should have seen it: about twenty undercover guys jumped on Norman (even a guy I thought was an old homeless man asleep on a bench) and dragged him, screaming, off to the mental ward!

I always have such a good time with Lilly.

Anyway, Lilly's parents told her Norman just got out of Bellevue, and that if she sees him, she's not to torment him any more, because he's just a poor obsessive-compulsive, with possible schizophrenic tendencies.

Lilly's devoting tomorrow's show to her feet. She's going to model every single pair of shoes she owns, but not once show her bare feet. She hopes that this will drive Norman over the edge, and he'll do something weirder than ever, like get a gun and shoot at us.

I'm not scared, though. Norman has kind of thick glasses, and I bet he couldn't actually hit anything, even with a machine-gun, which even a lunatic like Norman is allowed to buy in this country thanks to our totally unrestrictive gun laws, which Michael Moscovitz says in his webzine will ultimately result in the demise of democracy as we know it.

My mom was totally not buying this, though. She was all, 'Mia, I appreciate the fact that you want to help your friend through this difficult period with her stalker, but I really think you have more pressing responsibilities here at home.'

And I was all, 'What responsibilities?' thinking she was talking about the litter box, which I had totally cleaned two days ago.

And she was like, 'Responsibility towards your father and me.'

I just about lost it right there. Responsibilities? *Responsibilities*? *She's* telling *me* about responsibilities? When is the last time it ever occurred to *her* to drop the laundry off, let alone pick it up again? When is the last time *she* remembered to buy Q-Tips or toilet paper or milk?

And did she ever happen to think to mention, in all of my fourteen years, that I might possibly end up being the Princess of Genovia someday???

She thinks she needs to tell *me* about my responsibilities? HA!!!!!!

I nearly hung up on her. But Lilly was sort of standing nearby, practising her house manager duties by switching on and off the lights in the school lobby. Since I had promised not to act like a head case, and hanging up on my mother would definitely fall into the head case category, I said in this really patient voice, 'Don't worry, Mom, I won't forget to

53

stop at Genovese on my way home tomorrow and pick up new vacuum cleaner bags.'

And *then* I hung up.

Homework:

Algebra: Problems 1–12, pg. 119
English: Proposal
World Civ.: questions at end of Chapter 4
G & T: none
French: use avoir in neg. sentence, rd. lessons one to three, pas de plus
Biology: none

Saturday, October 4 - early, still Lilly's place

Why do I always have such a good time when I spend the night at Lilly's? I mean, it's not like they've got stuff that I don't have. In fact, my mom and I have better stuff: the Moscovitzes only get a couple of movie channels, and because I took advantage of the last Time Warner Cable bonus offer, we have all of them, Cinemax *and* HBO *and* Showtime, for the low, low rate of $19.99 per month.

Plus we have way better people to spy on through our windows, like Ronnie, who used to be a Ronald but is now called Ronette, and who has a lot of big fancy parties, and that skinny German couple who wear black all the time, even in summer, and never pull down their blinds. On Fifth Avenue, where the Moscovitzes live, there's *nobody* good to look at: just other rich psychoanalysts and their children. Let me tell you, you don't see anything good through *their* windows.

But it's like every time I spend the night here, even if all Lilly and I do is hang out in the kitchen, eating macaroons left over from Rosh Hashana, I have such a great time. Maybe that's because Maya, the Moscovitzes' Dominican maid, never forgets to buy orange juice, and she always remembers that I don't like the pulpy kind, and sometimes, if she knows I'm staying over, she'll pick up a vegetable lasagna from Balducci's, instead of a meat one, especially for me, like she did last night.

Or maybe it's because I never find mouldy old containers of anything in the Moscovitzes' refrigerator: Maya throws away anything that's even one day past its expiry date. Even sour cream that still has the protective plastic around the lid. Even cans of Tab.

And the Drs Moscovitz never forget to pay the electricity

bill: Con Ed has never once shut down *their* power in the middle of a *Star Trek* movie marathon. And Lilly's mom, she always talks about normal stuff, like what a great deal she got on Calvin Klein pantyhose at Bergdorf's.

Not that I don't love my mom or anything. I totally do. I just wish she could be more of a mom, and less of an artist.

And I wish my dad could be more like Lilly's dad, who always wants to make me an omelette, because he thinks I'm too skinny, and who walks around in his old college sweatpants when he doesn't have to go to his office to analyse anybody.

Dr Moscovitz would *never* wear a suit at seven in the morning.

Not that I don't love my dad. I do, I guess. I just don't understand how he could let something like this happen. He's usually so organized. *How could he have let himself become a prince?*

I just don't understand it.

The best thing, I guess, about going to Lilly's is that while I'm there, I don't even have to think about things like how I'm flunking Algebra or how I'm the heir to the throne of a small European principality. I can just relax and enjoy some real home-made Pop 'N Fresh Cinnamon Buns and watch Pavlov, Michael's sheltie, try to herd Maya back into the kitchen every time she tries to comes out.

Last night was *totally* fun. The Drs Moscovitz were out – they had to go to a benefit at the Puck Building for the homosexual children of survivors of the Holocaust – so Lilly and I made this huge vat of popcorn smothered in butter and climbed into her parents' giant canopy bed and watched all the James Bond movies in a row. We were able to definitively determine that Pierce Brosnan was the skinniest James Bond, Sean Connery the hairiest, and Roger

Moore the most tanned. None of the James Bonds took their shirts off enough for us to decide who had the best chest, but I think probably Timothy Dalton.

I like chest hair. I think.

It was sort of ironic that while I was trying to decide this, Lilly's brother came into the room. He had a shirt on, though. He looked kind of annoyed. He said my dad was on the phone. My dad was all mad because he'd been trying to get through for hours, only Michael was on the internet answering fanmail for his webzine, *Crackhead*, so he kept getting a busy signal.

I must have looked like I was going to throw up or something, because after a minute, Michael said, 'OK, don't worry about it, Thermopolis. I'll tell him you and Lilly already went to bed,' which is a lie my mother would never believe, but must have gone over pretty well with my dad, since Michael came back and reported that my dad had apologized for calling so late (it was only eleven) and that he'd speak to me in the morning.

Great. I can't wait.

I guess I must have still looked like I was going to throw up, because Michael called his dog and made him get into bed with us, even though pets aren't allowed in the Drs Moscovitzes' room. Pavlov crawled into my lap and started licking my face, which he'll only do to people he really trusts. Then Michael sat down to watch the movies with us, and in the interest of science, Lilly asked him which Bond girls were most attractive to him, the blondes who always needed James Bond to rescue them or the brunettes who were always pulling guns on him, and Michael said he couldn't resist a girl with a weapon, which got us started on his two favourite TV shows of all time, *Xena, Warrior Princess* and *Buffy the Vampire Slayer*.

So then not really in the interest of science, but more out of plain curiosity, I asked Michael if it was the end of the world and he had to repopulate the planet but he could only choose one life mate, who would it be, Xena or Buffy?

After telling me how weird I was for thinking of something like that, Michael chose Buffy, and then Lilly asked me if I had to choose between Harrison Ford or George Clooney, who would it be, and I said Harrison Ford even though he's so old, but the Harrison Ford from *Indiana Jones*, not *Star Wars*, and then Lilly said she'd choose Harrison Ford as Jack Ryan in those Tom Clancy movies, and then Michael goes, 'Who would you choose, Harrison Ford or Leonardo di Caprio?' and we both chose Harrison Ford because Leonardo is so passé, and then he went, 'Who would you choose, Harrison Ford or Josh Richter?' and Lilly said Harrison Ford, because he used to be a carpenter and if it was the end of the world, he could build her a house, but I said Josh Richter, because he'd live longer – Harrison is like SIXTY – and be able to give me a hand with the kids.

Then Michael started saying all this totally unfair stuff about Josh Richter, like how in the face of nuclear armageddon he'd probably show cowardice, but Lilly said fear of new things is not an accurate measure of one's potential for growth, with which I agreed. Then Michael said we were both idiots if we thought Josh Richter would ever give us so much as the time of day, that he only liked girls like Lana Weinberger who put out, to which Lilly responded that she would put out for Josh Richter if he was able to meet certain conditions, like bathing beforehand in an anti-bacterial solution, and wearing three condoms coated in spermicidal fluid during the act, in case one broke and one slipped off.

Then Michael asked me if I would put out for Josh Richter, and I had to think about it for a minute. Losing your virginity is a really big step, and you have to do it with the right person, or else you could be screwed up for the rest of your life, like the women in Dr Moscovitz's Over Forty And Still Single group, which meets every other Tuesday. So after I'd thought about it, I said I would put out for Josh Richter, but only if:

1. We'd been dating for at least a year.
2. He pledged his undying love to me.
3. He took me to see *Beauty and the Beast* on Broadway and didn't make fun of it.

Michael said the first two sounded all right, but if the third one was an example of the kind of boyfriend I expected to get, I'd be a virgin for a long, long time. He said he didn't know anyone with an ounce of testosterone who could watch *Beauty and the Beast* on Broadway without projectile vomiting. But he's wrong, because my dad definitely has testosterone – at least one testicle full – and he's never projectile vomited at the show.

Then Lilly asked Michael who he would choose if he had to, me or Lana Weinberger, and he said, 'Mia, of course,' but I'm sure he was just saying that because I was right there in the room and he didn't want to dis me to my face.

I wish Lilly wouldn't do things like that.

But she kept on doing it, wanting to know who Michael would choose, me or Madonna, or me or Buffy the Vampire Slayer (he chose me over Madonna, but Buffy won, hands down, over me).

And then Lilly wanted to know who I would choose, Michael or Josh Richter. I pretended to be seriously thinking about it, when to my total relief the Drs Moscovitz came home and started yelling at us for letting Pavlov in their room and eating popcorn in their bed.

So then later after Lilly and I had cleaned up all the

popcorn and gone back to her room, she asked me again who I would choose, Josh Richter or her brother, and I had to say Josh Richter, because Josh Richter is the hottest boy in our whole school, maybe the whole world, and I am completely and totally in love with him, and not just because of the way his blond hair sometimes falls into his eyes when he's bent over, looking for stuff in his locker, but because I know that behind that jock-facade he maintains, he is a deeply sensitive and caring person. I could tell by the way he said Hey to me that day in Bigelow's.

But I couldn't help thinking if it *really* were the end of the world, it might be better to be with Michael, even if he isn't so hot, because at least he makes me laugh. I think at the end of the world, a sense of humour would be important.

Plus, of course, Michael looks really good without a shirt.

And if it really was the end of the world, Lilly would be dead, so she'd never know her brother and I were procreating!

I'd *never* want Lilly to know that I feel that way about her brother. She'd think it was weird.

Weirder even than me turning out to be the Princess of Genovia.

Later on Saturday

The whole way home from Lilly's I worried about what my mom and dad were going to say when I got home. I had never disobeyed them before. I mean, really never.

Well, OK, there was that one time Lilly and Shameeka and Ling Su and I went to see that Christian Slater movie, but we ended up going to *The Rocky Horror Picture Show* instead, and I forgot to call until after the movie, which ended at, like, 2:30 in the morning and we were in Times Square and didn't have enough money left between us for a cab.

But that was just that one time! And I totally learned a lesson from it, without my mom having to ground me or anything. Not that she would ever do something like that – ground me, I mean. Who would go to the cash machine to get money for take-out if I were grounded?

But my dad's another story. He is totally rigid in the discipline department. My mom says that's because Grandmere used to punish him when he was a little boy by locking him into this one really scary room in their house.

Now that I think about it, the house my dad grew up in was probably the castle, and that scary room was probably the dungeon.

Geez, no wonder my dad does every single thing Grandmere says.

Anyway, when my dad gets mad at me, he *really* gets mad. Like the time I wouldn't go to church with Grandmere, because I refused to pray to a god who would allow rain-forests to be destroyed in order to make grazing room for cows who would later become Quarter Pounders for the ignorant masses who worship that symbol of all that is evil, Ronald McDonald. Not only did my dad tell me that if I didn't go to church, he'd wear out my behind, he wouldn't let me read Michael's webzine, *Crackhead*, again! He refused to let me go online again for the rest of the summer. He crushed my modem with a magnum of Chateauneuf du Pape.

Talk about reactionary!

So I was totally worried about what he was going to do when I got home from Lilly's. I tried to hang out at the Moscovitzes as long as possible: I loaded the breakfast dishes in the dishwasher for Maya, since she was busy writing a letter to her congressman asking him to please do something about her son Manuel, who was wrongfully imprisoned ten years ago for supporting a revolution in their country. I walked Pavlov, since Michael had to go to an astrophysics lecture at Columbia. I even unclogged the jets in the Drs Moscovitzes' Jacuzzi – boy, does Lilly's dad shed a lot.

Then Lilly had to go and announce that it was time to shoot the one-hour special episode of her show, the one dedicated to her feet. Only it turned out the Drs Moscovitz had not left, like we thought they had, for their rolfing sessions – which is like massage, only more expensive. They totally overheard and told me that I had to go home while they analysed Lilly about her need to taunt her sex-crazed stalker.

Here's the thing:

I am generally a very good daughter. I mean it. I don't smoke. I don't do drugs. I haven't given birth at any proms. I am completely trustworthy, and I do my homework most of the time. Except for one lousy F in a class that will be of no use to me whatsoever in my future life, I'm doing pretty well.

And then they had to spring the princess thing on me.

I decided on my way home that if my dad tried to punish

me, I was going to call Judge Judy, the family court judge who has her own show on Channel 4. He'd really be sorry if he landed on Judge Judy because of this. She'd let him have it, boy, let me tell you. People trying to make other people be princesses when they don't want to be? Judge Judy wouldn't stand for any of it. She'd probably award me five thousand dollars just for the mental anguish I've been put through.

Of course, when I got home, it turned out I didn't have to call Judge Judy at all.

My mom hadn't gone to her studio, which she does every Saturday without fail. She was sitting there waiting for me to come home, reading old copies of the subscription she got me to *Seventeen* magazine, before she realized I was too flat-chested to ever be asked out on a date, so all the information provided in that particular periodical was worthless to me.

Then there was my dad, who was sitting in the exact same spot as he'd been when I'd left the day before, only this time he was reading the *Sunday Times*, even though it was Saturday, and Mom and I have this rule that you can't start reading the Sunday sections until Sunday. To my surprise, he wasn't wearing a suit. Today he had on a sweater – cashmere, no doubt given to him by one of his many girlfriends – and corduroy trousers.

When I walked in, he folded the paper all carefully, put it down, and gave me this long, intent look, like Captain Picard right before he starts going on to Ryker about the Prime Directive. Then he goes, 'We need to talk.'

I immediately started in about how it wasn't like I hadn't told them where I was, and how I just needed a little time away to think about things, and how I'd been really careful and hadn't taken the subway or anything, and my dad just went, 'I know.'

63

Just like that. *I know.* He completely gave in without a fight.

My dad.

I looked at my mom to see if she'd noticed that he'd lost his mind. And then she did the craziest thing. She put the magazine down and came over and hugged me and said, 'We're so sorry, baby.'

Hello? These are my *parents?* Did the body snatchers come while I was gone and replace my parents with pod people? Because that was the only way I could think of that my parents would be so reasonable.

Then my dad goes, 'We understand the stress that this has brought you, Mia, and we want you to know that we'll do everything in our power to try to make this transition as smooth for you as possible.'

Then my dad asked me if I knew what a compromise was, and I said, yes, of course, I'm not in, like, the third grade any more, so he pulled out this piece of paper, and on it, we all drafted what my mom calls the Thermopolis–Renaldo Compromise. It goes like this:

I, the undersigned, Artur Christoff Phillipe Gerard Grimaldi Renaldo, agree that my sole offspring and heir, Amelia Mignonette Grimaldi Thermopolis Renaldo, may finish out her high school tenure at Albert Einstein School For Boys (made co-educational circa 1975) without interruption, save for Christmas and summer breaks, which she will spend without complaint in the country of Genovia.

I asked if that meant no more summers at Miragnac, and he said yes. I couldn't believe it. Christmas and summer, free of Grandmere? That would be like going to the dentist, only instead of having cavities filled, I'd just get to read *Teen People* and suck up a lot of laughing gas! I was so happy, I hugged him right there. But unfortunately, it turned out there was more to the agreement.

I, the undersigned, Amelia Mignonette Grimaldi Thermopolis Renaldo, agree to fulfil the duties of heir to Artur Christoff Phillipe Gerard Grimaldi Renaldo, prince of Genovia, and all that such a role entails, including but not exclusive to, assuming the throne upon the latter's demise, and attending functions of state at which the presence of said heir is deemed essential.

All of that sounded pretty good to me, except the last part. Functions of state? What were they?

My dad got all vague. 'Oh, you know. Attending the funerals of world leaders, opening balls, that sort of thing.'

Hello? Funerals? Balls? Whatever happened to smashing bottles of champagne against ocean liners, and going to Hollywood premieres, and that kind of thing?

'Well,' my dad said. 'Hollywood premieres aren't really all they're pegged up to be. Flashbulbs going off in your face, that kind of thing. Terribly unpleasant.'

Yeah, but *funerals*? *Balls*? I don't even know how to put on lip-liner, let alone curtsy . . .

'Oh, that's all right,' my dad said, putting the cap back on his pen. 'Grandmere will take care of that.'

Yeah, right. What can *she* do? She's in France!

Ha! Ha! Ha!

Saturday night

I can't even believe what a loser I am. I mean, Saturday night, alone with my DAD!

He actually tried to talk me into going to see *Beauty and the Beast*, like he felt sorry for me, because I didn't have a date!

I finally had to say, 'Look, Dad, I am not a child any more. Even the Prince of Genovia can't get tickets to a Disney show at last-minute notice on a Saturday night.'

He was just feeling left out, because Mom had taken off on another date with Mr Gianini. She wanted to cancel on him, given all the upheaval that has occurred in my life over the past twenty-four hours, but I totally made her go, because I could see her lips getting smaller and smaller, the more time she spent with Dad. Mom's lips only get small when she's trying to keep herself from saying something, and I think what she wanted to say to my dad was, '*Get out! Go back to your hotel! You're paying six hundred dollars a night for that suite! Can't you go stay in it?*'

My dad drives my mom completely insane, because he's always going around, digging her bank statements out from the big salad bowl where she throws all our mail, and trying to tell her how much she would save in interest if she would just transfer funds out of her checking account and into a Roth IRA.

So even though she felt like she should stay home, I knew if she did, she'd explode, so I said go, please go, and that Dad and I would discuss what it's like to govern a small principality in today's economic market. Only when Mom came out in her datewear – which included this totally hot black mini-dress from Victoria's Secret (my mom hates shopping, so she buys all her clothes from catalogues while she's soaking in the tub after a long day of painting) – my dad started

66

to choke on this ice cube. I guess he had never seen my mom in a mini-dress before – back in college, when they were going out, all she ever wore were overalls, like me – because he drank down his scotch and soda really fast and then said, '*That's* what you're wearing?', which made my mom go, 'What's wrong with it?' and look at herself all worriedly in the mirror.

She looked totally fine; in fact, she looked much better than she usually did, which I guess was the problem. I mean, it sounds weird to admit, but my mom can be a total Betty when she puts her mind to it. I can only *wish* that someday I'll be as pretty as my mom. I mean, *she* doesn't have Yield sign hair or a flat chest or size eight shoes. She is way hot, as far as moms go.

Then the buzzer rang and Mom ran out because she didn't want Mr Gianini to come up and meet her ex, the Prince of Genovia. Which was understandable, since he was still choking, and looked sort of funny. I mean, he looked like a red-faced bald man in a cashmere sweater, coughing up a lung. I mean, *I* would have been embarrassed to admit *I* had ever had sex with him, if I were her.

Anyway, it was good for me that she didn't buzz him up, because I didn't want Mr Gianini asking me in front of my parents why I hadn't gone to his review session on Friday.

So then after they were gone, I tried to show my dad how much better suited I am for life in Manhattan than in Genovia by ordering some really excellent food. I got us an insalata caprese, ravioli al funghetto, and a pizza margherita, all for under twenty bucks, but I swear, my dad wasn't a bit impressed! He just poured himself another scotch and soda and turned on the TV. He didn't even notice when Fat Louie sat down next to him. He started petting him like it was nothing. And my dad claims to be *allergic* to cats.

And then, to top it all off, he didn't even want to talk about Genovia. All he wanted to do was watch sports. I'm not kidding. Sports. We have seventy-seven channels, and all he would watch were the ones showing men in uniforms, chasing after a little ball. Forget the Dirty Harry movie marathon. Forget Pop Up Videos. He just turned on the sports channel and stared at it, and when I happened to mention that Mom and I usually watch whatever is on HBO on Saturday nights, he just turned up the volume!!!

What a baby.

And you think that's bad? You should have seen him when the food got here. He made Lars frisk the delivery man before he would let me buzz him up! Can you believe it? I had to give Antonio a whole extra dollar to make up for the indignity of it all. And then my dad sat down and ate, without saying a word, until, after another scotch and soda, he fell asleep, right on the futon, with Fat Louie on his lap!

I guess being a prince and having had testicular cancer can really make a person think he's something special. I mean, God forbid he should share some quality time with his only daughter, the heir to his throne.

So here I am again, home on a Saturday night. Not that I'm ever NOT home on a Saturday night, except when I'm with Lilly. Why am I so unpopular? I mean, I know I look weird and stuff, but I really try to be nice to people, you know? I mean, you'd think people would value me as a human being and invite me to their parties just because they like my company. It's not MY fault my hair sticks out the way it does, any more than it's Lilly's fault her face looks sort of squished.

I tried to call Lilly a zillion times, but her phone was busy, which meant Michael was probably home, working on his 'zine. The Moscovitzes are trying to have a second line installed so that people who call them can actually get through once in a while, but the phone company says it doesn't have any more 212 numbers to give out. Lilly's mom says she refuses to have two separate area codes in the same apartment, and that if she can't have 212, she'll just buy a beeper. Besides, Michael will be leaving for college next fall, and then their phone problems will be solved.

I really wanted to talk to Lilly. I mean, I haven't told her anything about the princess thing, and I'm not going to, *ever*, but sometimes even without telling her what's bothering me, talking to Lilly makes me feel better. Maybe it's just knowing that somebody else my age is also stuck at home on a Saturday night. I mean, most of the other girls in our class date. Even Shameeka has started dating. She's been quite popular since she developed breasts over the summer. True, her curfew is ten o'clock, even on weekends, and she has to introduce her date to her mom and dad, and her date has to provide a detailed itinerary of exactly where they're going and what they'll be doing, besides showing two pieces of photo ID for Mr Taylor to Xerox before he'll let Shameeka go out of the house with him.

But still, she's *dating*. Somebody *asked her out*.

Nobody has ever asked me out.

It was pretty boring, watching my dad snore, even though it was fairly comical the way Fat Louie kept glancing at him, all annoyed, every time he inhaled. I had already seen all the Dirty Harry movies, and there was nothing else on. I decided to try instant messaging Michael, telling him I really needed to talk to Lilly, and would he please go off-line so I could call her.

But Michael can be a total jerk sometimes. I printed out a copy of our conversation. Here it is:

```
CracKing: What do you want, Thermopolis?
>
FtLouie: I want to talk to Lilly. Please go
off-line so I can call her.
>
CracKing: What do you want to talk to her
about?
>
FtLouie: None of your business. Just go off-
line, please. You can't hog all the lines of
communication to yourself. It isn't fair.
>
CracKing: No one ever said life was fair,
Thermopolis. What are you doing home, anyway?
What's the matter? Dreamboy didn't call?
>
FtLouie: Who's Dreamboy?
>
CracKing: You know, your post-nuclear armaged-
don life mate of choice, Josh Richter.
```

Lilly told him! I can't believe she told him! I'm going to kill her.

```
FtLouie: WOULD YOU PLEASE GO OFF-LINE SO I CAN
CALL LILLY????
>
CracKing: What's the matter, Thermopolis? Did I
strike a nerve?
```

I logged off. He can be such a jerk sometimes.

But then about five minutes later the phone rang, and it was Lilly. So I guess even though Michael's a jerk, he can be a nice jerk, when he wants to be.

Lilly's very upset about how her parents are violating her First Amendment right to free speech by not letting her tape the episode of her show dedicated to her feet. She is going to call the ACLU as soon as it opens on Monday morning. Without her parents' financial support, which they have currently revoked, *Lilly Tells It Like It Is* cannot go on. It costs about $200 per episode, if you include the cost of tape and all. Public access is only accessible to people with cash.

Lilly was so upset, I didn't feel like yelling at her about telling Michael that I chose Josh. Now that I think about it, it's probably just better that way.

My life is a convoluted web of lies.

Sunday, October 5

I can't believe Mr Gianini told her. I can't believe he told my mother I skipped his stupid review session on Friday!!!!

Hello? Do I have no rights here? Can't I skip a review session and not get finked on by my mother's boyfriend?

I mean, it's not like my life isn't bad enough: I'm already deformed, *and* I have to be a princess. Do I have to have my every activity reported upon by my Algebra teacher????

Thanks a lot, Mr Gianini. Thanks to you, I got to spend my entire Sunday having the quadratic formula drilled into me by my demented father, who kept rubbing his bald head and screaming in frustration when he found out I don't know how to multiply fractions.

Hello? May I remind everyone that I'm supposed to have Saturday and Sunday OFF from school?

AND Mr Gianini had to go and tell my mother there's going to be a pop quiz tomorrow. I mean, I guess that was kind of nice of him and all, to give me a heads up, but you're not supposed to study for a pop quiz. The whole point is to test what you've retained.

Then again, since I've apparently retained nothing mathematical since about the second grade, I guess I can't really blame my dad for being so mad. He said if I don't pass Algebra, he's going to make me go to summer school. So then I pointed out that summer school was fine by me, since I'd already agreed to spend summers in Genovia. So then he said I'd have to go to summer school in GENOVIA!

I am so sure. I met some kids who went to school in Genovia and they didn't even know what a number line was. And they measure everything by kilos and centimetres. As if metric wasn't so totally over!

But just in case, I'm not taking any chances. I wrote out

the quadratic formula on the white rubber sole of my Converse high-top, right where it curves in between my heel and my toes. I'll wear them tomorrow, and cross my legs and take a peek, if I get stuck.

Monday, October 6, 3 a.m.

I've been up all night, worrying about getting caught cheating. What will happen if someone sees I have the quadratic formula written on my shoe? Will I be expelled? I don't want to be expelled! I mean, even though everybody at Albert Einstein High School thinks I'm a freak, I'm sort of getting used to it. I don't want to have to start over at a whole new school. I'll have to wear the scarlet mark of being a cheater for the rest of my high school career!

And what about college? I might not get into college, if it goes down on my permanent record that I'm a cheater.

Not that I want to go to college. But what about Greenpeace? I'm sure Greenpeace doesn't want cheaters. Oh my God, what am I going to do???

Monday October 6, 4 a.m.

I tried washing the quadratic formula off my shoe, but it won't come off! I must have used indelible ink or something! What if my dad finds out? Do they still behead people in Genovia?

Monday October 6, 7 a.m.

Decided to wear my Docs, and throw my high-tops away on the way to school – but then I broke one of the bootlaces! I can't wear any of my other shoes because they're all size 7 and a half, and my foot grew a whole half inch last month! I can barely walk in my loafers, and my heels hang out over the backs of my clogs. I have no choice but to wear my high-tops!

I'm going to get caught for sure, I just know it.

Monday, October 6, 9 a.m.

Realized in the car on the way to school that I could have taken the laces out of my high-tops and strung them through my Doc Martens. I am so stupid.

Lilly wants to know how much longer my dad is going to be in town. She doesn't like being driven to school. She likes to ride the subway, because then she can brush up on her Spanish, reading all the health awareness posters. I told her I didn't know how long my dad was going to be in town, but that I had a feeling I wasn't going to be allowed to ride the subway any more, anywhere.

Lilly observed that my father was taking this infertility thing too far, that just because he can longer render anyone *embarrazada* was no reason to get all overprotective of me. I noticed that in the driver's seat, Lars was sort of laughing to himself. I hope he doesn't speak Spanish. How embarrassing.

Anyway, Lilly went on to say I should take a stand right away, now, before things got worse, and that she could tell it was already starting to take a toll on me, since I seemed listless and there were circles under my eyes.

Of course I'm listless! I've been up since 3 a.m., trying to wash my shoes!

Went into the Girls' Room to try to wash them again. Lana Weinberger came in while I was there. She saw me washing my shoes, and she just rolled her eyes and started brushing her long, Marcia Brady hair and staring at herself in the mirror. I half expected her to walk right up to her reflection and kiss it, she is so obviously in love with herself.

The quadratic formula is smeared, but still legible, on my sneaker. But I won't look at it during the test, I swear.

Monday October 6, G & T

OK. I admit it. I looked.

Fat lot of good it did me too. After he'd collected the test, Mr Gianini went over the problems on the board, and I got every single one of them wrong anyway.

I CAN'T EVEN CHEAT RIGHT!!!

I have got to be the most pathetic human being on the planet.

polynomials
term: variables multiplied by a coefficient
degree of polynomial = the degree of the term with the highest degree

Hello? Does ANYONE care??? I mean, really, truly care about polynomials? I mean, besides people like Michael Moscovitz and Mr Gianini. Anyone? Anyone at all?

When the bell finally rang, Mr Gianini goes, 'Mia, will I have the pleasure of your company this afternoon at the review session?'

I said yes, but I didn't say it loud enough for anyone to hear but him.

Why me? *Why, why, why?* Like I don't have enough to worry about. I'm flunking Algebra, my mom's dating my teacher, and I'm the Princess of Genovia.

Something has just *got* to give.

Tuesday, October 7

Ode to Algebra

Thrust into this dingy classroom
we die like lampless moths
locked into the desolation of
fluorescent lights and metal desks.
Ten minutes until the bell rings.
What use is the quadratic formula
in our daily lives?
Can we use it to unlock the secrets
in the hearts of those we love?
Five minutes until the bell rings.
Cruel Algebra teacher,
Won't you let us go?

Homework:

Algebra: Problems 17–30 on handout
English: Proposal
World Civ.: questions at end of Chapter 7
G & T: none
French: huit phrase, ex. A, pg. 31
Biology: worksheet

Wednesday, October 8

Oh no.

She's here.

Well, not *here*, exactly. But she's in this country. She's in the city. She's only like fifty-seven blocks away, as a matter of fact. She's staying at the Plaza, with Dad. Thank God. Now I'll only have to see her after school and on the weekends. It would suck so bad if she were staying here.

It's pretty awful, seeing her first thing in the morning. She wears these really fancy negligees to bed, with big lace sections that everything shows through. You know. Stuff you wouldn't want to see. Plus, she still has on eyeliner, because she had it tattooed onto her eyelids back in the eighties when she went through a brief manic phase shortly after Princess Grace died (according to my mom). It looks pretty weird, seeing this old lady in a lace nightie with big black lines around her eyes first thing in the morning.

Actually, it's scary. Scarier than Freddie Kruger and Jason put together.

No wonder Grandpa died of a heart attack in bed. He probably rolled over one morning and got a real good look at his wife.

Somebody ought to warn the President she's here. I mean it, he really ought to know. Because if anybody could start World War III, it's my grandmother.

Last time I saw Grandmere, she was having this dinner party, and she served everybody foie gras except this one woman. She just had Marie, her cook, leave that lady's plate bare for the foie gras course. And when I tried to give the lady my foie gras, because I thought maybe they had run out, and anyway, I don't eat anything that once was alive, my grandmother was all, 'Amelia!' She said it so loud, she scared me. She made me drop my slice of foie gras on the floor. Her horrible miniature poodle pried it up off the parquet before I could even move.

And then later, after everybody left, when I asked her why she wouldn't give that lady any foie gras, Grandmere said it was because the lady had had a child out of wedlock.

Hello? Grandmere, may I point out that your own son had a child out of wedlock, namely me, Mia, *your granddaughter?*

But when I said that, Grandmere just yelled for her maid to bring her another drink. Oh, so I guess it's OK to have a child out of wedlock if you're a PRINCE. But if you're just a regular person, no foie gras for you.

Oh, no! What if Grandmere comes to the loft? She's never seen the loft before. She's never been below Fifty-Seventh Street before. She's going to hate it here in the Village, I'm telling you right now. People of the same sex kiss and hold hands in our neighbourhood all the time. Grandmere has a fit when she sees people of the *opposite* sex holding hands. What's she going to do during the Gay Pride Parade, when everybody is kissing and holding hands and shouting, 'We're Here, We're Queer, Get Over It?' Grandmere won't get over it. She might have a heart attack. She doesn't even like pierced ears, let alone pierced anything else.

Plus it's against the law to smoke in restaurants here, and Grandmere smokes all the time, even in bed, which is why Grandpere had these weird disposable oxygen masks installed in every single room at Miragnac, and had an underground tunnel dug that we could run through in case Grandmere fell asleep with a cigarette in her mouth and the chateau burst into flames.

Also, Grandmere hates cats. She thinks they jump on children while they're sleeping on purpose to suck out their breath. What's she going to say when she sees Fat Louie? He sleeps in bed with me every night. If he ever jumped on my face, he'd kill me instantly. He weighs twenty-five pounds and seven ounces, and that's before he's had his can of Fancy Feast in the morning.

And can you imagine what she'll do when she sees my mom's collection of wooden fertility goddesses?

Why did she have to come NOW? She's going to ruin EVERYTHING. There's no way I'm going to be able to keep this a secret from everyone with HER around.

Why?

Why??

WHY???

Thursday, October 9

I found out why.
    She's giving me princess lessons.
    In too much shock to write. More later.

Friday, October 10

Princess lessons.

I am not kidding. I have to go straight from my Algebra review session every day to princess lessons at the Plaza with my grandmother.

OK, so if there's a god, how could this have happened?

I mean it. Like, people always talk about how God doesn't ever give you more than you can handle, but I'm telling you right now, I cannot handle this. This is just *too much*! I *cannot* go to princess lessons every day after school. Not with Grandmere. I am seriously considering running away from home.

My dad says I have no choice. Last night, after I left Grandmere's room at the Plaza, I went straight down to his. I banged on the door, and when he answered it, I stalked straight in and told him I wasn't doing it. No way. Nobody had told me anything about princess lessons.

And do you know what he said? He says I signed the compromise, so I am obligated to attend princess lessons as part of my duties as his heir.

I said then we are just going to have to revise the compromise, because there was nothing in there about me having to meet with Grandmere every day after school for any princess lessons.

But my dad wouldn't even talk to me about it. He said he was late, and could we please talk about it later. And then while I was standing there, going on about how unfair this all was, in walks this reporter from ABC. I guess she was there to interview him, but it was kind of funny, because I've seen her interview people before, and normally she doesn't wear black sleeveless cocktail dresses when she's interviewing the President or somebody like that.

I'm going to have to take a good look at that compromise tonight, because I don't recall it saying anything about princess lessons.

Here is how my first 'lesson' went, yesterday after school:

First the doorman won't even let me in (big surprise). Then he sees Lars, who is like six foot seven and must weigh three hundred pounds. Plus Lars has this bulge sticking out of his jacket, and I only just now figured out that it's a gun and not the stump of an extraneous third arm, which is what I thought originally. I was too embarrassed to ask him about it, in case it dredged up painful memories for him, of being teased as a child in Amsterdam, or wherever Lars is from. I mean, I know what it's like to be a freak: it's just better not to bring that kind of thing up.

But no, it's a gun, and the doorman got all upset about it, and called the concierge over. Thank God the concierge recognized Lars, who's staying there, after all, in a room in Dad's suite.

So then the concierge himself escorted me upstairs to the penthouse, which is where Grandmere is staying. Let me tell you about this penthouse: it is very fancy. I thought the Ladies' Room at the Plaza was fancy. Those Ladies' Rooms are nothing compared to this penthouse.

First of all, everything is pink. Pink walls, pink carpet, pink curtains, pink furniture. There are pink roses everywhere, and these portraits hanging on the walls that all feature pink-cheeked shepherdesses and stuff.

And just when I thought I was going to drown in pinkness, out came Grandmere, dressed completely in purple, from her silk turban all the way down to her mules with the rhinestone clips on the toes.

At least, I think they're rhinestones.

Grandmere always wears purple. Lilly says people who

wear purple a lot usually have borderline personality disorders, because they have delusions of grandeur: traditionally, purple has always stood for the aristocracy, since for hundreds of years peasants weren't allowed to dye their clothes with indigo, and therefore couldn't make violet.

Of course, Lilly doesn't know my grandmother IS a member of the aristocracy. So while she is definitely delusional, it's not because she THINKS she's an aristocrat: she really IS aristocracy.

So Grandmere comes in off the terrace where she was standing, and the first thing she says to me is, 'What's that writing on your shoe?'

But I didn't need to worry about getting caught cheating, because Grandmere started in right away about everything else that was wrong with me.

'Why are you wearing tennis shoes with a skirt? Are those tights supposed to be clean? Why can't you stand up straight? What's wrong with your hair? Have you been biting your nails again, Amelia? I thought we agreed you were going to give up that nasty habit. My God, can't you stop growing? Is it your goal to be as tall as your father?'

Only it sounded even worse, because it was all in French.

And then, as if that wasn't bad enough, she goes, in her creaky old cigaretty voice, 'Haven't you a kiss for your grandmere, then?'

So I go up to her and bend down (my grandmother is, like, a foot shorter than me) and kiss her on the cheek (which is very soft because she rubs Vaseline on her face every night before she goes to bed), and then when I start to pull away she grabs me and goes, '*Pfui*! Have you forgotten *everything* I taught you?' and makes me kiss her on the other cheek too, because in Europe and SoHo that's how you say hello to people.

Anyway, I bent down and kissed Grandmere on the other cheek, and as I did so, I noticed Rommel peeking out from behind her. Rommel is Grandmere's fifteen-year-old miniature poodle. He is the same shape and size as an iguana, only not as smart. He shakes all the time and has to wear a fleece jacket. Today his jacket was the same purple as Grandmere's dress. Rommel won't let anyone touch him except for Grandmere, and even then, he rolls his eyes around as if he were being tortured while she's petting him.

If Noah had ever met Rommel, he might have changed his mind about letting two of *all* of God's creatures on the ark.

'Now,' Grandmere said, when she felt we'd been affectionate enough, 'let's see if I have this right: your father tells you that you are the Princess of Genovia, and you burst into tears. Why is this?'

All of a sudden, I got very tired. I had to sit down on one of the pink foofy chairs, before I fell down.

'Oh, Grandma,' I said, in English. 'I don't want to be a princess. I just want to be me, Mia.'

Grandmere said, 'Don't call me Grandma. It's vulgar. I am your grandmere. Speak French when you speak to me. Sit up straight in that chair. Do not drape your legs over the arm. And you are not Mia. You are Amelia. In fact, you are Amelia Mignonette Grimaldi Renaldo.'

I said, 'You forgot Thermopolis,' and Grandmere gave me the evil eye. She is very good at this.

'No,' she says. 'I did not forget Thermopolis.'

Then Grandmere sat down in the foofy chair next to mine and said, 'Are you telling me you have no wish to assume your rightful place upon the throne?'

'Grandma – I mean, Grandmere.' Boy, was I tired. 'You

know as well as I do that I'm not princess material, OK? So why are we even wasting our time?'

Grandmere looked at me out of her twin tattoos of eyeliner. I could tell she wanted to kill me, but probably couldn't figure out how to do it without getting blood on the pink carpet.

'You are the heir to the crown of Genovia,' she said, in this totally serious voice. 'And you will take my son's place on the throne when he dies. This is how it is. There is no other way.'

Oh, boy.

So I kind of went, 'Yeah, whatever, Grandmere. Look, I got a lot of homework. Is this princess thing going to take long?'

Grandmere just looked at me. 'It will take,' she said, 'as long as it takes. I am not afraid to sacrifice my time – or even myself – for the good of my country.'

Whoa. This was getting way patriotic. 'Um,' I said. 'OK.'

So then I stared at Grandmere for a while, and she stared back at me, and Rommel laid down on the carpet between our chairs, only he did it really slow, like his legs were too delicate to support all two pounds of him, and then Grandmere broke the silence by saying, 'We will begin tomorrow. You will come here directly after school.'

'Um, Grandma, I mean, mere. I can't come here directly after school. I'm flunking Algebra. I have to go to a review session every day after school.'

'Then after that. No dawdling. You will bring with you a list of the ten women you admire most in the world, and why. That is all.'

My mouth fell open. *Homework?* There's going to be *homework?* Nobody said anything about homework!

'And close your mouth,' she barked. 'It is uncouth to let it hang open like that.'

I closed my mouth. Homework???

'Tomorrow you will wear nylons. Not tights. Not knee-socks. You are too old for tights and knee-socks. And you will wear your school shoes, not tennis sneakers. You will style your hair, apply lipstick, and paint your fingernails – what's left of them, anyway.' Grandmere stood up. She didn't even have to push up with her hands on the arms of her chair, either. Grandmere's pretty spry, for her age. 'Now I must dress for dinner with the Shah. Goodbye.'

I just sat there. Was she insane? Was she completely nuts? Did she have the slightest idea what she was asking me to do?

Evidently she did, since the next thing I knew, Lars was standing there, and Grandmere and Rommel were gone.

Geez! Homework!!! Nobody said there was going to be homework.

And that's not the worst of it. Pantyhose? To school? I mean, the only girls who wear pantyhose to school are girls like Lana Weinberger, and seniors, and people like that. You know. Show-offs. None of *my* friends wear pantyhose.

And, I might add, none of my friends wear lipstick or nail polish or do their hair. Not for *school*, anyway.

But what choice did I have? Grandmere totally scared me, with her tattooed eyelids and all. I couldn't NOT do what she said.

So what I did was, I borrowed a pair of my mom's panty-hose. She wears them whenever she has an opening – and on dates with Mr Gianini, I've noticed. I took a pair of her pantyhose to school with me, in my backpack. I didn't have any fingernails to paint – according to Lilly, I am orally fixated: if it fits in my mouth, I'll put it there – but I did bor-row one of my mom's lipsticks too. And I tried some mousse I found in the medicine cabinet. It must have worked, since when Lilly got into the car this morning, she said, 'Wow. Where'd you pick up the Jersey girl, Lars?'

Which I guess meant that my hair looked really big, like girls in New Jersey wear it when they come into Manhattan for a romantic dinner in Little Italy with their boyfriends.

So then, after my review session with Mr G at the end of the day, I went into the Girls' Room and put on the pantyhose, the lipstick, and my loafers, which are too small and pinch my toes really badly. When I checked myself out in the mirror, I thought I didn't look so bad. I didn't think Grandmere would have any complaints.

I thought I was pretty slick, waiting to change until after school. I figured on a Friday afternoon, there wouldn't be anyone hanging around. Who wants to hang around school on a Friday?

I had forgotten, of course, about the Computer Club.

Everybody forgets about the Computer Club, even the people who belong to it. They don't have any friends, except each other, and they never go on dates – only unlike me, I think this is by choice: no one at Albert Einstein is smart enough for them – except, again, for each other.

Anyway, I walked out of the Girls' Room and ran smack into Lilly's brother, Michael. He's the Computer Club treasurer. He's smart enough to be president, but he says he has no interest in being a figurehead.

'Christ, Thermopolis,' he said, as I scrambled around, trying to pick up all the stuff I'd dropped – like my high-tops and socks and stuff – when I bumped into him. 'What happened to *you*?'

I thought he meant why was I there so late. 'You know I have to meet with Mr Gianini every day after school, because I'm flunking Alge—'

'I know *that*.' Michael held up the lipstick that had

exploded out of my backpack. 'I mean what's with the war-paint?'

I took it away from him. 'Nothing. Don't tell Lilly.'

'Don't tell Lilly what?' I stood up, and he noticed the pantyhose. 'Jesus, Thermopolis. Where are *you* going?'

'Nowhere.' Must I continuously be forced to lie all the time? I really wished he would go away. Plus a bunch of his computer nerd friends were standing there, staring at me, like I was some new kind of pixel, or something. It was making me pretty uncomfortable.

'Nobody goes *nowhere* looking like *that.*' Michael shifted his laptop from one arm to the other, then got this funny look on his face. 'Thermopolis, are you going out on a *date*?'

'*What*? No, I'm not going on a date!' I was completely shocked at the idea. A *date*? *Me*? I'm so sure! 'I have to meet my grandmother!'

Michael didn't look as if he believed me. 'And do you usually wear lipstick and pantyhose to meet your grandmother?'

I heard some discreet coughing, and looked down the hall. Lars was there by the doors, waiting for me.

I guess I could have stood there and explained that my grandmother had threatened me with bodily harm (well, practically) if I didn't wear make-up and nylons to meet her. But I sort of didn't think he'd believe me. So I said, 'Look, don't tell Lilly, OK?'

Then I ran away.

I knew I was dead meat. There was no way Michael wasn't going to tell his sister about seeing me coming out of the Girls' Room after school in lipstick and pantyhose. No way.

And Grandmere's was HORRIBLE. She said the lipstick I had on made me look like a *poulet*. At least that's what I thought she said, and I couldn't figure out why she thought

I looked like a chicken. But just now I looked up poulet in my English–French dictionary, and it turns out *poulet* can also mean prostitute! My grandmother called me a hooker!

Geez! Whatever happened to nice grandmothers, who bake brownies for you and tell you how precious you are? It's just my luck I get one who has tattooed eyeliner and tells me *I* look like a hooker.

And she said that the pantyhose I had on were the wrong colour. How could they be the wrong colour? They're panty-hose colour! Then she made me practise sitting down so my underwear didn't show between my legs for like two hours!

I'm thinking about calling Amnesty International. This has to constitute torture.

And when I gave her my essay on the ten women I admire most, she read it, and then ripped it up into little pieces! I am not even kidding!

I couldn't help screaming, 'Grandmere, why'd you do that?' and she went, all calmly, 'These are not the sort of women you should be admiring. You should be admiring *real* women.'

I asked Grandmere what she meant by *real women*, because all of the women on my list are real. I mean, Madonna might have had a little plastic surgery, but she's still *real*.

But Grandmere says real women are Princess Grace and Coco Chanel. I pointed out to her that Princess Diana is on my list, and you know what she said? She says she thinks Princess Diana was a 'twink'! That's what she called her. A 'twink'.

Only she pronounced it 'tweenk'.

Geez!

After we'd rehearsed sitting for another hour, Grandmere said she had to go and take a bath, since she's having dinner tonight with some prime minister. She told me to be at the Plaza tomorrow no later than ten o'clock. A.m. 10 a.m.!

'Grandmere,' I said. 'Tomorrow is Saturday.'

'I know it.'

'But Grandmere,' I said. 'Saturdays is when I help my friend Lilly film her TV show—'

But Grandmere asked me which was more important, Lilly's TV show, or the well-being of the people of Genovia, who, in case you didn't know, number in the 50,000 range.

I guess 50,000 people are more important than one episode of *Lilly Tells It Like It Is*. Still, it's going to be tough explaining to Lilly why I won't be there to hold the camera when she confronts Mr and Mrs Ho, owners of Ho's Deli across the street from Albert Einstein's, about their unfair pricing policies. Lilly has discovered that Mr and Mrs Ho give significant discounts to the Asian students who go to Albert Einstein's, but no discounts at all to the Caucasian, African American, Latino or Arab students. Lilly discovered this yesterday after play rehearsal when she went to buy ginkgo biloba puffs, and Ling Su, in front of her in line, bought the same thing. But Mrs Ho charged her (Lilly) *five whole cents more* than Ling Su for the same product.

And then when Lilly complained, Mrs Ho pretended like she couldn't speak English, even though she must speak some English, or why else would her mini-TV behind the counter always be tuned to Judge Judy?

Lilly has decided to secretly videotape the Hos to gather evidence of their blatantly preferential treatment of Asian Americans. She's calling for a school-wide boycott of Ho's Deli.

The thing is, I think Lilly's making a really big deal about five cents. But Lilly says it's the principle of the thing, and that maybe if people had made a big deal about how the

Nazis smashed up Jewish people's store windows on Kristallnacht, they wouldn't have ended up putting so many people in ovens.

I don't know. The Hos aren't exactly Nazis. They're very nice to the little cat they've raised from a kitten to chase rats away from the chicken wings in the salad bar.

Maybe I'm not too sorry about missing the taping tomorrow.

But I *am* sorry Grandmere tore up my list of the ten women I admire most. I thought it was *nice*. When I got home, I printed it out again, just because it made me so mad, her tearing it up like that. I put a copy in this book.

And after carefully reviewing my copy of the Renaldo–Thermopolis Compromise, I see *nothing* about princess lessons. Something is going to have be done about this. I have been leaving messages for Dad all night, but he doesn't answer. Where *is* he?

Lilly isn't home either. Maya says the Moscovitzes went to Great Shanghai for dinner as a family, in order to grow to understand one another better as human beings.

I wish Lilly would hurry up and get home and call me back. I don't want her to think I'm in any way against her ground-breaking investigation into Ho's Deli. I just want to tell her the reason I won't be able to be there is because I have to spend the day with my grandmother.

I hate my life.

The Ten Women I Admire Most In The Whole World
by
Mia Thermopolis

Madonna Madonna Ciccone revolutionized the fashion world with her iconoclastic sense of style, sometimes offending people who are not very open-minded – for instance, her rhinestone cross earrings, which made many Christian groups ban her CDs – or have no sense of humour – like Pepsi, which didn't like it when she danced in front of some burning crosses. It was because she wasn't afraid to make people like the Pope mad that Madonna became one of the richest female entertainers in the world, paving the way for women performers everywhere by showing them that it is possible to be sexy on stage and smart off it.

Princess Diana Even though she is dead, Princess Diana is one of my favourite women of all time. She, too, revolutionized the fashion world by refusing to wear the ugly old hats that her mother-in-law told her to wear, and instead wore Halston and Bill Blass. Also she visited a lot of really sick people, even though nobody made her do it. The night Princess Diana died I unplugged the TV and said I would never watch it again, since media was what killed her. But then I regretted it the next morning when I couldn't watch Japanese Anime on the Sci-Fi channel, because unplugging the TV scrambled our cable box.

Hillary Rodham Clinton Hillary Rodham Clinton totally recognized that her thick ankles were detracting from her image as a serious politician, and so she started wearing trousers. Also, even though everybody was talking bad about her all the time for not leaving her husband who was going around having sex with people behind her back she pretended like nothing was going on, and went on running the country, just like she'd always done, which is how a president should behave.

Picabo Street She won all those gold medals in skiing, all because she just practised like crazy and never gave up, even when she was crashing into fences and things. Plus she picked her own name, which is cool.

Leola Mae Harmon I saw a movie about her on the Lifetime Channel. Leola was an Air Force nurse who was in a car accident and the lower part of her face got all mangled, but then Armand Assante, who plays a plastic surgeon, said he could fix her. Leola had to endure hours of painful reconstructive surgery, during which her husband left her because she didn't have any lips (which I guess is why the movie is called *Why Me?*). Armand Assante said he would make her a new pair of lips, only the other Air Force doctors didn't like the fact that he wanted to make them out of skin from Leola's vagina. But he did it anyway, and then he and Leola got married, and worked together to help give other accident victims vagina lips. And the whole thing turned out to have been *based on a true story*.

Joan of Arc Joan of Arc, or Jeanne d'Arc as they say in France, lived in, like, the twelfth century and one day when she was my age, she heard this angel's voice tell her to take up arms and go help the French army fight against the British so she cut off her hair and got herself a suit of armour, just like Mulan in the Disney movie, and went and led the French forces to victory in a number of battles. But then, like typical politicians, the French government decided Joan was too powerful, so they accused her of being a witch and burned her to death at the stake. And unlike Lilly, I do NOT believe that Joan was suffering from adolescent onset schizophrenia. I think angels really DID talk to her. None of the schizophrenics in our school have ever had their voices tell them to do something cool like lead their country into battle. All Brandon Hertzenbaum's voices told him to do was go into the Boys' Room and carve *Satan* in the door of the bathroom stall with a protractor. So there you go.

Christy Christy is not really a person. She is the fictional

96

heroine of my favourite book of all time, which is called *Christy*, by Catherine Marshall. Christy is a young girl who goes to teach school in the Smokey Mountains at the turn of the century because she believes she can make a difference, and all these really hot guys fall in love with her and she learns about God and typhoid and stuff. Only I can't tell anyone, especially Lilly, that this is my favourite book, because it's kind of sappy and religious, and plus it doesn't have any spaceships or serial killers in it.

The Lady Cop I Once Saw give a truck driver a ticket for honking at a woman who was crossing the street (her skirt was kind of short). The lady cop told the truck driver it was a no-honking zone, and then when he argued about it, she wrote him another ticket, for arguing with an officer of the law.

Lilly Moscovitz Lilly Moscovitz isn't really a woman, yet, but she's someone I admire very much. She is very, very smart, but unlike many very smart people, she doesn't rub it in all the time, the fact that she's so much smarter than me. Well, at least, not much. Lilly is always thinking up fun things for us to do, like go to Barnes & Noble and secretly film me asking Dr Laura, who was signing books there, if she knows so much, how come she's divorced, then showing it on her (Lilly's) TV show, including the part where we got thrown out and banned from the Union Square Barnes & Noble forever after. Lilly is my best friend and I tell her everything, except the part about me being a princess, which I don't think she'd understand.

Helen Thermopolis Helen Thermopolis, besides being my mother, is a very talented artist who was recently featured in *Art In America* magazine as one of the most important painters of the new millennium. Her painting, *Woman Waiting For Price Check At The Grand Union*, won this big national award and sold for $140,000, only part of which my mom got to keep, since fifteen per cent of it went to her gallery and half of what was left went to taxes, which sucks, if you ask me. But even though she's such an important artist, my mom always has time for me. I also respect her because she is deeply principled: she says she would never think of inflicting her beliefs on others, and would thank others to pay her the same courtesy.

Can you believe Grandmere tore this up? I'm telling you, this is the sort of essay that could bring a country to its knees.

So I was right: Lilly *does* think the reason I'm not participating in the taping today is because I'm against her boycott of the Hos.

I told her that wasn't true, that I had to spent the day with my grandmother. But guess what? She doesn't believe me. The one time I tell the truth, and she doesn't believe me!

Lilly says that if I really wanted to get out of spending the day with Grandmere, I could, but because I'm so codependent, I can't say no to anyone. Which doesn't even make sense, since obviously I am saying no to *her*. When I pointed that out to Lilly, though, she just got madder. I can't say no to my grandmother, since she's like sixty-five years old, and she's going to die soon, if there's any justice at all in the world.

Besides, you don't know my grandmother, I said. You don't say no to my grandmother.

Then Lilly went, 'No, I don't know your grandmother, do I, Mia? Isn't that curious, considering the fact that you know all *my* grandparents—' The Moscovitzes have me over every year for Passover dinner. '—And yet I haven't met any of *yours*.'

Well, of course the reason for *that* is that my mom's parents are, like, total farmers who live in a place called Versailles, Indiana, only they pronounce it Ver-sales. My mom's parents are *afraid* to come to New York City because they say there are too many 'furinners' – by which they mean foreigners – here, and anything that isn't one hundred per cent American scares them, which is one of the reaso[n] my mom left home when she was eighteen and has o[nly] been back twice, and that was with me. Let me tell [y]o, Versailles is a small, small town. It's so small, that the a[...]

sign on the door at the bank that says, *If bank is closed, please slide money under door.* I am not lying, either. I took a photo of it and brought it back to show everyone because I knew they wouldn't believe me. It's hanging on our refrigerator.

Anyway, Grandpa and Grandma Thermopolis don't make it out of Indiana much.

And the reason I'd never introduced Lilly to Grandmere Renaldo is because Grandmere Renaldo hates children. And I can't introduce her now, because then Lilly will find out I'm the Princess of Genovia, and you can bet I'll never hear the end of *that*. She'd probably want to interview me, or something, for her TV show. That's all I need: my name and image plastered all over Manhattan Public Access.

So I was telling Lilly all of this – about how I had to go out with my grandmother, not about my being a princess, of course – and as I was talking, I could hear her breathing over the phone in that way she does when she's mad, and finally she just goes, 'Oh, come over tonight then, and help me edit', and slammed the phone down.

Geez.

Well, at least Michael didn't tell her about the lipstick and pantyhose. *That* would have really made her mad. She never would have believed I was only going to my grandmother's. No way.

This was all at, like, nine-thirty, while I was getting ready to go to Grandmere's. Grandmere told me that for today, I don't have to wear lipstick or pantyhose. She said I could wear anything I wanted. So I wore my overalls. I know she hates them, but hey, she said anything I wanted. Hee hee

Oops, gotta go. Lars just pulled up in front of the Plaza. here.

Later on Saturday

I can never go to school again. I can never go *anywhere* again. I will never leave this loft, ever, ever again.

You won't believe what she did to me. *I* can't believe what she did to me. I can't believe my dad *let* her do this to me.

Well, he's going to pay. He's totally paying for this, and I mean, BIG. As soon as I got home (right after my mom went, 'Well, hey, Rosemary. Where's your baby?' which I suppose was some kind of joke about my new haircut, but it was NOT funny), I marched right up to him and said, 'You are paying for this. Big-time.'

Who says I have a fear of confrontation?

He totally tried to get out of it, going, 'What do you mean? Mia, I think you look beautiful. Don't listen to your mother, what does she know? I like your hair. It's so . . . short.'

Gee, I wonder why? Maybe because his mother met Lars and me in the lobby as soon as we'd turned the car over to the valet, and just pointed at the door. Just pointed at the door again, and said, 'On y va,' which in English means, 'Let's go'.

'Let's go where?' I asked, all innocently (this was this morning, remember, back when I was still innocent).

'Chez Paolo,' Grandmere said. Chez Paolo means Paul's house. So I thought we were going to meet one of her friends, maybe for brunch, or something, and I thought, huh, cool, field trip. Maybe these princess lessons won't be so bad.

But then we got there, and I saw Chez Paolo wasn't a house at all. At first I couldn't tell what it was. It looked a little like a really fancy hospital – it was all frosted glass and these Japanese-looking trees. And then we got inside, all of these skinny young people were floating around, dressed all in black. They were all excited to see my grandmother, and took us to this little room, where there were these couches and all these magazines. So then I figured Grandmere maybe had some plastic surgery scheduled, and while I am sort of against plastic surgery – unless you're like Leola Mae and you need lips – I was like, Well, at least she'll be off my back for a while.

Boy, was I ever wrong! Paolo isn't a doctor. I doubt he's ever even been to college! Paolo is a *stylist*! Worse, he styles *people*! I'm serious. He takes unfashionable, frumpy people like me, and he makes them stylish – for a *living*. And Grandmere got him to do *me*! *Me*!! Like it's bad enough I don't have breasts. She has to tell some guy named *Paolo* that?

What kind of name is Paolo, anyway? I mean, this is America, for Pete's sake! YOUR NAME IS PAUL!!!

That's what I wanted to scream at him. But of course, I couldn't. I mean, it wasn't Paolo's fault my grandmother dragged me there. And as he pointed out to me, he only made time for me in his incredibly busy schedule because Grandmere told him it was this big emergency.

God, how embarrassing. *I'm* a fashion emergency.

Anyway, I was plenty peeved at Grandmere, but I couldn't start yelling at her right there in front of Paolo. She totally knew it too. She just sat there on this velvet couch, petting Rommel, who was sitting on her lap with his legs crossed – she's even taught her *dog* to sit lady-like, and *he's* a boy – sipping a Sidecar she got somebody to make for her and reading *W*.

Meanwhile, Paolo was picking up chunks of my hair and making this face and going, all sadly, 'It must go. It must *all* go.'

102

And it went. All of it. Well, almost all of it. I still have some, like, bangs, and a little fringe in back.

Did I mention that I'm no longer a dishwater blonde? No. I'm just plain old blonde, now.

And Paolo didn't stop there. Oh, no. I now have fingernails. I am not kidding. For the first time in my life, I have fingernails. They're completely fake, but I have them. And it looks like I'll have them for a while: I already tried to pull one off, and it HURT. What kind of secret astronaut glue did that manicurist use, anyway?

You might be wondering why, if I didn't want to have all my hair cut off, and fake fingernails glued over my real, stumpy fingernails, I let them do all that.

I'm sort of wondering that myself. I mean, I know I have a fear of confrontation. So it wasn't like I was going to throw down my glass of lemonade and say, 'OK, stop making a fuss over me, right now!' I mean, they gave me lemonade! Can you imagine that? At the International House of Hair, which is where my mom and I usually go, over on Sixth Avenue, they sure don't give you lemonade, but it *does* only cost $9.99 for a cut and blow dry.

And it is sort of hard when all these beautiful, fashionable people are telling you how good you'd look in *this*, and how much *that* would bring out your cheekbones, to remember you're a feminist and an environmentalist, and don't believe in using make-up or chemicals that might be harmful to the Earth. I mean, I didn't want to hurt their feelings, or cause a scene, or anything like that.

And I kept telling myself, She's only doing this because she loves you. My grandmother, I mean. I know she probably wasn't doing it for that reason – I don't think Grandmere loves me any more than I love her – but I *told* myself that anyway.

I told myself that after we left Paolo's, and went to Bergdorf Goodman, where Grandmere bought me four pairs of shoes that cost almost as much as the removal of that sock from Fat Louie's small intestines. I told myself that after she bought me a bunch of clothes I will never wear. I did tell her I would never wear these clothes, but she just waved at me. Like, Go on, go on. You tell such amusing stories.

Well, I for one will not stand for it. There isn't a single inch of me that hasn't been pinched, cut, filed, painted, sloughed, blown dry, or moisturised. I even have fingernails.

But I am not happy. I am not a bit happy. *Grandmere's* happy. *Grandmere's* head-over-heels happy about how I look. Because I don't look a thing like Mia Thermopolis. Mia Thermopolis never had fingernails. Mia Thermopolis never had blonde highlights. Mia Thermopolis never wore make-up or Gucci shoes or Chanel skirts or Christian Dior bras which, by the way, don't even come in 32A, which is my size. I don't even know who I am any more. It certainly isn't Mia Thermopolis.

She's turning me into someone else.

So I stood in front of my father, looking like a human cotton bud in my new hair, and I let him have it.

'First she makes me do homework. Then she rips the homework up. Then she gives me sitting lessons. Then she has all my hair dyed a different colour and most of it hacked off, makes someone glue tiny surfboards to my fingernails, buys me shoes that cost as much as small animal surgery, and clothes that make me look like Vicky, the captain's daughter, from that old seventies series, *The Love Boat.*

'Well, Dad, I'm sorry, but I'm not Vicky, and I never will be, no matter how much Grandmere dresses me up like her. I'm not going to do great in school, be super cheerful all the time, or have any shipboard romances. That's Vicky. That's not me!'

My mom was coming out of her bedroom, putting the last touches on her datewear, when I screamed this. She was wearing a new outfit. It was this sort of Spanish skirt in all these different colours, and a sort of off-the-shoulder top. Her long hair was all over the place, and she looked really great. In fact, my dad headed for the liquor cabinet again when he saw her.

'Mia,' my mom said, as she fastened on an earring. 'Nobody is asking you to be Vicky, the captain's daughter.'

'Grandmere is!'

'Your grandmother is just trying to prepare you, Mia.'

'Prepare me for what? I can't go to school looking like this, you know,' I yelled.

My mom looked kind of confused. 'Why not?'

Oh my God. Why me?

'Because,' I said, as patiently as I could, 'I don't want anyone at school finding out I'm the Princess of Genovia!'

My mom shook her head. 'Mia, honey, they're going to find out sometime.'

I don't see how. See, I have it all worked out: I'll only be a princess in Genovia, and since the chances of anybody I know from school ever actually going to Genovia are, like, none, no one here will ever find out, so I'm totally safe from being branded a freak, like Tina Hakim Baba. Well, at least, not the kind of freak who has to ride in a chauffeured limo to school everyday, and be followed by bodyguards.

'Well,' my mom said, after I'd told her all this. 'What if it's in the newspaper?'

'Why would it be in the newspaper?'

My mom looked at my dad. My dad looked away, and took a sip from his drink.

You wouldn't believe what he did next. He put down his drink, then he reached into his trouser pocket, took out his Prada wallet, opened it, and asked, 'How much?'

I was shocked. So was my mom.

'Phillipe,' she said, but my dad just kept looking at me.

'I'm serious, Helen,' he said. 'I can see the compromise we drew up is getting us nowhere. The only solution in matters like these is cold, hard cash. So how much do I have to pay you, Mia, to let your grandmother turn you into a princess?'

'Is that what she's doing?' I started yelling some more. 'Well, if that's what she's doing, she has it all screwed up. I never saw a princess with hair this short, or feet as big as mine, who didn't have breasts!'

My dad just looked at his watch. I guess he had somewhere to go. I bet it was another 'interview' with that blonde anchor woman from ABC News.

'Consider it a job,' he said, 'this learning how to be a princess business. I will pay your salary. Now, how much do you want?'

I started yelling even more about personal integrity and how I refused to sell my soul to the company store, that kind of thing. Stuff I got from some of my mom's old records. I think she recognized this, since she sort of started slinking away, saying she had to go get ready for her date with Mr G. My dad shot her the evil eye – he can do it almost as good as Grandmere – and then he sighed and went, 'Mia, I will donate one hundred dollars a day, in your name, to – what is it? Oh, yes – Greenpeace, so they can save all the whales they want, if you will make my mother happy by letting her teach you to be a princess.'

Well.

That's an entirely different matter. It would be one thing

if he were paying *me* to have my hair colour chemically altered. But paying one hundred dollars per day to Greenpeace? That's $356,000 per year! In my name! Why, Greenpeace will *have* to hire me after I graduate. I practically will have donated a million dollars, by that time!

Wait, maybe that's only $36,500. Where's my calculator????

Even later on Saturday

Well, I don't know who Lilly Moscovitz thinks she is, but I sure know who she isn't: my friend. I don't think anyone who was my friend would be as mean to me as Lilly was tonight. I couldn't believe it. And all because of my *hair*!

I guess I could understand it if Lilly was mad at me about something that mattered – like missing the taping of the Ho segment. I mean, I'm, like, the main cameraperson for *Lilly Tells It Like It Is*. I also do a lot of the prop work. When I'm not there, Shameeka has to do my job as well as hers, and Shameeka is already executive producer and location scout.

So I guess I could see how Lilly might kind of resent the fact that I missed today's taping. She thinks Ho-Gate – that's what she's calling it – is the most important story she's ever done. I think it's kind of stupid. Who cares about five cents anyway? But Lilly's all, 'We're going to break the cycle of racism that has been rampant in delis across the five boroughs.'

Whatever. All I know is, I walked into the Moscovitzes' apartment tonight, and Lilly took one look at my new hair and was like, 'Oh my God, what happened to you?'

Like I had frostbite all over my face, and my nose had turned black and fallen off, like those people who climbed Mt. Everest.

OK, I knew people were going to freak and stuff when they saw my hair. I totally washed it before I came over, and got all the mousse and goop out of it. Plus I took off all the make-up Paolo had slathered on me, and put on my overalls and high-tops (you can hardly see the quadratic formula any more). I really thought, except for my hair, I looked mostly normal. In fact, I kind of thought maybe I looked good – for me, I mean.

But I guess Lilly didn't think so.

I tried to be casual, like it was no big deal. Which it isn't, by the way. It wasn't as if I'd had breast implants, or something.

'Yeah,' I said, taking off my coat. 'Well, my grandmother made me go see this guy Paolo, and he—'

But Lilly wouldn't even let me finish. She was in this state of shock. She went, 'Your hair is the same colour as Lana Weinberger's.'

'Well,' I said. 'I know.'

'What's on your *fingers*? Are those fake fingernails? Lana has those too!' She stared at me all bug-eyed. 'Oh my God, Mia. You're turning into Lana Weinberger!'

Now, that kind of peeved me off. I mean, in the first place, I am *not* turning into Lana Weinberger. In the second place, even if I am, Lilly's the one who's always going on about how stupid people are, for not seeing that it doesn't matter what anybody looks like: what matters is what's going on on the inside.

So I stood there in the Moscovitzes' foyer, which is made out of black marble, with Pavlov jumping up and down against my legs, because he was so excited to see me, going, 'It wasn't me. It was my grandmother. I had to—'

'What do you mean, you had to?' Lilly got this really crabby look on her face. It was the same look she gets every year when our PE instructor tells us we have to run around the reservoir in Central Park for the Presidential Fitness test. Lilly doesn't like to run anywhere, particularly around the reservoir in Central Park (it's really big).

'What are you?' she wanted to know. 'Completely passive? You're mute, or something? Unable to say the word no? You know, Mia, we really need to work on your assertiveness. You seem to have real issues with your grandmother. I mean, you certainly don't have any trouble saying no to *me*. I could have really used your help today with the Ho segment, and you totally let me down. But you've got no problem letting your grandmother cut off all your hair and dye it yellow—'

OK, now keep in mind I'd just spent the whole day hearing how bad I looked – at least, until Paolo got ahold of me, and made me look like Lana Weinberger. Now I had to hear there was something wrong with my personality too.

So I cracked. I said, 'Lilly, *shut up*.'

I have never told Lilly to shut up before. Not ever. I don't think I have ever told anyone to shut up before. It's just not something I do. I don't know what happened, really. Maybe it was the fingernails. I never had fingernails before. They sort of made me feel strong. I mean, really, why was Lilly *always* telling me what to do?

Unfortunately, right as I was telling Lilly to shut up, Michael came out, holding an empty cereal bowl, and not wearing a shirt.

'Whoa,' he said, backing up. I wasn't sure if he said whoa and backed up because of what I'd said, or how I looked.

'What?' Lilly said. '*What* did you just say to me?'

Now she looked more like a pug than *ever*.

I totally wanted to back down. But I didn't, because I knew she was right: I *do* have problems being assertive.

So instead I said, 'I'm tired of you putting me down all the time. All day long, my mom and dad and grandmother and teachers are telling me what to do. I don't need my *friends* getting on my case too.'

'Whoa,' Michael said, again. This time I knew it was because of what I said.

'What,' Lilly said, her eyes getting all narrow, 'is your *problem*?'

I went, 'You know what? I don't have a problem. *You're* the one with the problem. You seem to have a big problem with me. Well, you know what? I'm going to solve your problem for you. I'm leaving. I never wanted to help you with your stupid Ho-Gate story anyway. The Hos are nice people. They haven't done anything wrong. I don't see why you have to pick on them. And—' I said this as I opened the door. 'My hair is *not* yellow.'

Then I left. I sort of slammed the door behind me too.

While I was waiting for the elevator, I sort of thought Lilly might come out and apologize to me.

But she didn't.

I came straight home, took a bath, and got into bed with my remote control and Fat Louie, who's the only person who likes me the way I am right now. I was thinking Lilly might call to apologize, but so far she hasn't.

Well, I'm not apologizing until she does.

And you know what? I looked in the mirror a minute ago, and my hair doesn't look that bad.

Saturday, October 11, 11:59 p.m.

She still hasn't called.

Sunday, October 12

Oh my God. I am so embarrassed. I wish I could disappear. You will never believe what just happened.

I walked out of my room to get breakfast, and there was my mom and Mr Gianini sitting at the table eating pancakes!

And Mr Gianini was wearing a T-shirt and boxer shorts!! My mom was in her kimono!!! When she saw me, she choked on her orange juice. Then she went, 'Mia, what are you doing here? I thought you spent the night at Lilly's.'

I wish I had. I wish I had never chosen to be assertive last night. I could have stayed over at the Moscovitzes' and never had to look at Mr Gianini in his boxer shorts. I could have lived a full and happy life without ever having seen *that*.

Not to mention him seeing me in my bright red flannel nightie.

How am I ever going to go to a review session again?

This is so horrible. I wish I could call Lilly, but I guess we are fighting.

Later on Sunday

Oh, OK. According to my mom, who just came into my room, Mr Gianini spent the night on the futon couch because a train on the line he normally takes to his apartment in Brooklyn derailed, and it was going to be out of service for hours, so she told him to just stay over.

If I were still friends with Lilly, she would probably say that my mother was lying to compensate for having traumatized my perception of her as a strictly maternal, and therefore non-sexual, being. That's what Lilly always says when anybody's mother has a guy over and then lies about it.

I prefer to believe my mom's lie, though. The only way I will ever pass Algebra is to believe my mother's lie, because I could never sit there and concentrate on polynomials knowing that the guy in front of me has not only probably stuck his tongue in my mom's mouth, but also probably seen her naked.

Why do all these bad things keep happening to me? I would think it would be time for something good to happen to me for a change.

After my mom came in and lied to me, I got dressed and went out into the kitchen to make breakfast. I had to, because my mom wouldn't bring me breakfast in my room, like I asked her. Actually, she went, 'Who do you think you are, anyway? The Princess of Genovia?'

Which I suppose she thinks is hysterically funny, but really, it isn't.

By the time I left my room, Mr Gianini had gotten dressed too. He was trying to be all jokey about what had happened, which is the only way you can be about it, I guess.

I wasn't feeling too jokey at first. But then Mr G started talking about what it would be like to see certain people from Albert Einstein's in their pyjamas. Like Principal Gupta. Mr G thinks Principal Gupta probably wears a football jersey to bed, with her husband's sweatpants. I kind of started to laugh, thinking about Principal Gupta in sweatpants. I said I bet Mrs Hill wears a negligee, one of those fancy ones with the feathers and stuff. But Mr G said he thought Mrs Hill was more into flannel than feathers. I wonder how Mr G knows. Did he go out with Mrs Hill too? For a boring guy with so many pens in his shirt pocket, he sure gets around.

After breakfast, my mom and Mr Gianini tried to get me to go to Central Park with them, because it was all nice outside and everything, but I said I had too much homework, which wasn't too big of a lie. I *do* have homework – Mr G should know – but not that much. I just didn't really want to be hanging around with a couple. It's like when Shameeka started going with Aaron Ben-Simon in the seventh grade, and she wanted us to go with her to the movies with him and stuff, because her dad wouldn't let her go anywhere with a guy alone (even a totally harmless guy like Aaron Ben-Simon, whose neck was as thick as my upper arm), but when we went with her she sort of ignored us, which I guess is the point. Only for the two weeks they went out, you sort of couldn't talk to Shameeka, because all she could talk about was Aaron.

Not that all my mom can talk about is Mr Gianini. She's not like that at all. But I had a feeling if I went to Central Park, I might have to see kissing. Not that there's anything wrong with kissing, like on TV. When it's your mom and your Algebra teacher, though . . .

You know what I mean, right?

Reasons I should make up with Lilly:

1. We've been best friends since kindergarten.
2. One of us has to be the bigger person and make the first move.
3. She makes me laugh.
4. Who else can I eat lunch with?
5. I miss her.

Reasons I should not make up with Lilly:

1. She's always telling me what to do.
2. She thinks she knows everything.
3. Lilly is the one who started it, so she should be the one to apologize.
4. I will never achieve self-actualization if I always back down from my convictions.
5. What if I apologize and she STILL won't talk to me????

Even later on Sunday

I just turned on my computer to look some stuff up about Afghanistan on the internet (I have to write a paper for World Civ. on a current event), and then I saw that I had an e-mail. I hardly ever get e-mails, so I was totally excited.

But then I saw who it was from: CracKing.

Michael Moscovitz? What could *he* want?

To meet him in a chat room, for one thing.

Here's what he wrote:

CracKing: Hey, Thermopolis. What happened to you last night? It's like you went mental, or something.

Me? Mental???

FtLouie: For your information, I did not go mental. I just got tired of your sister always telling me what to do. Not that it's any of your business.
>
CracKing: What are you being so snotty about? Of course it's my business. I have to live with her, don't I?
>
FtLouie: Why? Is she talking about me?
>
CracKing: You could say that.

I can't believe she's been talking about me. And you know she can't have been saying anything good.

FtLouie: What's she saying?
>
CracKing: I thought it wasn't any of my business.

I'm so glad I don't have a brother.

FtLouie: It isn't. What's she saying about me?
>
CracKing: That she doesn't know what's with you
these days, but ever since your dad came to
visit, you've been acting like a head case.
>
FtLouie: Me? A head case? What about her? She's
the one who's always criticizing me. I'm so
sick of it!! If she wants to be my friend, why
can't she just accept me the way I am???
>
CracKing: No need to yell.
>
FtLouie: I'm not yelling!!!
>
CracKing: You're using excessive amounts of
punctuation, and on-line, that's like yelling.
Besides, she's not the only one criticizing.
She says you won't support her boycott of Ho's
Deli.
>
FtLouie: Well, she's right. I won't. It's stu-
pid. Don't you think it's stupid?
>
CracKing: Sure, it's stupid. Are you still
flunking Algebra?

That was out of the blue.

```
FtLouie: I guess so. But considering the fact
that Mr G slept over last night, I'll probably
scrape by with a D. Why?
>
CracKing: What? Mr G slept over? At your place?
What was that like?
```

Now, why did I tell him that? It'll be all over school by tomorrow morning. Maybe Mr G will get fired! I don't know if teachers are allowed to date their pupils' mothers. Why did I tell Michael that?

```
FtLouie: It was pretty awful. But then he kind
of joked around, and made it OK. I don't know.
I should probably be more mad, but my mom's so
happy, it's hard.
>
CracKing: Your mom could do a lot worse than
Mr G. Imagine if she was going out with Mr
Stuart.
```

Mr Stuart teaches Health. He thinks he's God's gift to women. I haven't had him yet, since you don't have Health until sophomore year, but even I know that you should never go near Mr Stuart's desk, because if you do, he'll reach out and rub your shoulders, like he's giving you a massage, but everybody says he's really just trying to see whether or not you're wearing a bra.

If my mom ever went out with Mr Stuart, I would move to Afghanistan.

```
FtLouie: Ha ha ha. Why'd you want to know
whether or not I'm flunking Algebra?
>
CracKing: Oh, because I'm done with this
month's issue of Crackhead, and I thought if
you wanted, I could tutor you during G & T. If
you wanted.
```

Michael Moscovitz, offering to do something for me? I couldn't believe it. I nearly fell off my computer chair.

```
FtLouie: Wow, that would be great! Thanks!
>
CracKing: Don't mention it. Hang in there,
Thermopolis.
```

Then he signed off.

Can you believe it? Wasn't that nice? I wonder what's got into him.

I should definitely fight with Lilly more often.

Even later on Sunday

Just when I thought things might be looking very slightly up, my dad called. He said he was sending Lars over to pick me up, so he and me and Grandmere could have dinner together at the Plaza.

Notice the invitation didn't include Mom.

But I guess that's OK, since Mom didn't want to go anyway. When I told her I was going, she got really cheerful, in fact.

'Oh, that's OK,' she said. 'I'll just stay here and order in some Thai food and watch *Sixty Minutes*.'

She's been really cheerful ever since she got back from Central Park. She says she and Mr G went on one of those dorky carriage rides. I was shocked. Those carriage drivers don't take care of their horses at all. There's always some ancient carriage horse keeling over from lack of water. I had always vowed never to ride in one. At least not until they start giving those horses some rights, and I always thought my mom agreed with me.

Love can do strange things to people.

The Plaza wasn't that bad this time. I guess I'm getting used to it. The doormen know who I am now – or at least they know who Lars is – so they don't give me a hard time any more. Grandmere and my dad were both in kind of bad moods. I don't know why. I guess they're not getting paid to spend time with each other, like I kind of am.

Dinner was *so* boring. Grandmere went on and on about which fork to use with what and why. There were all these courses, and most of them were meat. One was fish, though, so I ate that, plus dessert, which was a big fancy tower of chocolate. Grandmere tried to tell me that when I am representing Genovia at state functions, I have to eat whatever is put down in front of me, or I will insult my hosts and possibly create an international incident. But I told her I would have my staff explain to my hosts ahead of time that I don't eat meat, so not to serve me any.

Grandmere looked kind of mad. I guess it never occurred to her that I might have watched that made-for-TV movie about Princess Diana. I know all about how to get out of eating stuff at state dinners, and also about throwing up what you did eat afterwards (only I would never do that).

All through dinner, Dad kept asking me these weird questions about Mom: like, was I uncomfortable about her relationship with Mr Gianini, and did I want him to say something to her? I think he was trying to get me to tell him whether or not I thought it was serious between the two of them – Mr G and my mom, I mean.

Well, I know it's pretty serious if he's spending the night. My mom only lets guys she really, really likes spend the night. So far, including Mr G, that's only been three guys in the past fourteen years: Wolfgang, who turned out to be gay; this guy, Tim, who turned out to be a Republican; and now my algebra teacher. That's not so many, really. It's only, like, one guy every four years.

Or something like that.

But of course I couldn't tell my dad that Mr G had spent the night, or I know he'd have had an embolism. He is such a chauvinist – he has girlfriends stay over at Miragnac every summer, sometimes a new one every two weeks! – but he expects Mom to stay pure as the driven snow.

If Lilly were still speaking to me, I know she'd say men are such hypocrites.

A part of me wanted to tell my dad about Mr G, just so he'd stop being so smug. But I didn't want to give my grandmother any more ammunition against my mom –

122

Grandmere says my mom is 'flighty' – so I just pretended like I didn't know anything about it.

Tomorrow Grandmere says we're going to work on my vocabulary. She says my French is atrocious, but my English is even worse. She says if she ever hears me say *Whatever* again, she's going to wash my mouth out with soap.

I said, 'Whatever, Grandmere', and she shot me this way dirty look. I wasn't trying to be smart-alecky, though. I really forgot.

To date, I've made $200 for Greenpeace. I'm probably going to go down in history as the girl who saved all the whales.

When I got home, I noticed there were *two* empty containers of pad thai in the trash. Also *two* sets of plastic chopsticks, and *two* bottles of Heineken in the recycled bin. I asked my mom if she'd had Mr G over for dinner – My God, she'd spent the whole day with him already! – and she said, 'Oh, no, honey. I was just really hungry.'

That's two lies she's told me in one day. This thing with Mr G must be pretty serious.

Lilly still hasn't called. I'm starting to think maybe *I* should call *her*. But what would I say? *I* didn't do anything. I mean, I know I told her to shut up, but that was only because she told me I was turning into Lana Weinberger. I had every right to tell her to shut up.

Or did I? Maybe nobody has a right to tell anybody to shut up. Maybe this is how wars get started, because someone tells someone else to shut up, and then no one will apologize.

If this keeps up, who am I going to eat lunch with tomorrow?

Monday, October 13, Algebra

When Lars pulled up in front of Lilly's building to pick her up for school, her doorman said she'd already left. Talk about holding a grudge.

This is the longest fight we've ever had.

When I walked into school, the first thing somebody did was shove a petition in my face.

> *Boycott Ho's Deli!*
> *Sign below and take a stand against racism!*

I said I wouldn't sign it, and Boris, who was the person holding it, told me I was ungrateful, and that in the country he came from, voices raised in protest had been crushed for years by the government, and that I should feel lucky I lived in a place where I could sign a petition and not live in fear that the secret police would come after me.

I told Boris that in America, we don't tuck our sweaters into our trousers.

One thing you have to say for Lilly: she acts fast. The whole school is plastered with *Boycott Ho's Deli* posters.

The other thing you have to say about Lilly: when she's mad, she stays mad. She is totally not speaking to me.

I wish Mr G would get off my case. Who *cares* about integers, anyway?

Operations on Real Numbers: negatives or opposites – numbers on opposite sides of the zero but the same distance from zero on the number line are called negatives or opposites

What to do during Algebra:

O, what to do during Algebra!
The possibilities are limitless:
There's drawing, and yawning,
and portable chess.

There's dozing, and dreaming,
and feeling confused.
There's humming, and strumming,
and looking bemused.

You can stare at the clock.
You can hum a little song.
I've tried just about everything
to pass the time along.

BUT NOTHING WORKS!!!!!

Later on Monday, French

So even if Lilly and I weren't in a fight, I wouldn't have been able to sit with her at lunch today. She's become the queen of the *cause célèbre*. All these people were clustered around the table where she and I and Shameeka and Ling Su normally eat our dumplings from Big Wong. *Boris Pelkowski* was sitting where I usually sit.

Lilly must be in heaven. She's always wanted to be worshipped by a musical genius.

So I was standing there like a total idiot with my stupid tray of stupid salad, which was the only vegetarian entree today, since they ran out of cans of Sterno for the bean and grain bar, and I was like, Who am *I* going to sit by? There are only about ten tables in our caff, since we have rotating lunch shifts: there's the table where I sit with Lilly, and then the jock table, the cheerleader table, the rich kid table, the hip hop table, the druggie table, the drama freak table, the National Honours Society table, the foreign exchange students table, and the table where Tina Hakim Baba sits every day with her bodyguard.

I couldn't sit with the jocks or the cheerleaders, because I'm not one. I couldn't sit at the rich kids table because I don't have a cell phone or a broker. I'm not into hip-hopping or drugs, I didn't get a part in the latest play, and with my F in Algebra, the chances of my getting into the National Honors Society is like nil, and I can't understand anything the foreign exchange students say.

I looked at Tina Hakim Baba. She had a salad in front of her, just like me. Only Tina eats salad because she has a weight problem, not because she's a vegetarian. She was reading a romance novel. It had a photograph on the front of a teenage boy with his arms around a teenage girl. The teenage girl had long blonde hair and pretty big breasts for someone with such thin thighs. She looked exactly the way I know my grandmother wants me to look.

I walked over and put my tray down in front of Tina Hakim Baba's.

'Can I sit here?' I asked.

Tina looked up from her book. She had an expression of total shock on her face. She looked at me, and then she looked at her bodyguard. He was a tall, dark-skinned man in a black suit. He had on sunglasses even though we were inside. I think Lars could probably have taken him, if it had come down to a fight between the two of them.

When Tina looked at her bodyguard, he looked at me – at least I think he did; it was hard to tell with those sunglasses – and nodded.

Tina smiled really big at me. 'Please,' she said, laying down her book. 'Sit with me.'

I sat down. I felt kind of bad, seeing Tina smile like that. Like maybe I should have asked to sit down with her before. But I used to think she was such a freak, because she rode to school in a limo and had a bodyguard.

I don't think she's as much of a freak now.

Tina and I ate our salads and talked about how much school food sucks. She told me about her diet. She wants to lose twenty pounds by the Cultural Diversity Dance. But the Cultural Diversity Dance is this Saturday, so I don't know how that's going to work out for her. I asked Tina if she had a date for the Cultural Diversity Dance or something, and she got all giggly and said yes she did. She's going with a guy from Trinity, which is another private school in Manhattan. The guy's name is Dave Farouq El-Abar.

Hello? It isn't fair. Even Tina Hakim Baba, whose father doesn't allow her to walk two blocks to school, has been asked out by someone.

Well, she's got breasts, so I guess that's why.

Tina is pretty nice. When she went up to go to the jet-line to get another diet soda – the bodyguard went with her: God, if Lars ever started shadowing me like that, I'd kill myself – I read the back of her book. It was called *I Think My Name Is Amanda*, and it was about a girl who woke up from a coma and couldn't remember who she was. This really cute boy comes to visit her in the hospital and tells her that her name is Amanda and that he's her boyfriend. She spends the rest of the book trying to figure out whether or not he's lying.

I am so sure! If some cute boy wants to tell you that he's your boyfriend, why wouldn't you just *let* him? Some girls don't know when they've got it made.

While I was reading the back of the book, this shadow fell over it, and I looked up and there was Lana Weinberger. It must have been a game day, because she had on her cheer-leader uniform, a green-and-white pleated mini-skirt and a tight white sweater with a giant A across the front of it. I think she stuffs her pom-poms down her bra when she isn't using them. Otherwise, I don't see how her chest could stick out so much.

'Nice hair, Amelia,' she said, in her snotty voice. 'Who are you supposed to be? Tank Girl?'

I looked past her. Josh Richter was standing there with some of his dumb jock friends. They weren't paying any attention to me and Lana. They were talking about a party they'd been to over the weekend. They were all 'wrecked' from having consumed too much beer.

I wonder if their coach knows.

128

'What do you call this colour, anyway?' Lana wanted to know. She touched the top of my head. 'Pus Yellow?'

Tina Hakim Baba and her bodyguard came back while Lana was standing there tormenting me. In addition to her diet soda, Tina had purchased a Nutty Royale ice cream cone, which she gave to me. I thought this was very nice of her, considering the fact that I'd hardly ever spoken to her before.

But Lana didn't see the niceness of this gesture. Instead she asked, all innocently, 'Oh, Tina, did you buy that ice cream for Mia here? Did your daddy give you an extra hundred dollars today, so you could buy yourself a new friend?'

Tina's dark eyes filled up with hurt. The bodyguard saw this and opened his mouth.

Then a strange thing happened. I was sitting there, looking at the tears welling up in Tina Hakim Baba's eyes, and then the next thing I knew, I'd taken my Nutty Royal and thrust it with all my might at the front of Lana's sweater.

Lana looked down at the vanilla ice cream, hard chocolate shell, and peanuts that were sticking to her chest. Josh Richter and the other jocks stopped talking and looked at Lana's chest too. The noise level in the cafeteria plummeted to the quietest I've heard it. *Everyone* was looking at the ice cream cone sticking to Lana's chest. It was so quiet, I could hear Boris breathing through the wires of his retainer.

Then Lana started to scream.

'You-you—' I guess she couldn't think of a word bad enough to call me. 'You-you . . . Look what you've done! Look what you've done to my sweater!'

I stood up and grabbed my tray. 'Come on, Tina,' I said. I was still really mad, so my voice didn't shake or anything. 'Let's go somewhere a little bit quieter.'

Tina, her big brown eyes on the sugar cone sticking out

the middle of the *A* on Lana's chest, picked up her tray and followed me. The bodyguard followed Tina. I could swear he was laughing.

As Tina and I walked past the table where Lilly and I usually sat, I saw Lilly staring at me with her mouth open. She had obviously seen the whole thing.

Well, I guess she's going to have to change her diagnosis: I am *not* unassertive. Not when I don't want to be.

I'm not sure, but as Tina and her bodyguard and I left, I thought I heard some applause coming from the geek table.

I think self-actualization might be right around the corner.

Later on Monday

Oh my God. I am in so much trouble. Nothing like this has ever happened to me before!

I am sitting in the principal's office!

That's right. I got sent to the principal's office for stabbing Lana Weinberger with a Nutty Royale!

I should have known she'd tell on me. She is such a big whiner.

I'm kind of scared. I've never disobeyed a student rule before. I've always been a really good kid. When the student worker came to our G & T class with the pink hall pass, I never thought for a minute it might be for me. I was sitting there with Michael Moscovitz. He was showing me that the way I subtract is all wrong. He says my main problem is that I don't write my numbers neat enough when borrowing. Also that I don't keep track of my notes, and scribble them in whatever notebook I happen to have handy. He says I should keep all my Algebra notes in one notebook.

Also, he says I seem to have trouble concentrating.

But the reason I couldn't concentrate was that I had never sat so close to a boy before! I mean, I realize it was only Michael Moscovitz, and that I see him all the time, and he'd never like me anyway, because I'm a freshman and he's a senior, and I'm his little sister's best friend and all – at least, I used to be.

But he's still a boy, a *cute* boy, even if he *is* Lilly's brother. It was really hard to pay attention to subtraction when I could smell this really nice clean boy smell coming from him. Plus every once in a while he would put his hand over mine and take my pencil away and go, 'No, like *this*, Mia.'

Of course, I was also having trouble concentrating because I kept feeling like Lilly was looking at us. She wasn't, of course. Now that she's fighting the evil forces of racism in our neighbourhood, she doesn't have time for the little people like me. She was sitting at this big table with all of her supporters, plotting their next move in the Ho Offensive. She even let Boris come out of the supply closet to help.

May I point out that he was all over her? How she can stand having his spindly little violin-stroking arm around the back of her chair, I can't imagine. And he *still* hasn't untucked his sweater.

So I really shouldn't have worried that anybody was going to notice me and Michael. I mean, he certainly didn't have his arm around the back of *my* chair. Although once, under the table, his knee touched my knee. I nearly died at the niceness of it all.

Then that stupid hall pass arrived with *my* name on it.

I wonder if I'm going to get expelled. Maybe if I get expelled I could go to a different school, where nobody knows that my hair used to be a different colour and that these fingernails aren't really real. That might be kind of nice.

From now on I will:

1. Think before I act.
2. Try to be gracious, no matter how much I am provoked to behave otherwise.
3. Tell the truth, except when doing so would hurt someone's feelings.
4. Stay as far away as possible from Lana Weinberger.

Uh-oh. Principal Gupta is ready to see me now.

Monday night

Well, I don't know what I'm going to do now. I have detention for a week, *plus* Maths review with Mr G, *plus* princess lessons with Grandmere.

I didn't get home until nine o'clock tonight. Something has *got* to give.

My father is furious. He says he is going to sue the school. He says no one can give his daughter detention for defending the weak. I told him that Principal Gupta can. She can do anything. She's the principal.

I can't say I really blame her. I mean, it wasn't like I said I was sorry, or anything. Principal Gupta is a nice lady, but what could she do? I admitted I had done it. She told me I'd have to apologize to Lana, and pay to have her sweater cleaned. I said I'd pay for the sweater but that I wouldn't apologize. Principal Gupta looked at me over the rims of her bifocals and went, 'I beg your pardon, Mia?'

I repeated that I wouldn't apologize. My heart was beating like crazy. I didn't want to make anybody mad, especially Principal Gupta, who can be very scary, when she wants to. I tried to picture her in her husband's sweatpants, but it didn't work. She still scared me.

But I won't apologize to Lana. I won't.

Principal Gupta didn't look mad, though. She looked concerned. I guess that's how educators are supposed to look. You know. Concerned about you. She went, 'Mia, I must say, when Lana came in here with her complaint, I was extremely surprised. It's usually Lilly Moscovitz I have to pull in here. I never expected I was going to have to pull *you* in. Not for disciplinary reasons. Academic reasons, maybe. I understand you aren't doing very well in

Algebra. But I've never known you to be a discipline problem before. I really feel I must ask you, Mia . . . is everything all right?'

For a minute I just stared at her.

Is everything all right? *Is everything all right?*

Hmm, hold on a minute, let me see . . . my mom is going out with my Algebra teacher, a subject I'm flunking, by the way; my best friend hates me; I'm fourteen years old and I've never been asked out; I don't have any breasts; and oh, I just found out I'm the Princess of Genovia.

'Oh, sure,' I said to Principal Gupta. 'Everything is fine.'

'Are you certain, Mia? Because I can't help wondering if this isn't all rooted in some problems you might be having – maybe at home?'

Who did she think I was, anyway? Lana *Whine*berger? Like I was really going to sit there and tell her my problems. Yeah, Principal Gupta. On top of all that other stuff, my grandmother is in town, and my dad is paying one hundred dollars a day for me to get lessons from her in how to be a princess. Oh, and this weekend, I ran into Mr Gianini in my kitchen, and all he was wearing was a pair of boxer shorts. Anything else you want to know?

'Mia,' Principal Gupta said. 'I want you to know that you are a very special person. You have many wonderful qualities. There is no reason for you to feel threatened by Lana Weinberger. None at all.'

Oh, OK. Just because she's the prettiest, most popular girl in my class, and she's going out with the handsomest, most popular boy in school, you're right, Principal Gupta. There's no reason at all to feel threatened by her. Especially since she puts me down every chance she gets and tries to humiliate me in public. Threatened? *Me*? Nah.

'You know, Mia,' Principal Gupta said. 'I bet if you took

the time to get to know Lana, you'd find that she's really a very nice girl. A girl just like you.'

Right. Just like me.

I was so upset, I actually told Grandmere all about it at our vocabulary lesson. She was surprisingly sympathetic.

'When I was a girl your age,' Grandmere said, 'there was a girl just like this Lana at my school. Her name was Genevieve. She sat behind me in Geography. Genevieve would take the end of my braid, and dip it in her inkwell, so that when I stood up, I got ink all over my dress. But the teacher would never believe me that Genevieve did it on purpose.'

'Really?' I was kind of impressed. That Genevieve had some guts. I never met anyone who'd try to dis my grandmother. 'What did you do?'

Grandmere let out this evil laugh. 'Oh, nothing.'

There is no way she did *nothing* to Genevieve. Not with a laugh like that. But no matter how hard I pestered her, Grandmere wouldn't tell me what she did to get back at Genevieve. I'm kind of thinking maybe she killed her.

Well? It could happen.

But I guess I shouldn't have pestered Grandmere so hard, because to shut me up, she gave me a quiz! I'm not kidding!

It was really hard too. I've stapled it in here, since I got a ninety-eight. Grandmere says I've really come a long way since we started:

Grandmere's Test:

In a restaurant, what does one do with one's napkin when one rises to go to the powder room?
If it's a four-star restaurant, hand it to the waiter who rushes over to help you with your chair. If it's a normal place, and no waiter rushes over, leave your napkin on your empty chair.
Under what circumstances is it acceptable to apply lipstick in public?
Never.
What are the characteristics of capitalism?
Private ownership of the means of production and distribution, and the exchange of goods based on the operations of the market.
What is the appropriate reply to make to a man who says he loves you?
Thank you. You are very kind.
What did Marx consider to be the contradiction in capitalism?
The value of any commodity is determined by the amount of labour needed to produce it. In denying workers the value of what they have produced, the capitalists are undermining their own economic system.
White shoes are unacceptable . . .
At funerals, after Labour Day, before Memorial Day, and anywhere there might be horses.
Describe an oligarchy:
Small group exercises control for generally corrupt purposes.
Describe a Sidecar:
⅓ lemon juice, ⅓ Cointreau, ⅓ brandy shaken well with ice, strained before serving.

The only one I missed was the one about what to say to a

136

man when he tells you he loves you. It turns out you aren't supposed to say thank you.

Not, of course, that this will ever happen to me. But Grandmere says I might be surprised someday.

I wish!

Tuesday, October 13, Homeroom

No Lilly again this morning. Not that I expected there to be. But I made Lars stop at her place anyway, just in case maybe she wanted to be friends again. I mean, she could have seen how assertive I was with Lana and decided she was wrong to criticize me so much.

But I guess not.

The funny thing is, when Lars was dropping me off at school, Tina Hakim Baba's chauffeur was dropping her off too. We sort of smiled at each other, then walked into school together, her bodyguard behind us. Tina said she wanted to thank me for what I had done yesterday. She said she told her parents about it, and that they want me to come over for dinner Friday night.

'And maybe,' Tina asked, all shyly, 'you could spend the night after, if you wanted.'

I said, 'OK.' I mostly said it because I feel sorry for Tina, since she doesn't have any other friends, because everybody thinks she's so weird, with the bodyguard and all. I also said it because I heard she has a fountain in her house, just like Donald Trump, and I wanted to see if that was true.

And I kind of like her too. She's *nice* to me.

It's nice to have somebody be nice to you.

I have GOT to:

1. Stop waiting for the phone to ring (Lilly is NOT going to call; neither is Josh Richter).
2. Make more friends.
3. Have more self-confidence.
4. Stop biting my fake fingernails.

5. Start acting more:
    A. Responsible
    B. Adult
    C. Mature
6. Be happier.
7. Achieve self-actualization.
8. Buy:
    trash bags
    napkins
    conditioner
    tuna
    toilet paper!!!!

More Tuesday, Algebra

Oh my God. I can't even believe this. But it must be true, since Shameeka just told me:

Lilly has a date to the Cultural Diversity Dance this weekend.

Lilly has a date. Even *Lilly* has a date. I thought all the boys in our school were terrified of Lilly.

But there's one boy who's not:

Boris Pelkowski.

AAAAHHHHHHHHHHHHHHHHHH!

More Tuesday, English

No boy will ever ask me out. Ever. EVERYONE has a date to the Cultural Diversity Dance: Shameeka, Lilly, Ling Su, Tina Hakim Baba. I'm the only one not going. The ONLY ONE.

Why was I born under such an unlucky star? Why did *I* have to be cursed with such freakishness? Why? WHY???

I would give anything if, instead of being a five-foot-nine flat-chested princess, I could be a five-foot-six normal person with breasts.

ANYTHING.

Satire – employs humour systematically for the purpose of persuasion
Irony – counter to expectation
Parody – close imitation that exaggerates ridiculous or objectionable features

More Tuesday, French

Today in G & T, in between showing me how to carry over, Michael Moscovitz complimented me on my handling of what he called the Weinberger Incident. I was surprised he'd heard about it. He said it was all over school, about how I'd decimated Lana in front of Josh. He said, 'Your locker is right next to Josh's, isn't it?'

I said yes it was.

He said, 'That must be awkward', but I told him actually it wasn't, since Lana seems to be avoiding that area lately, and Josh never talks to me at all, except to say, Can I get by here? once in a while.

I asked him if Lilly was still saying mean things about me, and he said, all taken aback, 'She's never said mean things about you. She just doesn't understand why you blew up at her like that.'

I said, 'Michael, she's always putting me down! I just couldn't take it any more. I have too many other problems without having friends who aren't supportive of me.'

He laughed. 'What kind of problems could *you* have?'

Like I was too much of a kid or something to have problems!

Boy, did I straighten him out. I couldn't exactly tell him about being the Princess of Genovia, or about not having any breasts or anything, but I did remind him that I'm flunking Algebra, I have detention for a week, and I had recently woken up to find Mr Gianini in his boxer shorts eating breakfast with my mom.

He said he guessed I did have some problems, after all.

The whole time Michael and I were talking, I saw Lilly shooting us these looks from behind the poster board she was writing Ho-Gate slogans on with a big black Magic

Marker. So I guess because I'm fighting with her, I'm not allowed to be friends with her brother.

Or maybe she's just sore because her boycott of Ho's Deli is creating serious turmoil within the school. First of all, all the Asian kids have started doing their shopping exclusively at Ho's. And why not? Because of Lilly's campaign, now they know they can get a five-cent discount on just about anything. The other problem is that there is no other deli within walking distance. This has caused some serious division within the ranks of the protesters. The non-smokers want to continue the boycott, but the smokers are all for writing the Hos a stern letter and then forgetting about it. And since all the popular kids in school smoke, they aren't honouring the boycott at all. They're going to Ho's just like they always did to get their Camel Lights.

When you can't get the popular kids on your side, you have to realize it's hopeless: without celebrity supporters, no cause stands a chance. I mean, where would all those starving kids be without Sally Struthers, star of some boring seventies show my mother used to watch when she was little, and who is always interrupting VH1's *Before They Were Rock Stars* and begging us to Save the Children when all we really want to know is whether Mrs Sumner calls her boy Sting or Gordon, and how come none of our teachers ever looked like that?

Anyway, then Michael asked me a strange question. He went, 'So are you grounded?'

I looked at him kind of funny. 'You mean for getting detention? No, of course not. My mom is totally on my side. My dad wants to sue the school.'

Michael said, 'Oh. Well, I was wondering because, if you aren't busy Saturday, I thought maybe we could—'

But then Mrs Hill came in, and made us all fill out

questionnaires for the Ph.D. she's doing on urban youth violence, even though Lilly complained that we're hardly qualified to comment, seeing as how the only youth violence any of us had ever experienced was when there was a sale on relaxed fit jeans at the Gap on Madison Avenue.

Then the bell rang, and I ran out as fast as I could. I knew what Michael was going to ask me, see: he was going to suggest we meet to go over my long division, which he says is a human tragedy. And I just didn't think I could take it. Maths? On the weekend? After spending almost every waking moment on it all week?

No, thank you.

But I didn't want to be rude, so I left before he could ask me. Was that terrible of me?

Really, a girl can only take so much criticism on her remainders.

ma	mon	tes
ta	ton	tes
sa	son	ses
notre	notre	nos
votre	votre	vos
leur	leur	leurs

Homework:

Algebra: pg.121, 1–57 odd only
English: ??? Ask Shameeka
World Civ.: questions at end of Chapter 9
G & T: none
French: pour demain, une vignette culturelle
Biology: none

Tuesday night

Grandmere says Tina Hakim Baba sounds like a much better friend for me than Lilly Moscovitz. But I think she is only saying that because Lilly's parents are psychoanalysts, and it turns out Tina's dad is this Arabian sheikh, and her mom is related to the King of Sweden, so they are more appropriate for the heir to the throne of Genovia to hang out with.

The Hakim Babas are also super-rich, according to my grandmother. They own about a gazillion oil wells. Grandmere told me when I go have dinner with them on Friday night, I have to bring a gift, and wear my Gucci loafers. I asked Grandmere what kind of gift and she said breakfast. She's special-ordering it from Balducci's, and having it delivered Saturday morning.

Being a princess is hard work.

I just remembered: at lunch today Tina had a new book with her. It had a cover just like the last one, only this time the heroine was a brunette. This one was called *My Secret Love*, and it was about a girl from the wrong side of the tracks who falls in love with a rich boy who never notices her. Then the girl's uncle kidnaps the boy and holds him for ransom, and she has to bathe his wounds and help him to escape and stuff, and of course he falls madly in love with her.

Tina said she already read the end, and the girl gets to go and live with the rich boy's parents after her uncle goes to jail and can no longer support her.

How come things like that don't ever happen to *me*?

Wednesday, October 14, Homeroom

No Lilly again today. Lars suggested we'd make better time if we just drove straight to school and didn't stop by her place every day. I guess he's right.

It was really weird when we pulled up to Albert Einstein's. All the people who normally hang around outside before school starts, smoking and sitting on Joe, the stone lion, were all clustered into these groups, looking at something. I suppose somebody's dad has been accused of money-laundering again. Parents can be so self-centred: before they do something illegal, they should totally stop and think about how their kids are going to feel if they get caught.

If I were Chelsea Clinton, I would change my name and move to Iceland.

I just walked right on by to show I wasn't going to have any part in gossip. A bunch of people stared at me. I guess Michael's right: it really *has* gotten around about me stabbing Lana with that Nutty Royale. Either that or my hair was sticking up in some weird way. But I checked in the mirror in the Girls' Room and it wasn't.

A bunch of girls ran out of the bathroom giggling like crazy when I went in, though.

Sometimes I wish I lived on a desert island. Really. With nobody else around for hundreds of miles. Just me, the ocean, the sand and a coconut tree.

And maybe a high definition 37-inch TV with a satellite dish and a Sony Playstation with Bandicoot, for when I get bored.

Little-Known Facts:

1. The most commonly asked question at Albert Einstein High School is, 'Do you have any gum?'
2. Bees and bulls are attracted to the colour red.
3. In my homeroom, it sometimes takes up to half an hour just to take attendance.
4. I miss being best friends with Lilly Moscovitz.

Later on Wednesday, before Algebra

This totally weird thing happened. Josh Richter came up to his locker to put his Trig book away, and he said, 'How you doin'?' to me as I was getting out my Algebra notebook.

I swear to God I am not making this up.

I was in such total shock, I nearly dropped my backpack. I don't have any idea what I said to him. I think I said I was fine. I *hope* I said I was fine.

Why is Josh Richter speaking to me?

It must have been another one of those synaptic break-downs, like the one he had at Bigelow's.

Then Josh slammed his locker closed, *looked right down into my face* – he's really tall – and said, 'See you later.'

Then he walked away.

It took me five minutes to stop hyperventilating.

His eyes are so blue they hurt to look at.

Wednesday, Principal Gupta's office

It's over.

I'm dead.

That's it.

Now I know what everyone was looking at outside. I know why they were whispering and giggling. I know why those girls ran out of the bathroom. I know why Josh Richter talked to me.

My picture is on the cover of the *Post*.

That's right. The *New York Post*. Read by millions of New Yorkers daily.

Oh, yeah. I'm dead.

It's a pretty good picture of me, actually. I guess somebody took it as I was leaving the Plaza Sunday night, after dinner with Grandmere and my dad. I'm going down the steps just outside the revolving door. I'm sort of smiling, only not at the camera. I don't remember anybody taking my picture, but I guess somebody did.

Superimposed over the photo are the words, *Princess Amelia*, and then in smaller letters, *New York's Very Own Royal*.

Great. Just great.

Mr Gianini was the one who figured it out. He said he was walking to catch the subway to work, and he saw it on the news-stand. He called my mother. My mom was taking a shower, though, and didn't hear the phone. Mr G left a message. But my mom never checks the machine in the morning, because everyone who knows her knows she is not a morning person, so nobody ever calls before noon. When Mr G called again, she had already left for her studio, where she never answers the phone, because she wears a Walkman when she paints, so she can listen to Howard Stern.

So then Mr G had no choice but to call my dad at the Plaza, which was pretty nervy of him, if you think about it. According to Mr G, my dad blew a gasket. He told Mr G that until he could get there, I should be sent to the principal's office, where I would be 'safe'.

My dad has obviously never met Principal Gupta.

Actually, I shouldn't say that. She hasn't been so bad. She showed me the paper and said, kind of sarcastically, but in a nice way, 'You might have shared this with me, Mia, when I asked you the other day if everything was all right at home.'

I blushed. 'Well,' I said. 'I didn't think anybody would believe me.'

'It is,' Principal Gupta said, 'a bit unbelievable.'

That's what the story on page 2 of the *Post* said too. *Fairy Tale Comes True For One Lucky New York Kid* was how the reporter, one Ms. Carol Fernandez, put it. Like I had won the Lottery, or something. Like I should be *happy* about it.

Ms Carol Fernandez goes on at length about my mom, 'the raven-haired avant-garde painter, Helen Thermopolis', and about my dad, 'the handsome Prince Phillipe of Genovia, who's successfully battled his way back from a bout of testicular cancer'. Oh, thanks, Carol Fernandez for letting all of New York know my dad's only got one you-know-what.

Then she went on to describe me as 'the statuesque beauty who is the product of Helen and Phillipe's tempestuous whirlwind college romance'.

HELLO??? CAROL FERNANDEZ, WHAT ARE YOU ON????

I am NOT a statuesque beauty. Yeah, I'm TALL. I'm way TALL. But I am no beauty. I want what Carol Fernandez has been smoking, if she thinks *I'M* beautiful.

No wonder everybody was laughing at me. This is SO embarrassing. I mean, really.

Oh, here comes my dad. Boy, does *he* look mad . . .

More Wednesday, English

It isn't fair.

This is totally, completely unfair.

I mean, anybody else's dad would have let them come home. Anybody else's dad, if his kid's picture was on the front of the *Post*, would say, 'Maybe you should skip school for a few days, until things calm down.'

Anybody else's dad would have been like, 'Maybe you should change schools. How do you feel about Iowa? Would you like to go to school in Iowa?'

But oh, no. Not *my* dad. Because *he's* a prince. And he says members of the royal family of Genovia do not 'go home' when there is a crisis. No, they stay where they are and slug it out.

Slug it out. I think my dad has something in common with Carol Fernandez: they're BOTH on something.

Then my dad reminded me that it's not like I'm not getting paid for this. Right! One hundred lousy bucks! One hundred lousy bucks a day to be publicly ridiculed and humiliated.

Those baby seals better be grateful, that's all I have to say.

So here I am in English, and everybody is whispering about me and pointing at me like I'm a victim of alien abduction, or something, and my dad expects me to sit here and let them, because I'm a princess, and that's what princesses do.

But these kids are *brutal*.

I tried to tell my dad that. I was like, 'Dad, you don't understand. They're all laughing at me.'

And all he said was, 'I'm sorry, honey. You're just going to have to tough it out. You knew this was going to happen eventually. I'd hoped it wouldn't be quite this soon, but it's probably just as well to get it over with . . .'

Um, hello? I did *not* know this was going to happen eventually. I thought I was going to be able to keep this whole princess thing a secret. My lovely plan about only being a princess in Genovia is falling apart. I have to be a princess right here in Manhattan, and believe me, that is no picnic.

I was so mad at my dad for telling me I had to go back to class, I accused him of having ratted me out to Carol Fernandez himself.

He got all offended. '*Me*? *I* don't know any Carol Fernandez.' He shot this funny look at Mr Gianini, who was standing there with his hands in his pockets, looking all concerned.

'What?' Mr G said, going from concerned to surprised real fast. '*Me*? I'd never even *heard* of Genovia until this morning.'

'Geez, Dad,' I said. 'Don't blame Mr G. *He* had nothing to do with it.'

My dad didn't look very convinced. 'Well, *somebody* leaked the story to the press . . .' He said it in this mean way too. You could totally tell he thought Mr G had done it. But it couldn't have been Mr Gianini. Carol Fernandez wrote about stuff in her story that there's no way Mr G could know, because even *Mom* doesn't know about it. Like how Miragnac has a private airstrip. I never told her about that.

But when I told my dad that, he just shot Mr G a suspicious look. 'Well,' he said, again. 'I'm just going to give this Carol Fernandez a call, and see who her source is.'

And while my dad was doing that, I got stuck with Lars. I'm not kidding. Just like Tina Hakim Baba, I now have a bodyguard trailing around after me from class to class. Like I'm not enough of a laughing stock already.

I now have an armed escort.

I totally tried to get out of it. I was like, 'Dad, I can seriously take care of myself,' but he was completely rigid, and said that even though Genovia is a small country, it is a very wealthy country, and he cannot take the risk of me being kidnapped and held for ransom like the boy in *My Secret Love*, only my dad didn't say that because he's never read *My Secret Love*.

I said, 'Dad, no one is going to kidnap me. This is *school*,' but he wouldn't go for it. He asked Principal Gupta if it was all right, and she said, 'Of course, Your Highness.'

Your Highness! Principal Gupta called my dad Your Highness! If it hadn't been all serious and stuff, I would have wet my pants laughing.

The only good thing that has come out of this is that Principal Gupta let me off detention for the rest of the week, claiming that having my picture in the *Post* is punishment enough.

But really the only reason is that she is totally charmed by my father. He pulled such a Jean-Luc Picard on her, you wouldn't believe it, calling her Madam Principal and apologizing for all the fuss. I practically expected him to kiss her hand, he was flirting so hard with her. And Principal Gupta has been married a million years, and has this big black mole on the side of her nose. And she totally fell for it! She was eating it up!

I wonder if Tina Hakim Baba will still sit with me at lunch. Well, if she does, at least our bodyguards will have something to do: they can compare civilian defence tactics.

More Wednesday, French class

I guess I should have my picture on the front of the *Post* more often.

Suddenly I am very popular.

I walked into the cafeteria (I told Lars to keep five paces behind me at all times; he kept stepping on the backs of my combat boots) and Lana Weinberger, of all people, came up to me while I was in the jet-line getting my tray, and said, 'Hey, Amelia. Why don't you come and sit with us?'

I am not even kidding. That lousy hypocrite wants to be friends with me, now that I'm a princess.

Tina was right behind me in line (well, Lars was behind me; Tina was behind Lars, and Tina's bodyguard was behind her). But did Lana invite Tina to join her? Of course not. The *New York Post* hadn't called *Tina* a statuesque beauty. Short, heavy-set girls – even one whose father is an Arab sheikh – aren't good enough to sit by *Lana*. Oh, no. Only pure-bred Genovian princesses are good enough to sit by *Lana*.

I nearly threw up all over my lunch tray.

'No, thanks, Lana,' I said. 'I already have someone to sit with.'

You should have seen Lana's face. The last time I saw her look that shocked, a sugar cone had been stuck to her chest.

Later, when we were sitting down, Tina could only nibble at her salad. She hadn't said a word about the princess thing. Meanwhile, though, everybody in the whole cafeteria – including the geeks, who never noticed anything – were staring at our table. Let me tell you, it was way uncomfortable. I could feel Lilly's eyes boring into me. She hadn't said anything to me yet, but I think she had to have known. Nothing much escapes Lilly.

Anyway, after a while, I couldn't stand it any more. I put down a forkful of rice and beans and said, 'Look, Tina. If you don't want to sit with me any more, I understand.'

Tina's big eyes filled up with tears. I mean it. She shook her head, and her long black braid swayed. 'What do you mean?' she asked. 'You don't like me any more, Mia?'

It was my turn to be shocked. 'What? Of course I like you. I thought maybe you might not like *me*. I mean, everyone is staring at us. I could see why you might not want to sit with me.'

Tina smiled sadly. 'Everyone always stares at me,' she said. 'Because of Wahim, you see.'

Wahim is her bodyguard. Wahim and Lars were sitting next to us, arguing over whose gun had the most firepower, Wahim's 357 Magnum, or Lars's 9mm Glock. It was kind of a disturbing topic, but they both seemed happy as could be. In a minute or two, I expected they'd start to arm-wrestle.

'So you see,' Tina said, '*I'm* used to people thinking I'm weird. It's *you* I feel sorry for, Mia. You could be sitting with anyone – anyone in this whole cafeteria – and yet you're stuck with me. I don't want you to feel you have to be nice to me, just because no one else is.'

I got really mad, then. Not at Tina. But at everybody else at Albert Einstein's. I mean, Tina Hakim Baba is really, really nice, and no one knows it, because no one ever talks to her, because she isn't thin and she's kind of quiet and she's stuck with a stupid bodyguard. While people are worrying about things like the fact that a deli is over-charging some people by five cents for gingko biloba rings, there are human beings walking around our school in abject misery because no one will even say Good Morning to them, or How Was Your Weekend?

And then I felt guilty, because a week ago, *I* had been one of those people. I had always thought Tina Hakim Baba was a freak. The whole reason I hadn't wanted anyone to find out I was a princess was that I was afraid they'd treat me the way they treated Tina Hakim Baba. And now that I know Tina, I know just how wrong I'd been to think badly of her.

So I told Tina I didn't want to sit with anybody but her. I told her I thought we needed to stick together, and not just for the obvious reason (Wahim and Lars). I told her we needed to stick together because everyone else at this stupid school is completely NUTS.

Tina looked a lot happier then, and started filling me in on the new book she's reading. This one is called *Love Only Once*, and it's about a girl who falls in love with a boy who has terminal cancer. I told Tina it seemed like kind of a bummer thing to read, but she told me she'd already read the end, and that the boy's terminal cancer goes away. So I guess that's OK then.

As we cleared our trays, I saw Lilly staring in my direction. It wasn't the kind of stare someone who was about to apologize would use. So I wasn't too surprised when later, after I got to G & T, Lilly sat there and stared at me some more. Boris kept on trying to talk to her, but she obviously wasn't listening. Finally he gave up, and picked up his violin and went back into the supply closet, where he belongs.

Meanwhile, this is how my tutoring session with Lilly's brother went:

Me: Hi, Michael. I did all those problems you gave me. But I still don't see why you couldn't just look at the train schedule to find out what time a train travelling at 67 miles per hour will arrive in Fargo, North Dakota, if it leaves Salt Lake City at 7 a.m.

Michael: So. Princess of Genovia, huh? Were you ever going

157

to share that little piece of info with the group, or were we all supposed to guess?

Me: I was kind of hoping no one would ever find out.

Michael: Well, that's obvious. I don't see why, though. It's not like it's a bad thing.

Me: Are you kidding me? Of course it's bad!

Michael: Did you *read* the article in today's *Post*, Thermopolis?

Me: No way. I'm not going to read that trash. I don't know who this Carol Fernandez thinks she is, but—

Then Lilly got into the act. It was like she couldn't stand not to get involved.

Lilly: So you're not aware that the Crown Prince of Genovia – namely your father – has a total personal worth which, including real estate property and the palace's art collection, is estimated at over three hundred million dollars?

Well, I guess it's pretty obvious that *Lilly* read the article in today's *Post*.

Me: Um . . .

Hello? Three hundred million dollars?? And I get a lousy $100 a day???

Lilly: I wonder how much of that fortune was amassed by taking advantage of the sweat of the common labourer.

Michael: Considering that the people of Genovia have traditionally never paid income or property taxes, I would say none of it. What is *with* you, anyway, Lil?

Lilly: Well, if *you* want to tolerate the excesses of the monarchy, you can be my guest, Michael. But I happen to think that it's disgusting, with the world economy in the state it's in today, for anyone to have a total worth of three hundred million dollars . . . especially someone who never did a day's work for it!

Michael: Pardon me, Lilly, but it's my understanding that

Mia's father works extremely hard for his country. His father's historic pledge, after Mussolini's forces invaded in 1939, to exercise the rights of sovereignty in accordance with the political and economic interests of neighbouring France, in exchange for military and naval protection in the event of war, might have tied the hands of a lesser politician, but Mia's father has managed to work around that agreement. His efforts have resulted in a nation that has the highest literacy rate in Europe, some of the best educational attainment rates, and the lowest infant mortality, inflation, and unemployment rates in the Western hemisphere.

I could only stare at Michael after that. *Wow.* Why doesn't Grandmere teach me stuff like *that* at our princess lessons? I mean, this is information I could actually use. I don't exactly need to know which direction to tip my soup bowl. I need to know how to defend myself from virulent anti-royalists like my ex-best friend Lilly.

Lilly (to Michael): Shut up. (To me): I see they already having you spouting off their populist propaganda like a good little girl.

Me: *Me?* Michael's the one who—

Michael: Aw, Lilly, you're just jealous.

Lilly: I am not!

Michael: Yes, you are. You're jealous because she got her hair cut without consulting you. You're jealous because you stopped talking to her, and she went out and got a new friend. And you're jealous because all this time, Mia's had this secret she didn't tell you.

Lilly: Michael, SHUT UP!

Boris: (leaning out of supply closet door) Lilly? Did you say something?

Lilly: I WASN'T TALKING TO YOU, BORIS!

Boris: Sorry. (Goes back in closet)

Lilly: (really mad now) Gosh, Michael, you sure are quick to come to Mia's defence all of a sudden. I wonder if maybe it ever occurred to you that your argument, while ostensibly based on logic, might have less intellectual than libidinous roots?

Michael: (turning red for some reason) Well, what about your persecution of the Hos? Is that rooted in intellectual reasoning? Or is it more an example of vanity run amok?

Lilly: That's a circular argument.

Michael: It isn't. It's empirical.

Wow. Michael and Lilly are so smart. Grandmere's right: I need to improve my vocabulary.

Michael: (to me) So does this guy (he pointed at Lars) have to follow you around everywhere from now on?

Me: Yes.

Michael: Really? *Everywhere?*

Me: Everywhere except the Ladies' Room. Then he waits outside.

Michael: What if you were to go on a date? Like to the Cultural Diversity Dance this weekend?

Me: That hasn't exactly been an issue, considering that no one's asked me.

Boris: (leaning out of supply closet) Excuse me. I accidentally knocked over a bottle of rubber cement with my bow, and it's getting hard to breathe. Can I come out now?

Everyone in the G & T room: NO!!!

Mrs Hill: (poking head in from hallway) What's all this noise in here? We can hardly hear ourselves think in the teachers' lounge. Boris, why are you in the supply closet? Come out now. Everybody else, get back to work!

I need to take a closer look at that article in today's *Post*.

Three hundred million dollars?? That's as much as Oprah made last year!

So if we're so rich, how come the TV in my room is only black and white?

Note to self: Look up the words *empirical* and *libidinous*

Wednesday night

No wonder my dad was so mad about Carol Fernandez's article! When Lars and I walked out of Albert Einstein's after my review session, there were reporters all over the place. I am not even kidding. It was just like I was a murderer, or a celebrity, or something.

According to Mr Gianini, who walked out with us, reporters have been arriving all day. There were vans there from New York One, Fox News, CNN, *Entertainment Tonight* – you name it. They've been trying to interview all the kids who go to Albert Einstein's, asking them if they know me (for once, being unpopular pays off: I can't imagine they were able to find anybody who could actually remember who I was – at least, not with my new non-triangular hair). Mr G says Principal Gupta finally had to call the police, because Albert Einstein's is private property and the reporters were trespassing all over, dropping cigarette butts on the steps and blocking the sidewalk and leaning on Joe and stuff.

Which if you think about it, is exactly what all the popular kids do when they hang around the school grounds after the last bell rings, and Principal Gupta never calls the cops on *them* . . . but then again, I guess their parents are paying tuition.

I have to say, I sort of know now how Princess Diana must have felt. I mean, when Lars and Mr G and I came out, the reporters started trying to swarm all over, waving microphones at us, and yelling stuff like, 'Amelia, how about a smile?' and 'Amelia, what's it like to wake up one morning the product of a single-parent family and go to bed the next night a royal princess worth over three hundred million dollars?'

162

I was kind of scared. Even if I'd wanted to, I couldn't have answered their questions, because I didn't know which microphone to talk into. Plus I was practically rendered blind by all the flashbulbs going off in front of my face.

Then Lars went into action. You should have seen it. First, he told me not to say anything. Then he put his arm around me. He told Mr G to put his arm around my other side. Then, I don't know how, but we ducked our heads and barrelled through all the cameras and microphones and the people attached to them, until the next thing I knew, Lars was pushing me into the back seat of my dad's car, and jumping in after me.

Hello! I guess all that training in the Israeli army paid off (I overheard Lars telling Wahim that's where he'd learned how to work an Uzi. Wahim and Lars actually have some mutual friends, it turns out. I guess all bodyguards go to the same training school out in the Gobi Desert).

Anyway, as soon as Lars slammed the back door shut, he said, 'Drive,' and the guy behind the wheel hit the gas. I didn't recognize him, but sitting in the passenger seat beside him was my dad. And while we're pulling away, brakes squealing, flashbulbs going off, reporters jumping onto the windshield to get a better shot, my dad goes, all casual, 'So. How was your day, Mia?'

Geez!

I decided to ignore my dad. Instead, I turned around in my seat to wave goodbye to Mr G. Only Mr G had been swallowed up in a sea of microphones! He wouldn't talk to them, though. He just kept waving his hands at them, and trying to head for the subway, so he could take the E train home.

I felt sorry for poor Mr Gianini then. True, he had probably stuck his tongue in my mom's mouth, but he's a really nice guy, and doesn't deserve to be harassed by the media.

I said so to my dad, also that we should have given Mr G a ride home, and he just got huffy and tugged on his seat belt. He said, 'Damn these things. They always choke me.'

So then I asked my dad where I was going to go to school now.

My dad looked at me like I was nuts. 'You said you wanted to stay at Albert Einstein's!' he kind of yelled.

I said, Well, yes, but that was before Carol Fernandez outed me.

Then my dad wanted to know what outing was, so I explained to him that outing is when somebody reveals your sexual orientation on national TV, or in the newspaper, or some other large public forum. Only in this case, I explained, instead of my sexual orientation, my royal status had been revealed.

So then my dad said I couldn't go to a new school just because I'd been outed as being a princess. He said I have to stay at Albert Einstein's, and Lars will go to class with me and protect me from reporters.

So then I asked him who'll drive him around and he pointed to the new guy and said Hans.

The new guy nodded to me in the rear view mirror and said, 'Hi.'

So then I said Lars is going to go with me everywhere I go? Like how about if I just wanted to walk over to Lilly's? I mean, if Lilly and I were still friends. Which is certainly never going to happen now.

And my dad said, Lars would go with you.

So basically, I am never going anywhere alone again.

This made me kind of mad. I sat in the back seat with red from a traffic light flashing down on my face and I said,

'OK, well, that's it. I don't want to be a princess any more. You can take back your one hundred dollars a day and send Grandmere back to France. I quit.'

And my dad said, in this tired voice, 'You can't quit, Mia. The article today closed the deal. Tomorrow your face will be in every newspaper in America – maybe even the world. Everyone will know that you are the Princess Amelia of Genovia. And you cannot quit being who you are.'

I guess it wasn't a very princessy thing to do, but I cried all the way to the Plaza. Lars gave me his handkerchief, which I thought was very nice of him.

More Wednesday

My mom thinks the person who tipped off Carol Fernandez is Grandmere.

But I really can't believe Grandmere would do something like that – you know, give the *Post* the inside scoop on me. Especially when I'm so far behind in my princess lessons. You know? It's almost guaranteed that now I'm going to have to start acting like a princess – I mean, *really* acting like one – but Grandmere hasn't even gotten to all the really important stuff yet, the stuff like how to argue knowledgeably with virulent anti-royalists like Lilly. So far all Grandmere has taught me is how to sit, how to dress, how to use a fish fork, how to address senior members of the royal household staff, and how to say thank you so much and, no, I don't care for that in seven languages, how to make a Sidecar, and some Marxist theory.

What good is any of THAT going to do me?

But my mom is convinced. Nothing will change her mind. My dad got really mad at her, but she still wouldn't budge. She says Grandmere is the one who tipped off Carol Fernandez, and that all my dad has to do is ask her, and he'll find out the truth.

My dad did ask her – not Grandmere. Mom. He asked her why she never bothered to consider that her boyfriend might be the one who spilled the beans to Carol Fernandez.

The minute he said it, I think my dad probably regretted it. Because my mom's eyes got the way they do when she's really mad – I mean *really* mad, like the time I told her about the guy in Washington Square Park who flashed his you-know-what at me and Lilly one day when we were filming for her show. Her eyes got narrower and narrower, until they're nothing more than little slits. Then, next thing I knew, she was putting on her coat and going out to kick some flasher butt.

Only she didn't put on her coat when my dad said that about Mr Gianini. Instead, her eyes got very narrow, and her lips almost disappeared, she pressed them together so hard, and then she went, 'Get . . . out,' in a voice that kind of sounded like the poltergeist in that movie *Amityville Horror*.

But my dad wouldn't get out, even though technically, the loft belongs to my mom (thank God Carol Fernandez didn't put the loft's address in the paper; and thank God my mom is so paranoid about Christian right-winger Jesse Helms telling the Central Intelligence Agency about socio-political artists like herself, in order to yank out their National Endowment for the Arts grants, that she keeps our phone number unlisted. No reporters have discovered the loft, so we can at least order in Chinese without fear of hearing a story on *Extra* on how much the Princess Amelia likes moo shu vegetable).

Instead, my dad went, 'Really, Helen. I think you're letting your dislike of my mother blind you to the real truth.'

'The real truth?' my mom yelled. 'The real truth, Phillipe, is that your mother is—'

At this point, I decided it might be best to retire to my room. I put my headphones on so I wouldn't have to listen to them fight. This is a trick I learned from watching kids on made-for-TV movies whose parents are divorcing. My favourite CD right now is the latest Britney Spears, which I know is really dorky, and I could never tell Lilly, but secretly I sort of want to be Britney Spears. Once I had a dream I *was* Britney, and I was performing in the auditorium at Albert Einstein's, and I had this little pink mini-dress on, and Josh Richter complimented me on it right before I went on stage.

167

Isn't that an embarrassing thing to admit? The funny thing is, while I know I could never tell Lilly about that dream without her going all Freudian on me, and telling me how the pink dress is a phallic symbol and being Britney signifies my low self-esteem or something, I know I could tell Tina Hakim Baba, and she would totally get into it, and just want to know whether or not Josh was wearing leather trousers.

I don't think I've ever mentioned this, but it's really hard to write with my new fake fingernails.

The more I think about it, the more I wonder whether or not Grandmere really is the one who tipped off Carol Fernandez. I mean, when I went to my princess lesson today, I was still crying, and Grandmere was totally unsympathetic about it. She was all, 'And these tears are because . . .?' and when I told her, she just raised her painted-on eyebrows – she plucks hers all out and draws on new ones every day, which kind of defeats the purpose, if you ask me, but whatever – and went, '*C'est la vie*,' which means 'Well, that's life', in French.

Only in life, I don't think a whole lot of girls get their face plastered across the cover of the *Post*, unless they've won the Lottery or had sex with the President or something. *I* didn't do anything except get born.

I don't think 'that's life' at all. I think that sucks, is what I think.

Then Grandmere started talking about how she'd been fielding calls all day from representatives of the media, and how all these people want to interview me, like Leeza Gibbons and Barbara Walters and stuff, and she said I ought to have a press conference, and that she'd already talked to the Plaza people about it, and they'd set aside this special room with a podium and a pitcher of ice water and some potted palms and stuff.

I couldn't believe it! I was like, 'Grandmere! I don't want to talk to Barbara Walters! God! Like I really want everyone knowing my business!'

And Grandmere said, all prissy, 'Well, if you don't try to accommodate the media, they're just going to try to get the story any way they can, which means they'll keep showing up at your school. And at your friends' houses, and at your grocery store, and at the place where you rent those movie videos you like so much.'

Grandmere doesn't believe in VCRs. She says if God meant for us to watch movies at home, He wouldn't have invented coming attractions.

Then Grandmere wanted to know where my sense of civic duty was. She said it would greatly promote tourism in Genovia if I just went on *Dateline*.

I really want to do what's best for Genovia. I really do. But I also have to do what's best for Mia Thermopolis. And going on *Dateline* would definitely not be good for me.

But Grandmere seems really gung-ho on the whole promoting Genovia thing. So I sort of started to wonder if maybe, just maybe, my mom is right. Maybe Grandmere *did* talk to Carol Fernandez.

But would Grandmere do something like that?

Well. Yeah.

I just lifted up my headphones. They're still at it.

Looks like it's going to be a long night.

Thursday, October 15, Homeroom

Well, this morning my face was on the covers of the *Daily News* and *New York Newsday*. My picture was also in the Metro Section of the *New York Times*. They used my school photo, and let me tell you, my mom wasn't too happy about that, since that meant either somebody in our family, to whom she sent copies of that photo, or someone at Albert Einstein's must have leaked it, which looks bad for Mr Gianini. I wasn't too happy about it because my school photo was taken before Paolo fixed my hair and I look like one of those girls who are always going on TV to talk about their bad experience being in a cult or escaping from an abusive husband or something.

There were more reporters than ever in front of Albert Einstein's when Hans pulled up in front of it this morning. I guess all the morning news shows needed something they could report from live. Usually it's an overturned chicken truck on the Palisades Parkway, or a crackhead holding his wife and kids hostage in Queens. But today, it was me.

I had sort of anticipated that this might happen, and I was a little more prepared today than I was yesterday. So, in flagrant violation of my grandmother's fashion dictums, I wore my newly re-laced combat boots (in case I had to kick anybody holding a microphone who got too close) and I also wore all of my Greenpeace and anti-fur badges, so at least my celebrity status will be put to good use.

It was the same drill as the day before. Lars took me by the arm and the two of us sprinted through a sea of TV cameras and microphones into the school. As we ran, people shouted stuff at me like, 'Amelia, do you intend to follow the example of Princess Diana and become the queen of people's hearts?' and 'Amelia, who do you like better,

Leonardo di Caprio or Prince William?' and 'Amelia, what are your feelings on the meat industry?'

They almost got me on that one. I started to turn around, but Lars dragged me on into the school.

Here's what I need to do:

1. Think of some way to get Lilly to like me again.
2. Stop being such a wimp.
3. Stop lying
   and/or
   Think of better lies.
4. Stop being so dramatic.
5. Start being more
   A. independent.
   B. self-reliant.
   C. mature.
6. Stop thinking about Josh Richter.
7. Stop thinking about Michael Moscovitz.
8. Get better grades.
9. Achieve self-actualization.

Thursday, French class

Today in Algebra Mr Gianini was totally trying to teach us about the Cartesian plane, but nobody could pay attention because of all the news vans outside. People kept jumping up to lean out the windows and yell at the reporters, like 'Go find some real news,' and 'Hey, take a picture of this,' accompanied by a rude gesture.

Mr Gianini kept trying to bring people to order, but it was impossible. Lilly was getting all burned up because everyone was coming together against the reporters, but no one had wanted to stand outside Ho's Deli and do her chant, which was 'We oppose/the racist Hos.'

So then in the general confusion Lana Weinberger asked me how long I'd known I was a princess, and I couldn't believe she was actually asking me a question without being snotty about it, and I was like, well, I don't know, a couple of weeks or something, and then Lana said if she found she was a princess she would go straight to Disneyworld, and I said, No, you wouldn't, because you'd miss cheerleading practice, and then she said she didn't see why I didn't go to Disneyworld since I'm not even that involved in extracurricular activities, and then Lilly started in about the Disneyfication of America and how Walt Disney was actually a fascist, and then everybody started wondering if it was really true about his body being cryogenically frozen under the castle in Anaheim, and then Mr Gianini was like, Could we please return to the Cartesian plane?

Which is probably a safer plane to be on, if you think about it, than the one we live on, since there aren't any reporters there.

Cartesian coordinate system
divides the plane into 4 parts called quadrants

Thursday, G & T

So I was eating lunch with Tina Hakim Baba and Lars and Wahim, and Tina was telling me about how in Saudi Arabia, where her father comes from, girls have to wear this thing called a chadrah, which is like a huge blanket that covers them from head to foot, with just a slit for them to see out of. It's supposed to protect them from the lustful eyes of men, but Tina says her cousins wear Gap jeans underneath their chadrahs, and as soon as there aren't any adults around, they take their chadrahs off and hang out with boys just we like do.

Well, like we *would* do, if any boys liked us.

I take that back. I forgot that Tina has a boy to hang out with, her Cultural Diversity date, Dave Farouq El-Abar.

Geez. What is *wrong* with me, anyway? How come no boys like *me*?

So Tina was telling me all about chadrahs, when all of a sudden, Lana Weinberger set her tray down next to ours.

I am not even kidding. *Lana Weinberger.*

I of course thought she was going to whip out the receipt for the Nutty Royaled sweater's dry cleaning or start shaking Tabasco sauce all over our salads or something, but instead, she just went, all breezy, 'You guys don't mind if we join you, do you?'

And then I saw this tray sliding over next to mine. It was loaded down with two double cheeseburgers, large fries, two chocolate milks, a bowl of chilli, a bag of Doritos, a salad with French dressing, a pack of Yoo Hoos, an apple, and a large Coke. When I looked up to see who could possibly be ingesting that many saturated fats, I saw Josh Richter pulling out the chair next to mine.

I am not even kidding. *Josh Richter.*

He went, 'Hey', to me and sat down and started eating.

I looked at Tina, and Tina looked at me, and then both of us looked at our bodyguards. But they were busy arguing over whether rubber-tipped bullets really did hurt rioters, or if it was better just to use hoses.

Tina and I looked back at Lana and Josh.

Really attractive people, like Lana and Josh, don't ever go anywhere alone. They always have this sort of entourage that follows them around. Lana's entourage consists of a bunch of other girls, most of whom are junior varsity cheerleaders like she is. They are all really pretty, with long hair and breasts and stuff, like Lana.

Josh's entourage consists of a bunch of senior boys who are all on the crew team with him. They are all really large and handsome, and they were all eating excessive amounts of animal by-products, just like Josh.

Josh's entourage put their trays down beside Josh's. Lana's entourage put their trays beside Lana's. And soon, our table, which had consisted only of two geeky girls and their bodyguards, was being graced by the most beautiful people in Albert Einstein's – maybe even in all of Manhattan.

I got a good look at Lilly and her eyes were bugging out the way they do when she sees something she thinks would make a good episode of her show.

'So,' Lana said, all chatty-like, while she picked at her salad – no dressing, and only water on the side. 'What are you up to this weekend, Mia? Are you going to the Cultural Diversity Dance?'

It was the first time she'd ever called me Mia, and not Amelia.

'Uh,' I said, brilliantly. 'Let me see . . .'

'Because Josh's parents are going away, and we were thinking about having a thing at his place on Saturday night, after the dance, and all. You should come.'

'Huh,' I said. 'Well, I don't—'

'She should totally come,' Lana said, stabbing at a cherry tomato with her fork. 'Shouldn't she, Josh?'

Josh was shovelling his chilli into his mouth using Doritos instead of a spoon. 'Sure,' he said, with his mouth full. 'She should come.'

'It's going to be so *cool*,' Lana said. 'Josh's place is like *great*. It's got six bedrooms. On Park Avenue. And there's a Jacuzzi in the master bedroom. Isn't there a Jacuzzi, Josh?'

Josh said, 'Yeah, there's—'

Pierce, a member of Josh's entourage, and a six foot two inch rower, interrupted. 'Hey, Richter, remember after the last dance? When Bonham-Allen passed out in your mom's Jacuzzi? That was *rad*.'

Lana giggled. 'Oh, God! She chugged that whole bottle of Bailey's Irish Cream. Remember, Josh? She drank practically the whole thing herself – what a hog! – and then she wouldn't stop throwing up.'

'Major vomitage,' Pierce agreed.

'She had to have her stomach pumped,' Lana said, to Tina and me. 'The paramedics said if Josh hadn't phoned them when he did, she'd have died.'

We all turned to look at Josh. He said, modestly, 'It was *way* uncool.'

Lana stopped giggling. 'It was,' she said, all solemn now that Josh Richter had declared the incident uncool.

I didn't know what I was supposed to say about that, so I just said, 'Wow.'

'So,' Lana said. She ate a shred of lettuce and swished some water around in her mouth. 'Are you coming, or not?'

'I'm sorry,' I said. 'I can't.'

A lot of Lana's friends, who'd been talking amongst

themselves, stopped talking and looked at me. Josh's friends, however, went right on eating.

'You *can't*?' Lana said, making this very astonished face.

'No,' I said. 'I can't.'

'What do you mean, you *can't*?'

I thought about lying. I could have said something like, Lana, I can't go because I have to have dinner with the Prime Minister of Iceland. I could have said I can't go because I have to go christen a cruise ship. There were all sorts of excuses I could have made up. But for once, for once in my stupid life, I went and told the truth.

'I can't go,' I said, 'because my mom wouldn't let me go to a party like that.'

Oh, my God. Why did I say that? Why, why, why? I should have lied. I totally should have lied. Because how did I sound, saying something like that? Uh, like a total freak. Worse than a freak. A dork. A Grade-A nerd.

I don't know what compelled me to tell the truth in the first place. It wasn't even the *real* truth. I mean, it was *a* truth, but it wasn't the *real* reason I was saying no. I mean, it's true there was no way my mom was going to *let* me go to a party in a boy's apartment when his parents are out of town. Even with a bodyguard. But the real reason, of course, is that I wouldn't know how to *act* at a party like that. I mean, I've heard about these kinds of parties. There are like *whole rooms* reserved for people to go into to make out. We're talking major French kissing. Maybe even MORE than French kissing. Maybe even like above-the-waist touching. Maybe even below-the-waist touching. I don't know for sure, because no one I know has ever been to one of those parties. No one I know is popular enough to get invited.

Plus everybody drinks. But I don't drink, and I don't have anybody to make out with. So what would I *do* there?

Lana looked at me, and then she looked at her friends, and then she burst out laughing. Loud. I mean, REALLY loud.

Well, I guess I can't really blame her.

'Oh, my God,' Lana said, when she had gotten over laughing so hard that she couldn't talk. 'You can't be serious.'

I knew right then Lana had just latched upon a whole new thing to torture me about. I didn't really care so much about me, but I felt bad for Tina Hakim Baba, who'd managed to keep such a low profile for so long. Suddenly, because of me, she was being sucked into the middle of the popular girl torture zone.

'Oh, my God,' Lana said. 'Are you kidding me?'

'Um,' I said. 'No.'

'Well, you're not supposed to tell her the *truth*,' Lana said, all snotty again.

I didn't know what she was talking about.

'Your mom. *Nobody* tells their mom the *truth*. You tell her you're spending the night at a girlfriend's house. *Duh*.'

Oh.

She meant lie. To my mom. Lana had obviously never met my mom. *Nobody* lies to my mom. You just can't. Not about something like that. No way.

So I said, 'Look, it's not like I don't appreciate being asked, and all, but I really don't think I can come. Besides, I don't even drink . . .'

OK, *that* was another big mistake.

Lana looked at me like I'd just said I'd never watched *Party of Five*, or something. She went, 'You don't *drink*?'

I just looked at her. The truth is, at Miragnac, I do drink. We drink wine with dinner every night. That's just what you do in France. You don't drink it for *fun*, though. You drink it

177

because it goes with the food. It's supposed to make the foie gras taste better. I wouldn't know about that, since I don't eat foie gras, but I can tell you from experience that wine goes better with goat cheese than Dr Pepper does.

I certainly wouldn't chug a whole bottle of it, though, not even on a dare. Not even for Josh Richter.

So I just shrugged and went, 'No. I try to be respectful of my body, and not put a whole lot of toxins into it.'

Lana snorted at that, but across from her – beside me – Josh Richter swallowed the mouthful of burger he was chewing and said, 'I can respect that.'

Lana's mouth dropped open. So, I'm sorry to say, did mine. Josh Richter respected something *I* had said? Are you *kidding* me?

But he looked perfectly serious. More than serious. He looked the way he had that day at Bigelow's, like he could see into my soul with those electric blue eyes of his . . . Like he already *had* seen into my soul . . .

I guess Lana didn't notice her boyfriend looking into my soul, though. Because she said, 'God, Josh. You drink more'n anybody else in this whole *school*.'

Josh turned his head and looked at her with those hypnotic eyes. He said, without smiling, 'Well, maybe I should quit, then.'

Lana started laughing. She said, 'Oh, right! That'll happen!'

Josh didn't laugh, though. He just went on looking at her.

That's when I started to get the heebie-jeebies. Josh just kept staring at Lana. I was glad he wasn't staring at *me* like that: those blue eyes of his are no joke.

I got up real fast, and grabbed my tray. Tina, seeing what I was doing, did the same.

'Well,' I said. 'Bye.'

Then we booked out of there.

On the way to drop off our trays, Tina was like, 'What was *that* all about?' and I said I didn't know. But one thing for sure:

For once, I'm kind of glad I'm not Lana Weinberger.

More Thursday, French

When I went to my locker after lunch to get my books for French, Josh was there. He was sort of leaning on his closed locker door, looking around. When he saw me coming, he straightened up, and went, 'Hey.'

And then he smiled. A big smile, that showed all of his white teeth. His perfectly straight white teeth. I had to look away, those teeth were so perfect and so blindingly white.

I said, 'Hey,' back. I was really embarrassed, and all, since I had sort of seen him fighting with Lana a few minutes before. I figured he was probably waiting for her, and that the two of them would make up, and probably French kiss all over the place, so I tried to work my combination as quickly as possible and get the heck out of there, so I wouldn't have to watch.

But Josh started *talking* to me. He said, 'I really agree with what you said in the caff just now. You know, about respecting your body, and everything. I think that's really, you know, a cool attitude.'

I could feel my face start to burn. It was sort of like I was on fire. I concentrated on not dropping anything as I moved books around in my locker. It's too bad my hair is so short now. I couldn't duck my head to hide the fact that I was blushing. 'Huh,' I said, real intelligently.

'So,' Josh said. 'Are you going to the dance with anyone, or not?'

I dropped my Algebra book. It went skittering across the hall. I stooped down to pick it up.

'Um,' I said, by way of answering his question.

I was down on my hands and knees, picking up old worksheets that had slid out of my Algebra book, when I saw these knees covered in grey flannel bend. Then Josh's face was right next to mine.

'Here,' he said, and handed me my favourite pencil, the one with the feathery pom-pom on the end.

'Thanks,' I said. Then I made the mistake of looking into his too blue eyes.

'No,' I said, real faintly, because that's how his eyes made me feel: faint. 'I'm not going to the dance with anyone.'

Then the bell rang.

Josh said, 'Well, see you.' And then he left.

I am still in shock.

Josh Richter *spoke* to me. He actually *spoke* to me. *Twice.*

For the first time in like a month, I don't care that I'm flunking Algebra. I don't care that my mom is dating one of my teachers. I don't care that I'm the heir to the throne of Genovia. I don't even care that my best friend and I aren't speaking.

I think Josh Richter might *like* me.

Homework:

Algebra: ??? Can't remember!!!
English: ??? Ask Shameeka
World Civ.: ??? Ask Lilly. Forgot. Can't ask Lilly. She's not speaking to me.
G & T: none
French: ???
Biology: ???

God, just because a boy might like me, I completely lose my head. I disgust myself.

Thursday night

Grandmere says, 'Well, of course the boy likes you. What wouldn't he like? You are turning out very well, thanks to Paolo's handiwork and my tutelage.'

Geez, Grandmere, thanks. Like it would be impossible for any guy to like me for *me*, and not because all of a sudden I'm a princess, with a two-hundred dollar haircut.

I think I sort of hate her.

I mean it. I know it's wrong to hate people, but I really do sort of hate my grandmother. At least, I strongly dislike her. I mean, besides the fact that she's totally vain and thinks only about herself, she's also kind of mean to people.

Like tonight, for instance:

Grandmere decided that for my lesson today, we would go to dinner somewhere outside of the hotel, so she could teach me how to deal with the press. Only there wasn't a whole lot of press around when we went outside, just some kid reporter from *Tiger Beat*, or something. I guess all the real reporters had gone home to get their dinner (plus it's no fun for the press to stalk you when you're ready for them. It's only when you least expect them that they come around. This is how they get their kicks, at least as far as I can figure out).

Anyway, I was pretty happy about this, because who needs the press around, yelling questions and setting off flashbulbs in your face? Believe me, as it is, I see big purple splotches everywhere I go.

But then as I was getting into the car Hans had brought around, Grandmere said, 'Wait one moment', and went back inside. I thought maybe she'd forgotten her tiara, or something, but she came back out a minute later looking no different than before.

But then, when we pulled up in front of the restaurant, which was the Four Seasons, there were all these reporters there! At first I thought somebody important had to be inside, like Shaquille O'Neal or Madonna, but then they all started taking pictures of me, and yelling, 'Princess Amelia, how does it feel to grow up in a single-parent household, then find out your mom's ex has three million dollars?' and 'Princess, what kind of running shoes do you wear?'

I totally forgot my whole fear of confrontation thing. I was mad. I turned to Grandmere in the car, and I said, 'How did they know we were coming here?'

Grandmere just dug around in her purse for her cigarettes. 'Now, what did I do with that lighter?' she asked.

'You called them, didn't you?' I was so mad, I could hardly even see straight. 'You called and told them we were coming here.'

'Don't be ridiculous,' Grandmere said. 'I had no time to call all these people.'

'You didn't have to. You'd just have to call one, and they'd all follow. Grandmere, *why*?'

Grandmere lit her cigarette. I hate when she smokes in the car. 'This is an important part of being a royal, Amelia,' she said, between puffs. 'You must learn to handle the press. Why are you taking on so?'

'You're the one who told all that stuff to Carol Fernandez.' I said it totally calmly.

'Of course I did,' Grandmere said, with a kind of *So what?* shrug.

'Grandma,' I yelled. 'How could you?'

She looked totally taken aback. She said, 'Don't call me Grandma.'

'Seriously,' I yelled. 'Dad thinks Mr Gianini did it! He and

Mom had this totally big fight about it. She said it was you, but he wouldn't believe her!'

Grandmere blew cigarette smoke out of her nostrils. 'Phillipe,' she said, 'always was incredibly naive.'

'Well,' I said. 'I'm telling him. I'm telling him the truth.'

Grandmere just waved a hand, as if to say, *Whatever*.

'Seriously,' I said. 'I'm telling him. He's going to be really mad at you, Grandmere.'

'He won't. You needed the practice, darling. That piece in the *Post* was only the beginning. Soon you'll be on the cover of *Vogue*, and then—'

'Grandmere!' I yelled. 'I DO NOT WANT TO BE ON THE COVER OF VOGUE! DON'T YOU UNDERSTAND? I JUST WANT TO PASS THE NINTH GRADE!'

Grandmere looked a little startled. 'Well, all right, darling, all right. You needn't *shout*.'

I don't know how much of that sunk in, but after dinner, I noticed the reporters had all gone home. So maybe she heard me.

When I got home, Mr Gianini was here, AGAIN. I had to go into my room to call my dad. I said, 'Dad, it was Grandma, not Mr Gianini, who told Carol Fernandez everything,' and he said, 'I know', in this miserable way.

'You *know*?' I could hardly believe it. 'You *know*, and you haven't said anything?'

He went, 'Mia, your grandmother and I have a very complicated relationship.'

He means he's scared of her. I guess I can't really blame him, considering the fact that she used to lock him in the dungeon, and everything.

'Well,' I said. 'You could still apologize to Mom for what you said about Mr Gianini.'

184

He went, still sounding all miserable, 'I know.'

So I said, 'Well? Are you going to?'

And he said, 'Mia . . .' Only now he sounded all exasperated. I figured I'd done enough good deeds for one day, and hung up.

After that, I sat around while Mr Gianini helped me with my homework. I was too distracted by Josh Richter talking to me today to pay attention while Michael was trying to help me in G & T.

I guess I can sort of see how my mom likes Mr G. He's OK to just hang out with, you know, like in front of the TV. He doesn't hog the remote, like some of my mom's past boyfriends. And he doesn't seem to care about sports at all.

About a half hour before I went to bed, my dad called back, and asked to speak to my mother. She went into the room to talk to him, and when she came out again, she looked all happy, in a I-told-you-so sort of way.

I wish I could tell Lilly about Josh Richter talking to me.

Friday, October 16, English

OH MY GOD!!!
 JOSH AND LANA BROKE UP!!!!
 I am not even kidding. It's all over school. Josh broke up with her last night after crew practice. They were having dinner together at the Hard Rock Café, and he asked for his class ring back!!! Lana was completely humiliated under the pointy cone bra Gaultier made for Madonna!
 I wouldn't wish that on my worst enemy.
 Lana wasn't hanging around Josh's locker this morning, like usual. And then when I saw her in Algebra, her eyes were all red and squinty, and her hair looked like it hadn't been brushed, let alone washed, and her thigh-highs had come unglued, and were all baggy around her knees. I never thought I'd see Lana Weinberger looking like a mess!!! Before class started, she was on her cell phone with Bergdorf's, trying to convince them to take her Cultural Diversity Dance dress back, even though she'd already removed the tags. Then during class, she sat there with a big black marker crossing out *Mrs Josh Richter* from where she'd written it all over her book covers.
 It was so depressing. I could hardly factor my integers, I was so distracted.

I wish I were:

1. Size 36 double-D bra.
2. Good at maths.
3. A member of a world-famous rock band.
4. Still friends with Lilly Moscovitz.
5. Josh Richter's new girlfriend.

More Friday

You will not even believe what just happened. I was putting my Algebra book away in my locker, and Josh Richter was there getting his Trig notes, and he goes, in this totally casual way, 'Hey, Mia, who you going to the dance with tomorrow?'

Needless to say, the fact that he actually spoke to me at all practically caused me to pass out. And then the fact that he was actually saying something that sounded like it might be a prelude to asking me out – well, I nearly threw up. I mean it. I felt really sick, but in a good way.

I think.

Somehow, I managed to stammer out, 'Uh, no one,' and he goes, and I kid you not:

'Well, why don't we go together?'

OH MY GOD!!!!! JOSH RICHTER ASKED ME OUT!!!!!

I was so shocked I couldn't say anything at all for like a minute. I thought I was going to hyperventilate, like I did the time I saw that documentary about how cows become hamburgers. I could only stand there and look up at him (he's so tall!).

Then a funny thing happened. This tiny part of my brain – the only part that wasn't completely stunned by his asking me out – went, He's only asking you out because you're the Princess of Genovia.

Seriously. That's what I thought, for just a second.

Then this other part of my brain, a much bigger part, went, SO WHAT???

I mean, maybe he asked me to the dance because he respects me as a human being and wants to get to know me better and maybe, just maybe, likes me, sort of.

It could happen.

So the part of my brain that was rationalizing all this made me go, all nonchalantly, 'Yeah, OK. That might be fun.'

Then Josh said a bunch of stuff about how he'd pick me up and we'd have dinner beforehand or something. But I barely heard him. Because inside my head, this voice was going:

Josh Richter just asked you out. Josh Richter just asked YOU out. JOSH RICHTER JUST ASKED YOU OUT!!!!

I think I must have died and gone to heaven. Because it had happened. It had finally happened: Josh Richter had finally looked into my soul. He had looked into my soul, and saw the real me, the one beneath the flat chest. AND THEN HE'D ASKED ME OUT.

Then the bell rang, and Josh went away, and I just kept standing there, until Lars poked me in the arm.

I don't know what Lars's problem is. I *know* he's not my personal secretary.

But thank God he was there, or I'd never have known Josh was picking me up tomorrow night at seven. I'm going to have to learn not to be so shocked the next time he asks me out, or I'll never get the hang of this dating thing.

Things to do:

(I think: never having been on a date before, I am not exactly sure WHAT to do)

1. Get a dress.
2. Get hair done.
3. Get nails redone (stop biting fake ones off).

188

Friday, G & T

OK, so I don't know who Lilly Moscovitz thinks she is. First she stops talking to me. Then, when she finally does deign to speak to me, it's only to criticize me some more. What right has she got, I ask you, to dump all over my Cultural Diversity Dance date? I mean, *she's* going with Boris Pelkowski. *Boris Pelkowski*. Yeah, he might be a musical genius and all, but he's still *Boris Pelkowski*.

Lilly goes: 'Well, at least I know Boris isn't on the rebound.'

Excuse me. Josh Richter is *not* on the rebound. He and Lana had been broken up for sixteen whole hours before he asked me out.

Lilly goes: 'Plus Boris doesn't do *drugs*.'

I swear, for someone so smart, Lilly sure does go for the whole rumour and innuendo thing in a major way. I asked her if she'd ever *seen* Josh do drugs, and she looked at me all sarcastically.

But really, if you think about it, there isn't any *proof* Josh does drugs. He definitely hangs out with people who do drugs, but hey, Tina Hakim Baba hangs out with a princess, and that doesn't make *her* one.

Lilly didn't like that argument, though. She went, 'You're over-rationalizing. Whenever you over-rationalize, Mia, I know you're worried.'

I am *not* worried. I am going to the biggest dance of the fall semester with the cutest, most sensitive boy in school, and nothing anyone can do or say will make me feel bad about that.

Except that it does kind of make me feel weird, seeing Lana looking so sad, and Josh looking like he doesn't care at all. Today at lunch, he and his entourage sat with Tina and

189

me, and Lana and her entourage sat back with the other cheerleaders. It was just so *strange*. Plus neither Josh nor any of his friends talked to me or to Tina. They just talked to each other. Which didn't bother Tina any, but it kind of bothered me. Especially since Lana kept trying so hard not to look over at our table.

Tina didn't say anything bad about Josh when I told her the news. She just got very excited and said tonight, when I spend the night, we can try on different outfits and experiment with our hair to see what will look best for tomorrow night. Well, I have no hair to experiment with, but we can experiment with her hair. Actually, Tina's almost more excited than I am. She is a much more supportive friend than Lilly, who went, all sarcastically, when she heard, 'Where's he taking you to dinner? The Harley-Davidson Café?'

I said, 'No,' very sarcastically back. 'Tavern on the Green.'

Lilly went, 'Oh, how imaginative.'

I suppose super-artsy Boris is taking *her* somewhere in the Village.

Then Michael, who had been pretty quiet (for him) all through class, looked at Lars and went, 'You're going too, right?'

And Lars went, 'Oh, yes.' And the two of them looked at each other in that infuriating way guys look at each other sometimes, like they have this secret. You know in sixth grade, when they made all of us girls go into this other room and watch a video about getting our periods and stuff? I bet while we were gone, the boys were watching a video about how to look at each other in that infuriating way.

Or maybe a cartoon, or something.

But now that I think of it, Josh *is* kind of dissing Lana. I mean, he probably shouldn't have asked out another girl so soon after breaking up with her – at least, not to something he was going to go to with her. Know what I mean? I kind of feel bad about the whole thing.

But not bad enough not to go.

From now on I will:

1. Be nicer to everyone, even Lana Weinberger.
2. Never ever bite my fingernails, even the fake ones.
3. Write faithfully in this journal every day.
4. Stop watching old *Baywatch* re-runs and use my time wisely, like to study Algebra, or maybe improve the environment, or something.

Friday night

Abbreviated lesson with Grandmere today, because of me spending the night at Tina's. Grandmere had pretty much gotten over me yelling at her yesterday about the press. She was totally into helping me figure out what I'm going to wear tomorrow night, just like I knew she would. She got on the phone with Chanel, and set up an appointment for tomorrow to pick something out. It will have to be a rush job, and will cost a fortune, but she says she doesn't care: it will be my first formal event as a representative of Genovia, and I have to 'sparkle' (her word, not mine).

I pointed out to her that it was a school dance, not an inauguration ball, or anything, and that it wasn't even prom, just a stupid dance to celebrate the diversity of the various racial and cultural groups that attend Albert Einstein High School. But Grandmere went ape anyway, and kept on worrying there wouldn't be time to dye shoes to match my gown.

There's a lot of stuff about being a girl I never realized. Like having your shoes match your gown. I didn't know that was so important.

But Tina Hakim Baba sure knows. You should see her room. She must have every women's magazine ever printed. They are in order on shelves all around her room, which, by the way, is huge and pink, much like the rest of her apartment, which takes up the entire top floor of her building. You hit PH on the elevator buttons, and the elevator opens in the Hakim Babas' marble foyer, which really does have a fountain, only you're not supposed to throw pennies in it, I found out.

And then there's just room after room after room. They have a maid, a cook, a nanny, and a driver, all of whom live-in. So you can imagine how many rooms there are, on top of the fact that Tina has three little sisters and a baby brother, and all of *them* have their own rooms too.

Tina's room has its own thirty-seven inch TV with a Sony Playstation. I can see now that I have been living a life of monastic simplicity compared to Tina.

Some people have all the luck.

Anyway, Tina is a lot different at home than she is at school. At home, she's totally bubbly and outgoing. Her parents are pretty nice too. Mr Hakim Baba is really funny. He had a heart attack last year and isn't allowed to eat practically anything but vegetables and rice. He has to lose twenty more pounds. He kept pinching my arm and going, 'How do you stay so skinny?' I told him about my strict vegetarianism, and he went, 'Oh,' and shuddered really hard. The Hakim Babas' cook has orders to only prepare vegetarian meals, which was good for me. We had couscous and vegetable goulash. It was all quite delicious.

Mrs Hakim Baba is beautiful, but in a different way from my mom. Mrs Hakim Baba is British and very blonde. I think she's pretty bored, living here in America and having a job and all. Mrs Hakim Baba used to be a model, but she quit when she got married. Now she doesn't get to meet all the interesting people she used to meet when she was modelling.

Mrs Hakim Baba is as tall as me, which makes her about five inches taller than Mr Hakim Baba. But I don't think Mr Hakim Baba minds.

Tina's little sisters and brother are really cute. After we messed around with the fashion magazines, looking up hairstyles, we tried some of them out on Tina's sisters. They looked pretty funny. Then we put butterfly clips in Tina's little brother's hair and gave him a French manicure like mine, and he got very excited and changed into his Batman suit and ran around the apartment, screaming. I thought it was cute, but Mr and Mrs Hakim Baba didn't think so. They made the nanny put little Bobby Hakim Baba to bed right after dinner.

Then Tina showed me her dress for tomorrow. It's by a designer called Nicole Miller. It's so pretty, like sea foam. Tina Hakim Baba looks much more like a princess than I ever could.

Then it was time for *Lilly Tells It Like It Is*, which comes on on Friday nights at nine. This was the episode dedicated to exposing the unjust racism at Ho's Deli. It was filmed before Lilly called off the boycott due to lack of interest. It was a very hard-hitting piece of television news journalism, and I can say that without bragging, since I wasn't involved in its creation. If *Lilly Tells It Like It Is* ever went network, I bet it would be as highly rated as *Sixty Minutes*.

At the end, Lilly came on and did a segment she must have shot the night before, with a tripod in her bedroom. She sat on her bed and said that racism is a powerful force of evil that all of us must work to combat. She said that even though to some of us, paying five cents more for a bag of gingko biloba rings might not seem like much, victims of real racism, like the Armenians and the Rwandans and the Ugandans and the Bosnians, would recognize that that five cents was only the first step on the road to genocide. Lilly went on to say that because of her daring stand against the Hos, there was a little bit more justice on the side of right today.

I don't know about that, but I did sort of start to miss her when she waggled her feet, in their furry bear claw slippers, into the camera, as a tribute to Norman. Tina is a fun friend, and everything, but I've known Lilly since kindergarten. It's kind of hard to forget that.

We stayed up really late reading Tina's teenage love novels. I swear, there wasn't a single one where the boy broke up with a snotty girl and started going out with the heroine right away. Usually he waited a tactful amount of time, like a summer or at least a weekend, before asking her out. The only ones with a guy who started going out with the heroine right away turned out to be ones where the guy was just using the girl to get revenge or something.

But then Tina said even though she loves reading those books, she never takes them as a guide to real life. Because how many times in real life does anybody ever get amnesia? And when do cute young European terrorists ever take anybody hostage in the girls' locker room? And if they did, wouldn't it be on the day when you're wearing your worst underwear, the kind with the holes and loose elastic, and a bra that doesn't match, and not a pink silk camisole and French knickers, like the heroine of that particular book?

She has a point.

Tina's turning out the light now, because she's tired. I'm glad. It's been a long day.

Saturday, October 17

When I got home, the first thing I did was check to make sure Josh hadn't called to cancel.

He hadn't.

Mr Gianini was there, though (of course. This time he had trousers on, though, thank God). When he heard me ask my mom if a boy named Josh had called, he was all, 'You don't mean Josh Richter, do you?'

I got kind of mad, because he sounded . . . I don't know. Shocked, or something.

I said, 'Yes, I mean Josh Richter. He and I are going to the Cultural Diversity Dance tonight.'

Mr Gianini raised his eyebrows. 'What about that Weinberger girl?'

It kind of sucks to have a parent who's dating a teacher in your school. I went, 'They broke up.'

My mom was watching us pretty closely, which is unusual for her, since most of the time, she's in her own world. She went, 'Who's Josh Richter?'

And I went, 'Only the cutest, most sensitive boy in school.'

Mr Gianini snorted and said, 'Well, most popular, anyway.'

To which my mom replied, with a lot of surprise, 'And he asked *Mia* to the dance?'

Needless to say, this was not very flattering. When your own mother knows it's weird for the cutest, most popular boy in school to ask you to the dance, you know you're in trouble.

'Yes,' I said, all defensively.

'I don't like this,' Mr Gianini said. And when my mom asked him why, he said, 'Because I know Josh Richter.'

My mom went, 'Uh oh. I don't like the sound of that,' and before I could say anything in Josh's defence, Mr Gianini went, 'That boy is going one hundred miles per hour,' which doesn't even make any sense.

At least it didn't until my mom pointed out that since I'm only going five miles per hour (FIVE!) she was going to have to consult my father 'about this'.

Hello? Consult him about what? What am I, a car with a faulty fan belt? What's this five miles per hour stuff?

'He's fast, Mia,' Mr Gianini translated.

Fast? FAST? What is this, the Fifties? Josh Richter is a rebel without a cause all of a sudden?

My mom went, as she was dialling my dad's phone number, over at the Plaza, 'You're just a freshman. You shouldn't be going out with seniors anyway.'

How unfair is THAT? I finally get a date, and all of a sudden, my parents turn into Mike and Carol Brady? I mean, come on!

So I was standing there, listening to my mom and dad go on about how they both think I'm too young to date, and that I SHOULDN'T date, since this has been a very confusing time for me, what with finding out I'm a princess and all. They were planning out the rest of my life for me (no dating until I'm eighteen, all-girls dorm when I get to college, etc) when the buzzer to the loft went off, and Mr G went to answer it. When he asked who it was, this all-too familiar voice went, 'This is Clarisse Marie Grimaldi Renaldo. Who is *this*?'

Across the room, my mom nearly dropped the phone. It was Grandmere. Grandmere had come to the loft!

I never in my life thought I'd be grateful to Grandmere for something. I never thought I'd be glad to see her. But when she showed up at the loft to take me shopping for my dress,

I could have kissed her – on both cheeks, even – I really could have. Because I met her at the door, and I was like, 'Grandmere, they won't let me go!'

I forgot Grandmere had never even been to the loft before. I forgot Mr Gianini was there. All I could think about was the fact that my parents were trying to low-ball me about Josh. Grandmere would take care of it, I knew.

And boy, did she ever.

Grandmere came bursting in, giving Mr Gianini a very dirty look – 'This is *he*?' she stopped long enough to ask, and when I said yes, she made this sniffing sound and walked right by him – and heard Dad on the speaker phone. She shouted, 'Give me that phone', at my mother, who looked like a kid who'd just gotten caught jumping a turnstile by the transit authority.

'Mother?' my dad's voice shouted over the speaker phone. You could tell he was in almost as much shock as Mom. 'Is that you? What are *you* doing there?'

For someone who claims to have no use for modern technology, Grandmere sure knew how to work that speaker phone. She took Dad right off it, snatched the receiver out of my mother's hand, and went, 'Listen, here, Phillipe', into it. 'Your daughter is going to the dance with her beau. I travelled fifty-seven blocks by limo to take her shopping for a new dress, and if you think I'm not going to watch her dance in it, than you can just—'

Then my grandmother used some pretty strong language. Only since she said it all in French, only my dad and I understood. My mom and Mr Gianini just stood there. My mom looked mad. Mr G looked nervous.

After my grandmother had finished telling my dad just where he could get off, she slammed the phone down, then looked around the loft. Let's just say Grandmere has never been one for hiding her feelings, so I wasn't too surprised when the next thing she said was, '*This* is where the Princess of Genovia is being brought up? In this . . . *warehouse?*'

Well, if she had lit a firecracker under my mom, she couldn't have made her madder.

'Now look here, Clarisse,' my mother said, stomping around in her Birkenstocks. 'Don't you dare try to tell me how to raise my child! Phillipe and I have already decided she isn't going out with this boy. You can't just come in here and—'

'Amelia,' my grandmother said. 'Go and get your coat.'

I went. When I got back, my mom's face was really red, and Mr Gianini was looking at the floor. But neither of them said anything as Grandmere and I left the loft.

Once we were outside, I was so excited, I could hardly stand it. 'Grandmere!' I yelled. 'What'd you *say* to them? What'd you say to convince them to let me go?'

But Grandmere just laughed in this scary way and said, 'I have my ways.'

Boy, did I ever not hate her then.

More Saturday

Well, I'm sitting here in my new dress, my new shoes, my new nails, and my new pantyhose, with my newly waxed legs and underarms, my newly touched-up hair, my professionally made-up face, and it's seven o'clock, and there's no sign of Josh, and I'm wondering if maybe this whole thing was a joke, like in the movie *Carrie*, which is too scary for me to watch but Michael Moscovitz rented it once, and then he told Lilly and me what it was about: this homely girl gets asked to a dance by the most popular boy in school, just so he and his popular friends can pour pig blood on her. Only he doesn't know Carrie has psychic powers, and at the end of the night she kills everyone in the whole town, including Stephen Spielberg's first wife and the mom from *Eight Is Enough*.

The problem is, of course, I don't have psychic powers, so if it turns out that Josh and his friends pour pig blood on me, I won't be able to kill them all. I mean, unless I call in the Genovian national guard, or something. But that would be difficult, since Genovia doesn't have an air force or navy, so how would the guards get here? They'd have to fly commercially, and it costs A LOT to buy tickets at the last minute. I doubt my dad would approve such an exorbitant expenditure of government funds – especially for what he'd be bound to consider a frivolous reason.

But if Josh Richter stands me up, I can assure you, I will *not* have a frivolous reaction. I got my LEGS waxed for him. OK? And you think that doesn't hurt, think about having your UNDERARMS waxed, which I also had done for him. OK? That waxing stuff HURTS. I practically started to cry, it hurt so bad. So don't be telling ME we can't call out the Genovian national guard if I get stood up.

I know my dad thinks Josh has stood me up. He's sitting at the kitchen table right now, pretending to read *TV Guide*. But I see him sneaking peeks at his watch all the time. Mom too. Only she never wears a watch, so she keeps sneaking peeks at the blinking-eye cat clock on the wall.

Lars is here too. He isn't checking the clock, though. He keeps checking his ammunition clip, to make sure he has enough bullets. I suppose my dad told him to shoot Josh if he makes a move on me.

Oh, yes. My dad said I can go out with Josh, but only if Lars goes too. This is no big thing since I always expected Lars would go, anyway. But I pretended to be all mad about it, so my dad wouldn't think I was getting off too easy. I mean, HE's in BIG trouble with Grandmere. She told me while I was being fitted for my dress that my dad has always had a problem with commitment, and that the reason he doesn't want me to go out with Josh is that he can't stand to see me dumped the way my dad has dumped countless models all over the world.

God! Assume the worst, why don't you, Dad?

Josh can't dump me. He's never even been out with me yet.

And if he doesn't show up soon, well, all I can say is HIS LOSS. I look better than I have ever looked in my whole entire life. Old Coco Chanel, she really outdid herself – my dress is HOT: pale, pale blue silk, all scrunched up on top like an accordion, so my being flat-chested doesn't even show, then straight and skinny the rest of the way down, all the way to my matching pale, pale blue silk high heels. I think I kind of resemble an icicle, but according to the ladies at Chanel, this is the look of the new millennium. Icicles are *in*.

The only problem is I can't pet Fat Louie, or I'll get

orange cat hair on myself. I should have got one of those masking tape roller thingies last time I was at Rite Aid, but I forgot. Anyway, he's sitting beside me on the futon, looking all sad because I won't pet him. I picked up all my socks, just in case he got it into his head to punish me or something by eating one.

My dad just looked at his watch and went, 'Hmm. Seven-fifteen. I can't say much for this boy's promptness.'

I tried to remain calm. 'I'm sure there's a lot of traffic,' I said in as princessy a voice as I could.

'I'm sure,' said my dad. He didn't sound very sad, though. 'Well, Mia, we can still make it to *Beauty and the Beast*, if you want to go. I'm sure I can get—'

'Dad!' I was horrified. 'I am NOT going to *Beauty and the Beast* with you tonight.'

Now he sounded sad. 'But you used to love *Beauty and the Beast* . . .'

THANK GOD the intercom just rang. It's him. My mom just buzzed him up. The other stipulation, before my dad would let me go, is that besides Lars going, Josh has to meet both my parents, and probably submit proof of ID, though I'm not sure Dad's thought of that yet.

I'm going to have to leave this book here, because there's no room for it in my 'clutch', which is what my skinny flat purse is called.

Oh my God, my hands are sweating so hard! I should have listened when Grandmere suggested those elbow-length gloves—

Saturday night, Ladies' Room,
Tavern on the Green

OK, so I lied. I brought this book anyway. I made Lars carry it. Well, it's not like he doesn't have room in that brief-case he carries around. I know it's filled with silencers and grenades and stuff, but I knew he could fit one measly jour-nal into it.

And I was right.

So I'm in the bathroom at the Tavern on the Green. The Ladies' Room here isn't as nice as the one at the Plaza. There isn't a little stool to sit on in my stall, so I'm sitting on the toilet with the lid down. I can see a lot of fat ladies' feet moving around outside my stall door. There are a whole lot of fat ladies here, mostly for this wedding between a very Italian-looking, dark-haired girl who needs a good eyebrow waxing and a skinny red-headed boy named Fergus. Fergus gave me the old eyeball when I walked into the dining room. I am not kidding. My first married man, even if he has only been married about an hour and looks my age. This dress is the BOMB!

Dinner's not so great as I thought it would be, though. I mean, I know from Grandmere which fork to use and all that, and to tilt my soup bowl away from me, but that's not it:

It's Josh.

Don't get me wrong. He looks totally hot in his tux. He told me he owns it. Last year, he escorted his girlfriend before Lana to all the debutante events in the city, his girl-friend before Lana having been related to the guy who invented those plastic bags you put vegetables in when you go to the grocery store. Only his were the first to say *Open*

Here so you knew which end was the one you were supposed to try to open. Those two little words earned the guy half a billion dollars, Josh says.

I don't know why he told me this. Am I supposed to be impressed by something his ex-girlfriend's dad did? He isn't acting very sensitively, to tell you the truth.

Still, he was really good with my parents. He came in, gave me a corsage (tiny white roses tied together with pink ribbon, totally gorgeous: it must have cost him ten dollars *at least*. I couldn't help thinking, though, that he'd originally picked it out for another girl, with a different colour dress) and shook my dad's hand. He said, 'It's a pleasure to meet you, Your Highness', which made my mom start laughing really loud. She can be so embarrassing some-times.

Then he turned to my mom and said, 'You're Mia's mother? Oh my gosh, I thought you must be her college-age sister', which is a totally foolish thing to say, but my mom actually fell for it, I think. She BLUSHED as he was shak-ing her hand. I guess I am not the only Thermopolis woman to fall under the spell of Josh Richter's blue eyes.

Then my dad cleared his throat and started asking Josh a whole lot of questions about what kind of car he was driv-ing (his dad's BMW), where we were going (duh), what time we would be back (in time for breakfast, Josh said)! My dad didn't like that, though, and Josh said, 'What time would you like her back, sir?'

SIR! Josh Richter called my dad SIR!

And my dad looked at Lars and said, 'One o'clock at the latest,' which I thought was pretty decent of him, since my normal curfew is eleven on weekends. Of course, con-sidering that Lars was going to be there, and there wasn't anything that could actually happen to me, it was kind of bogus that I couldn't stay out as late as I wanted, but Grandmere told me a princess should always be prepared to compromise, so I didn't say anything.

Then my dad asked Josh some more questions, like where was he going to college in the fall (he hasn't decided yet, but he's applying to all the Ivy Leagues) and what does he plan on studying (business), and then my mom asked him what was wrong with a liberal arts education and Josh said he was really looking for a degree that would guarantee him a minimum salary of eighty thousand a year, to which my mom replied that there are more important things than money, and then I said, 'Gosh, look at the time,' and grabbed Josh and headed out the door.

Josh and Lars and I went down to Josh's dad's car, and Josh held the door to the front seat open for me, and then Lars said why didn't he drive, so Josh and I could sit in the back and get to know each other. I thought this was way nice of Lars, but when Josh and I got in the back, we didn't have a whole lot to say to each other. I mean, Josh was like, 'You look really nice in that dress,' and I said I liked his tux, and thanked him for my corsage. And then we didn't say anything for, like, twenty blocks.

I am not even kidding. I was so embarrassed! I mean, I don't hang around with boys that much, but I've never had that problem with the ones I HAVE hung around with. I mean, Michael Moscovitz practically never shuts up. I couldn't understand why Josh wasn't SAYING anything. I thought about asking him who he'd rather spend eternity with if it was the end of the world and he had to choose, Winona Ryder or Nicole Kidman, but I didn't feel like I knew him well enough . . .

But finally Josh broke the silence by asking if it was true my mom was dating Mr Gianini. Well, I should have expected *that* to get around. Maybe not as fast as my being a princess, but it had gotten around, all right.

So I said, Yes, it's true, and then Josh wanted to know what that was like.

But then for some reason I couldn't tell him about seeing Mr G in his underwear at my kitchen table. It just didn't seem . . . I don't know. I just couldn't tell him. Isn't that funny? I had told Michael Moscovitz without even having been asked. But I couldn't tell Josh, even though he had looked into my soul and everything. Weird, huh?

Then after like a zillion more blocks of silence we pulled up in front of the restaurant, and Lars surrendered the car to the valet and Josh and I went in (Lars promised he wouldn't eat with us. He said he'd just stand by the door and look at everybody who came in in a mean way, like Arnold Schwarzenegger) and it turned out all of Josh's entourage was meeting us here, which I didn't know, but was kind of relieved to see. I mean, I'd sort of been dreading sitting there for another hour or so with nothing to say . . .

But, thank God, all the guys on the crew team were at this big long table with their cheerleader girlfriends, and at the head of this table were these two empty places, one for Josh and one for me.

I have to say, everyone has been pretty nice. The girls all complimented me on my dress, and asked me questions about being a princess, like how weird was it to wake up and see your picture on the front of the *Post*, and do you ever wear a crown, and stuff like that. They're all much older than me – some of them are seniors – so they're pretty mature. None of them have made any comments about how I have no chest, or anything, like Lana would have, if she'd been here.

But then, if Lana were here, I wouldn't be.

The thing that most surprised me is that Josh ordered champagne, and nobody even questioned his ID, which of course was totally fake. The table's been through three bottles already, and Josh just keeps ordering more, since his dad gave him his platinum American Express card for the occasion. I just don't get it. Can't the waiters tell he's only eighteen, and that most of his guests are even younger than that?

And how can Josh sit there and drink so much? What if Lars hadn't been here to drive? Josh would be driving his dad's BMW, and driving it half-sloshed. How irresponsible can you get? And Josh is our class valedictorian!

And then, without even asking me, Josh ordered dinner for the whole table: filet mignon for everyone. I guess that's very nice and all, but I won't eat meat, not even for the most sensitive boy in the world. I really wish Josh had asked me.

And he hasn't even noticed I haven't touched my food! I totally had to fill up on salad and bread rolls to keep from starving to death.

Maybe I could sneak out of here and get Lars to pick up a veggie wrap for me from Emerald Planet.

And the funny thing is, the more champagne Josh has to drink, the more he keeps on touching me. Like he keeps on putting his hand on my leg under the table. At first I thought it was a mistake, but he's done it four times now. The last time, he squeezed!

I don't think he's drunk, exactly, but he's certainly friend-lier than he was in the car on the way up. Maybe he's just feeling less inhibited, with Lars not hovering around, two feet away.

Well, I guess I should go back out there. I just wish Josh had told me we were meeting his friends. Then maybe I could have invited Tina Hakim Baba and her date – or even Lilly and Boris. Then at least I'd have someone fun to talk to.

Oh, well. Here goes nothing.

Later Saturday night, Girls' Room, Albert Einstein High School

Why?

Why??

Why???

I can't even believe this is happening. I can't believe it's happening to ME!

WHY? WHY ME? WHY IS IT ALWAYS ME these things have to happen to????

I'm trying to remember what Grandmere told me, about how to act under duress. Because I am definitely under duress. I keep trying to breathe in through my nose, out through my mouth, like Grandmere said. In through my nose, out through my mouth. In through my nose, out through my—

HOW COULD HE DO THIS TO ME???? HOW, HOW, HOW?????!!!

I could rip his stupid face off, I really could. I mean, who does he think he is? Do you know what he did? Do you know what he did? Well, let me tell you what he did:

So after polishing off NINE bottles of champagne – that's practically one bottle per person, except I only had a couple of sips, so somebody drank my bottle as well as theirs – Josh and his friends finally decided it was time to go to the dance. Oh, gee, let me see, the dance had only started an HOUR earlier. It was only about TIME we left.

So we go and wait for the valet to bring the car around, and I was thinking maybe everything would be all right, since while we were waiting, Josh had his arm around my shoulders, which was really nice, since my dress is sleeveless, and even though I have a wrap, it's just this shimmery see-through veil thing. So I'm appreciative of this arm, since it's keeping me warm. It's a nice arm, really, very muscular from all that rowing. The only problem is, Josh doesn't smell that good, not a bit like Michael Moscovitz, who always smells like soap. No, I think Josh must have taken a bath in Drakkar Noir, which in large doses actually smells pretty vile. I could hardly breathe, but whatever. In spite of that, I'm thinking, OK, things aren't so bad. Yes, he didn't respect my rights as a vegetarian, but you know, everybody makes mistakes. We'll go to the dance and he'll look into my soul again with those electric blue eyes and everything will be all right.

Boy, was I ever wrong.

First of all, we can barely pull up to the school, there's so much traffic. At first I couldn't figure it out. Yes, it was Saturday night, but there shouldn't be THAT much traffic in front of Albert Einstein's, right? I mean, it's just a school dance. Most kids in New York City don't even have access to cars, right? We're probably, like, the only people who go to Albert Einstein's who drove.

And then I realize why there's so much congestion. There are news vans parked all over the place. They're shining these big bright lights all over the steps to Albert Einstein's. There are reporters swarming around all over the place, smoking cigarettes, talking on cell phones, waiting.

Waiting for what?

Waiting for me, it turns out.

As soon as Lars saw the lights, he started to swear very colourfully in some language that wasn't English or French. But you could tell they were swear words by his voice. I leaned forward and was like, 'How could they have known? How could they have known? Could Grandmere have told them?'

But you know, I really don't think Grandmere would have

done this. I really don't. Not after our talk. I laid it on the line for Grandmere. I came down on her like a New York cop on a game of three card monte. Grandmere would not, I'm sure, EVER call the press on me again, without my permission.

But there they all were, and SOMEBODY called them, all right, and if it wasn't Grandmere, then who was it?

Josh was totally unconcerned by all the lights and cameras and everything. He goes, 'So what? You ought to be used to it by now.'

Oh, right. Let me tell you how used to it I am by now. So used to it that the thought of getting out of that car, even with the arm of the cutest boy in the school around me, made me feel like I was going to barf up all of that salad and bread.

'Come on,' Josh said. 'You and I can make a run for it while Lars goes and parks the car.'

Lars totally did not like that idea. He went, 'I think not. *You* will park the car, and the princess and *I* will make a run for it.'

But Josh was already opening his door. He had hold of my hand. He said, 'Come on. You only live once,' and started dragging me out of the car.

And like the really stupid chump that I am, I let him.

That's right. I let him drag me out of the car. Because his hand felt so nice over mine, so big and protective, so warm and secure, I thought, Oh, what could happen? So a bunch of flashbulbs will go off. So what? We'll just make a run for it, like he said. Everything will be fine.

So I said to Lars, 'That's OK, Lars. You park the car. Josh and I'll go on inside.'

Lars said, 'No, Princess, wait—'

Which were the last words I heard out of him – for a

while, anyway – since by that time Josh and I were out of the car, and he had slammed the door shut behind us.

And then, instantly, the press was on us, everyone throwing down their cigarettes and pulling the lens caps off their cameras, yelling, 'It's her! It's her!'

And then Josh was pulling me up the steps, and I was sort of laughing, since for the first time, it *was* sort of fun. Flashbulbs were going off everywhere, blinding me, so that all I could see were the steps underneath us as we ran up them. I was totally concentrating on holding up the hem of my dress so I didn't trip on it, and had put all my faith in those fingers wrapped around my other hand. I was completely dependent on Josh to lead the way, since I couldn't see a blessed thing.

So when he suddenly stopped, I thought it was because we were at the school doors. I thought we'd stopped because Josh was opening the doors for me. I know it's stupid, but that's what I thought. I could see the doors. We were standing right in front of them. Below us, on the stairs, the reporters were screaming questions and taking pictures. Some moron was yelling, 'Kiss her! Kiss her!' which I don't need to tell you was way embarrassing.

And so I just stood there, like a complete IDIOT, waiting for Josh to open the doors, instead of doing the smart thing, which was open the doors myself and get inside where it was safe, where there weren't any cameras or reporters or people yelling *Kiss her, kiss her*.

And then, I don't know how, the next thing I knew, Josh had put his arm around me again, dragged me to him, and smashed his mouth against mine.

I swear, that's exactly what it felt like. He just smashed his mouth up against mine, and all these flashes started going off, but believe me, it wasn't like in those books Tina is always reading, where the boy kisses the girl and she sees, like, fireworks and stuff behind her eyelids. I really WAS seeing lights go off, but they weren't fireworks, they were flashes from cameras. EVERYONE was taking a picture of Princess Mia getting her first kiss.

I am not even kidding. Like it wasn't bad enough that this was my first kiss.

It was my first kiss, and *Teen People* was photographing it.

And another thing about those books Tina reads: in those books, when the girl gets her first kiss, she gets this warm gushy feeling inside. She feels like the guy is drawing her soul up from deep within her. I didn't get that feeling. I didn't get that feeling at all. All I got was embarrassed. It didn't feel especially good, having Josh Richter kiss me. All it felt, really, was strange. It felt strange, having this guy stand there and smash his mouth against mine. And you would think that after I'd spent so much time thinking this guy was the greatest thing on earth, I'd have felt SOMETHING when he kissed me.

But all I felt was embarrassed.

And like our car ride to the restaurant, I just kept wishing it would end. All I could think was, When is he going to stop doing this? Am I even doing this right? In the movies they move their heads around a lot. Should I move my head around? What am I going to do if he tries to stick his tongue in there, like I used to see him do to Lana? I can't let *Teen People* take a picture of me with some guy's tongue in my mouth: my dad will kill me.

Then, just when I thought I couldn't stand it another minute, that I was going to DIE of embarrassment right there on the steps of Albert Einstein High School, Josh lifted up his head, waved to the reporters, opened the doors to the school, and pushed me inside.

Where, I swear to God, every single person I knew was standing, looking at us.

I am not kidding. There was Tina and her date from Trinity, Dave, looking at me in a sort of shocked way. There was Lilly and Boris, and for once Boris hadn't tucked in anything that wasn't supposed to be tucked in. In fact, he almost looked handsome, in a geeky musical genius kind of way. And Lilly, in a beautiful white dress with spangles all over it, and white roses in her hair. And there was Shameeka and Ling Su, with their dates, and a bunch of other people I probably knew but didn't recognize out of their school uniforms, all looking at me with the same sort of expression Tina was wearing, one of total and complete astonishment.

And there was Mr G, standing by the ticket booth in front of the doors to the cafeteria, where the dance was being held, looking more astonished than anybody.

Except maybe me. I would have to say, out of everybody there, I was the person in the most shock. I mean, Josh Richter HAD just kissed me. JOSH RICHTER had just KISSED me. Josh Richter had just kissed ME.

Did I mention that he'd kissed me ON THE LIPS?

Oh, and that he did it in front of reporters from *TEEN PEOPLE*?

So I'm standing there, and everybody is looking at me, and outside, I could still hear the reporters yelling, and inside the cafeteria, I could hear the thump, thump, thump of the sound system as it ground out some hip hop, a tribute to our Latino student population, and these thoughts are moving really sluggishly through my head, these thoughts that are saying:

He set you up.

He only asked you out so he could get his picture in the paper.

214

He's the one who notified the press that you'd be here tonight.

He probably only broke up with Lana just so he could tell his friends he's dating a girl worth three hundred million dollars. He never even noticed you until your picture was on the cover of the *Post*. Lilly was right: that day in Bigelow's, he WAS only suffering from a synaptic breakdown when he smiled at you. He probably thinks his chances of getting into Harvard or whatever are way enhanced by the fact that he's the Princess of Genovia's boyfriend.

And like a big idiot, I fell for it.

Great. Just great.

Lilly says I'm not assertive enough. Her parents say I have a tendency to internalize everything, and fear confrontation.

My mom says the same thing. That's why she gave me this book, in the hope that what I won't tell her, I'll at least get out into the open somehow.

If it hadn't turned out that I'm a princess, maybe I might still be all that stuff. You know, unassertive, fearful of confrontation, an internalizer. I probably wouldn't have done what I did next.

Which was turn to Josh and ask, 'Why did you do that?'

He was busy patting himself down, trying to find the dance tickets to hand to the sophomores who were manning the ticket table. 'Do what?'

'Kiss me like that, in front of everybody.'

He found the tickets in his wallet. 'I don't know,' he said. 'Didn't you hear them? They were yelling at me to kiss you. So I did. Why?'

'Because I didn't appreciate it.'

'You didn't appreciate it?' Josh looked confused. 'You mean you didn't like it?'

'Yes,' I said. 'That's exactly what I mean. I didn't like it. I

215

didn't like it at all. Because I know you didn't kiss me because you like me. You just kissed me because I'm the Princess of Genovia.'

Josh looked at me like he thought I was crazy.

'That's crazy,' he said. 'I like you. I like you a lot.'

I said, 'You can't like me a lot. You don't even *know* me. That's why I thought you asked me out. So you could get to know me better. But you haven't tried to get to know me at all. You just wanted to get your picture on *Extra*.'

He laughed at that, but I noticed he didn't look me in the eye when he said, 'What do you mean, I don't even know you? Of course I know you.'

'No, you don't. Because if you did, you wouldn't have ordered me a steak for dinner.'

I heard a murmur go around through all of my friends. I guess they recognized the seriousness of Josh's mistake, even if he didn't. He heard them too, so when he replied, he was talking to them too. 'So I ordered the girl a steak,' he said, with his arms open in a So-sue-me sort of way. 'That's a crime? It was *filet mignon*, for God's sake.'

Lilly said, in her meanest voice, 'She's a vegetarian, you sociopath.'

This information didn't seem to bother Josh very much. He just shrugged and went, 'Oops, *so* sorry.'

Then he turned to me and said, 'Ready to slide?'

But I had no intention of sliding with Josh. I had no intention of doing anything with Josh, ever again. I couldn't believe, after what I'd just said to him, he thought I'd still *want* to. The guy really *was* a sociopath. How could I ever have thought he'd seen into my soul? How???

Disgusted, I did the only thing a girl can be expected to do, under those circumstances:

I turned my back on him and walked out.

Only, since of course I couldn't go back outside – not if I didn't want *Teen People* to get a nice close-up of me crying – my only recourse was to walk out into the Girls' Room.

It finally registered on Josh that I was ditching him. By that time, all of his friends had shown up, and they came tumbling through the doors just as Josh said, sounding totally peeved, 'Jesus! It was just a kiss!'

I whirled around. 'It wasn't just a kiss,' I said. I was getting really mad. 'Maybe that's how you wanted it to look, like it was just a kiss. But you and I both know what it really was: a media event. And one that you've been planning since you saw me in the *Post*. Well, thank you, Josh, but I can get my own publicity. I don't need *you*.'

Then, after holding out my hand to Lars for my journal, I took it and stalked into the Girls' Room. Which is where I am now, writing this.

God! Can you BELIEVE that? I mean, I ask you: my first kiss – my first kiss ever – and next week it's going to be in every teen magazine in the country. Probably even some international magazines will pick it up, like *Majesty* magazine, which follows the lives of all the young royals in Great Britain and Monaco. They ran a whole article on the wardrobe of Prince Edward's wife Sophie once, rating each one of her outfits on a scale of one to ten. They called it *Out of the Closet*. I don't suppose it will be too long before *Majesty* magazine starts following me around, rating my wardrobe – and boyfriends – too. I wonder what the headline under the picture of me and Josh will be? *Young Royal In Love?*

Excuse me, but *ew*.

And the kicker of it all is that I am totally NOT in love with Josh Richter. I mean, it would have been nice – Who am I kidding? It would have been GREAT – to have a

217

boyfriend. Sometimes I think there really is something wrong with me, that I don't have one.

But the thing is, I would rather not have a boyfriend at all than have one who is only using me for my money or the fact that my father is a prince or for any reason, really, except that he likes me for *me*, and nothing else.

Of course, now that everyone knows I'm a princess, it's going to be kind of hard to tell which guys like me for me, and which guys like me for my tiara. But at least I realized the truth about Josh before things went on too long.

How could I have ever liked him? He's such a user. He totally used me! He purposefully hurt Lana, and then tried to use me. And I played right into his hands like the stupid sap that I am.

What am I going to do? When my dad sees that photograph, he is going to FLIP OUT. There is no way I will ever be able to explain that it wasn't my fault. Maybe if I'd punched Josh in the stomach in front of all those cameras. Maybe then my dad would believe I was an innocent bystander . . .

But probably not.

I will never be allowed out of the house with a boy again, ever, for the rest of my natural life.

Uh oh. I see shoes outside my stall. Somebody is talking to me.

It's Tina. Tina wants to know if I'm all right. Somebody is with her.

Oh, my God, I recognize those feet! It's Lilly! Lilly and Tina both want to know if I'm all right!

Lilly is actually speaking to me again. Not criticizing me, or complaining about my behaviour. She is actually speaking to me in a friendly manner. She's saying through the stall door that she's sorry for laughing at my hair and that she knows she's controlling and that she suffers from a border-line authoritarian personality disorder, and she says she's going to make a concerted effort to stop telling everyone, especially me, what to do.

Wow! Lilly is admitting she did something wrong! I can't believe it! I CAN'T BELIEVE IT!

She and Tina want me to come out and hang out with them. But I told them I don't want to. It would be too awkward, all of them with dates, and me by myself like a big dope.

And then Lilly goes, 'Oh, that's OK. Michael's here. He's been hanging around by himself like a big dope all night.'

Michael Moscovitz came to a school event??? I can't believe it!! He never goes anywhere, except to, like, lectures in quantum physics and stuff!!

I have got to see this for myself. I am going out there right now.

More later.

Sunday, October 18

I just woke up from the strangest dream:

In my dream, Lilly and I weren't fighting any more; she and Tina had become friends; Boris Pelkowski actually turned out to be not so bad when you got him away from his violin; Mr Gianini said he was raising my nine-week grade from an F to a D; I slow-danced with Michael Moscovitz; and Iran bombed Afghanistan, so there wasn't a single picture of me and Josh kissing in any newspaper on the news-stand, since all the papers were filled with photos of war carnage.

But it wasn't a dream. It wasn't a dream at all, none of it! It had all really happened!

Because I woke up this morning with something wet on my face, and when I opened my eyes, I saw that I was lying in the spare bed in Lilly's room, and her brother's sheltie was licking me all over my face. I mean it. I have dog spit all over me.

And I don't even care! Pavlov can drool all over me if he wants to! I have my best friend back! I'm not going to flunk out of ninth grade! My dad isn't going to kill me for kissing Josh Richter!

Oh, and I think Michael Moscovitz might like me!

I can hardly write for happiness.

Little did I know when I came out of the Girls' Room last night with Lilly and Tina that all this happiness lay in store for me. I was morbidly depressed – yes, *morbidly*. Isn't that a good word? I learned it from Lilly – over what had happened with Josh.

But when I came out of the Girls' Room, Josh was gone. Lilly told me later that after I publicly humiliated him and then went storming off into the bathroom, Josh went on into the dance, not looking as if he cared too much. Lilly isn't sure what happened after that, because Mr G asked her and Tina to go and check on me (wasn't that sweet of him?), but I have a feeling Lars may have used one of his special nerve-paralysing holds on Josh, because the next time I saw him, Josh was slumped over at the Pacific Islander display table, with his forehead resting on a model of Krakatowa. He didn't move all night, either, but maybe that was because of all the champagne he'd had to drink.

Anyway, me and Lilly and Tina joined Boris and Dave – who is really nice, even if he does go to Trinity – and Shameeka and her boyfriend Allan and Ling-Su and her date Clifford at this table they had snagged. It was the Pakistani table, with a display sponsored by the Economics Club, detailing how the market for maunds (a Pakistani unit of measurement) of rice was falling. We moved some of the maunds and sat there anyway, right on the tabletop, so we could see everything.

And then Michael suddenly appeared out of nowhere, looking crescent-fresh – isn't that a funny expression? I learned it from Michael – in the tux his mom made him get for his cousin Steve's bar mitzvah. Michael really didn't have anyone else to hang out with, since Principal Gupta ruled that the internet is not a culture, and therefore cannot have its own table, and so the Computer Club boycotted the Cultural Diversity Dance on principle.

But Michael didn't seem to care what the Computer Club thought; and he's the treasurer! He sat down next to me and asked if I was all right, and then we had fun for a while cracking jokes about how all the cheerleaders sure don't practise any cultural diversity, since they were all dressed in practically the same gown, a slinky black number by Donna Karan. Then somebody started talking about *Star Trek: Deep*

Space Nine, and whether or not there's caffeine in replicator coffee, and Michael insisted that the matter used to make the things that come out of the replicator is from refuse, which means maybe when you order an ice cream sundae, it might be made out of urine, but with the germs and impurities extracted. And we were all getting kind of grossed out when the music changed, and a slow song came on, and everybody left the table to go and dance.

Except for me and Michael, and of course. We just sat there amidst the maunds of rice.

Which wasn't too bad, actually, since Michael and I never run out of things to talk about – unlike me and Josh. We kept on arguing about the replicator, and then we moved on to who was the more effective leader, Captain Kirk or Captain Picard, when Mr Gianini came over and asked me if I was OK.

I said of course, and that was when Mr G told me he was glad to hear it, and, by the way, based on my latest scores on the practice sheets he'd been giving me every day, I had brought my F in Algebra up to a D, for which he congratulated me, and urged me to keep up the hard work.

But I credited my improved Maths performance to Michael, who taught me to stop writing my Algebra notes in my journal, not be so messy with my columns, and to cross things out when I borrow during subtraction. Michael got all embarrassed and claimed not to have had anything to do with it, but Mr G didn't hear him since he had to hurry off and dissuade a group of Goths from embarking upon a demonstration over the unfair exclusion of a table dedicated to Satan worshippers by the event organizers.

Then a fast song came on and everybody came back, and we sat around and talked about Lilly's show, which Tina

Hakim Baba is now going to be producer of, since we found out she gets fifty dollars a week in allowance (she is going to start borrowing teen romances from the library instead of buying them new so that she can use all of her funds for promoting *Lilly Tells It Like It Is*). Lilly asked if I'd mind being the topic for next week's show, entitled The New Monarchy: Royals Who Make a Difference. I gave her exclusive rights to my first public interview, if she'd promise to ask me about my feelings on the meat industry.

Then another slow song came on, and everybody went to go and dance to it. Michael and I were left sitting amidst the rice again and I was about to ask him who he'd choose to spend eternity with if nuclear armaggedon wiped out the rest of the population, Buffy The Vampire Slayer or Sabrina The Teenage Witch, when he asked me if I wanted to dance!

I was so surprised, I said sure, without even thinking about it. And then the next thing I knew, I was dancing my first dance with a boy who wasn't my dad!

And it was a *slow* one!

Slow-dancing is *strange*. It isn't even dancing, really. It's more like standing there with your arms around the other person, moving from one foot to the other in time to the music. And I guess you aren't supposed to talk – at least, nobody else around us was talking. I guess I could sort of see why, since you're so busy *feeling* stuff, it's hard to think of anything to say. I mean, Michael *smelled* so good – like Ivory soap – and *felt* so good – the dress Grandmere picked out for me was pretty and everything, but I was kind of cold in it, so it was nice to stand close to Michael, who was so warm – that it was next to impossible to *say* anything.

I guess Michael felt the same way, because even though when we were sitting there on the table with all the rice, neither of us ever shut up, we had so much to talk about, when we were dancing together, neither of us said a word.

But the minute the song was over, Michael started talking again, asking me if I wanted some Thai iced tea from the Thai Culture table, or maybe some edamame from the Japanese Anime Club's table. For somebody who'd never been to a single school event – aside from Computer Club meetings – Michael sure was making up for lost time in his enthusiasm over being at this one.

And that was how the rest of the night went: we sat around and talked during the fast songs, and danced during the slow ones.

And you know, to tell the truth, I couldn't say which I liked better, talking to Michael, or dancing with him. They were both so . . . interesting.

In different ways, of course.

When the dance was over, we all piled into the limo Mr Hakim Baba sent to pick Tina and Dave up (the news vans had all left by then, since the story about the bombing had broken: I suppose they went to go stake out the Iranian embassy). I called my mom on the limo cell phone and told her where I was, and asked if I could spend the night at Lilly's, since that's where we were all headed. She said yes without asking any questions, which led me to believe that she'd already talked to Mr G, and that he'd filled her in on the night's events. I wonder if he told her he'd raised my F to a D.

You know, he could have given me a D plus. I have been nothing but supportive of his relationship with my mother. That kind of loyalty ought to be rewarded.

Dr and Dr Moscovitz seemed kind of surprised when all ten of us – twelve, if you count Lars and Wahim – showed up at their door. They were especially surprised to see

Michael; they hadn't realized he'd left his room. But they let us take over the living room, where we played End of the World until Lilly and Michael's dad finally came out in his pyjamas and said everybody had to go home: he had an early appointment with his t'ai chi instructor.

Everybody said goodbye and piled into the elevator, except for me and the Moscovitzes. Even Lars hitched a ride back to the Plaza – once I had been locked down for the night, his responsibilities were over. I made him promise not to tell my dad about the kiss. He said he wouldn't, but you can never tell with guys: they have this weird code of their own, you know? I was reminded of it when I saw Lars and Michael giving each other high fives right before he left.

The strangest thing out of everything that happened last night is that I found out what Michael does in his room all the time. He showed me, but he made me swear never to tell anyone, including Lilly. I probably shouldn't even write it down here, in case someone ever finds this book and reads it. All I can say is Lilly's been wasting her time worshipping Boris Pelkowski: there's a musical genius in her very own family.

And to think, he's never had one lesson! He taught himself how to play the bass – and he writes all his own songs! The one he played for me is called 'Tall Drink of Water'. It's about this very tall pretty girl who doesn't know this boy is in love with her. I predict that one day it will be number one on the *Billboard* chart. Michael Moscovitz could one day be as famous as Puff Daddy.

It wasn't until everyone was gone that I realized how tired I was. It had been a really long day. I had broken up with a boy I had only been out on half a date with. That can be very emotionally wearing.

Still, I woke up way early, like I always do when I spend

the night at Lilly's. I lay there with Pavlov in my arms and listened to the sound of the morning traffic on Fifth Avenue, which isn't really very loud, since the Moscovitzes had their windows sound-proofed. As I lay there, I thought, Really, I am a very lucky girl. Things had looked pretty bad there, for a while. But isn't it funny how everything kind of works itself out in the end?

I hear stirrings in the kitchen. Maya must be here, pouring out glasses of pulpless orange juice for breakfast. I'm going to go see if she needs any help.

I don't know why, but I AM SO HAPPY!

I guess it doesn't take much, does it?

Sunday night

Grandmere showed up at the loft today, with Dad in tow. Dad wanted to find out how things went at the dance. Lars didn't tell him! God, I *love* my bodyguard. And Grandmere wanted to let me know that she has to go away for a week, so our princess lessons are suspended for the time being. She says it's time to pay her yearly visit to somebody named Baden-Baden. I suppose he's friends with that other guy she's always hanging around with, Boutros-Boutros Something or other.

Even *my grandmother* has a boyfriend.

Anyway, she and Dad just showed up out of the blue, and you should have seen my mom's face. She looked about ready to heave. Especially when Grandmere started bossing her around about how messy the loft is (I've been too busy lately to clean).

To distract Grandmere from my mom, I told her I'd walk her back to her limo, and on the way, I told her all about Josh, and she was way interested, since the story had everything in it that she likes, reporters and cute boys and people getting their heart totally stomped on and stuff like that.

Anyway, while we were standing on the corner saying goodbye until next week (*YES*! No princess lessons for a whole week! She shoots, she scores!) the Blind Guy walked by, tapping his cane. He stopped at the corner and stood there, waiting for his next victim to come along and help him cross the street. Grandmere saw this, and totally fell for it. She was like, 'Amelia, go and help that poor young man.'

But of course, I knew better. I said, 'No way.'

'Amelia!' Grandmere was shocked. 'One of the most important traits in a princess is her unfailing kindness to strangers. Now go and help that young man cross the street.'

227

I said, 'No way, Grandmere. If you think he needs help so much, *you* do it.'

So Grandmere, all bent out of shape – and I guess intent on showing me how unfailingly kind she is – went up to the Blind Guy and said in this fakey voice, 'Let me help you, young man . . .'

The Blind Guy grabbed Grandmere by the arm. I guess he liked what he felt because the next thing I knew, he was going, 'Oh, thank you so much, ma'am,' and he and Grandmere were crossing Spring Street.

I didn't think the Blind Guy was going to try to feel up my grandmother. I really didn't, or I wouldn't have let her help him. I mean, Grandmere is no spring chicken, if you know what I mean. I couldn't imagine any guy, even a blind one, feeling her up.

But next thing I knew, Grandmere was yelling her head off, and both her driver and our neighbour who used to be a man came running out to help her.

But Grandmere didn't need any help. She whacked the Blind Guy across the face with her purse, so hard his sunglasses went flying off. After that, there was no doubt about it: the Blind Guy can see.

And let me tell you something: I don't think he'll be taking any more trips down our street for a while.

Grandmere seemed way more upset about the whole thing than I would have thought, considering she's faced worse things than some guy trying to feel her up – like Nazis, for instance, and interior decorators. I sort of started feeling bad I hadn't warned her about the Blind Guy, especially when she sputtered a bunch of stuff about how dreadful New York City is, with its sexual perverts and traffic lights, and how she can't wait to leave it.

This burned me up a little. I'm not saying New York City

is the best place to live in the world, or anything. I'm just saying I'll bet it's way more interesting than Genovia. And I thought it would be a shame for Grandmere to leave – even if only for a week – thinking bad things about the city where I live.

So I said, 'Come with me,' and I dragged her back into my building.

But instead of heading up to the loft, I took Grandmere to the roof, which is only about ten storeys in the air – still, it's higher than all the roofs around it. From the roof of the building my mom and I live in, you can see all of downtown Manhattan, including the World Trade Center. On the Fourth of July, you can see the fireworks from there, both the ones on the East River and the ones down at the Seaport. What's more, any old day you can see all the way to the Hudson River . . . which just happened, as we were gazing at it, to have this great big ocean liner sliding along it.

No, really.

And as if that wasn't enough, the sun was going down, and the sky was all purple and pink and orange and stuff. Just looking at all that majestic natural beauty it made me feel that maybe everything was going to be all right, you know? I mean about the whole princess thing.

Then as we were standing there, watching the sun set, my mom and dad came out onto the roof too.

'I thought you'd be up here,' my mother said.

'We were looking for you,' my father said. 'You shouldn't go off on your own like this without telling anyone where you're going.'

Then my mom noticed the sunset and went, 'Oh, isn't that beautiful?' Even my dad said, 'I never knew you could see sunsets like that in New York.'

And then all four of us just stood and watched the sun go down.

And as we stood there, I couldn't help thinking how great it was that we could all put aside our differences and just watch a sunset and really be *in* the moment, you know? And my heart was totally filled with this sense of inner peace, and I thought to myself, You know, I think it's true. It's really true. I've finally achieved self-actualization . . .

At least until my mom went, 'For God's sake, Philippe, must you breathe so loud?'

And my dad went, 'I'll stop breathing loud when you start balancing your chequebook.'

And Grandmere started digging in her purse for a handkerchief. 'What is that foul odour?' she wanted to know. 'I thought barbecuing was illegal in Manhattan.'

Oh, well, I thought. Maybe tomorrow. For the self-actualization thing, I mean. For now, I guess I'll settle for what I've got. Because it's actually a lot, now that I think about it.

The
PRINCESS
DIARIES
Take Two

'When things are horrible – just horrible – I think as hard as ever I can of being a princess. I say to myself, "I am a princess." You don't know how it makes you forget.'

A Little Princess
Frances Hodgson Burnett

Monday, October 19, 8 a.m.

OK. So I was just in the kitchen, eating cereal – you know, the usual Monday morning routine – when my mom comes out of the bathroom with this funny look on her face. I mean, she was all pale and her hair was kind of sticking out and she had on her terry cloth robe instead of her kimono, which usually means she's premenstrual.

So I was all, 'Mom, you want some aspirin? Because no offence, but you look like you could use some.'

Which is sort of a dangerous thing to say to a premenstrual woman, but you know, she's my mom, and all. It's not like she was going to karate chop me, the way she would if anybody else said that to her.

But she just went, 'No. No, thanks,' in this dazed voice.

So then I assumed something really horrible had happened. You know, like the cat had eaten another sock, or they were cutting off our electricity again because I'd forgotten to fish the bill out of the salad bowl where Mom keeps stuffing them.

So I grabbed her and I was like, 'Mom? Mom, what is it? What's wrong?'

She sort of shook her head, like she does when she's confused over the microwave instructions on a frozen pizza. 'Mia,' she said, in this shocked but happy way, 'Mia. I'm pregnant.'

Oh my God. OH MY GOD.

My mother is having my Algebra teacher's baby.

Monday, October 19, Homeroom

I am really trying to take this calmly. You know? Because there isn't any point in getting upset about it.

But how can I NOT be upset? My mother is about to become a single parent. AGAIN.

You would think she'd have learned a lesson with me and all, but apparently not.

As if I don't have enough problems. As if my life isn't over already. I just don't see how much more I can be expected to take. I mean, apparently, it is not enough that:

1. I am the tallest girl in the freshman class.
2. I am also the least endowed in the chest area.
3. Last month, I found out that my mother was dating my Algebra teacher.
4. Also last month, I found out that I am the sole heir to the throne of a small European country – Genovia.
5. I have to take princess lessons.
6. In December, I am supposed to be introduced to my new countrymen and women on national television in Genovia (population 30,000, but still).
7. I don't have a boyfriend.

Oh, no. You see, all of that isn't enough of a burden, apparently. Now my mother has to get pregnant out of wedlock. AGAIN.

Thanks, Mom. Thanks a whole lot.

Monday, October 19, Still Homeroom

And what *about* that? Why weren't she and Mr Gianini using birth control? Could someone please explain that to me? Whatever happened to her diaphragm? I know she has one. I found it once in the shower when I was a little kid. I took it and used it as a birdbath for my Barbie townhouse for a few weeks, until my mom finally found out and took it away.

And what about condoms??? Do people my mother's age think they are immune to sexually transmitted diseases? They are obviously not immune to pregnancy, so what gives?

This is so like my mother. She can't even remember to buy toilet paper. How is she going to remember to use birth control????????

Monday, October 19, Algebra

I can't believe this. I really can't believe this.

She hasn't told him. My mother is having my Algebra teacher's baby, *and she hasn't even told him.*

I can tell she hasn't told him, because when I walked in this morning, all Mr Gianini said was, 'Oh, hi, Mia. How are you doing?'

OH, HI, MIA. HOW ARE YOU DOING?????

That is not what you say to someone whose mother is having your baby. You say something like, 'Excuse me, Mia, can I see you a moment?'

Then you take the daughter of the woman with whom you have committed this heinous indiscretion out into the hallway, where you fall on bended knee to grovel and beg for her approval and forgiveness. That is what you do.

I can't help staring at Mr G and wondering what my new baby brother or sister is going to look like. My mom is totally hot, like Carmen Sandiego, only without the trench coat – further proof that I am a biological anomaly, since I inherited neither my mother's thick curly black hair nor her C-cup. So there's nothing to worry about *there*.

But Mr G, I just don't know. Not that Mr G isn't good-looking, I guess. I mean, he's tall and has all his hair (score one for Mr G, since my dad's bald as a parking meter). But what is with his nostrils? I totally can't figure it out. They are just so . . . big.

I sincerely hope the kid gets my mom's nostrils and Mr G's ability to divide fractions in his head.

The sad thing is, Mr Gianini doesn't have the slightest idea what is about to befall him. I would feel sorry for him if it weren't for the fact that it is all his fault. I know it takes two to tango, but please, my mother is a painter. He is an Algebra teacher.

You tell me who is supposed to be the responsible one.

Monday, October 19, English

Great. Just great.

As if things aren't bad enough, now our English teacher says we have to complete a *journal* this semester. I am not kidding. A *journal*. Like I don't already keep one.

And get this: at the end of every week, we're supposed to *turn our journals in*. For Mrs Spears to *read*. Because she wants to get to know us. We are supposed to begin by introducing ourselves, and listing our pertinent stats. Later, we are supposed to move on to recording our innermost thoughts and emotions.

She has got to be joking. Like I am going to allow Mrs Spears to be privy to my innermost thoughts and emotions. I won't even tell my innermost thoughts and emotions to my *mother*. Would I tell them to my *English teacher*?

And I can't possibly turn *this* journal in. There's all sorts of stuff in here I don't want anyone to know. Like how my mother is pregnant by my Algebra teacher, for instance.

Well, I will just have to start a new journal. A *fake* journal. Instead of recording my innermost emotions and feelings in it, I'll just write a bunch of lies, and hand that in instead.

I am such an accomplished liar, I very highly doubt Mrs Spears will know the difference.

MY ENGLISH JOURNAL
by Mia Thermopolis

An Introduction

Name: *Amelia Mignonette Grimaldi Thermopolis Renaldo*
Known as Mia for short.
Her Royal Highness Princess Mia in some circles.

Age: *Fourteen*

Yr in School: *Freshman*

Sex: *Haven't had it yet. Ha, ha, just kidding, Mrs Spears!*
Ostensibly female, but lack of breast size lends disturbing androgyny.

Description: *Five foot nine*
Short mouse brown hair (new blonde highlights)
Grey eyes
Size eight shoe

Parents:

Mother:	*Helen Thermopolis*
Occupation:	*Painter*
Father:	*Artur Christoff Philippe Gerard Grimaldi Renaldo*
Occupation:	*Prince of Genovia*
Marital Status:	*Because I am the result of a*

*fling my mother and father
had in college, they never
married (each other) and are
both currently single.
It is probably better this
way, since all they ever do is
fight.
With each other, I mean.*

Pets: *One cat, Fat Louie. Orange and white, Louie
weighs over twenty-five pounds. Louie is eight years
old, and has been on a diet for approximately six
of those years. When Louie is upset with us for,
say, forgetting to feed him, he eats any socks he
might find lying around. Also, he is attracted to
small glittery things, and has quite a collection of
beer bottle caps and tweezers which he thinks I
don't know about, hidden behind the toilet in my
bathroom.*

Best Friend: *My best friend is Lilly Moscovitz. Lilly has been
my best friend since kindergarten. She is fun to
hang out with because she is very very smart and
has her own public access television show,* Lilly
Tells It Like It Is. *She is always thinking up
fun things to do, like stealing the foam board
sculpture of the Parthenon that the Greek and
Latin Derivatives class made for Parents' Night
and holding it for a ransom of ten pounds of lime
Starbursts.
Not that that was us, Mrs Spears. I am just using
that as an example of the type of crazy thing
Lilly might do.*

242

Boyfriend: *Ha! I wish.*

Address: *I have lived all of my life in New York City with my mother, except for summers, which I have traditionally spent with my father at his mother's chateau in France. My father's primary residence is Genovia, a small country in Europe located on the Mediterranean between the Italian and French border. For a long time, I was led to believe that my father was an important politician in Genovia, like the mayor, or something. Nobody told me that he was actually a member of the Genovian royal family – that he was, in fact, the reigning monarch, Genovia being a principality. I guess nobody ever would have told me, either, if my dad hadn't gotten testicular cancer and become sterile, making me – his illegitimate daughter – the only heir he'll ever have to his throne. Ever since he finally let me in on this slightly important little secret (a month ago) Dad has been living at the Plaza Hotel here in New York, while his mother, my grandmere, the Dowager Princess, gives me princess lessons so I won't make a fool of myself when I ascend the throne.*

For which I can only say: thanks. Thanks a whole lot.

And do you want to know what the *really* sad part is? None of that was lies.

Monday, October 19, Lunch

OK, Lilly knows.

All right, maybe she doesn't KNOW, but she knows something is wrong. I mean, come on: she's been my best friend since for ever. We totally bonded in first grade, the day Orville Lockhead dropped his pants in front of us in the line to the music room. I was appalled, having never seen male genitalia before. Lilly, however, was unimpressed. She has a brother, you see, so it was no big surprise to her. She just looked Orville straight in the eye and said, 'I've seen bigger.'

And he never did it again.

So you can see that Lilly and I share a bond that is stronger than mere friendship.

Which was why she took just one look at my face when she sat down at our lunch table today and went, 'What's wrong? Something's wrong. It's not Louie, is it? Did Louie eat another sock?'

As if. This is so much more serious. Not that it isn't totally scary when Louie eats a sock. I mean, we have to rush him to the cat hospital and all, and right away, or he could die. A thousand bucks later, we get an old half-digested sock as a souvenir.

But at least the cat is back to normal.

But this? A thousand bucks won't cure *this*. And nothing will ever be back to normal again.

It is so incredibly embarrassing. I mean, that my mom and Mr Gianini, you know, Did It.

Worse, that they Did It without using anything. I mean, please. Who DOES that any more?

I told Lilly there wasn't anything wrong, that it was just PMS. It was totally embarrassing to admit this in front of my bodyguard, Lars, who was sitting there eating a lamb kebab that Tina Hakim Baba's bodyguard Wahim – Tina has a bodyguard because her father is a sheik who fears that she will be kidnapped by executives from a rival oil company; I have one because . . . well, just because I'm a princess, I guess – had bought off the vendor in front of Ho's Deli across the street from the school.

The thing is, who announces the vagaries of her menstrual cycle in front of her bodyguard?

But what else was I supposed to say?

I noticed Lars totally didn't finish his kebab though. I think I completely grossed him out.

Could this day get any worse?

Anyway, even then, Lilly didn't drop it. Sometimes she really does remind me of one of those little pug dogs you always see old ladies walking in the park. I mean, not only is her face kind of small and squashed in (in a nice way), but sometimes when she gets hold of something, she simply will not let it go.

Like this thing at lunch, for instance. She was all, 'If the only thing bothering you is PMS, then why are you writing in your journal so much? I thought you were mad at your mom for giving that to you. I thought you weren't even going to use it.'

Which reminds me that I *was* mad at my mom for giving it to me. She gave me this journal because she says I have a lot of pent-up anger and hostility, and I have to get it out somehow, since I'm not in touch with my inner child and have an inherent inability to verbalize my feelings.

I think my mom must have been talking to Lilly's parents, who are both psychoanalysts, at the time.

But then I found out I was the Princess of Genovia, and I started using this journal to record my feelings about that

246

which, looking back at what I wrote, really were pretty hostile.

But that's nothing compared with how I feel now.

Not that I feel *hostile* towards Mr Gianini and my mother. I mean, they're adults, and all. They can make their own decisions. But don't they see that this is one decision that is going to affect not just them, but everyone around them? I mean, Grandmere is NOT going to like it when she finds out my mother is having ANOTHER child out of wedlock.

And what about my father? He's already had testicular cancer this year. Finding out that the mother of his only child is giving birth to another man's baby just might kill him. Not that he's still in love with my mom, or anything. I don't think.

Also, has Mom even thought about her folic acid intake? I know for a fact she has not. And may I just point out that alfalfa sprouts can be deadly for a newly developing foetus? We have alfalfa spouts in our refrigerator. Our refrigerator is a deathtrap for a gestating child. There is BEER in the vegetable crisper.

Still Monday, October 19, Gifted and Talented

Lilly caught me looking up stuff about pregnancy on the Internet.

She went, 'Oh, my God! Is there something you haven't told me???'

Which I really didn't appreciate, since she said it right in front of her brother Michael – not to mention Lars, Boris Pelkowski, and the rest of the class. She said it really loud too.

You know, these kinds of things wouldn't happen if the teachers of this school would do their jobs and actually teach once in a while. I mean, except for Mr Gianini, every teacher in this school seems to think it is perfectly acceptable to toss out an assignment and then leave the room to go have a smoke in the teachers' lounge.

Which is probably a health violation, you know.

And Mrs Hill is the worst of all. I mean, I know Gifted and Talented isn't a real class at all. It's more like study hall for the socially impaired. But if Mrs Hill would be in here once in a while to supervise, people like me who are neither gifted nor talented and only ended up in this class because they happen to be flunking Algebra and need the extra study time, might not get picked on all the time by the resident geniuses.

Anyway, I exited really fast from the You and Your Pregnancy site I was on, but not fast enough for Lilly. She kept going, 'Oh, my God, Mia, why didn't you tell me?'

It was getting kind of embarrassing, even though I explained that I was doing an extra-credit report for Biology, which isn't really a lie, since my lab partner Kenny Showalter and I are ethically opposed to dissecting frogs, which the rest of the class will be doing next. Mrs Sing said we could do a term paper instead.

Only the term paper is supposed to be on the life cycle of the mealworm. But Lilly doesn't know that.

I tried to change the subject by asking Lilly if she knew the truth about alfalfa sprouts, but she just kept blabbing on and on about my phantom pregnancy. I really wouldn't have minded so much if it hadn't been for her brother Michael sitting right there, listening, instead of working on his webzine, *Crackhead*, like he was supposed to be doing. I mean, it's not like I haven't had a crush on him since for ever.

Not that he's noticed, of course. To him, I'm just his kid sister's best friend, that's all. He has to be nice to me, or Lilly will tell everyone in school how she once caught him getting teary-eyed over an old *7th Heaven* re-run.

Besides which, I'm just a lowly freshman. Michael Moscovitz is a senior and has the best grade point average in the whole school (after Lilly) and is co-valedictorian of his class. And he didn't inherit the squashed-in-face gene like his sister. Michael could go out with any girl at Albert Einstein High School that he wanted to.

Well, except for the cheerleaders. They only date jocks.

Not that Michael isn't athletic. I mean, he doesn't believe in organized sports, but he has excellent quadriceps. All his 'ceps are nice, actually. I noticed last time he came into Lilly's room to yell at us for screaming obscenities too loudly during a Christina Aguilera video, and he didn't happen to be wearing a shirt.

So I really didn't appreciate Lilly standing there talking about how I might be pregnant, right in front of her brother.

Top Five Reasons Why It's Hard to Be Best Friends with a Certified Genius

1. She usually uses words I don't understand.
2. She is often incapable of admitting that I might make a meaningful contribution to any conversation or activity.
3. In group situations, she has trouble relinquishing control.
4. Unlike normal people, when solving a problem she does not go from A to B, but from A to D, making it difficult for us lower human life forms to follow along.
5. You can't tell her anything without her analysing it half to death.

Homework:

Algebra: problems on pg. 133
English: write a brief family history
World Civ.: find an example of negative stereotyping of Arabs (film, television, literature) and submit with explanatory essay
Gifted and Talented: N/A
French: ecrivez une vignette parisiene
Biology: reproductive system (get answers from Kenny)

ENGLISH JOURNAL
My Family History:

*The ancestry of my family on my father's side can be traced back to
AD 568.*

*That is the year when a Visogothic warlord named Alboin, who
appeared to be suffering from what today would be called an authoritarian personality disorder, killed the king of Italy and all these other
people, then made himself king. And after he made himself king, he
decided to marry Rosagunde, the daughter of one of the old king's gen-
erals.*

*Only Rosagunde didn't much like Alboin after he made her drink
wine out of her dead dad's skull, and so she got him back the night of
their wedding, by strangling him with her braids while he slept.*

*With Alboin dead, the old king of Italy's son took over. He was so
grateful to Rosagunde that he made her princess of an area that is today
known as the country of Genovia. According to the only existing records
of that time, Rosagunde was a kind and thoughtful ruler. She is my
great-grandmother times about sixty. She is one of the primary reasons
why today Genovia has some of the best literacy, infant mortality, and
employment rates in all of Europe: Rosagunde implemented a highly
sophisticated (for its time) system of governmental checks and balances,
and did away entirely with the death penalty.*

*On my mom's side of the family, the Thermopolises were goat
herders on the island of Crete until the year 1904, when Dionysius
Thermopolis, my mom's great-grandfather, couldn't take it any more,
and ran away to America. He eventually settled in Versailles, Indiana,
where he opened an appliance store. His offspring have been running the
Handy Dandy Hardware store on the Versailles, Indiana, courthouse
square ever since, but my mom says her upbringing would have been
much less oppressive, not to mention more liberal, back in Crete.*

A Suggested Daily Diet for Pregnancy

- Two to four protein servings of meat, fish, poultry, cheese, tofu, eggs, or nut-grain-bean-dairy combinations.

- One pint of milk (whole, skim buttermilk) or milk equivalents (cheese, yogurt, cottage cheese).

- One or two vitamin C rich foods – whole potato, grapefruit, orange, melon, green pepper, cabbage, strawberries, fruit, orange juice.

- A yellow or orange fruit or vegetable.

- Four to five slices of whole-grain bread, pancakes, tortillas, cornbread, or a serving of whole-grain cereal or pasta. Use wheat germ and brewers' yeast to fortify other foods.

- Butter, fortified margarine, vegetable oil.

- Six to eight glasses of liquid – fruit and vegetable juices, water and herb teas. Avoid sugar sweetened juices, colas, alcohol, and caffeine.

- For snacks – dried fruits, nuts, pumpkin and sunflower seeds, popcorn.

My mom is so not going to go for this. Unless she can smother it in hoisin sauce from Number One Noodle Son, she is just not interested.

To do before Mom gets home

Throw out: Heineken
cooking sherry
alfalfa sprouts
Colombian roast
chocolate chips
salami
Don't forget the bottle of Absolut in the freezer!

Buy: Multi-vitamins
fresh fruit
wheat germ
yogurt

Monday, October 19, After school

Just when I thought things couldn't get any worse, suddenly, they did:

Grandmere called.

This is so unfair. She was supposed to have gone to Baden-Baden for a little R and R. I was fully looking forward to a respite from her torture sessions – also known as princess lessons, which I am forced by my father, the despot, to attend. I mean, I could use a little vacation myself. Do they really think anyone in Genovia cares whether I know how to use a fish fork? Or if I can sit down without getting wrinkles in the back of my skirt? Or if I know how to say 'Thank you' in Swahili? Shouldn't my future countrymen and women be more concerned with my views on the environment? And gun control? And overpopulation?

But according to Grandmere, the people of Genovia don't care about any of that. They just want to know that I won't embarrass them at any state dinners.

As if. Grandmere's the one they should be worried about. I mean, *I* didn't have eyeliner permanently tattooed onto *my* eyelids. *I* don't dress *my* pet up in chinchilla bolero jackets. *I* was never a close personal friend of Richard Nixon.

But, oh no, it's *me* everyone is supposedly so worried about. Like *I* might commit some huge social gaffe at my introduction to the Genovian people in December.

Right.

But whatever. It turns out Grandmere didn't go on her trip after all, on account of the Baden-Baden baggage-handlers being on strike.

I wish I knew the head of the baggage-handler union in Baden-Baden. If I did, I would totally offer him the one hundred dollars per day my dad has been donating in my name to Greenpeace for performing my duties as Princess of Genovia, just so he and the other baggage-handlers would go back to work, and get Grandmere out of my hair for a while.

Anyway, Grandmere left a very scary message on the answering machine. She says she has a 'surprise' for me. I'm supposed to call her right away.

I wonder what her surprise is. Knowing Grandmere, it's probably something totally horrible, like a coat made out of the skin of baby poodles.

Hey, I wouldn't put it past her.

I'm going to pretend like I didn't get the message.

Monday, October 19, Later

Just got off the phone with Grandmere. She wanted to know why I hadn't returned her call. I told her I didn't get the message.

Why am I such a liar? I mean, I can't even tell the truth about the simplest things. And I'm supposed to be a princess, for crying out loud. What kind of princess goes around lying all the time?

Anyway, Grandmere says she is sending a limo to pick me up. She and my dad and I are going to have dinner in her suite at the Plaza. Grandmere says she is going to tell me all about my surprise then.

Tell me all about it. Not *show me*. Which hopefully rules out the puppy skin coat.

I guess it's just as well I'm having dinner with Grandmere tonight. My mom invited Mr Gianini over to the loft tonight so they can 'talk'. She's not very happy with me for throwing out the coffee and beer (I didn't actually throw it away. I gave it to our neighbour Ronnie). Now my mom is stomping around complaining that she has nothing to offer Mr G when he comes over.

I pointed out that it's for her own good, and that if Mr Gianini is any sort of gentleman, he'll give up beer and coffee anyway, to support her in her time of need. I know I would expect the father of my unborn child to pay me that courtesy.

That is, in the unlikely event that I were ever actually to have sex.

Monday, October 19, 11 p.m.

Some surprise *that* was.

Somebody really needs to tell Grandmere that surprises are supposed to be pleasant. I mean, I guess I'm not really shocked that she doesn't seem to know the difference between a nice surprise and a bad one, considering that she once 'surprised' my dad (who was ten years old at the time) with a new horse – but only after having his old beloved pony 'put out to pasture' (read: shipped off to the glue factory) because it had gone lame, a story he told me one Christmas after he'd had too many egg-nogs.

To this day Grandmere doesn't get it. She still insists that was one heck of a great surprise: 'That horse,' she reminds my dad, whenever he brings it up, 'was a Thoroughbred, seventeen hands high if he was an inch!'

Well, my surprise wasn't quite *that* bad, but it was still pretty grim: a primetime interview for me with Beverly Bellerieve on *Twenty Four/Seven*.

I don't care if it *is* the most highly rated television news show in America. I told Grandmere a million times I don't want to have my picture taken, let alone be on TV. I mean, it's bad enough that everyone I know is aware that I look like a walking cotton bud, what with my lack of breasts and my temperamental hair. I don't need all of America finding it out.

But now Grandmere says it's my duty as a member of the Genovian royal family. Also, that it will be good practice for my debut on Genovian television in December.

She even got my dad into the act. He was all, 'Your grandmother's right, Mia.'

It would have taken a *lot* for him to admit something like *that*. I mean, considering the fact that about the only thing my dad and Grandmere have ever agreed on is that I shouldn't get a navel ring.

So I get to spend next Saturday afternoon being interviewed by Beverly Bellerieve.

I told Grandmere I thought this interview thing was a really bad idea. I told her I wasn't ready for anything this big yet. I said maybe we could start small, and have Carson Daly or somebody like that interview me.

But Grandmere didn't go for it. I never met anybody who needed to go to Baden-Baden so badly for a little rest and relaxation. Grandmere looks about as relaxed as Fat Louie right after the vet sticks a thermometer you-know-where in order to take his temperature.

Of course, this might have had something to do with the fact that Grandmere shaves off her eyebrows and draws on new ones every morning. Don't ask me why. I mean, she has perfectly good eyebrows. I've seen the stubble. But lately I've noticed those eyebrows are getting drawn on higher and higher up her forehead, which gives her this look of perpetual surprise. I think that's because of all her plastic surgery. If she doesn't watch it, one of these days her eyelids are going to be up in the vicinity of her frontal lobes.

And my dad was no help at all. He was asking all these questions about Beverly Bellerieve, like was it true she was Miss America in 1991, and did Grandmere happen to know if she (Beverly) was still going out with Ted Turner, or was that over?

I swear, for a guy who only has one testicle, my dad sure spends a lot of time thinking about sex.

We argued about it all through dinner. Like, were they going to shoot the interview at the hotel, or back in the loft? If they shot it at the hotel, people would be given a false impression about my lifestyle. But if they shot it at the loft,

Grandmere insisted, people would be horrified by the squalor in which my mother has brought me up.

Which is totally unfair. The loft is not squalid. It just has that nice lived-in look.

'Never-been-cleaned look, you mean,' Grandmere said, correcting me. But that isn't true, because just the other day I dusted the whole place.

'With that animal, I don't know how you can ever get the place really clean,' Grandmere said.

But Fat Louie isn't responsible for the mess. Dust, as everyone knows, is ninety-five per cent human skin tissue.

The only good thing I can see about all this is that at least the film crew isn't going to follow me around at school and stuff. That's one thing to be thankful for, anyway. I mean, could you imagine them filming me being tortured by head cheerleader Lana Weinberger, who has always had it in for me, during Algebra? She would so totally start flipping her pom-poms in my face, or something, just to show the producers what a wimp I can be sometimes. People all over America would be like, What is wrong with that girl? Why isn't she self-actualized?

And what about G & T? In addition to there being absolutely no teacher supervision in that class, there's the whole thing with us locking Lilly's boyfriend Boris in the supply closet so we don't have to listen to him practise his violin. That has to be some kind of health codes violation.

Anyway, the whole time we were arguing about it, a part of my brain was going, *Right now, as we're sitting here arguing over this whole interview thing, fifty-seven blocks away, my mother is breaking the news to her lover – my Algebra teacher – that she is pregnant with his child.*

What was Mr G going to say? I wondered. If he expressed

anything but joy, I was going to set Lars on him. I really was. Lars would beat up Mr G for me, and he probably wouldn't charge me very much for it, either. He has three ex-wives he's paying alimony to, so he can always use an ten extra bucks, which is all I could afford to pay a hired thug.

I really need to see about getting more of an allowance. I mean, who ever heard of a princess who only gets ten bucks a week spending money? You can't even go to the movies on that.

Well, you can, but you can't get popcorn.

The thing was, though, when I got back to the loft, I couldn't tell whether I would need Lars to beat up my Algebra teacher or not. Mr G and my mom were talking in hushed voices in her room.

I can't hear anything going on in there, even when I press my ear to the door.

I hope Mr G takes it well. He's the nicest guy my mom's ever dated, despite that F he almost gave me in Algebra. I don't think he'll do anything stupid, like dump her, or try to sue for full custody.

Then again, he's a man, so who knows?

It's funny, because as I was writing that, an instant message came over my computer. It was from Michael, Lilly's brother! He wrote:

CracKing: What was with you at school today? It was like you were off in this whole other world or something.

I wrote back:

FtLouie: I don't have the slightest idea what you are talking about. Nothing is wrong with me. I'm totally fine.

I am such a liar.

```
CracKing: Well, I got the impression that you
didn't hear a word that I said about negative
slopes.
```

Since I found out my destiny is to rule a small European principality someday, I have been trying really hard to understand Algebra, as I know I will need it to balance the budget of Genovia, and all. So I have been attending review sessions every day after school and, during G & T, Michael has been helping me a little too.

But it's very hard to pay attention when Michael tutors me. This is because he smells really, really good.

How can I think about negative slopes when this guy I've had a major crush on since, oh, I don't know, for ever, practically, is sitting there right next to me, smelling like soap and sometimes brushing my knee with his?

I replied:

```
FtLouie:I heard everything you said about
negative slopes. Given slope m, +y-intercept
(O,b) equation y+mx+b Slope-intercept.
>
CracKing: WHAT???
>
FtLouie: Isn't that right?
>
CracKing: Did you copy that out of the back of
the book?
```

Of course.
Uh-oh, my mom is at the door.

Monday, October 19, Late

My mom just came in. I thought Mr G had left, so I went, 'How'd it go?'

Then I saw she had tears in her eyes, so I went over and gave her this big hug.

'It's OK, Mom,' I said. 'You'll always have me. I'll help with everything – the midnight feeds, the diaper changing, everything. Even if it turns out to be a boy.'

My mom hugged me back, but it turned out she wasn't crying because she was sad. She was crying because she was so happy.

'Oh, Mia,' she said. 'We want you to be the first to know.'

Then she pulled me out into the living room. Mr Gianini was standing there with this really dopey look on his face. Dopey happy.

I knew before she said it, but I pretended to be surprised anyway.

'We're getting married!'

My mom pulled me into this big group hug between her and Mr G.

It's sort of weird to be hugged by your Algebra teacher. That's all I have to say.

Tuesday, October 20, 1 a.m.

Hey, I thought my mom was a feminist who didn't believe in the male hierarchy and was against the subjugation and obfuscation of the female identity that marriage necessarily entails.

At least, that's what she always used to say when I asked her why she and my dad didn't ever get married.

I always thought it's because he just never asked her.

Maybe that's why she told me not to tell anyone just yet . . . she wants to let my dad know in her own way, she says.

All of this excitement has given me a headache.

Tuesday, October 20, 2 a.m.

Oh my God. I just realized that if my mom marries Mr
Gianini, it means he'll be living here. I mean, my mom
would never move to Brooklyn, where he lives. She always
says the subway aggravates her antipathy towards the cor-
porate hordes.

I can't believe it. I'm going to have to eat breakfast every
morning with my *Algebra teacher*.

And what happens if I accidentally see him naked, or
something? My mind could be permanently warped.

I'd better make sure the lock on the bathroom door is
fixed before he moves in.

Now my throat hurts, in addition to my head.

Tuesday, October 20, 9 a.m.

When I woke up this morning, my throat hurt so much, I couldn't even talk. I could only croak.

I tried croaking for my mom for a while, but she couldn't hear me. So then I tried banging on the wall, but all that did was make my Greenpeace poster fall down.

Finally I had no choice but to get up. I wrapped my comforter around me so I wouldn't get a chill and get even sicker, and went down the hall to my mom's room.

To my horror, there was not one lump in my mom's bed, but TWO!!!! Mr Gianini stayed over!!!!

Oh, well. It's not like he hasn't already promised to make an honest woman of her.

Still, it's a little embarrassing to stumble into your mom's bedroom at six in the morning and find your *Algebra teacher* in there with her. I mean, that kind of thing might seriously damage the mind of a lesser person than myself.

But whatever. I stood there croaking in the doorway, totally too freaked out to go in, and finally my mom cracked an eye open. Then I whispered to her that I was sick, and told her that she'd have to call the attendance office and explain that I wouldn't be in school today.

I also asked her to call and cancel my limo, and to let Lilly know we wouldn't be stopping by to pick her up.

I also told her that if she was going to go to the studio, she'd have to get my dad or Lars (please not Grandmere) to come to the loft and make sure no one tried to kidnap or assassinate me while she was gone and I was in my weakened physical state.

I think she understood me, but it was hard to tell.

I tell you, this princess business is no joke.

Later on Tuesday

My mom stayed home from the studio today.

I croaked to her that she shouldn't. She has a show at the Mary Boone Gallery in about a month, and I know she only has about half the paintings done that she's supposed to have. If she should happen to succumb to morning sickness, she is one dead realist.

But she stayed home anyway. I think she feels guilty. I think she thinks my getting sick is her fault. Like all my anxiety over the state of her womb weakened my auto-immune system, or something.

Which totally isn't true. I'm sure whatever it is I have, I picked it up at school. Albert Einstein High School is one giant Petri dish of bacteria, if you ask me, what with the astonishing number of mouth-breathers who go there.

Anyway, about every ten minutes, my guilt-ridden mother comes in and asks me if I want anything. I forgot she has a Florence Nightingale complex. She keeps making me tea and cinnamon toast with the crusts cut off. This is very nice, I must say.

Except then she tried to get me to let some zinc dissolve on my tongue, as one of her friends told her this is supposedly a good way to combat the common cold.

That was not so nice.

She felt bad about it when the zinc made me gag a whole bunch. She even ran down to the deli and bought me one of those king-size Crunch bars to make up for it.

Later she tried to make me bacon and eggs in order to build up my strength, but there I drew the line: just because I'm on my deathbed does not mean it's OK to abandon all of my vegetarian principles.

My mother just took my temperature. Ninety-nine point six.

If this were medieval times, I would probably be dead.

Temperature Chart
11:45 a.m. – 99.2
12:14 p.m. – 99.1
1:27 p.m. – 98.6
This stupid thermometer must be broken!
2:05 p.m. – 99.0
3:35 p.m. – 99.1

Clearly, if this keeps up, I will be unable to be interviewed by Beverly Bellerieve on Saturday.

YIPPEE!!!!!!!!!!!!!!!!!

Even later on Tuesday

Lilly just stopped by. She brought me all of my homework. She says I look wretched, and that I sound like Linda Blair in *The Exorcist*. I've never seen *The Exorcist*, so I don't know if this is true or not. I don't like movies where people's heads spin round, or where things come bursting out of their stomach. I like movies with beauty makeovers and dancing.

Anyway, Lilly says the big news at school is that the It Couple, Josh Richter and Lana Weinberger, got back together, after having been broken up one whole entire week (a personal record for the both of them: last time they broke up, it was for only three days). Lilly says when she went by my locker to get my books, Lana was standing there in her cheerleader uniform, waiting for Josh, whose locker is next to mine.

Then, when Josh showed up, he laid a big wet one on Lana that Lilly swears was the equivalent to an F5 on the Fujimoto scale of tornado suck zone intensity, making it impossible for Lilly to close my locker door again (how well I know that problem). Lilly resolved the situation pretty quickly, however, by accidentally-on-purpose stabbing Josh in the spine with the tip of her number two pencil.

I thought about telling Lilly my own Big News: you know, about my mom and Mr G. I mean, she's going to find out about it anyway.

Maybe it was the infection coursing through my body, but I just couldn't bring myself to do it. I just couldn't bear the thought of what Lilly might say regarding the potential size of my future brother or sister's nostrils.

Anyway, I have about a ton of homework. Even the father of my unborn sibling, who you would think would feel an iota of sympathy towards me, loaded me down with it. I tell you, there isn't a single perk to having your mother engaged to your Algebra teacher. Not a single one.

Well, except when he comes over for dinner and helps me with the assignment. He doesn't give me the answers, though, so I mostly get sixty-eights. And that's still a D.

And I am really sick now! My temperature has gone up to ninety-nine point eight! Soon it will reach one hundred.

If this were an episode of *ER*, they'd have practically put me on a respirator already.

There is no way I'll be able to be interviewed by Beverly Bellerieve now. NO WAY.

Tee hee.

My mom has her humidifier in here, going on full blast. Lilly says my room is just like Vietnam, and why don't I at least crack the window, for God's sake.

I never thought of it before, but Lilly and Grandmere sort of have a lot in common. For instance, Grandmere called a little while ago. When I told her how sick I was, and how I probably wouldn't be able to make it to the interview on Saturday, she actually *chastised* me.

That's right. Chastised me, like it was *my* fault I got sick. Then she starts going on about how on her wedding day she had a fever of one hundred and two, but did she let that stop her from standing through a two-hour wedding ceremony, then riding in an open coach through the streets of Genovia waving to the populace, and then dining on prosciutto and melon at her reception and waltzing until four in the morning?

No, you might not be too surprised to learn. It did not.

That, Grandmere said, is because a princess does not use poor health as an excuse to shirk her duties to her people.

As if the people of Genovia care about me doing some lousy interview for *TwentyFour/Seven*. They don't even get that show there. I mean, except for the people who have satellite dishes, maybe.

Lilly is just about as unsympathetic as Grandmere. In fact, Lilly isn't really a very soothing visitor to have at all when you are sick. She suggested it was possible that I have consumption, just like Elizabeth Barrett Browning. I said I thought it was probably only bronchitis, and Lilly said that's probably what Elizabeth Barrett Browning thought too . . . before she *died*.

Homework:

Algebra: problems at the end of chapter ten
English: in your journal: list your favourite TV show, movie, book, food, etc.
World Civ.: one thousand word essay explaining the conflict between Iran and Afghanistan
Gifted and Talented: as if
French: ecrivez une vignette amusant (Oh, *right*)
Biology: endocrine system (get answers from Kenny)

God! What are they trying to do over there, anyway? Kill us?

Wednesday, October 21

This morning my mom called my dad where he's staying at the Plaza, and made him bring the limo over so I could go to the doctor. This is because when she took my temperature after I woke up, it was one hundred and two, just like Grandmere's on her wedding day!

Only I can tell you, I didn't feel much like waltzing. I could hardly even get dressed. I was so feverish I actually put on one of the outfits Grandmere bought me. So there I was in Chanel from head to toe, with my eyes all glassy and this sheen of sweat all over me. My dad jumped about a foot and a half when he saw me, I think because he thought for a minute that I *was* Grandmere.

Only of course I am much taller than Grandmere. Though my hair isn't as big.

It turns out that Dr Fung is one of the few people in America who hadn't heard yet that I'm a princess now, so we had to sit in the waiting room for like ten minutes before he could see me. My dad spent the ten minutes talking to the receptionist. That's because she was wearing an outfit that showed her navel, even though it is practically winter.

And even though my dad is completely bald and wears suits all the time instead of khakis, like a normal dad, you could tell the receptionist was completely into him. That's because in spite of his incipient Europeaness, my dad is still something of a hottie.

Lars, who is also a hottie, but in a different sort of way, being extremely large and hairy, sat next to me, reading *Parenting* magazine. I could tell he would have preferred the latest copy of *Soldier of Fortune*, but they don't have a subscription to that at the SoHo Family Medical Practice.

Finally Dr Fung saw me. He took my temperature (one

271

hundred and one point seven) and felt my glands to see if they were swollen (they were). Then he tried to take a throat culture to check for strep.

Only when he jabbed that thing into my mouth, it made me gag so hard, I started coughing uncontrollably. I couldn't stop coughing, so I told him between coughs that I was going to get a drink of water. I think I must have been delusional because of my fever and all, since what I did instead of getting water was walk right out of the doctor's office. I got back into the limo and told the chauffeur to take me to Emerald Planet right away, so I could get a smoothie.

Fortunately the chauffeur knew better than to take me somewhere without my bodyguard. He got on the radio and said some stuff, and then Lars came out to the limo with my dad, who asked me what on earth I thought I was doing.

I thought about asking him the exact same thing, only about the receptionist with the pierced belly button. But my throat hurt too much to talk.

Dr Fung was pretty nice about it in the end. He gave up on the throat culture and just prescribed some antibiotics and this cough syrup with codeine in it.

But not until he had one of his nurses take a picture of us shaking hands together inside the limo, so he could hang it on his wall of celebrity photos. He has pictures of himself up there shaking hands with other famous patients of his, like Rex Harrison and Lou Reed.

Now that my raging fever has gone down, I can see that I was behaving completely irrationally. I would have to say that that trip to the doctor's office was probably one of the most embarrassing moments of my life. Of course, there's been so many, it's hard to tell where this one ranks. I think I would chalk it up there with the time I accidentally dropped my dinner plate in the buffet line at Lilly's bat mitzvah, and everybody kept stepping in gefiltefish for the rest of the night.

Mia Thermopolis's Top Five
Most Embarrassing Moments

1. The time when I was six and Grandmere ordered me to hug her sister, Tante Jean Marie, and I started to cry because I was afraid of Jean Marie's moustache, and hurt Jean Marie's feelings.

2. The time when I was seven and Grandmere forced me to attend a boring cocktail party she gave for all her friends, and I was so bored I picked up this little ivory coaster holder which was shaped like a rickshaw, and then I wheeled it around the coffee table, making noises like I was speaking Chinese, until all the coasters fell out the back of the rickshaw and rolled around on the floor very noisily, and everyone looked at me. (This is even more embarrassing when I think of it now, because imitating Chinese people is very politically incorrect.)

3. The time when I was ten and Grandmere took me and some of my cousins to the beach and I forgot my bikini top and Grandmere wouldn't let me go back to the chateau to get it, she said this was France for God's sake and I should just go topless like everybody else. Even though I had even less up there to show than I do now, I was mortified and wouldn't take my shirt off and everyone looked at me because they thought I had a rash or disfiguring birthmark.

4. The time when I was twelve and I got my first period, and I was at Grandmere's house and I had to tell her about it because I didn't have any pads or anything, and later that night as I walked in for dinner I overheard Grandmere announcing it to all her friends, and then for the rest of the night all they did was make jokes about the joys of womanhood.

5. The time when I was thirteen and Grandmere told the totally hot guy who came to fix the pool at the chateau that my favourite band was Hanson.

Now that I think about it, almost all of the most embarrassing moments of my life have something to do with Grandmere.

I wonder what Lilly's parents, who are both psychoanalysts, would have to say about this.

Temperature Chart
5:20 p.m. – 99.3
6:45 p.m. – 99.2
7:52 p.m. – 99.1

Is it possible I am getting better *already*???? This is horrible. If I get better, I'll have to do that stupid interview . . .

This calls for drastic measures: tonight I fully intend to take a shower and go to bed with my hair wet.

That will show them.

Thursday, October 22

Oh my God. Something so exciting just happened, I can hardly write.

This morning as I was lying in my sick bed, my mom handed me a letter that she said had come in the mail yesterday, only she forgot to give it to me.

This wasn't like the electricity or cable bills my mom usually forgets about after they have arrived. This was a personal letter to me.

Still, since the address on the front of it was typed, I didn't suspect anything out of the ordinary. I thought it was a letter from school, or something. Like maybe I'd made honour roll (HA HA). Except that there was no return address, and usually mail from Albert Einstein High School has Albert's thoughtful face in the left-hand corner, along with the school's address.

So you can imagine my surprise when I opened the letter and found not a flier asking me to show my school spirit by making Rice Krispie treats for a bake sale to raise money for the crew team, but the following . . . which, for want of a better word, I can only call a love letter:

Dear Mia (the letter went)

I know you will think it's strange, receiving a letter like this. I feel strange writing it. And yet I am too shy to tell you face-to-face what I'm about to tell you now: that I think you are the Josiest girl I've ever met.

I just want to make sure you know that there's one person, anyway, who liked you long before he found out you were a princess . . .

And will keep on liking you, no matter what.

Sincerely,
A Friend

Oh my God!

I can't believe it! I've never gotten a letter like this before. Who could it be from? I seriously can't figure it out. The letter is typed, like the address on the envelope. Not by a typewriter, either, but obviously on a computer.

So even if I wanted to compare keystrokes, say, on a suspect's typewriter (like Jan did on *The Brady Bunch* when she suspected Alice of sending her that locket), I couldn't. You can't compare the type on laser printers, for God's sake. It's always the same.

But who could have sent me such a thing?

Of course, I know who I *want* to have sent it.

But the chances of a guy like Michael Moscovitz ever actually liking me as more than just a friend are like zero. I mean, if he liked me, he has had more than ample opportunity to tell me so. How many times have we totally hung out? I mean, his sister is my best friend. It's not like we don't see each other on practically a daily basis.

And he has never said a word.

And why would he? I mean, I am a complete freak, what with my noticeable lack of mammary glands, my gigantism, and my utter inability ever to mould my hair into something remotely resembling a style.

We just got through studying people like me in Bio., as a matter of fact. Biological sports, we are called. A biological sport occurs when an organism shows a marked change from the normal type or parent stock, typically as a result of mutation.

That is me. That is so totally me. I mean, if you looked at me, and then you looked at my parents, who are both very attractive people, you would be all, What *happened*?

Seriously. I should go and live with the X-men, I am such a mutant.

Besides, is Michael Moscovitz really the type of guy who'd say I was the *Josiest* girl in school? I mean, I am assuming the author is referring to Josie, the lead singer of Josie and the Pussycats, that cartoon that was made into a movie about a girl band that solve mysteries. I sincerely doubt Michael's ever seen *Josie and the Pussycats*. He doesn't even watch the Cartoon Network, as far as I know.

Michael generally only watches PBS, the Sci Fi Channel and *Buffy the Vampire Slayer*. Maybe if the letter had said *I think you are the* Buffiest *girl I've ever met . . .*

But if it isn't from Michael, who could it be from?

This is all so exciting, I want to call someone and tell them. Only who? Everyone I know is in school.

WHY DID I HAVE TO GET SICK????

Forget going to bed with my hair wet. I have to get better right away so I can go back to school and figure out who my secret admirer is!!!!!!!!!!!!!!!!!!!!

Temperature Chart
10:45 p.m. – 99.2
11:15 p.m. – 99.1
12:27 p.m. – 98.6
Yes! YES! I am getting better!!!!
Thank you, Selman Waksman, inventor of the antibiotic.
2:05 p.m. – 99.0
No. Oh no.
3:35 p.m. – 99.1
Why is this happening to me???????

Later on Thursday

This afternoon while I was lying around with ice-packs under the covers, trying to bring my fever down so I can go to school tomorrow and find out who my secret admirer is, I happened to see the best episode of *Baywatch* ever.

Really.

See, Mitch met this girl with this very fake French accent during a boat race, and they totally fell in love and ran around in the waves to this excellent soundtrack, and then it turned out the girl was engaged to Mitch's opponent in the boat race, and not only that, but she was actually the *princess of this small European country Mitch had never heard of*. Her fiancé was this prince her father had betrothed her to at birth!

While I was watching this, Lilly came over with my new homework assignments, and she started watching with me, and she totally missed the deep philosophical importance of the episode. All she said was, 'Boy, does that royal chick need an eyebrow waxing.'

I was appalled.

'Lilly,' I croaked. 'Can't you see that this episode of *Baywatch* is prophetic? It is entirely possible that I have been betrothed since birth to some prince I've never even met, and my dad just hasn't told me yet. And I could very likely meet some lifeguard on a beach and fall madly in love with him, but it won't matter, because I will have to do my duty and marry the man my people have picked out for me.'

Lilly said, 'Hello, exactly how much of that cough medicine have you had today? It says one *tea*spoon every four hours, not *table*spoon, dorkus.'

I was annoyed at Lilly for failing to see the bigger picture. I couldn't, of course, tell her about the letter I'd gotten. Because what if her brother was the one who wrote it? I wouldn't want him thinking I'd gone blabbing about it to everyone I knew. A love letter is a very private thing.

But still, you would think she'd be able to see it from my perspective.

'Don't you understand?' I rasped. 'What is the point of me liking anybody, when it's entirely possible that my dad has arranged a marriage for me with some prince I've never met? Some guy who lives in Dubai, or somewhere, and who gazes daily at my picture and longs for the day when he can finally make me his own?'

Lilly said she thought I'd been reading too many of my friend Tina Hakim Baba's teen romances. And I will admit, that is sort of where I got the idea. But that is not the point.

'Seriously, Lilly,' I said. 'I have to guard diligently against falling in love with somebody like David Hasselhoff or your brother, because in the end I might have to marry Prince William.' Not that that would be such a great sacrifice.

Lilly got up off my bed and stomped out into the loft's living room. Only my dad was around, because when he'd come over to check on me, my mom had suddenly remembered an errand she had to get done, and dashed off.

Only of course there was no errand. My mom still hasn't told my dad about Mr G and her pregnancy, and how they're getting married and all. I think she's afraid that he might start yelling at her for being so irresponsible (which I could totally see him doing).

So instead she flees from Dad in guilt every time she sees him. It would almost be funny, if it wasn't such a pathetic way for a thirty-six-year-old woman to behave. When I am thirty-six, I fully intend to be self-actualized, so you will not catch me doing any of the things my mother is always doing.

'Mr Renaldo,' I heard Lilly say, as she went out into the living room. She calls my dad Mr Renaldo even though she knows perfectly well he is the prince of Genovia. She doesn't care though, because she says this is America and she isn't calling anybody Your Highness. She is fundamentally opposed to monarchies – and principalities, like Genovia, fall under that heading. Lilly believes that sovereignty rests with the people. In Colonial times, she'd probably have been branded a Whig.

'Mr Renaldo,' I heard her ask my dad. 'Is Mia secretly betrothed to some prince somewhere?'

My dad lowered his newspaper. I could hear it crinkling all the way from my bedroom. 'Good God, no,' he said.

'Moron,' she said to me, when she came stomping back into my room. 'And while I can see why you might want to guard diligently against falling in love with David Hasselhoff, who is, by the way, old enough to be your father, and hardly a hottie, what does my *brother* have to do with any of this?'

Too late, I realized what I'd said. Lilly has no idea how I feel about her brother Michael. Actually, *I* don't really have any idea how I feel about him either. Except that he looks extremely Casper Van Dien with his shirt off.

I *so* want him to be the one who'd written that letter. I really, really do.

But I'm not about to mention this to his sister.

Instead, I told her I think it unfair of her to demand explanations for stuff I said under the influence of codeine cough syrup.

Lilly just got that expression she gets sometimes when teachers ask a question and she knows the answer, only she wants to give someone else in the class a chance to answer for a change.

It can really be exhausting sometimes, having a best friend with an IQ of 170.

Homework:

Algebra: problems 1–20, pg. 115
English: chapter 4 of Strunk and White
World Civ.: two-hundred word essay on the conflict between India and Pakistan
Gifted and Talented: yeah, right
French: chaptre huit
Biology: pituitary gland (ask Kenny!)

Lilly Moscovitz and Mia Thermopolis's List of Celebrities and Their Breasts

	Lilly	Mia
Britney Spears	Fake	Real
Jennifer Love Hewitt	Fake	Real
Winona Ryder	Fake	Real
Courtney Love	Fake	Fake
Jennie Garth	Fake	Real
Tori Spelling	Fake	Fake
Brandy	Fake	Real
Neve Campbell	Fake	Real
Sarah Michelle Gellar	Real	Real
Christina Aguilera	Fake	Real
Lucy Lawless	Real	Real
Melissa Joan Hart	Fake	Real
Mariah Carey	Fake	Fake

Even later on Thursday

After dinner I felt well enough to get out of bed, and so I did.

I checked my e-mail. I was hoping there might be something from my mysterious 'friend'. If he knew my 'snail mail' address, I figured he'd know my e-mail address too. Both are listed in the school directory.

Tina Hakim Baba was one of the people who had e-mailed me. She sent get-well wishes. So did Shameeka. Shameeka mentioned that she was trying to talk her father into letting her have a Halloween party, and that if she succeeded, would I come? I wrote back to say of course, if I wasn't too weak from coughing.

There was also a message from Michael. It was a get-well message too, but it was animated, like a little film. It showed a cat that looked a lot like Fat Louie doing a little get-well dance. It was very cute. Michael signed it *Love, Michael*.

Not Sincerely.

Not Yours Truly.

Love.

I played it four times, but I still couldn't tell whether he was the one who'd sent me that letter. The letter, I noticed, never once mentioned the word 'love'. It said the sender *liked* me. And he signed it *sincerely*.

But there was no love. Not a hint of love.

Then I saw a message from someone whose e-mail address I didn't recognize. Oh my God! Could it be my anonymous liker? My fingers were trembling on my mouse . . .

And then I opened it and saw the following message from JoCrox:

285

```
JoCrox: Just a note to say hope you are
feeling better. Missed you in class today! Did
you get my letter? Hope it made you feel at
least a little better, knowing there's someone
out there who thinks you rock. Get well soon.
Your Friend
```

Oh my God! It's *him*! My anonymous admirer!

But who is Jo Crox? I don't know anyone named Jo Crox. He says he missed me in class today, which means we must be in one together. But there are no Jos in any of my classes.

Maybe Jo Crox isn't really his name. In fact, Jo Crox doesn't sound like a name at all. Maybe that actually stands for Joc Rox.

But I don't know any jocks, either. I mean, not personally.

Oh, no, wait, I get it:

Jo-C-rox.

Josie Rocks! Oh my God! Josie from *Josie and the Pussycats*! That is just so *cute*.

But who? *Who is it?*

I figured there was only one way to find out, so I wrote back right away:

```
FtLouie: Dear Friend, I got your letter. Thank
you very much. Thanks also for the get-well
wishes.
WHO ARE YOU? (I swear I won't tell anyone.)
Mia
```

I sat around for half an hour, hoping he would write back, but he never did.

WHO IS IT??? WHO IS IT??

I have GOT to get well by tomorrow so I can go to school

and figure out who Jo-C-rox is. Otherwise, I will go mental, just like Mel Gibson's girlfriend in *Hamlet*, and I'll end up floating in my Lanz of Salzburg nightie in the Hudson with the rest of the medical waste.

Friday, October 23, Algebra

I AM BETTER!!!!!

Well, actually, I don't feel all that great, but I don't care. I don't have a temperature, so my mother had no choice but to let me go to school. There was no way I was going to lie in bed another day. Not with Jo-C-rox out there somewhere, possibly loving me.

But so far, nothing. I mean, we swung by Lilly's in the limo and picked her up, as usual, and Michael was with her and all, but by the casual way he said hello to me, you would hardly have known that he'd ever sent me a get-well e-mail signed *Love, Michael,* let alone ever called me the Josiest girl he's ever met. It is so very clear that he isn't Jo-C-rox.

And that *Love* at the end of his e-mail was just a platonic *Love.* I mean, Michael's *Love* obviously didn't mean he actually *loves* me.

Not that I ever thought he did. Or might. Love me, I mean.

He did walk me to my locker though. This was extremely nice of him. Granted, we were in the middle of a heated discussion about last week's episode of *Buffy the Vampire Slayer,* but still, no boy has ever walked me to my locker before. Boris Pelkowski meets Lilly at the front doors to the school and walks her to her locker *every single morning,* and has done ever since the day she agreed to be his girlfriend.

And OK, I admit that Boris Pelkowski is a mouth-breather who continues to tuck his sweaters into his trousers despite my frequent hints that in America, this is considered a Glamour Don't. But still, he is a boy. And it is always cool to have a boy – even one who wears a brace – walk you to your locker. I know I have Lars, but it's different having your *bodyguard* walk you to your locker, as opposed to an actual *boy.*

I just noticed that Lana Weinberger has purchased all new notebook binders. I guess she threw away the old ones. She had written *Mrs Josh Richter* all over them, then crossed it out when she and Josh broke up. They are back together now. I guess she's willing once again to have her identity obfuscated by taking her husband's name, since she's already got three *I Love Joshes* and seven *Mrs Josh Richters* on her Algebra notebook alone.

Before class started, Lana was telling everyone who would listen about some party she is going to tonight. None of us are invited, of course. It's a party given by one of Josh's friends.

I never get invited to parties like that. You know, like the ones in movies about teenagers, where somebody's parents go out of town, so everybody in the school comes over with kegs of beer and trashes the house?

I do not actually know anybody who lives in a house. Just apartment buildings. And if you start trashing an apartment, you can bet the people next door will call the doorman to complain. And that could get you in major trouble with the co-op board.

I don't suppose Lana has ever considered these things, however.

The 3rd power of x is called cube of x
The 2nd power of x is squared

Ode to the View from the Window in My Algebra Class

Sun-warmed concrete benches
next to tables with built-in checkerboards
and the graffiti left by hundreds
before us in
Day-Glo spray paint:

Joanne Loves Richie
Punx Rule
Nuke Fags and Lesbos
And
Amber Is A Slut.

The dead leaves and plastic bags scatter
in the breeze from the park
and men in business suits try to keep the
last few remaining strands of hair covering
their pink bald spots.
Cigarette packets and used-up chewing gum
coat the grey sidewalk.

And I think
What does it matter
that it is not a linear equation if any variable is raised
to a power?
We're all just going to die anyway.

Friday, October 23, World Civ.

List five basic types of government

monarchy
aristocracy
dictatorship
oligarchy
democracy

List five people who could conceivably be Jo-C-rox

Michael Moscovitz (I wish)
Boris Pelkowski (please no)
Mr Gianini (in a misguided attempt to cheer me up)
My dad (ditto)
That weird boy I see sometimes in the cafeteria who gets so
upset whenever they serve chilli and there's corn in it (please
please no)

AAAAARRRRRGGGGGGGHHHHHH!!!!!!!!!!!!

Friday, October 23, G & T

It turns out that since I've been gone, Boris has started learning some new music on his violin. Right now he is playing a concerto by someone named Bartok.

And let me tell you, that's exactly how it sounds. Even though we locked him and his violin into the supply closet, it isn't doing any good. You can't even hear yourself think. Michael had to go to the nurse's office for aspirin.

But before he left, I tried to steer the conversation in the direction of mail. You know, casually, and all.

Just in case.

Anyway, Lilly was talking about her show, *Lilly Tells It Like It Is*, and I asked her if she's still getting a lot of fan mail – one of her biggest fans, her stalker Norman, sends her free stuff all the time, with the understanding that he wants her to show her bare feet on the air: Norman is a foot fetishist.

Then I mentioned that I'd received some *intriguing* mail lately . . .

Then I looked at Michael real fast, to see how he responded.

But he didn't even glance up from his laptop.

And now he is back from the nurse's office. She wouldn't give him any aspirin because it is a violation of the school drug code. So I gave him some of my codeine cough syrup. He says it cleared his headache right up.

But that might also have been because Boris knocked over a can of paint thinner with his bow and we had to let him out of the supply closet. He was hyperventilating too hard to continue playing.

Here is what I have to do

1. Stop thinking so much about Jo-C-rox.
2. Ditto Michael Moscovitz.
3. Ditto my mother and her reproductive issues.
4. Ditto my interview tomorrow with Beverly Bellerieve.
5. Ditto Grandmere.
6. Have more self-confidence.
7. Stop biting off fake fingernails.
8. Self-actualize.
9. Pay more attention in Algebra.
10. Wash PE shorts.

Later on Friday

Talk about embarrassing! Principal Gupta found out somehow about my giving Michael some of my codeine cough syrup, and I got called out of Bio. and sent to her office to discuss my trafficking of controlled substances on school grounds!

Oh my God! I really and truly thought I was going to get expelled then and there.

I explained to her about the aspirin and the Bartok, but Principal Gupta was totally unsympathetic. Even when I brought up all the kids who stand outside the school and smoke. Do they get in trouble for bumming cigarettes off one another?

And what about the cheerleaders and their diet pills?

But Principal Gupta said cigarettes and diet pills are different from narcotics. She took my codeine cough syrup away and told me I could have it back after school. She also told me not to bring it to school on Monday.

She doesn't have to worry. I was so embarrassed about the whole thing, I am seriously considering never coming back to school at all, let alone on Monday.

I don't see why I can't be home-schooled, like the boys from Hanson. Look how they turned out.

Homework:

Algebra: problems on pg. 129
English: describe an experience that moved you profoundly
World Civ.: two-hundred words on the rise of the Taliban in Afghanistan
Gifted and Talented: please
French: devoirs – les notes grammaticals: 141–143
Biology: central nervous system

ENGLISH JOURNAL

My Favourite Things

Food: *Vegetarian lasagne.*

Movie: *My favourite movie of all time is one I first saw on HBO when I was twelve. It has remained my favourite movie in spite of my friends' and family's efforts to introduce me to so-called finer examples of cinematic art. But quite frankly, I think that* Dirty Dancing, *starring Patrick Swayze and a pre-nose job Jennifer Grey, has everything films like* Breathless *and* September, *created by supposed 'auteurs' of the medium, lack. For instance,* Dirty Dancing *takes place at a summer resort. Movies that take place in resorts (other good examples include* Cocktail *and* Aspen Extreme) *are just plain better, I've noticed, than other movies. Also,* Dirty Dancing *has dancing. Dancing in movies is always good. Think how much better Oscar-Award-winning films like* The English Patient *or* Schindler's List *would be if they had dancing in them. I am always so much less bored at the movies when there are people dancing on the screen. So all I have to say to the many, many people who disagree with me about* Dirty Dancing *is:*
Nobody Puts Baby in the Corner.

TV Show: *My favourite TV show is* Baywatch. *I know people think it is very lame and sexist, but it actually isn't. The boys are as scantily clad as the girls and, in the later episodes at least, a woman is in charge of the whole life-guarding operation. And the truth of the* *matter is, whenever I watch this show, I feel happy. That is because I know whatever jam Hobie gets into, whether it is giant electric eels or emerald smugglers, Mitch will get him out of it, and everything will be done to an excellent soundtrack, and with stunning shots of the ocean. I wish there was a Mitch in my life to make everything all right at the end of the day. Also that my breasts were as big as Carmen Electra's.*

Book: *My favourite book is called* IQ 83. *It is by the bestselling author of* The Swarm, *Arthur Herzog.* IQ 83 *is about a bunch of doctors who mess around with DNA, and they unwittingly cause an accident that makes everyone in the world lose a bunch of IQ points and start acting dumb. Seriously! Even the president of the United States. He ends up drooling like an idiot! And it's up to Dr James Healey to save the country from being populated by a bunch of overweight morons who do nothing but watch Jerry Springer and eat Ho Hos all day. This book has never gotten the attention it should receive. It hasn't even been made into a movie! This is a literary travesty.*

Even later on Friday

What am I supposed to do about this stupid English journal assignment, 'Describe an experience that moved you profoundly'? I am so sure. What do I write about? The time I walked into the kitchen and found my Algebra teacher standing there in his underwear? That didn't move me, exactly, but it was certainly an experience.

Or should I talk about the time my dad spilled his guts out about how it turns out I am the heir to the throne of the principality of Genovia? That was an experience, although I don't know if it was profound, and even though I was crying, I don't think it was because I was moved. I was just mad nobody had told me before. I mean, I guess I can understand that it might be embarrassing for him to have to admit to the Genovian people that he had a child out of wedlock, but to hide that fact for fourteen years? Talk about denial.

My Bio. partner Kenny, who also has Mrs Spears for English, says he is going to write about his family's trip to India last summer. He contracted cholera there, and nearly died. As he lay in his hospital bed in that far-off foreign land, he realized that we are only on this planet for a short while, and that it is vital we use every moment we have left as if it were our last. That is why Kenny is devoting his life to finding a cure for cancer, and promoting Japanese anime.

Kenny is so lucky. If only I could contract a potentially fatal disease.

I am beginning to realize that the only thing profound about my life so far is its complete and utter lack of profundity.

Jefferson Market
The freshest produce – guaranteed
Fast, Free Delivery

Order no. 2764

1 package soybean curd
1 bottle wheat germ
1 loaf whole-grain bread
5 grapefruits
12 oranges
1 bunch bananas
1 package brewer's yeast
1 container skimmed milk
1 container orange juice (not from concentrate)
1 pound butter
Dozen eggs
1 bag unsalted sunflower seeds
1 box whole-grain cereal
Toilet paper
Cotton buds

Deliver To: Mia Thermopolis, 1005 Thompson Street, Loft 4A

Saturday, October 24, 2 p.m., Grandmere's suite, The Plaza

I am sitting here waiting for my interview. In addition to my throat hurting, I feel like I am going to throw up. Maybe my bronchitis has turned into the flu, or something. Maybe the falafel I ordered in for dinner last night was made from rotten chick peas, or something.

Or maybe I'm just totally nervous, since this interview is going to be broadcast into an estimated twenty-two million homes on Monday night.

Although I find it very hard to believe that twenty-two million families could possibly be interested in anything *I* have to say.

I read that when Prince William is interviewed, he gets the questions about a week before, so he has time to think up really smart and incisive answers. Apparently, members of the Genovian royal family do not get extended that same courtesy. Not that, even with a week's worth of notice, I could ever think of anything smart and incisive. Well, OK, maybe smart, but definitely not incisive.

Well, probably not even smart, either, depending on what they ask.

So I am sitting here and I really do feel like I am going to throw up, and I wish I could hurry up and get this over with. It was supposed to start two hours ago.

But Grandmere isn't satisfied with the way the cosmetic technician (make-up lady) did my eyes. She says I look like a *poulet*. That means hooker in French. Or chicken. But when my grandmere says it, it always means hooker.

Why can't I have a nice, normal Grandma, who makes borchst and thinks I look wonderful no matter what I have on? Lilly's grandma has never said the word hooker in her life, even in Yiddish. I know that for a fact.

So the make-up lady had to go down to the hotel gift shop to see if they have any blue eyeshadow. Grandmere wants blue, because she says it matches my eyes. Except that my eyes are grey. I wonder if Grandmere is colour blind.

That would explain a lot.

I met Beverly Bellerieve. The one good thing about all this is that she actually seems semi-human. She told me that if she asked anything I felt was too personal or embarrassing, I could just say I don't want to answer. Isn't that nice?

Plus she is very beautiful. You should see my dad. I can already tell that Beverly is going to be this week's girlfriend. Well, she's better than the women he usually hangs around with. At least Beverly looks as if she probably isn't wearing a thong. And that her brain stem is fully functional.

So, considering that Beverly Bellerieve turns out to be so nice and all, you'd think I wouldn't be so nervous.

And truthfully, I'm not so sure it's just the interview that's making me feel like I'm going to hurl. It's actually something my dad said to me, when I came in. It was the first time I'd seen him since he'd come over to the loft while I was sick. Anyway, he asked me how I was feeling and all, and I lied and said fine, and then he went, 'Mia, is your Algebra teacher—'

And I was all, 'Is my Algebra teacher what?' thinking he was going to ask me if Mr Gianini was teaching me about parallel numbers.

But that is so totally NOT what he asked me. Instead, he asked me, 'Is your Algebra teacher living in the loft?'

Well, I was so shocked, I didn't know what to say. Because of course Mr Gianini isn't living there. Not really.

But he will be. And probably pretty shortly too.

So I just went, 'Um, no.'

And my dad looked relieved! He actually looked relieved! So how is he going to look when he finds out the *truth*?

It is very hard to concentrate on the fact that I am about to be interviewed by this world-renowned television news journalist, when all I can think about is how my poor dad is going to feel when he finds out my mother is marrying my Algebra teacher, and also having his baby. Not that I think my dad still loves my mom, or anything. It's just that, as Lilly once pointed out, his chronic bed-hopping is a clear indication that he has some serious intimacy issues.

And with Grandmere as a mother, you can see why that might be.

I think he really would like to have with someone what my mom has with Mr Gianini. Who knows how he is going to take the news about their impending marriage when my mom finally works up the guts to tell him? He might completely freak out. He might even want me to come live with him in Genovia, to comfort him in his grief!

And of course I will have to say yes, because he is my dad and I love him and all.

Except that I really don't want to live in Genovia. I mean, I would miss Lilly and Tina Hakim Baba and all my other friends. And what about Fat Louie? Would I get to keep him, or what? He is very well behaved (except when it comes to ingesting socks, and that whole thing with the sparkly objects) and if there was a rodent problem in the castle, he would totally solve it. But what if they don't let cats in the palace? I mean, he hasn't had his claws removed, so if there's any sort of valuable furniture or tapestries or whatever, you can pretty much kiss them goodbye . . .

Mr G and my mom are already talking about where his stuff is going to go when he moves into the loft. And Mr G has some really cool sounding stuff. Like a foozball table, a drum kit (who knew Mr Gianini was *musical*?) a pinball machine, AND a thirty-six inch flat-screen TV.

I am not even kidding. He is *way* cooler than I ever thought.

If I move to Genovia, I will totally miss out on having my own foozball table.

But if I don't move to Genovia, who will comfort my poor dad in his chronic loneliness?

Oops, the cosmetic technician is back with the blue eye-shadow.

I swear I am going to heave. Good thing I was too nervous to eat anything all day.

Saturday, October 24, 7 p.m.,
On the way to Lilly's house

Oh, God, oh, God, oh, God, oh, God, oh, God, OH, GOD.

I screwed up. I REALLY screwed up.

I don't know what happened. I honestly don't. Everything was going along fine. I mean, that Beverly Bellerieve, she's so . . . *nice*. I was really, really nervous, and she did her very best to try to calm me down.

Still, I think I did some major babbling.

Think??? I KNOW I did.

And because of it, my poor Dad . . . oh, my poor, poor Dad.

He knows now. About my mom and Mr G, I mean.

I didn't mean for it to happen. I really didn't. I don't even know how it slipped out. I was just so nervous and hyper, and there were those lights and that microphone and everything. I felt like . . . I don't know. Like I was back in Principal Gupta's office, living through that whole codeine cough syrup thing again.

So when Beverly Bellerieve went, 'Mia, didn't you have some exciting news recently?' I totally freaked out. Part of me was like, How did she know? And another part of me was like, Millions of people are going to see this. Act happy.

So I went, 'Oh. Yes. Well, I'm pretty excited. I've always wanted to be a big sister. But they don't really want to make a big deal out of it, you know. It's just going to be a very small ceremony at City Hall, with me as their witness—'

That's when my dad dropped the glass of Perrier he'd been drinking. Then Grandmere started hyperventilating and had to breathe into a paper bag.

303

And I sat there going, Oh, my God. Oh, my God, what have I done?

Of course it turned out that Beverly Bellerieve hadn't been referring to my mother's pregnancy at all. Of course not. How could she have known about it?

What she'd actually been referring to, of course, was my F in Algebra being raised to a D.

I tried to get up and go to my dad to comfort him, since I could see he'd sunk into a chair and had his head in his hands. But I was all tangled up in my microphone wires. It had taken about half an hour for the sound guys to get the wires right, and I didn't want to mess them up, or anything, but I could see that my dad's shoulders were all slumped over, and I was sure he was crying, just like he always does at the end of *Free Willy*, though he tries to pretend it's just allergies.

Beverly, seeing this, made a slashing motion with her hand to the camera guys, and very nicely helped me get untangled.

But when I finally got to my dad, I saw that he wasn't crying . . .

But he certainly didn't look too good. He didn't sound very good, either, when he croaked for someone to bring him a whiskey.

After three or four gulps, though, he got a little of his colour back. Which is more than I can say for Grandmere. I don't think she will ever recover. Last time I saw her, she was downing a Sidecar that someone had dropped some Alka-Seltzer tablets into.

I don't even want to think about what my mom is going to say when she finds out what I've done. I mean, even though my dad said not to worry, that he'll explain to Mom what happened, I don't know. He had kind of a weird look

304

on his face. I hope he doesn't plan on popping Mr G one in the pie hole.

Me and my big mouth. My HUGE, GROTESQUE, DISPROPORTIONATELY MASSIVE mouth.

There's no telling what else I said, once the interview got underway again. I was so completely freaked out by that first thing, I can't remember a single other thing Beverly Bellerieve might have asked.

My dad has assured me – after three whiskies: I counted – that he's not in the least jealous of Mr Gianini, that he is very happy for my mother, and that he thinks she and Mr G make a great couple.

Well, that's what he *said*, anyway.

Thank God I am going straight from the hotel to Lilly's. She is having us all over to film next week's episode of her show. I think I'll see if I can spend the night.

The coward's way out, I know. But maybe this way, by the time my mom sees me tomorrow, she and Dad will have had their little talk. And maybe Mom will have had time to process the whole thing, and will have forgiven me.

I hope.

Sunday, October 25, 2 a.m., Lilly's bedroom

OK, I just have one question: Why does it always have to go from bad to worse for me?

I mean, apparently it is not enough that:

1. I was born lacking any sort of mammary growth gland.
2. My feet are as long as a normal person's thigh.
3. I'm the sole heir to the throne of a European principality.
4. My grade point average is still slipping in spite of everything.
5. I have a secret admirer who will not declare himself.
6. My mother is pregnant with my Algebra teacher's baby, and
7. all of America is going to know it after Monday night's broadcast of my exclusive interview on *TwentyFour/Seven*.

No, in addition to all of that, I happen to be the only one of my friends who has yet to be French kissed.

Seriously. For next week's show, Lilly insisted on shooting what she calls a Scorsesian confessional, in which she hopes to illustrate the degenerate lows to which today's youth has sunk. So she made us all confess to the camera our worst sins, and it turns out Shameeka, Tina Hakim Baba, Ling Su, and Lilly have ALL had boys' tongues in their mouths. *All of them.*

Except for me.

OK, I'm not so surprised about Shameeka. Ever since she got breasts over the summer, boys have been buzzing around her like she was the newest version of Lara Croft, or something. And Ling Su and that Clifford guy she has been seeing are way into each other.

But Tina? I mean, she has a bodyguard, just like me. When has *she* ever been alone long enough with a boy for him to French her?

And Lilly? Excuse me, but Lilly, MY BEST FRIEND? Who I thought tells me everything (even though I don't necessarily always return the favour)? She has known the touch of a boy's tongue upon her own, and she never thought to tell me until NOW????

Boris Pelkowski is apparently a much smoother operator than you would suspect, considering that whole sweater thing.

I am sorry, but that is just sick. Sick, sick, sick, sick. I would rather die a dried-up, never-been-kissed old maid than be French kissed by Boris Pelkowski. I mean, he always has FOOD in his brace. And not just any food, either, but usually weird, multi-coloured foods like Gummi bears and Jelly Babies.

Lilly says he takes it out when they kiss though.

God, I am such a reject.

And since I have never been French kissed, and had nothing good to confess on the show, Lilly decided to punish me by giving me a Dare. You know, as in Truth or Dare? Since I had no Truth, I got a Dare:

Lilly dared me I wouldn't drop an eggplant onto the sidewalk from her sixteenth-storey bedroom window.

And I said I most certainly would, even though of course, I totally didn't want to. I mean, how stupid. Somebody could seriously get hurt. I am all for illustrating the degenerate lows to which America's teens have sunk, but I wouldn't want anybody to get their head bashed in.

But what could I do? It was a Dare. I had to go along with it. I mean, it's bad enough I've never been Frenched. I don't want to be branded a coward too.

And I couldn't exactly stand there and go, well, all right, I may never have been French kissed by a boy, but I have been the recipient of a love letter that was written by one. A boy, I mean.

Because what if Michael is Jo-C-rox? I mean, I know he probably isn't, but . . . well, what if he is? I don't want Lilly to know. Any more than I want her to know about my interview with Beverly Bellerieve, or the fact that my mom and Mr G are getting married. I am trying very hard to be a normal girl, and frankly, none of the aforementioned can be even remotely construed as normal.

I guess the knowledge that somewhere in the world there is a boy who likes me gave me a sense of empowerment – something I certainly could have used during my interview with Beverly Bellerieve, but whatever. I may not be able to form a coherent sentence when there is a television camera aimed in my direction, but I am at least capable, I decided, of throwing an eggplant out the window.

Lilly was shocked. I had never accepted a Dare like that before.

I can't really explain why I did it. Maybe I was just trying to live up to my new reputation as a very Josie-ish type of girl.

Or maybe I was more scared of what Lilly would try to make me do if I said no. Once she made me run up and down the hallway naked. Not the hallway in the Moscovitzes' apartment, either. The hallway *outside* of it.

Whatever my reasons, I soon found myself sneaking past the Drs Moscovitz, who were lounging around in sweatpants in the living room, with stacks of important medical journals all around their chairs – though Lilly's father was reading a copy of *Sports Illustrated*, and Lilly's mom was reading *Cosmo* – and creeping into the kitchen.

'Hello, Mia,' Lilly's father called from behind his magazine. 'How are you doing?'

'Um,' I said, nervously. 'Fine.'

'And how is your mother?' Lilly's mother asked.

'She's fine,' I said.

'Is she still seeing your Algebra teacher in a social capacity?'

'Um, yes, Dr Moscovitz,' I said. More than you know.

'And are you still amenable to the relationship?' Lilly's father wanted to know.

'Um,' I said. 'Yes, Dr Moscovitz.' I didn't think it would be appropriate to mention the whole thing about how my mom is having Mr G's baby. I mean, I was supposed to be on a Dare, after all. You aren't supposed to stop for psychoanalysis when you are on a Dare.

'Well, tell her hello from me,' Lilly's mother said. 'We can't wait until her next show. It's at the Mary Boone Gallery, right?'

'Yes, ma'am,' I said. The Moscovitzes are big fans of my mother's work. One of her best paintings, *Woman Enjoying a Quick Snack at Starbucks*, is hanging in their dining room.

'We'll be there,' Lilly's father said.

Then he and his wife turned back to their magazines, so I hurried into the kitchen.

I found an eggplant in the vegetable crisper. I hid it under my shirt so the Drs Moscovitz wouldn't see me sneaking back into their daughter's room holding a giant ovoid fruit, something sure to cause unwanted questions. While I carried it, I thought, This is how my mother is going to look in a few months. It wasn't a very comforting thought. I don't think my mother is going to dress any more conservatively pregnant than she did not pregnant.

Then, while Lilly narrated gravely into the microphone

about how Mia Thermopolis was about to strike a blow for good girls everywhere, and Shameeka filmed, I opened up the window, made sure no innocent bystanders were below, and then . . .

'Bombs away,' I said, like in the movies.

It *was* kind of cool seeing this huge purple eggplant – it was the size of a football – tumbling over and over in the air as it fell. There are enough street lamps on Fifth Avenue, where the Moscovitzes live, for us to see it as it plummeted downwards, even though it was night. Down and down the eggplant went, past the windows of all the psychoanalysts and investment bankers (the only people who can afford apartments in Lilly's building) until suddenly—

SPLAT!

The eggplant hit the sidewalk.

Only it didn't just hit the sidewalk. It *exploded* against the sidewalk, sending bits of eggplant flying everywhere – mostly over an M1 city bus that was driving by at the time, but quite a lot over this Jaguar that had been idling nearby.

While I was leaning out the window, admiring the splatter pattern the eggplant's pulp had made against the street and sidewalk, the driver's door of the Jaguar opened up and a man got out from behind the wheel, just as the doorman to Lilly's building stepped out from beneath the awning over the front doors and looked up—

Suddenly, someone threw an arm around my waist and yanked me backwards, right off my feet.

'Get down!' Michael hissed, pulling me down to the parquet.

We all ducked. Well, Lilly, Michael, Shameeka, Ling Su, and Tina ducked. I was already on the floor.

Where had Michael come from? I hadn't even known he was home – and I'd asked, believe me, on account of the

310

whole running down the hallway naked thing. Just in case, and all. But Lilly had said he was at a lecture on quasars over at Columbia and wouldn't be home for hours.

'Are you guys stupid, or what?' Michael wanted to know. 'Don't you know, besides the fact that it's a good way to kill someone, it's also against the law to drop things out the window in New York City?'

'Oh, Michael,' Lilly said, disgustedly. 'Grow up. It was just a common garden vegetable.'

'I'm serious.' Michael looked mad. 'If anyone saw Mia do that just now, she could be arrested.'

'No, she couldn't,' Lilly said. 'She's a minor.'

'She could still go to juvenile court. You better not be planning on airing that footage on your show,' Michael said.

Oh my God, Michael was defending my honour! Or at least trying to make sure I didn't end up in juvenile court. It was just so sweet. So . . . well, Jo-C-rox of him.

Lilly went, 'I most certainly am.'

'Well, you better edit out the parts that show Mia's face.'

Lilly stuck her chin out. 'No way.'

'Lilly, everybody knows who Mia is. If you air that segment, it will be all over the news that the Princess of Genovia was caught on tape dropping projectiles out the window of her friend's high-rise apartment. Get a clue, will you?'

Michael, I noticed with regret, had let go of my waist.

'Lilly, Michael's right,' Tina Hakim Baba said. 'We better edit that part out. Mia doesn't need any more publicity than she has already.'

And Tina didn't even *know* about the *TwentyFour/Seven* thing.

Lilly got up and stomped back towards the window. She started to lean out – checking, I guess, to see whether the doorman and the owner of the Jaguar were still there – but Michael jerked her back.

'Rule number one,' he said. 'If you insist on dropping something out the window, never, ever check to see if anybody is standing down there, looking up. They will see you look out and figure out what apartment you are in. Then you will be blamed for dropping whatever it was. Because no one but the guilty party would be looking out the window under such circumstances.'

'Wow, Michael,' Shameeka said, admiringly. 'You sound like you've done this before.'

Not only that. He sounded like Dirty Harry.

Which was just how I felt when I dropped that eggplant out the window. Like Dirty Harry.

And it had felt good.

But not quite so good as having Michael rush to my defence like that.

Michael said, 'Let's just say I used to have a very keen interest in experimenting with the earth's gravitational pull.'

Wow. There is so much I don't know about Lilly's brother. Like he used to be a juvenile delinquent!

Could a computer genius/juvenile delinquent ever be interested in a flat-chested princess like myself? He did save my life tonight (well, OK: he saved me from possible community service).

It's not a French kiss, or a slow dance, or even an admission he's the author of that anonymous letter.

But it's a start.

Things To Do:

1. English journal.
2. Stop thinking about that stupid letter.
3. Ditto Michael Moscovitz.
4. Ditto the interview.
5. Ditto Mom.
6. Change cat litter.
7. Drop off laundry.
8. Get super. to put lock on bathroom door.
9. Buy: Dishwashing liquid.
      Cotton buds.
      Canvas stretchers (for Mom).
      That stuff you put on your fingernails that makes
      them taste bad.
      Something nice for Mr Gianini to say welcome to
      the family.
      Something nice for Dad to say don't worry, some-
      day you will find true love too.

Sunday, October 25, 7 p.m.

I was really nervous that when I got home, my mom was going to be way disappointed in me. You know, for spilling the beans to my dad about her and Mr G's zygote.

Not that she would yell at me, or anything. My mom is really not a yelling kind of person.

But she does get disappointed in me, like when I do something stupid like not call and tell her where I am if I am out late (which, given my social life, or lack thereof, hardly ever happens).

But on this I really did screw up big-time. It was really really hard to leave the Moscovitzes apartment this morning and come home, knowing the potential for disappointment that awaited me there.

Of course, it's always hard to leave Lilly's. Every time I go there, it's like taking a vacation from my real life. Lilly has such a nice, normal family. Well, as normal as two psycho-analysts whose son has his own webzine and whose daughter has her own cable access television show can be. At the Moscovitzes, the biggest problem is always whose turn is it to walk Pavlov, their sheltie, or whether to order Chinese or Thai take-out.

At my house, the problems always seem to be a little more complicated.

But of course when I finally did work up the courage to come home, my mom was totally happy to see me. She gave me a big hug, and told me not to worry about what had happened at the interview taping. She said Dad had talked to her, and that she completely understood. She even tried to get me to believe that it was *her* fault for not having said anything to him right away.

314

Which I know isn't true – it's still my fault, me and my idiot mouth – but it was nice to hear, just the same.

So then we had a fun time sitting around planning her and Mr G's wedding. My mom decided Halloween would be an excellent day to get married, because the idea of marriage is so scary.

Since it was Halloween, my mom thought that instead of a wedding dress, she would go to the courthouse dressed as King Kong. She wants me to dress up as the Empire State Building (God knows I am tall enough). She was trying to convince Mr G to dress as Fay Ray when the phone rang, and she said it was Lilly, for me.

I was surprised, since I had just left Lilly's, but I figured I must have left my toothbrush there, or something.

But that wasn't why she was calling. That wasn't why she was calling at all.

As I found out when she demanded, tartly, 'What's this I hear about you being interviewed on *TwentyFour/Seven* this week?'

I was stunned. I actually thought Lilly had ESP or something, and had been hiding it from me all these years. I went, 'How did you know?'

'Because there are commercials announcing it every five minutes, dorkus.'

I switched on the TV. Lilly was right! No matter what station you put it on, there are ads urging viewers to tune in tomorrow night to see Beverly Bellerieve's exclusive interview with 'America's Royal, Princess Mia'.

Oh my God. My life is so over.

'So why didn't you tell me you were going to be on TV?' Lilly wanted to know.

'I don't know,' I said, feeling like I was going to throw up all over again. 'It just happened yesterday. It's no big deal.'

Lilly started yelling so loud I had to hold the phone away from my ear.

'*No big deal*??? *You were interviewed by Beverly Bellerieve and it was no big deal*??? *Don't you realize that Beverly Bellerieve is one of America's most popular and hardest-hitting journalists and that she is my all-time role model and hero*???'

When she finally calmed down enough to let me talk, I tried to explain to Lilly that I had no idea about Beverly's journalistic merits, much less that she was Lilly's all-time role model and hero. She just seemed, I said, like a very nice lady.

But by that time, Lilly was totally fed up with me. She said, 'The only reason I'm not mad at you is that tomorrow you are going to tell me every single little detail about it.'

'I am?'

Then I asked a more important question. 'Why should you be mad at me?' I really wanted to know.

'Because you gave me exclusive first rights to interview you,' Lilly pointed out. 'For *Lilly Tells It Like It Is.*'

I have no memory of this, but I guess it must be true.

Grandmere, I could see from the ads, had been right about the blue eyeshadow. Which was surprising, because she's never been right about much else.

Top Five Things Grandmere Has Been Wrong About

1. That my dad would settle down when he met the right woman.
2. That Fat Louie would suck out my breath as I slept and suffocate me.
3. That if I didn't attend an all-girls school, I would contract a social disease.
4. That if I got my ears pierced, they would get infected and I would die of blood poisoning.
5. That my figure would fill out by the time I hit my teens.

Sunday, October 25, 8 p.m.

You will not believe what got delivered to our house while I was gone. I insisted it was a mistake, until the delivery guy showed me the attached. I am going to kill my mother.

Jefferson Market
The freshest produce – guaranteed
Fast, Free Delivery

Order no. 2803

1 package microwave cheese popcorn
1 case Yoo Hoo chocolate drink
1 jar cocktail olives
1 bag oreos
1 container fudge ripple ice cream
1 package all-beef hot dogs
1 package hot dog buns
1 package string cheese
1 bag milk chocolate chips
1 bag barbecue potato chips
1 container beer nuts
1 bag Milano cookies
1 jar sweet gherkins
Toilet paper
6 pound ham

Deliver To: Helen Thermopolis, 1005 Thompson Street, Loft 4A

Hasn't she the slightest idea how adversely all this saturated fat and sodium will affect her unborn child? I can see that Mr Gianini and I will have to be hypervigilant for the next nine months. I have given everything except the toilet paper to Ronnie, next door. Ronnie says she is going to hand out the junkiest stuff to any trick-or-treaters who might come by. She has to watch her figure since her sex change operation. Now that she's taking all those oestrogen injections, everything goes right to her hips.

Sunday, October 25, 9 p.m.

Another e-mail from Jo-C-rox!!!!!!!!!!!!!!!
   This one went:

```
JoCrox: Hi, Mia. I just saw the ad for your
interview. You look great. Sorry I can't tell
you who I am. I'm surprised you haven't guessed
by now. Now stop checking your e-mail and get
to work on your Algebra homework. I know how
you are about that. It's one of the things I
like best about you.
Your Friend
```

   OK, this is going to drive me insane. Who could it be? Who????
   I wrote back right away:

```
FtLouie: WHO ARE YOU????????????????????????????
????????????????????????????????????????????????
```

I was hoping that would get the point across, but he so totally did not write back. I was trying to figure out who I know who knows that I always wait until the last minute to do my Algebra homework. Unfortunately, though, I think *everyone* knows it.

   But the person who knows it best of all is Michael. I mean, doesn't he help me every day with my Algebra homework in G & T??? And he is always chastising me for not putting my carry overs in straight enough lines and all of that.

   If ONLY Jo-C-rox were Michael Moscovitz. If only, if only, if ONLY.

But I'm sure it isn't. That would simply be too good to be true. And really excellent things like that only happen to girls like Lana Weinberger, never to girls like me.

Knowing my luck, it will totally be that weird chilli guy. Or some guy who breathes out of his mouth, like Boris. WHY ME??????????????????????????

Monday, October 26, G & T

Unfortunately, it appears that Lilly is not the only one who noticed the ads for tonight's broadcast.

Everybody is talking about it. I mean, EVERYBODY.

And everybody says they are going to watch it.

Which means by tomorrow, everyone will know about my mom and Mr Gianini.

Not that I care. There is nothing to be ashamed of. Nothing at all. Pregnancy is a beautiful and natural thing.

Still, I wish I could remember more about what Beverly and I talked about. Because I am sure my mom's impending marriage was not all we discussed. And I am totally worried I said other stuff that will come out sounding stupid.

I have decided that I should look more closely into that home-schooling idea, just in case . . .

Tina Hakim Baba told me that her mother, who was a supermodel in England before she married Mr Hakim Baba, used to get interviewed all the time. Mrs Hakim Baba says that as a courtesy, the interviewers would send her a copy of the tape before it aired, so if she had any objections she could straighten them out before the thing was broadcast.

This sounded like a good idea, so at lunch I called my dad in his hotel suite and asked him if he could get Beverly to do that for me.

He said, 'Hold on,' and asked her. It turns out Beverly was right there! In my dad's hotel room! On a Monday afternoon!

What is *with* my parents? They are completely oversexed. *I* am the teenager. *I* am supposed to be the one with the raging hormones.

But am I getting any action?

That would be a big N-O.

Then, to my utter mortification, Beverly Bellerieve actually got on the phone and went, 'What's the matter, Mia?'

I told her I was still pretty nervous about the interview, and was there any chance I could see a copy of it before it aired.

Beverly said a bunch of stuff about how adorable I was and how that wouldn't be necessary. Now that I think about it, I can't remember exactly what she said, but I just got this overwhelming feeling that everything would be just fine.

Beverly is just one of those people who make you feel good about yourself. I don't know how she does it.

No wonder my dad hasn't let her out of his hotel room since Saturday.

Two cars, one going north at 40 mph and one going south at 50 mph, leave town at the same time. In how many hours will they be 360 miles apart?

Why does it matter? I mean, really.

Monday, October 26, Bio.

Mrs Sing, our Biology teacher, says it is physiologically impossible to die of either boredom or embarrassment, but I know that isn't true, because I am experiencing heart failure right now.

That is because after G & T, Michael and Lilly and I were walking down the hall together, since Lilly was going to Psych. and I was going to Bio. and Michael was going to Trig., which are all right across the hall from each other, and Lana Weinberger walked right up to us – RIGHT UP TO MICHAEL AND ME – held up two of her fingers and waggled them at us, and went, 'Are you two going out?'

I could seriously die right now. I mean, you should have seen Michael's face. It was like his head was about to explode, he turned that red.

And I'm sure I wasn't all that pale myself.

Lilly didn't help by letting out this giant horse laugh and going, 'As if!'

Which caused Lana and her cronies to burst out laughing too.

I don't see what's so funny about it. Those girls obviously haven't seen Michael Moscovitz with his shirt off. Believe me, I have.

I guess because the whole thing was so ridiculous and everything, Michael just kind of ignored it. But I'm telling you, it's getting harder and harder for me not to ask him if he is Jo-C-rox. Like I keep trying to find ways to work *Josie and the Pussycats* into the conversation. I know I shouldn't, but I just can't help it!

I don't know how much longer I can stand being the only girl in the ninth grade who doesn't have a boyfriend.

Homework:

Algebra: problems on pg. 135
English: 'Make the most of yourself, for that is all there is of you.' Ralph Waldo Emerson
Write feelings about this quote in journal.
World Civ.: questions at the end of chapter nine
Gifted and Talented: N/A
French: plan an itinerary for a make-believe trip to Paris
Biology: Kenny's doing it

Remind Mom to make appointment with licensed geneticist. Could she or Mr G be a carrier for the genetic mutation Tay-Sachs? It is common in Jews of Eastern European origin and in French Canadians. Are there any French-Canadians in our family? FIND OUT!!

Monday, October 26, After school

I never thought I would say this, but I am worried about Grandmere.

I am serious. I think she has officially lost it.

I walked into her hotel suite for my princess lesson today – since I am scheduled to have my official introduction to the Genovian people sometime in December, and Grandmere wants to be sure I don't insult any dignitaries or whatever during it – and guess what Grandmere was doing?

Consulting with the royal Genovian event planner about my mother's wedding.

I am totally serious. Grandmere had the guy flown in. All the way from Genovia!

There they sat at the dining table with this huge sheet of paper stretched in front of them, on which were drawn all these circles, and to which Grandmere was attaching these tiny slips of paper. She looked up when I came in and went, in French, 'Oh, Amelia. Very nice. Come and sit down. We have much to discuss, you and Vigo and I.'

I think my eyes must have been bulging out of my head. I couldn't believe what I was seeing. I was totally hoping what I was seeing was, you know . . . not what I was seeing.

'Grandmere,' I said. 'What are you *doing*?'

'Isn't it obvious?' Grandmere looked at me with her drawn-on eyebrows raised higher than ever. 'Planning a wedding, of course.'

I swallowed. This was bad. WAY bad.

'Um,' I said. 'Whose wedding, Grandmere?'

She looked at me very sarcastically. 'Guess,' she said.

I swallowed some more. 'Uh, Grandmere?' I said. 'Can I talk to you a minute? In private?'

But Grandmere just waved her hand and said, 'Anything

you have to say to me, you can say in front of Vigo. He has been dying to meet you. Vigo, her royal highness, the Princess Amelia Mignonette Grimaldi Renaldo.'

She left out the Thermopolis. She always does.

Vigo jumped up from the table and came rushing over to me. He was way shorter than me, about my mom's age, and had on a grey suit. He seemed to share my grandmother's penchant for purple, since he was wearing a lavender shirt in some kind of very shiny material, along with an equally shiny dark purple tie.

'Your Highness,' he gushed. 'The pleasure is all mine. So delightful finally to meet you.' To Grandmere, he said, 'You're right, madame, she has the Renaldo nose.'

'I told you, did I not?' Grandmere sounded smug. 'Uncanny.'

'Positively.' Vigo made a little picture frame out of his index fingers and thumbs and squinted at me through it.

'Pink,' he said, decidedly. 'Absolutely pink. I do so love a pink maid of honour.'

'It's really nice to meet you,' I said to Vigo. 'But the thing is, I think my mom and Mr Gianini were kind of planning on having a private ceremony down at—'

'City Hall.' Grandmere rolled her eyes. It is very scary when she does this, because of the black eyeliner she had tattooed all around her eyelids, so she wouldn't have to waste valuable time putting on make-up when she could be, you know, terrorizing someone. 'Yes, I heard all about it. It is ridiculous, of course. They will be married in the White and Gold Room at the Plaza, with a reception directly afterwards in the Grand Ballroom, as befits the mother of the future princess of Genovia.'

'Um,' I said. 'I really don't think that's what they want.'

Grandmere looked incredulous. 'Why ever not? Your

father is paying for it, of course. And I have been very generous. They are each allowed to invite twenty-five guests.'

I looked down at the sheet of paper in front of her. There were way more than fifty slips of paper in front of her.

Grandmere must have noticed the direction of my gaze, since she went, 'Well, I, of course, require at least three hundred.'

I stared at her. 'Three hundred what?'

'Guests, of course.'

I could see that I was way out of my depth. I was going to have to call for reinforcements if I hoped to get anywhere with her.

'Maybe,' I said, 'I should just give Dad a call and run this by him . . .'

'Good luck,' Grandmere said, with a snort. 'He went off with that Bellerieve woman, and I haven't heard from him since. If he is not careful, he is going to end up in the same situation as your Algebra teacher.'

Except it's totally unlikely Dad would be getting anybody pregnant, since the whole reason I was his heir, instead of some legitimately produced offspring, is that he is no longer fertile due to the massive doses of chemotherapy that cured his testicular cancer. But I suppose Grandmere is still in denial about this, considering what a disappointing heir I've turned out to be.

It was at this point that a strange moaning noise came out from under Grandmere's chair. We both looked down. Rommel, Grandmere's miniature poodle, was cowering in fright at the sight of me.

I know I am hideous, and all of that, but really, it's ridiculous how scared that dog is of me. And I love animals!

But even St Francis of Assisi would have a hard time appreciating Rommel. I mean, first of all, he has recently

329

developed a nervous disorder (if you ask me, it's from living in such close proximity to my grandmother) that made all his fur fall out, so Grandmere dresses him up in little sweaters and coats so he won't catch cold.

Today Rommel had on a mink bolero jacket. I am not even joking. It was dyed lavender to match the one slung across Grandmere's shoulders. It is horrifying enough to see a person wearing fur, but it is a thousand times worse to see an animal wearing another animal's fur.

'Rommel,' Grandmere yelled at the dog. 'Stop that growling.'

Except that Rommel wasn't growling. He was moaning. Moaning with fright. At the sight of me. ME!!!

How many times in one day must I be humiliated?

'Oh, you stupid dog.' Grandmere reached down and picked Rommel up, much to his unhappiness. You could tell her diamond brooches were poking him in the spine (there is no fat on him at all, and since he doesn't have any fur, he is especially sensitive to pointy objects), but even though he wriggled to be free, she wouldn't let go of him.

'Now, Amelia,' Grandmere said. 'I need your mother and whatever-his-name-is to write their guests' names and addresses down tonight so I can have the envelopes engraved tomorrow. I know your mother is going to want to invite some of those more, ahem, free-spirited friends of hers, Amelia, but I think it would be better if perhaps if they just stood outside with the reporters and tourists and waved as she climbed in and out of the limo. That way they'll still have a feeling of belonging, but they won't make anyone uncomfortable with their unattractive hair styles and ill-fitting attire.'

'Grandmere,' I said. 'I really think—'

'And what do you think about this dress?' Grandmere

held up a picture of a Vera Wang wedding gown with a big poofy skirt that my mom wouldn't be caught dead in.

Vigo went, 'No, no, Your Highness. I really think this more the thing.' Then he held up a photo of a slinky Armani number that my mom similarly wouldn't be caught dead in.

'Uh, Grandmere,' I said. 'This is all really nice of you, but my mom definitely doesn't want a big wedding. Really. Definitely.'

'*Pfuit*,' Grandmere said. *Pfuit* is French for *No, duh*. 'She will when she sees the luscious hors d'oeurves they'll be serving at the reception. Tell her about them, Vigo.'

Vigo said, with relish, 'Truffle-filled mushroom caps, asparagus tips wrapped in salmon slivers, pea pods stuffed with goat cheese, endive with crumbles of blue cheese inside each gently furled leaf . . .'

I went, 'Uh, Grandmere? No, she won't. Believe me.'

Grandmere went, 'Nonsense. Trust me, Amelia, your mother is going to appreciate this some day. Vigo and I will make her wedding day an event she will never forget.'

I had no doubt about that.

I went, 'Grandmere, Mom and Mr G were really planning on something very casual and simple—'

But then Grandmere threw me one of those looks of hers – they are really very scary – and said, in this deadly serious voice, 'For three years, while your grandfather was off having the time of his life fighting the Germans, I held those Nazis – not to mention that fascist, Mussolini – at bay. They lobbed mortars at the palace doors. They tried to drive tanks across my moat. And yet I persevered, through sheer will power alone. Are you telling me, Amelia, that I cannot convince one pregnant woman to see things my way?'

Well, I'm not saying my mom has anything in common

with Mussolini or Nazis, but as far as putting up a resistance to Grandmere? I'd place my money on my mom over a fascist dictator any day.

I could see that reasoning wasn't going to be effective in this particular case. So I went along with it, listening to Vigo gush over the menu he had picked out, the music he had selected for the ceremony, and later even admiring the portfolio of the photographer he had chosen for the reception.

It wasn't until they actually showed me one of the invitations that I realized something.

'The wedding's this Saturday?' I squeaked.

'Yes,' Grandmere said.

'That's Halloween!' The same day as my mom's courthouse wedding. Also, incidentally, the same night as Shameeka's party.

Grandmere looked bored. 'What of it?'

'Well, it's just . . . you know. Halloween.'

Vigo looked at my grandmother. 'What is this Halloween?' he asked. Then I remembered they don't go in for Halloween much in Genovia.

'A pagan holiday,' Grandmere replied, with a shudder. 'Children dress up in costumes and demand candy from strangers. Horrible American tradition.'

'It's in less than a *week*,' I pointed out.

Grandmere raised her drawn-on eyebrows. 'And so?'

'Well, that's so . . . you know. Soon. People—' like me ' –might have other plans already.'

'Not to be indelicate, Your Highness,' Vigo said. 'But we do want to get the ceremony out of the way before your mother begins to . . . well, *show*.'

Great. So even the royal Genovian event organizer knows my mother is expecting. Why doesn't Grandmere just rent the Goodyear blimp and have it broadcast all over the tristate area?

Then Grandmere started telling me that, since we were on the topic of weddings and all, it might be a good opportunity for me to start learning what will be expected out of any future consorts I might have.

Wait a minute. 'Future *what*?'

'Consorts,' Vigo said, excitedly. 'The spouse of the reigning monarch. Prince Philip is Queen Elizabeth's *consort*. Whomever you choose to marry, Your Highness, will be *your* consort.'

I blinked at him. 'I thought you were the royal Genovian event organizer,' I said.

'Vigo not only serves as our event organizer, but also the royal protocol expert,' Grandmere explained.

'Protocol? I thought that was something to do with the army.'

Grandmere rolled her eyes. 'Protocol is the form of ceremony and etiquette observed by foreign dignitaries at state functions. In your case, Vigo can explain the expectations of your future consort. Just so there won't be any unpleasant surprises later.'

Then Grandmere made me get out a piece of paper and write down exactly what Vigo said, so that, she informed me, in four years, when I am in college, and I take it into my head to enter into a romantic liaison with someone completely inappropriate, I will know why she is so mad.

College? Grandmere obviously does not know that I am being actively pursued by would-be consorts at this very moment.

Of course, I don't even know Jo-C-rox's real name, but hey, it's something, at least.

But then I found out what, exactly, consorts have to do.

And now I sort of doubt I'll be French kissing anyone soon. In fact, I can totally see why my mother didn't want to marry my dad – that is, if he ever asked her.

I have glued the piece of paper here:

Expectations of Any Royal Consort of the Princess of Genovia

- *The consort will ask the princess's permission before he leaves a room.*
- *The consort will wait for the princess to finish speaking before speaking himself.*
- *The consort will wait for the princess to lift her fork before lifting his own at mealtimes.*
- *The consort will not sit until the princess has been seated.*
- *The consort will rise the moment the princess rises.*
- *The consort will not engage in any sort of risk-taking behaviour – such as racing, either car or boat, mountain-climbing, sky-diving, et cetera – until such time as an heir has been provided.*
- *The consort will give up his right, in the event of annulment or divorce, to custody of any children born during the marriage.*
- *The consort will give up the citizenship of his native country in favour of citizenship of Genovia.*

OK. Seriously. What kind of dweeb am I going to end up with?

Actually, I'll be lucky if I can get anybody to marry me at all. What schmuck would want to marry a girl he can't interrupt? Or can't walk out on during an argument? Or has to give up citizenship of his own country for?

I shudder to think of the total loser I will one day be forced to marry. I am already in mourning for the cool race-car driving, mountain-climbing, sky-diving guy I could have had, if it weren't for this whole crummy princess thing.

Top Five Worst Things About Being a Princess

1. Can't marry Michael Moscovitz (he would never renounce his American citizenship in favour of Genovian).
2. Can't go anywhere without a bodyguard (I like Lars, but come on: even the Pope gets to pray by himself sometimes).
3. Must maintain neutral opinion on important topics such as the meat industry and smoking and the Taliban.
4. Princess lessons with Grandmere.
5. Still forced to learn Algebra.

Later on Monday

I figured as soon as I got home, I would tell my mom that she and Mr G need to elope, and right away. Grandmere had brought in a professional! I knew it would be a pain, what with Mom's latest show opening being so soon and all, but it was either that, or a royal wedding the likes of which this city hasn't seen since . . .

Well, ever.

But when I got home, my mom had her head in the toilet.

It turns out her morning sickness has begun, and isn't at all exclusive. She'll throw up just about any time, not just in the a.m.

She was so sick, I didn't have the heart to make her feel worse by telling her what Grandmere had planned.

'Be sure to put a video in,' my mom kept calling from the bathroom. I didn't know what she was talking about, but Mr G did.

She meant to be sure to tape my interview. My interview with Beverly Bellerieve!

I had completely forgotten about it, in light of what had happened at Grandmere's. But my mom hadn't.

Since my mom was incapacitated, Mr G and I settled in to watch my interview together – well, in between running into the bathroom to offer my mom seltzer and saltines.

I figured I would tell Mr G about Grandmere and the wedding at the first commercial break.

But I sort of forgot, in the unbelievable horror of what followed.

TWENTYFOUR/SEVEN for Monday 26 October

AMERICA'S PRINCESS
B. Bellerieve int. w/ M. Renaldo

<u>Ext. Thompson Street, south of Houston (SoHo). World Trade in background.</u>
<u>Beverly Bellerieve (BB)</u>: Imagine, if you will, an ordinary teenage girl. Well, as ordinary as a teenage girl who lives in New York City's Greenwich Village with her single mom, acclaimed painter Helen Thermopolis, can be. Mia's life was filled with the normal things most teenagers' lives are full of – homework, friends, and the occasional F in Algebra . . . until one day, it all changed.

<u>Int. penthouse suite, Plaza Hotel.</u>
<u>BB</u>:   Mia – may I call you Mia? Or would you prefer that I call you Your Highness? Or Amelia?
<u>Mia Renaldo (MR)</u>: Um, no, you can call me Mia.
<u>BB</u>:   Mia. Tell us about that day. The day life as you know it changed completely.
<u>MR</u>: Well, um, what happened was, my dad and I were here at the Plaza, you know, and I was drinking tea, and I got the hiccups, and everyone was looking at me, and my dad was, you know, trying to tell me I was the heir to the throne of Genovia, the country where he lives, and I was like, Look, I gotta go to the bathroom, and so I did, and I waited there until my hiccups stopped and then I came back to my chair and he told me that I was a princess and I completely flipped out and I ran to the zoo and I sat and looked at the penguins for a

339

while and I totally couldn't believe it because in the seventh grade they made us do fact sheets on all the countries in Europe, but I totally missed the part about my dad being prince of it. And all I could think was that I was going to die if people in school found out, because I didn't want to end up being a freak like my friend Tina, who has to go around school with a bodyguard. But that's exactly what happened. I am a freak, a huge freak.

This is the part where she tries to salvage the situation:

BB: Oh, Mia, I can't believe that's true. I'm sure you're quite popular.

MR: No, I'm not. I'm not popular at all. Only jocks are popular in my school. And cheerleaders. But I'm not popular. I mean, I don't hang out with the popular people. I never get invited to parties, or anything. I mean, the cool parties, where there is beer and making out and stuff. I mean, I'm not a jock, or a cheerleader, or one of the smart kids—

BB: Oh, but aren't you one of the smart kids though? I understand one of your classes is called Gifted and Talented.

MR: Yes, but see, G &T is just like study hall. We don't actually do anything in this class – except goof around because the teacher is never there. She's always in the teachers' lounge across the hall so she has no idea what we're doing. Which is goofing off.

Obviously still thinking she can make something out of this interview:

BB: But I don't imagine you have much time for
      goofing off, do you, Mia? For instance, we are sit-
      ting here in the penthouse suite belonging to
      your grandmother, the celebrated Dowager
      Princess of Genovia, who is, I understand, instruct-
      ing you in royal decorum.
MR: Oh, yes. She's giving me princess lessons after
      school. Well, after my Algebra review sessions,
      which are after school.
BB: Mia, didn't you have some exciting news recently?
MR: Oh. Yes. Well, I'm pretty excited. I've always
      wanted to be a big sister. But they don't really
      want to make a big deal out of it, you know. It's
      just going to be a very small ceremony at City
      Hall, with me as their witness—

There's more. A lot more, actually. It's too excruciating to go
into. I mean, thinking about it just brings back the memory
of how my dad's face looked. You know, when I said the
words 'big sister'.

And of course, the whole part where Grandmere had to
breathe into a paper bag.

But it turns out I'll be able to remember for all of eternity,
because not only did we tape the interview, but Beverly
Bellerieve very nicely messengered over a transcript. I guess
so I could put it in my scrapbook, or something. Like I
would seriously ever want to remember ANY of this.

But especially that interview. Basically, I just babbled
like an idiot for about another ten minutes, while Beverly
Bellerieve frantically attempted to steer me back towards
something resembling the actual question she'd asked
me.

But it was completely beyond even her impressive journalistic abilities. I was gone. A combination of nerves and, I'm afraid to say, codeine cough syrup, put me over the edge.

Ms Bellerieve tried though. I have to give her that. The interview ended with this:

Ext. Thompson Street, SoHo.

BB: She's not a jock, nor is she a cheerleader. What Amelia Mignonette Thermopolis Renaldo is, ladies and gentlemen, defies the societal stereotypes that exist in today's modern educational institutions. She's a princess. An American princess.

And yet she faces the same problems and pressures that teenagers all over this country face every day . . . with a twist: one day, she'll grow up to govern a nation.

And come spring, she'll be a big sister. Yes, TwentyFour/Seven has discovered that Helen Thermopolis and Mia's Algebra teacher, Frank Gianini – who are unmarried – are expecting their first child in July. When we come back, an exclusive interview with Mia's father, the prince of Genovia . . . next on TwentyFour/Seven.

What it all boils down to is that, basically, I'm moving to Genovia.

My mom – who finally came out of the bathroom towards the end of the interview – and Mr G tried to convince me that it wasn't that bad.

But it was. Oh, believe me, it was.

And I knew I was in for it the minute the phone started ringing, right after the segment aired.

'Oh, God,' my mother said, suddenly remembering

something. 'Don't pick it up! It's my mother! Frank, I forgot to tell my mother about us!'

Actually, I was kind of hoping it *was* Grandma Thermopolis. Grandma Thermopolis was infinitely preferable, in my opinion, to who it actually turned out to be: Lilly.

And boy, was she mad.

'What do you mean, calling us a bunch of freaks?' she screamed into the phone.

I said, 'Lilly, what are you talking about? I didn't call you a freak.'

'You basically informed the entire nation that the population of Albert Einstein High School is divided into various socio-economic cliques, and that you and your friends are too uncool to be in any of them!'

'Well,' I said. 'We are.'

'Speak for yourself! And what about G & T?'

'What about G & T?'

'You just told the entire country that we sit in there and goof off because Mrs Hill is always in the teachers' lounge! What are you – stupid? You've probably got her into trouble!'

I felt something inside of me clench, as if someone was squeezing my intestines very, very tightly.

'Oh, no,' I breathed. 'Do you really think so?'

Lilly just let out a frustrated scream, then snarled, 'My parents say to tell your mother mazel tov.'

Then she slammed the phone down.

I felt worse than ever. Poor Mrs Hill!

Then the phone rang again. It was Shameeka.

'Mia,' she said. 'Remember how I invited you to my Halloween party this Saturday?'

'Yes,' I said.

'Well, my dad won't let me have it now.'

343

'*What*? Why?'

'Because thanks to you he is under the impression that Albert Einstein High School is filled with sex addicts and alcoholics.'

'But I didn't say that!' Not in those exact words, anyway.

'Well, that's what he heard. He is currently in the next room surfing the Internet for a girls' school in New Hampshire he can send me to next semester. And he says he's not letting me go out with a boy again until I'm thirty.'

'Oh, Shameeka,' I said. 'I'm so sorry.'

Shameeka didn't say anything. In fact, she had to hang up, because she was sobbing too hard to speak.

The phone rang again. I didn't want to answer it, but I had no choice: Mr Gianini was holding my mom's hair back while she threw up some more.

'Hello?'

It was Tina Hakim Baba.

'Oh my gosh!' she shouted.

'I'm sorry, Tina,' I said, figuring I better just start apologizing instantly to every single person who called.

'Sorry? What are you sorry for?' Tina was practically hyperventilating. 'You said my name on TV!'

'Um . . . I know.' I had also called her a freak.

'I can't believe it!' Tina yelled. 'That was so cool!'

'You aren't . . . you aren't mad at me?'

'Why should I be mad at you? This is the most exciting thing that has ever happened to me. I've never had my name said on television before!'

I was filled with love and appreciation for Tina Hakim Baba.

'Um,' I asked, carefully. 'Did your parents see it?'

'Yes! They're excited too. My mom said to tell you that the blue eyeshadow was a stroke of genius. Not too much, just enough to catch the light. She was very impressed. Also she said to tell your mother she has some excellent stretch mark cream that she got in Sweden. You know, for when she starts getting big. I'll bring it to school tomorrow, and you can give it to your mother.'

'What about your dad?' I asked, carefully. 'He's not planning on sending you to a girls' school or anything?'

'What are you talking about? He's delighted that you mentioned my bodyguard. Now he thinks anyone who'd had plans to kidnap me will definitely think twice. Oops, there's another call. It's probably my grandmother in Dubai. They have a satellite dish. I'm sure she heard you mention me! Bye!'

Tina hung up. Great. Even people in Dubai have seen my interview. I don't even know where Dubai is.

The phone rang again. It was Grandmere.

'Well,' she said. 'That was just terrible, wasn't it?'

I said, 'Is there any way I can demand a retraction? Because I didn't mean to say that my Gifted and Talented teacher doesn't do anything and that my school is full of sex addicts. It's not, you know.'

'I cannot imagine what that woman was thinking,' Grandmere said. I was pleased she was on my side for once. Then she went on, and I saw that she wasn't talking about anything to do with me. 'She failed to show a single picture of the palace! And it is at its most beautiful in the autumn. The palm trees look magnificent. This is a travesty, I tell you. A travesty. Do you realize the promotional opportunities that have been wasted here? Absolutely wasted?'

'Grandmere, you have to do something,' I wailed. 'I don't know if I'm going to be able to show my face at school tomorrow.'

'Tourism has been down in Genovia,' Grandmere

reminded me, 'ever since we banned cruise ships from docking in the bay. But who needs day-trippers? With their sticky-film cameras and their awful Bermuda shorts. If that woman had only shown a few shots of the casinos. And the beaches! Why, we have the only naturally white sand along the Riviera. Are you aware of that, Amelia? Monaco has to import its sand.'

'Maybe I could transfer to another school. Do you think there's a school in Manhattan that will take someone with a 1.0 in Algebra?'

'Wait—' Grandmere's voice became muffled. 'Oh, no, there we are. It's back on, and they're showing some simply lovely shots of the palace. Oh, and there's the beach. And the bay. Oh, and the olive groves. Lovely. Simply lovely. That woman might have a few redeeming qualities after all. I suppose I will have to allow your father to continue seeing her.'

She hung up. My own grandmother hung up on me. What kind of a reject am I, anyway?

I went into my mom's bathroom. She was sitting on the floor, looking unhappy. Mr Gianini was sitting on the edge of the bathtub. He looked confused.

Well, who can blame him? A couple of months ago, he was just an Algebra teacher. Now he's the father of the future sibling of the princess of Genovia.

'I need to find another school to go to from now on,' I informed them. 'Do you think you could help me out with that, Mr G? I mean, do you have any pull with the teachers' association, or anything?'

My mother went, 'Oh, Mia. It wasn't that bad.'

'Yes, it was,' I said. 'You didn't even see most of it. You were in here throwing up.'

'Yes,' my mother said. 'But I could hear it. And what did you say that wasn't true? People who excel at sports have traditionally been treated like gods in our society, while people whose brilliance is cerebral are routinely ignored – or worse, mocked as nerds or geeks. Frankly, I believe scientists working on cures for cancer should be paid the salaries professional athletes are receiving. Professional athletes aren't out there saving lives, for God's sake. They entertain. And actors. Don't tell me acting is art. Teaching. Now there's an art. Frank should be making what Tom Cruise does, for teaching you how to multiply fractions the way he did.'

I realized my mother was probably delusional with nausea. I said, 'Well, I think I'll just be going to bed now.'

Instead of replying, my mother leaned over the toilet and threw up some more. I could see that in spite of all my warnings about the potential lethality of shellfish for a developing foetus, she'd ordered jumbo prawns in garlic sauce from Number One Noodle Son.

I went to my room and went on-line. Maybe, I thought, I could transfer to the same school Shameeka's father is shipping her off to. At least then I'd already have one friend.

If Shameeka would even speak to me after what I'd done, which I doubted. No one at Albert Einstein High, with the exception of Tina Hakim Baba, who was obviously clueless, was ever going to speak to me again.

Then an instant message flashed across my computer screen. Someone wanted to talk to me.

But who? Jo-C-rox??? Was it Jo-C-rox?????

No. Even better!!! It was Michael. Michael, at least, still wanted to talk to me.

I have printed out our conversation and stuck it here:

```
CracKing: Hey. Just saw you on TV. You were
good.
>
```

FtLouie: What are you talking about? I made a complete and utter ass of myself. And what about Mrs Hill? They're probably going to fire her now.
>
CracKing: Well, at least you told the truth.
>
FtLouie: But all these people are mad at me now! Lilly's furious!
>
CracKing: She's just jealous because you had more people watching you in that one fifteen minute segment than all the people who've ever watched all of her shows put together.
>
FtLouie: No, that's not why. She thinks I've betrayed our generation, or something, by revealing that cliques exist at Albert Einstein High School.
>
CracKing: Well, that, and the fact that you claimed you don't belong to any of them.
>
FtLouie: Well, I don't.
>
CracKing: Yes, you do. Lilly likes to think you belong to the exclusive and highly selective Lilly Moscovitz clique. Only you neglected to mention this, and that has upset her.
>
FtLouie: Really? Did she say that?
>

```
CracKing: She didn't say it, but she's my
sister. I know the way she thinks.
>
FtLouie: Maybe. I don't know, Michael.
>
CracKing: Look, are you all right? You were a
mess at school today . . . although now it's
clear why. That's pretty cool about your mom
and Mr Gianini. You must be excited.
>
FtLouie: I guess so. I mean, it's kind of
embarrassing. But at least this time my mom's
getting married, like a normal person.
>
CracKing: Now you won't need my help with your
Algebra homework any more. You'll have your own
personal tutor right there at home.
```

I had never thought of this. How awful! I don't want my
own personal tutor. I want Michael to keep helping me during G & T! Mr Gianini is all right, and everything, but he's
certainly not *Michael*.

I wrote really fast:

```
FtLouie: Well, I don't know. I mean, he's going
to be awfully busy for a while, moving in, and
then there'll be the baby and everything.
>
CracKing: God. A baby. I can't believe it. No
wonder you were wigging out so badly today.
>
FtLouie: Yeah, I really was. Wigging out, I
mean.
```

>

```
CracKing: And what about that thing this
afternoon with Lana? That couldn't have helped
much. Though it was pretty funny, her thinking
we were going out, huh?
```

Actually, I didn't see anything particularly funny about it.
But what was I supposed to say? Gee, Michael, why don't we
give it a try?

As if.

Instead I said:

```
FtLouie: Yeah, she's such a headcase. I guess
it's never occurred to her that two people of
the opposite sex can just be friends, with no
romantic involvement.
```

Although I have to admit the way I feel about Michael –
particularly when I'm over at Lilly's and he comes out of his
room with no shirt on – is quite romantic.

```
CracKing: Yeah. Listen, what are you doing
Saturday night?
```

Was he asking me out? Was Michael Moscovitz finally asking me OUT???

No. It wasn't possible. Not after the way I'd made a fool
of myself on national television.

Just to be safe, though, I figured I'd try for a neutral reply,
in case what he wanted to know was whether I could come
over and walk Pavlov because the Moscovitzes were going to
be out of town, or something.

```
FtLouie:I don't know. Why?
>
CracKing: Because it's Halloween, you know. I
thought a bunch of us could get together and
go see The Rocky Horror Picture Show over at
the Village Cinema . . .
```

OK. Not a date.

But we'd be sitting beside one another in a darkened room! That counted for something! And *Rocky Horror* is sort of scary, so if I reached over and grabbed him, it might be OK.

Sure, I started to write. That sounds . . .

Then I remembered. Saturday night was Halloween, all right. But it was also the night of my mom's royal wedding! I mean, if Grandmere gets her way.

```
FtLouie: Can I get back to you? I may have a
family commitment that evening.
>
CracKing: Sure. Just let me know. Well, see you
tomorrow.
>
FtLouie: Yeah. I can't wait.
>
CracKing: Don't worry. You were telling the
truth. You can't get in trouble for telling the
truth.
```

Ha! That's what he thinks. There's a reason I lie all the time, you know.

Top Five Best Things About Being In Love With Your Best Friend's Brother

1. Get to see him in his natural environment, not just at school, thus allowing you access to vital information, like difference between his 'school' personality and real personality.
2. Get to see him without a shirt on.
3. Get to see him all the time.
4. Get to see how he treats his mother/sister/housekeeper (critical clues as to how he will treat any prospective girlfriend).
5. Convenient: you can hang out with your friend and spy on the object of your affections at the same time.

Top Five Worst Things About Being In Love With Your Best Friend's Brother

1. Can't tell her.
2. Can't tell him, because he might tell her.
3. Can't tell anyone else, because they might tell him or, worse, her.
4. He will never admit to his true feelings because you are his little sister's best friend.
5. You are continuously thrust into his presence, knowing that he will never think of you as anything but his little sister's best friend for as long as you live, and yet you continue to pine for him until every fibre of your being cries out for him and you think you are probably going to die even though your biology teacher says it is physiologically impossible to die from a broken heart.

Tuesday, October 27, Principal Gupta's office

Oh, God! No sooner had I set foot in Homeroom today than I was summoned to the principal's office!

I was hoping it was so that she could make sure I'm not carrying any contraband cough syrup, but it's more likely because of what I said last night on TV. Particularly, I would guess, the part about how divisive and clique-ridden it is around here.

Meanwhile, all the other people in this school who have never been invited to a party given by a popular kid have rallied round me. It's like I've struck a blow for dweebs everywhere, or something. The minute I walked into school today, the hip-hoppers, the brainiacs, the drama freaks, they were all, 'Hey! Tell it like it is, sistah.'

No one's ever called me sistah before. It is somewhat invigorating.

Only the cheerleaders treat me the way they always have. As I walk down the hall, their eyes flick over me, from the top of my head all the way down to my shoes. And then they whisper to each other and laugh.

Well, I suppose it is amusing to see a five foot ten, flat-chested amazon like myself roaming loose in the halls. I'm surprised no one has thrown a net over me and hauled me off to the Natural History Museum.

Of my own friends, only Lilly – and Shameeka, of course – aren't entirely thrilled with last night's performance. Lilly's still unhappy about my spilling the beans about the socio-economic division of our school population. Not unhappy enough to turn down a ride to school in my limo this morning, however.

Interestingly, Lilly's chilly treatment of me has only served to bring her brother and I closer. This morning on the way to school, Michael offered to go over my Algebra homework for me, and make sure my equations were all right.

I was touched by his offer, and the warm feeling I had when he pronounced all my problems correct didn't have anything to do with pride, but everything to do with the way his fingers brushed against mine as he handed the piece of paper back to me. Could he be Jo-C-rox? *Could he*????

Uh-oh. Principal Gupta is ready to see me now.

Tuesday, October 27, Algebra

Principal Gupta is way concerned about my mental health.

'Mia, are you really so unhappy here at Albert Einstein?'

I didn't want to hurt her feelings or anything, so I said no. I mean, the truth is, it probably wouldn't matter what school somebody stuck me in. I will always be a five foot ten freak with no breasts, no matter where I go.

Then Principal Gupta said something surprising. She went, 'I only ask because last night during your interview, you said you weren't popular.'

I wasn't quite sure where she was going with this. So I just said, 'Well, I'm not,' with a shrug.

'That isn't true,' Principal Gupta said. 'Everyone in the school knows who you are.'

I still didn't want her to feel bad, like it was her fault I'm a biological sport, so I explained very gently, 'Yes, but that's only because I'm a princess. Before that, I was pretty much invisible.'

Principal Gupta said, 'That simply isn't true.'

But all I could think was, How would you even know? You aren't out there. You don't know what it's like.

And then I felt even worse for her, because she is so obviously living in principal fantasy world.

'Perhaps,' Principal Gupta said, 'if you took part in more extracurricular activities, you'd feel a better sense of belonging.'

This caused my jaw to drop.

'Principal Gupta,' I couldn't help exclaiming. 'I am barely passing Algebra. All of my free time is spent attending review sessions so that I can scrape by with a D.'

'Well,' Principal Gupta said, 'I am aware of that—'

'Also, after my review sessions, I have princess lessons with my grandmother, so that when I go to Genovia in December for my introduction to the people I will one day rule, I do not make a complete idiot of myself, like I did last night on TV.'

'Well,' Principal Gupta said. 'I think the word *idiot* might be a little strong.'

'I really don't have time,' I went on, feeling more sorry for her than ever, 'for extracurricular activities.'

'The yearbook committee meets only once a week,' Principal Gupta said. 'Or perhaps you could join the track team. They won't begin training until the spring, and by that time, you hopefully won't be having princess lessons any more.'

I just blinked at her, I was so surprised. *Me? Track?* I can barely walk without tripping over my own gargantuan feet. God knows what would happen if I tried running.

And the yearbook committee? Did I really look like someone who wants to remember one single thing about my high school experience?

'Well,' Principal Gupta said, I guess realizing from my facial expression that I was not enthused by either of these suggestions. 'It was just an idea. I do think you would be much happier here at Albert Einstein if you joined a club. I am aware, of course, of your friendship with Lilly Moscovitz, and I sometimes wonder if she might not be . . . well, a negative influence on you. That television show of hers is quite acerbic.'

I was shocked by this. Poor Principal Gupta is more deluded than I thought!

'Oh, no,' I said. 'Lilly's show is actually quite positive. Didn't you see the episode dedicated to fighting racism in Korean delis? Or the one about how a lot of clothing stores that cater for teens are prejudiced against larger sized girls, since they don't carry enough things in size 12, the size of the average American woman? Or the one where we tried to hand-deliver a pound of Vaniero cookies to Freddie Prinze Jr.'s apartment because he'd been looking a little thin?'

Principal Gupta held up her hand. 'I see that you feel very passionately about this,' she said. 'And I must say, I am pleased. It is good to know you feel passionate about something, Mia, other than your antipathy towards athletes and cheerleaders.'

Then I felt worse than ever. I said, 'I don't feel antipathy towards them. I'm just saying that sometimes . . . well, sometimes it feels like they run this school, Principal Gupta.'

'Well, I can assure you,' Principal Gupta said. 'That is not true.'

Poor, poor Principal Gupta.

Still, I did feel that I had to intrude just a little upon the fantasy world in which she so obviously lives.

'Um,' I said. 'Principal Gupta. About Mrs Hill . . . '

'What about her?' Principal Gupta asked.

'I didn't mean it when I said she's always in the teachers' lounge during my Gifted and Talented class. That was an exaggeration.'

Principal Gupta smiled at me in this very brittle way.

'Don't worry, Mia,' she said. 'Mrs Hill has been taken care of.'

Taken care of! What does *that* mean?

I am almost scared to find out.

Tuesday, October 27, G & T

Well, Mrs Hill didn't get fired.

Instead, I guess they gave her a warning, or something. The upshot of it is, Mrs Hill won't budge from behind her desk here in the G & T lab.

Which means we have to sit at our desks and actually do work and not talk.

And we can't lock Boris in the supply closet. We actually have to sit here and listen to him play.

Play *Bartok*.

And we can't talk to one another, because we are supposed to be working on our individual projects.

Boy, is everyone mad at me.

But no one is madder than Lilly.

It turns out Lilly's been secretly writing a book about the socio-economic divisions that exist within the walls of Albert Einstein High School! Really! She didn't want to tell me, but finally Boris blurted it out at lunch today. Lilly threw a fry at him and got ketchup all over his sweater.

I can't believe Lilly has told Boris things that she hasn't told me. I'm supposed to be her best friend. Boris is just her boyfriend. Why is she telling him cool things, like about how she's writing a book, and not me?

'Can I read it?' I begged.

'No.' Lilly was really mad. She wouldn't even look at Boris. He has already totally forgiven her about the ketchup, even though he will probably have to get that sweater dry-cleaned.

'Can I read just one page?' I asked.

'No.'

'Just one sentence?'

'No.'

Michael didn't know about the book either. He told me

right before Mrs Hill came in that he offered to publish it in his on-line 'zine *Crackhead*, but Lilly said, in quite a snotty voice, that she was holding out for a 'legitimate' publisher.

'Am I in it?' I wanted to know. 'Your book? Am I in it?'

Lilly said if people don't stop bothering her about it, she is going to fling herself off the top of the school water tower. She is exaggerating, of course. You can't even get up to the water tower any more, since the seniors, as a prank a few years ago, poured a bunch of tadpoles into it.

I can't believe Lilly's been working on a book and never told me. I mean, I always knew she was going to write a book about the adolescent experience in post-Cold War America. But I didn't think she was going to start it before we had even graduated. If you ask me, this book can't be very balanced. Because I hear things get way better sophomore year.

Still, I guess it does make sense that you would tell someone whose tongue has been in your mouth things you wouldn't necessarily tell your best friend. But it makes me mad Boris knows things about Lilly that I don't know. I tell Lilly everything.

Well, everything except how I feel about her brother.

Oh, and about my secret admirer.

And about my mom and Mr Gianini.

But I tell her practically everything else.

Don't forget

Stop thinking about M.M.
English journal! Profound moment!
cat food
toothpaste
TOILET PAPER!!!

Tuesday, October 27, Bio.

I am winning friends and influencing people everywhere I go today. Kenny just asked me what I'm doing for Halloween. I said I might have a family commitment to attend, and he said if I could get out of it, he and a bunch of his friends from the Computer Club are going to *Rocky Horror*, and that I should come along.

I asked him if one of his friends was Michael Moscovitz, because Michael is treasurer of the Computer Club, and he said yes.

I thought about asking Kenny if he's heard Michael mention whether or not he likes me, you know, in any special way, but I decided not to.

Because then Kenny might think I like him. Michael, I mean. And how pathetic would I look *then*?

Ode to M
Oh, M,
why can't you see
that x = you
and y = me?
And that
you + me
= ecstasy,
and together we'd B
4ever happy?

Tuesday, October 27, 6 p.m., On the way back to the loft from Grandmere's

Oh God. What with all the backlash about my interview on *TwentyFour/Seven*, I completely forgot about Grandmere and Vigo, the Genovian event organizer!

I mean it. I swear I didn't remember a thing about Vigo and the asparagus tips, not until I walked into Grandmere's suite tonight for my princess lesson, and there were all these people scurrying around, doing things like barking into the phone, 'No, that's four *thousand* long-stemmed pink roses, not four *hundred*,' and calligraphying place cards.

I found Grandmere sitting in the midst of all this activity, Rommel – stylishly dressed in a chinchilla cape, dyed mauve – in her lap, sampling truffles.

I'm not kidding. Truffles.

'No,' Grandmere said, putting a gooey half-eaten chocolate ball back into the box Vigo was holding out to her. 'Not that one, I think. Cherries are so *vulgar*.'

'Grandmere.' I couldn't believe this. I was practically hyperventilating, the way Grandmere had when she'd found out my mom was pregnant. 'What are you *doing*? Who are all these people?'

'Ah, Amelia,' Grandmere said, looking pleased to see me. Even though, judging from the remains in the box Vigo was holding, she'd been eating a lot of stuff with nougat in it, none of it got onto her teeth. This was one of the many royal tricks Grandmere had yet to teach me. 'Lovely. Sit down and help me decide which of these truffles we should put in the gift box the wedding guests are getting as party favours.'

'Wedding guests?' I sank onto the chair Vigo had pulled up for me, and dropped my backpack. 'Grandmere, I told you. My mom is never going to go along with this. She wouldn't *want* something like this.'

Grandmere just shook her head and said, 'Pregnant women are never the most rational creatures.'

I pointed out that, judging from my research into the matter, while it was true that hormonal imbalances often cause pregnant women discomfort, I saw no reason to suppose that these imbalances in any way invalidated my mother's feelings on the matter – especially since I knew that they'd have been exactly the same if she weren't pregnant. My mom is not a royal wedding type of gal. I mean, she gets together with her girlfriends for margarita-poker night once a month.

'Your mother,' Vigo pointed out, 'is the matriarch of the future reigning monarch of Genovia, Your Highness. As such, it is vital that she be extended every privilege and courtesy the palace can offer.'

'Then how about offering her the privilege of planning her wedding for herself?' I said.

Grandmere had a good laugh at that one. She practically choked on the swig of Sidecar she was taking after each bite of truffle in order to cleanse her palate.

'Amelia,' she said, when she was through coughing – something Rommel had found extremely alarming, if the way he rolled his eyes back up into his head was any indication. 'Your mother will be eternally grateful to us for all the work we are doing on her behalf. You'll see.'

I realized it was no good arguing with them. I knew what I was going to have to do.

And right after my lesson – which was on how to write a royal thank you note, a lesson that arose out of necessity, since Grandmere's suite was crammed with wedding presents and baby stuff that people have started sending my

362

mother, care of the Genovian royal family at the Plaza Hotel – I did it. I marched up to the door to my father's hotel suite, and banged on it.

But he wasn't home! And when I asked the concierge down in the lobby if she knew where my dad had gone, she said she wasn't sure.

One thing she was quite certain of, however, was that Beverly Bellerieve had been with my dad when he'd left.

Well, I'm glad my dad's found a new friend, I guess, but hello? Is he not aware of the impending disaster growing under his own royal nose?

Tuesday, October 27, 10 p.m., The loft

Well, it happened. The impending disaster is now officially a *real* disaster.

Because Grandmere has gotten completely out of hand. I didn't even realize how badly, either, until when I got home tonight from my lesson and saw this *family* sitting at my dining room table.

That's right. An entire *family*. Well, a mom and a dad and a kid, anyway.

I am not kidding. At first I thought they were tourists that had maybe taken a wrong turn – our neighbourhood is very touristy. Like maybe they thought they were going to Washington Square Park, but ended up following a Chinese food delivery guy to our loft instead.

The woman, who was wearing pink jogging pants – a clear indication that she was from out of town – looked at me and went, 'Oh my Lord! Are you telling me that you actually wear your hair like that in real life? I felt sure it was just that way for TV.'

My jaw dropped. I went, '*Grandmother Thermopolis?*'

'Grandmother Thermopolis?' The woman squinted at me. 'I guess all this royal stuff really *has* gone to your head. Don't you remember me, honey? I'm *Mamaw*.'

Mamaw! My grandmother from my mother's side!

And there, sitting beside her – roughly half her size and wearing a baseball cap that had John Deere Tractors written just above the brim – was my mother's father, Papaw! The hulking boy in a flannel shirt and overalls I didn't recognize, but that hardly mattered. What were my mother's estranged parents, who had never left Versailles, Indiana, before in their lives, doing in our downtown Village loft?

A quick consultation with my mother explained it. I was

able to find her by following the phone cord first into her bedroom, then into her walk-in closet, where she was huddled behind her shoe rack (empty – all her shoes were on the floor, as usual) in whispered conspiracy with my father.

'I don't care how you do it, Philippe,' she was hissing into the phone. 'You tell that mother of yours she's gone too far this time. My *parents*, Philippe? *You know how I feel about my parents.* If you don't get them out of here, Mia is going to end up paying visits to me through a slot in the door up at Bellevue's mental ward.'

I could hear my father murmuring reassurances through the phone. My mom noticed me and whispered, 'Are they still out there?'

I said, 'Um, yes. You mean you didn't invite them?'

'Of course not!' My mother's eyes were as wide as Calamata olives. 'Your grandmother invited them for some cock-a-mamie wedding she thinks she's throwing for me and Frank on Saturday!'

I gulped guiltily. Oops.

Well, all I can say in my own defence is that things have been very very hectic lately. I mean, what with finding out my mother is pregnant, and then getting sick, and the whole thing with Jo-C-rox, and then the interview . . .

Oh, all right. There's no excuse. I am a horrible daughter.

My mom held out the phone to me. 'He wants to talk to you,' she said.

I took the phone and went, 'Dad? Where are you?'

'I'm in the car,' he said. 'Listen, Mia, I got the concierge to arrange for rooms for your grandparents at a hotel near your place – the SoHo Grand. OK? Just put them in the limo and send them there.'

'OK, Dad,' I said. 'But what about Grandmere and this whole wedding thing? I mean, it's sort of out of control.' Understatement of the year.

'I'll take care of Grandmere,' my dad said, sounding very Captain Picardish. You know, from *Star Trek, Next Generation*. I got the feeling Beverly Bellerieve was there in the car with him, and he was trying to sound all princely in front of her.

'OK,' I said. 'But . . .'

It's not that I didn't trust my dad, or anything, to take care of the situation. It's just – well, we are talking about Grandmere. She can be very scary, when she wants to be. Even, I am sure, to her own son.

I guess he must have known what I was thinking, since he went, 'Don't worry, Mia. I'll take care of it.'

'OK,' I said, feeling bad for doubting him.

'And, Mia?'

I'd been about to hang up. I went, 'Yeah, Dad?'

'Assure your mother I didn't know anything about this. I *swear* it.'

'OK, Dad.'

I hung up the phone. 'Don't worry,' I said to my mom. 'I'll take care of this.'

Then, my shoulders back, I returned to the living room. My grandparents were still sitting at the table. Their farmer friend, however, had got up. He was in the kitchen, peering into the refrigerator.

'This all you got to eat around here?' he asked, pointing to the carton of soy milk and the bowl of edamame on the first shelf.

'Um,' I said. 'Well, yes. We are trying to keep our refrigerator free from any sort of contaminants that might harm a developing foetus.'

When the guy looked blank, I said, 'We usually order in.'

366

He brightened at once, and closed the refrigerator door. 'Oh, Dominos?' he said. 'Great!'

'Um,' I said. Dominos! There are three thousand restaurants in New York City, almost all of which will deliver, and this guy wants Dominos, which you can get anywhere? Unreal. 'Well, you can certainly order Dominos, if that's what you want. They'll probably have a phone book or something in your hotel room, so you can look up the number—'

'*Hotel room?*'

I spun around. Mamaw had snuck up behind me.

'Um, yes,' I said. 'You see, my father thought you might be more comfortable at a nice hotel than here in the loft—'

'Well, if that doesn't beat all,' Mamaw said. 'Here your Papaw and Hank and I come all the way to see you, and you stick us in a hotel?'

I looked at the guy in the overalls with renewed interest. *Hank?* As in my *cousin* Hank?

Why, the last time I'd seen Hank had been during my second – and ultimately final – trip to Versailles, back when I'd been about ten or so. Hank had been dropped off at the Thermopolis homestead the year before by his globe-trotting mother – my aunt Marie, who my mom can't stand, primarily because, as my mother puts it, she exists in an intellectual and spiritual vacuum (meaning that Marie is a Republican).

Back then, Hank had been a skinny, whiny thing with a milk allergy, who had followed me around everywhere, pestering me with questions about what it was like to live in Noo York City. It had been very annoying.

Anyway, during one particularly boring interrogation session, Hank had asked me, in complete sincerity, if, when I grew up, I would marry him.

And even though I'd been sickened and appalled – I mean, we're first cousins, after all – I hadn't wanted to hurt his feelings, and since I didn't figure I'd ever see him again, I'd said, Yeah, sure, Hank, I'll marry you.

I had no way of telling whether or not Hank remembered that long ago exchange. I certainly hoped not! Even though he wasn't as skinny as he'd once been, he still looked a little lactose intolerant, if you ask me.

'Nobody said anything about us being hauled off to an expensive New York City hotel when that French woman called.' Mamaw had followed me into the kitchen, and now she stood with her hands on her generous hips. 'She said she'd pay for everything,' Mamaw said, 'free and clear.'

I realized at once where Mamaw's concern lay.

'Oh, um, Mamaw,' I said. 'My father will take care of the bill, of course.'

'Well, that's different.' Mamaw beamed. 'Let's go!'

I figured I'd better go with them, just to make sure they got there all right. As soon as we got into the limo, Hank forgot all about how hungry he was, in his delight over all the buttons there were to push. He had a swell time sticking his head in and out of the sun roof. At one point he stuck his whole body out of the sun roof, and then spread his arms out wide and yelled, 'I'm the king of the world!'

I couldn't help feeling mortified, but fortunately the limo's windows are tinted, so I don't think anyone from school could have recognized me.

So you can understand why, after I got them all checked into the hotel and everything, and Mamaw asked me if I would take Hank to school with me in the morning, I nearly passed out.

'Oh, you don't want to go to school with me, Hank,' I said, quickly. 'I mean, you're on vacation. You could go do

368

something really fun.' I tried to think of something that might seem really fun to Hank. 'Like go to the Harley Davidson Café.'

But Hank said, 'Heck, no. I want to go to school with you, Mia. I always wanted to see what it was like at a real Noo York City high school.' He lowered his voice, so Mamaw and Papaw wouldn't hear. 'I hear the girls in Noo York City have all got their belly buttons pierced.'

Hank was in for a real big disappointment if he thought he'd see any pierced navels in my school – we wear uniforms, and Principal Gupta frowns upon us tying the ends of our shirts into halter tops, like Britney Spears always does.

But I couldn't see a way to get out of having him accompany me for the day. Grandmere was always going on about how princesses have to be gracious. Well, I guess this was my big test.

So I went, 'OK.' Which didn't sound very gracious, but what else could I say?

Then Mamaw surprised me by grabbing me and giving me a hug goodbye. I don't know why I was so surprised. This was a very grandmotherly thing to do, of course. But I guess, seeing as how the grandmother I spend the most time with is Grandmere, I wasn't expecting it.

As she hugged me, Mamaw went, 'Why, you aren't anything but skin and bones, are you?' Yes, thank you, Mamaw. It is true, I am mammarily challenged. But must you shout it out in the lobby of the SoHo Grand? 'And when are you going to stop shooting up so high? I swear, you're almost taller than Hank!'

Which was, unfortunately, true.

Then Mamaw made Papaw give me a hug goodbye too. Mamaw had been very soft when I hugged her. Papaw was the exact opposite, very bony. It was sort of amazing to me that these two people had managed to turn my strong-willed, independent-minded mother into such a gibbering mess. I mean, Grandmere used to lock my dad into the castle dungeon when he was a kid, and he wasn't half as resentful towards her as my mom was towards her parents.

On the other hand, my dad is in deep denial and suffers from classic Oedipal issues. At least according to Lilly.

When I got home, my mom had moved from the closet to her bed, where she lay covered with Victoria's Secret and J Crew catalogues. I knew she must be feeling a little better. Ordering things is one of her favourite hobbies.

I said, 'Hi, Mom.'

She looked out from behind the Spring Bathing Suit edition. Her face was all bloated and splotchy.

I was glad Mr Gianini wasn't around. He might have had second thoughts about marrying her if he'd got a good look at her just then.

'Oh, Mia,' she said when she saw me. 'Come here and let me give you a hug. Was it horrible? I'm sorry I'm such a bad mother.'

I sat down on the bed beside her. 'You aren't a bad mother,' I said. 'You're a good mother. You just aren't feeling well.'

'No,' my mother said. She was sniffling, so I knew the reason she looked bloated and horrible was that she'd been crying. 'I'm a terrible person. My parents came all the way from Indiana to see me, and I sent them to a hotel.'

I could tell my mom was having a hormonal imbalance and wasn't herself. If she'd been herself, she wouldn't have thought twice about sending her parents to a hotel. She has never forgiven them for

1. not supporting her decision to have me,
2. not approving of the way she was raising me, and

370

3. voting for George Bush Sr, as well as his son.

Hormonal imbalance or not, though, the truth is, my mother does not need this kind of stress. This should be a really happy time for her. It says in all the stuff I've read about pregnancy that preparing for the birth of your child should be a time of joy and celebration.

And it would be, if Grandmere hadn't come around and ruined it all by sticking her nose in where no one wants it.

She has *got* to be stopped.

And I'm not just saying that on account of how much I really, really want to go to *Rocky Horror* on Saturday with Michael.

Tuesday, October 27, 11 p.m.

Another e-mail from Jo-C-rox!!!!!
  This one said:

```
JoCrox: Dear Mia,
Just a note to tell you I saw you last night
on TV. You looked beautiful, as always. I know
some people at school have been giving you a
hard time. Don't let them get you down. The
majority of us think you rock the world.
Your Friend
```

  Isn't that the sweetest? I wrote back right away:

```
FtLouie: Dear Friend,
Thank you so much. PLEASE won't you tell me
who you are? I swear I won't tell a
soul!!!!!!!!!!!!
Mia
```

He hasn't written back yet, but I think my sincerity really shows, considering all the exclamation points.
  I am slowly wearing him down, I just know it.

ENGLISH JOURNAL

My most profound moment was

ENGLISH JOURNAL

'Make the most of yourself, for that is all there is of you.'
Ralph Waldo Emerson

I believe that Mr Emerson was talking about the fact that you are only given one life to live, and so you had better make the best of it. This idea is best illustrated by a movie I saw on the Lifetime channel while I was sick. The movie was called Who Is Julia?. *In this movie, Mare Winningham portrays Julia, a woman who wakes up one day after an accident to discover that her body has been completely destroyed and her brain transplanted into someone whose body was OK but whose brain had ceased functioning. Since Julia was formerly a fashion model, and now her brain is in a housewife's body (Mare Winningham's), she is understandably upset. She goes around banging her head against things because she is no longer blonde, five foot ten, and a hundred and ten pounds.*

But finally, through Julia's husband's undying devotion to her – despite her new looks – and a brief kidnapping by the housewife's psychotic husband, who wants her to come back home to do his laundry, Julia realizes that looking like a model isn't as important as not being dead.

This movie raises the all important question, If your body was destroyed in an accident, and they had to transplant your brain into someone else's body, whose body would you want it to be? *After considerable thought, I have decided that I would most want to be in the body of Michelle Kwan, the Olympic ice-skater, since she is very pretty, has a marketable skill, and as everyone knows, it is quite stylish these days to be Asian.*

Either Michelle, or Britney Spears so I could finally have breasts.

Wednesday, October 28, English

Well, one thing is for sure:

Having a guy like my cousin Hank follow you around from class to class certainly keeps people's minds off the idiot you made of yourself on TV the other night.

Seriously. Not that the cheerleaders have forgotten all about the whole *TwentyFour/Seven* thing – I'm still getting the evil eye in the hallway every once in a while. But as soon as their gazes flick over me and settle on Hank, something seems to happen to them.

I couldn't figure out what it was, at first. I thought it was just that they were so stunned to see a guy in a flannel shirt and overalls in the middle of Manhattan.

Then I slowly started realizing it was something else. I guess Hank is sort of buff, and he does have sort of nice blond hair that kind of hangs in his pretty-boy-blue eyes.

But I think it's something even more than that. It's like Hank is giving off those pheromones we studied in Bio., or something.

Only I can't sense them, because I am related to him.

As soon as girls notice Hank, they sidle up to me and whisper 'Who is *that*?' while gazing longingly at Hank's biceps, which are actually quite pronounced beneath all that plaid.

Take Lana Weinberger, for instance. There she was, hanging around my locker, waiting for Josh to show up so the two of them could take part in their morning face-suckage ritual, when Hank and I appeared. Lana's eyes – heavily circled in Clinique – widened, and she went, 'Who's your friend?' in this voice I had never heard her use before. And I've known her a while.

I said, 'He's not my friend, he's my cousin.'

Lana said to Hank, in the same strange voice, 'You can be *my* friend.'

To which Hank replied, with a big smile, 'Gee, thanks, ma'am.'

And don't think in Algebra Lana wasn't doing everything she could to get Hank to notice her. She swished her long blonde hair all over my desk. She dropped her pencil like four times. She kept crossing and re-crossing her legs. Finally Mr Gianini was like, 'Miss Weinberger, do you need a bathroom pass?' That calmed her down, but only for like five minutes.

Even Miss Molina, the school secretary, was strangely giggly when she was making out a guest pass for Hank.

But that's nothing compared to Lilly's reaction as she climbed into the limo this morning, when we swung by to pick up her and Michael. She looked across the seat and her jaw dropped open and this piece of Pop Tart she'd been chewing fell right out onto the floor. I'd never seen her do anything like that before in my life. Lilly is generally very good at keeping things in her mouth.

Hormones are very powerful things. We are helpless in their wake.

Which would certainly explains the whole Michael thing.

I mean, about my being so deeply besotted by him and all.

T. Hardy – buried his heart in Wessex, body in Westminster. Um, excuse me, but *gross*.

I don't believe this. I really don't.

Lilly and Hank are missing.

That's right. *Missing.*

Nobody knows where they are. Boris is beside himself. He won't stop playing Mahler. Even Mrs Hill agreed that shutting him into the supply closet was the best way to maintain our sanity. She let us sneak into the gymnasium and steal some exercise mats and lean them up against the supply closet door to muffle the sound.

It isn't working though.

I guess I can understand Boris's despair. I mean, when you're a musical genius and the girl you've been French kissing on a fairly regular basis suddenly disappears with a guy like Hank, it has to be fairly demoralizing.

I should have seen it coming. Lilly was excessively flirty at lunch. She kept asking Hank all these questions about life back in Indiana. Like if he was the most popular boy in his school, and all. Which of course he said he was. Though I personally don't believe being the most popular boy at Versailles (which is properly pronounced Ver-Sales, by the way) High School is such a big accomplishment.

Then she was all, 'Do you have a girlfriend?'

Hank got bashful and said that he used to, only 'Amber' had ditched him a couple weeks ago for a guy whose father owns the local Australian Outback Steakhouse. Lilly acted all shocked, and said Amber must be suffering from a borderline personality disorder if she couldn't see what a fully self-actualized individual Hank was.

I was so revolted by this display, I could hardly keep my veggie burger down.

Then Lilly started talking about all the fabulous things

there are to do in the city, and how Hank really ought to take advantage of them, rather than hanging around here at school with me. She said, 'For instance, there's the Transit Museum, which is fascinating.'

Seriously. She actually said the *Transit Museum* was fascinating. *Lilly Moscovitz.*

I swear, hormones are way dangerous.

Then she went, 'And on Halloween, there's a parade in the Village, and then we are all going to the *Rocky Horror Picture Show.* Have you ever been to that before?'

Hank said that no, he hadn't.

I should have known right then that something was up, but I didn't. The bell rang, and Lilly said she wanted to take Hank to the auditorium to show him the part of the *My Fair Lady* set that she had painted herself (a street lamp). Feeling that even a momentary alleviation from Hank's constant stream of reminders of our last visit together – 'Remember that time we went crawdadding, and you wouldn't touch any of 'em, on account of how you said they looked just like great big cockroaches?' – would be a relief, I went, 'OK.'

And that was the last any of us saw of them.

I blame myself. Hank is apparently simply too attractive to be released amongst the general population. I ought to have recognized that. I ought to have recognized that the pull of an uneducated but completely gorgeous farmboy from Indiana would be stronger than the pull of a not-so-attractive musical genius from Russia.

Now I have turned my best friend into a two-timer AND a class-ditcher. Lilly has never skipped a class in her life. If she gets caught, she will get detention. I wonder if she'll think sitting in the cafeteria for an hour after school with the other juvenile delinquents will be worth the fleeting moments of teenage lust she and Hank are sharing.

Michael is no help. He isn't worried about his sister at all. In fact, he seems to find the situation highly amusing. I have pointed out to him that for all we know, Lilly and Hank could have been kidnapped by Libyan terrorists, but he says he finds that unlikely. He thinks it more reasonable to assume that they are enjoying an afternoon showing at the Sony Imax.

As if. Hank is totally prone to motion sickness. He told us all about it when we drove past the cable car to Roosevelt Island this morning on the way to school.

What are Mamaw and Papaw going to say when they find out I lost their grandson?????

Top Five Places Lilly and Hank Could Be

1. Transit Museum.
2. Enjoying some corned beef at 2nd Avenue Deli.
3. Looking up Dionysius Thermopolis's name on the wall of immigrants at Ellis Island.
4. Getting tattoos on St Marks' Place.
5. Making wild passionate love back at his room at the SoHo Grand.

OH GOD!!!!!!!!!!!!!!!

Wednesday, October 28, World Civ.

Still no sign of them.

Wednesday, October 28, Bio.

Still nothing.

Homework:

Algebra: solve problems #3, 9, 12 on pg. 147
English: Profound Moment!!
World Civ.: read chapter 10
Gifted and Talented: please
French: 5 sentences: une blague, la montagne, la mer, il y a du soleil, une vacance
Biology: ask Kenny

I am so sure, who can concentrate on homework when your best friend and cousin are missing in New York City????

Wednesday, October 28, Algebra Review

Lars says he thinks it would be precipitous at this point to call the police. Mr Gianini agrees with him. He says Lilly is ultimately quite sensible, and it is unrealistic to believe that she might let Hank fall into the hands of Libyan terrorists. I was, of course, only using Libyan terrorists as an example of the type of peril that might befall the two of them. There is another scenario which is much more disturbing:

Supposing Lilly is in love with him.

Seriously. Supposing Lilly, against all reason, has fallen madly in love with my cousin Hank, and he has fallen in love with her. Stranger things have happened. I mean, maybe Lilly is starting to realize that, yeah, Boris is a genius, but he still dresses funny and is incapable of breathing through his nose. Maybe she's willing to sacrifice those long intellectual conversations she and Boris used to have for a boy whose only asset is what is commonly referred to as booty.

And Hank, maybe he's been dazzled by Lilly's superior intellect. I mean, her IQ is easily a hundred points higher than his.

But can't they see that in spite of their mutual attraction, this relationship can only lead to ruin? I mean, suppose they DO IT, or something? And suppose that in spite of all those public service announcements on MTV, they neglect to practise safe sex, like my mom and Mr G? They'll have to get married, and then Lilly will have to go live in Indiana in a trailer park, because that's where all teen mothers live. And she'll be wearing Wal-Mart housedresses and smoking Kools while Hank goes off to the rubber tyre factory and makes five-fifty an hour.

Am I the only one who can see where all of this is heading? What is wrong with everyone?????

First – grouping (evaluate with grouping symbols beginning with the inner most one)
Second – evaluate all powers
Third – multiply and division left to right
Fourth – add and subtract in order left to right

Wednesday, October 28, 7 p.m.

It's all right. They're safe.

Apparently, Hank got back to the hotel around five, and Lilly showed up at her apartment, according to Michael, a little before that.

I would seriously like to know where they were, but all either of them will say is, 'Just walking around.'

Lilly adds, 'God, could you be a little more possessive?'

I am so sure.

But I have bigger things to worry about. Right as I was about to step into Grandmere's suite at the Plaza for my princess lesson today, Dad appeared, looking nervous.

Only two things make my dad nervous. One is my mother.

And the other is his mother.

He said in a low voice, 'Listen, Mia, about the wedding situation . . . '

I said, 'I hope you had a chance to talk to Grandmere.'

'Your grandmother has already sent out the invitations. To the wedding, I mean.'

'*What?*'

Oh my God. Oh my God. This is a disaster. A *disaster*!

My dad must have known what I was thinking from my expression, since he went, 'Mia, don't worry. I'll take care of it. Just leave it to me, all right?'

But how can I not worry? My dad is a good guy and all. At least he tries to be, anyway. But we're talking *Grandmere* here. GRANDMERE. Nobody goes up against *Grandmere*, not even the prince of Genovia.

And whatever he might have said to her so far, it certainly hasn't worked. She and Vigo are more deeply absorbed than ever in their nuptial planning.

'We have had acceptances already,' Vigo informed me proudly when I walked in, 'from the mayor, and Mr Donald Trump, and Miss Diane von Fustenberg, and the royal family of Sweden, and Mr and Mrs Michael Douglas and Mr Phil Collins, and of course the Duchess of York.'

I didn't say anything. That's because all I could think was what my mother was going to say, if she walked down the aisle and there was Catherine Zeta Jones-Douglas and Phil Collins. She might actually run screaming from the room.

'Your dress arrived,' Vigo informed me, his eyebrows waggling suggestively.

'My what?' I said.

Unfortunately Grandmere overheard me, and clapped her hands so loudly she sent Rommel scurrying for cover, apparently thinking a nuclear missile or something had gone off.

'Do not ever let me hear you say *what* again,' Grandmere fire-breathed at me. 'Say, *I beg your pardon*.'

I looked at Vigo, who was trying not to smile. Really! Vigo actually thinks it's funny when Grandmere gets mad.

If there is a Genovian medal for valour, he should totally get it.

'I beg your pardon, Mr Vigo,' I said, politely.

'Please, please,' Vigo said, waving his hand. 'Just Vigo, none of this mister business, Your Highness. Now tell me. What do you think of this?'

And suddenly, he pulled this dress from a box.

And the minute I saw it, I was lost.

Because it was the most beautiful dress I have ever seen. It looked just like Glinda the Good Witch's dress from *The Wizard of Oz* – only not as sparkly. Still, it was pink with this big poofy skirt, and it had little rosettes on the sleeves. I had never wanted a dress as much as I wanted that one the minute I laid eyes on it.

I had to try it on. I just had to.

Grandmere supervised the fitting, while Vigo hovered nearby, offering often to refresh her Sidecar. In addition to enjoying her favourite cocktail, Grandmere was smoking one of her long cigarettes, so she looked even more officious than usual. She kept pointing with the cigarette and going, 'No, not that way,' and 'For God's sake, stop slouching, Amelia.'

It was determined that the dress was too big in the bust (what else is new?) and would have to be taken in. The alterations would take until Saturday, but Vigo assured us he'd see that they were done in time.

And that's when I remembered what this dress was actually for.

God, what kind of daughter am I? I am terrible. I don't want this wedding to happen. My mother doesn't want this wedding to happen. So what am I doing, trying on a dress I'm supposed to be wearing at this event nobody but Grandmere wants to see happen, and which, if my dad succeeds, isn't going to happen anyway?

Still, I thought my heart might break as I took off the dress and put it back on its satin hanger. It was the most beautiful thing I had ever seen, let alone worn. If only, I couldn't help thinking, Michael could see me in this dress.

Or even Jo-C-Rox. He might overcome his shyness and be able to tell me to my face what he'd been able to tell me before only in writing . . . and if it turns out he isn't that chilli guy, maybe we could actually go out.

But there was only one appropriate place to wear a dress like this, and that was in a wedding.

And no matter how much I wanted to wear that dress, I

certainly didn't want there to be a wedding. My mother was barely holding onto her sanity as it was. A wedding at which Phil Collins was in attendance – and who knows, maybe even playing – might push her over the edge.

Still, I've never in my life felt as much like a princess as I did in that dress.

Too bad I'll never get to wear it.

Wednesday, October 28, 10 p.m.

OK, so I was just casually flipping through the channels, you know, taking a little study break and all from thinking up a profound moment to write about in my English journal, when all of a sudden I hit Channel 67, one of the public access channels, and there is an episode of Lilly's show, *Lilly Tells It Like It Is*, that I have never seen before. Which was weird, because *Lilly Tells It Like It Is* is usually on Friday nights.

But then I figured Lilly's show was being pre-empted for coverage of a mayoral address on Friday or something.

So I'm sitting there, watching the show, and it turns out to be the slumber party episode. You know, the one we taped on Saturday, with all the other girls confessing their French kissing exploits, and me dropping the eggplant out the window . . . ? Only Lilly had edited out any scene showing my face, so unless you knew Mia Thermopolis was the one in the pyjamas with the strawberries all over them, you would never have known it was me.

All in all, pretty tame stuff. Maybe some really puritanical moms would get upset about the French kissing, but there aren't too many of those in the five boroughs, which is the extent of the broadcast region.

Then the camera did this funny skittering thing, and when the picture got clear again, there was this close-up of my face. That's right. MY FACE. I was lying on the floor with this pillow under my head, talking in this sleepy way.

Then I remembered: at the slumber party, after everyone else had fallen asleep, Lilly and I had stayed awake, chatting.

And it turned out she'd been FILMING ME THE WHOLE TIME!

I was lying there going, 'The thing I most want to do is

389

start a place for stray and abandoned animals. Like I went to Rome once, and there were about eighty million cats there, roaming around the monuments. And they totally would have died if these nuns hadn't fed them and stuff. So the first thing I think I'll do is, I'll start a place where all the stray animals in Genovia will be taken care of. You know? And I'd never have any of them put to sleep, unless they were really sick or something. And there'll just be like all these dogs and cats, and maybe some dolphins and ocelots—'

Lilly's voice, disembodied, went, 'Are there ocelots in Genovia?'

I went, 'I hope so. Maybe not though. But whatever. Any animals that need a home, they can come live there. And maybe I'll hire some seeing-eye dog trainers, and they can come and train all the dogs to be seeing-eye dogs. And then we can give them away free to blind people who need them. And then we can take the cats to hospitals and old people's homes, and let the patients pet them, because that always makes people feel better. Except the people like my grand-mere who hate cats. We can take dogs for them. Or maybe one of the ocelots.'

Lilly's voice: 'And that's going to be your first act when you become the ruler of Genovia?'

I went, sleepily, 'Yeah, I think so. Maybe we could just turn the whole castle into an animal shelter, you know? And like all the strays in Europe can come live there. Even those cats in Rome.'

'Do you think your grandmere is going to like that? I mean, having all those stray cats around the castle?'

I went, 'She'll be dead by then, so who cares?'

Oh my God! I hope they don't have public access on the TVs up at the Plaza!

Lilly asked me, 'What part of it do you hate the most? Being a princess, I mean.'

'Oh, that's easy. Not being able to go to the deli to buy milk or Lottery tickets without having to call ahead and arrange for a bodyguard to escort me. Not being able just to come over and hang out with you without it being this big production. This whole thing with my fingernails. I mean, who cares how my fingernails look, right? Why does it even matter? That kind of stuff.'

Lilly went, 'Are you nervous? About your formal introduction to the people of Genovia, in December?'

'Well, not really nervous, just . . . I don't know. What if none of them like me? Like the ladies-in-waiting and stuff? I mean, nobody at school likes me. So chances are, nobody in Genovia will like me, either.'

'People at school like you,' Lilly said.

Then, right in front of the camera, I drifted off to sleep. Good thing I didn't drool, or worse, snore. I wouldn't have been able to show my face at school tomorrow.

Then these words floated up over the screen. They said, *Don't Believe the Hype! This Is the* Real *Interview with the Princess of Genovia!*

As soon as it was over, I called Lilly and asked her exactly what she thought she'd been doing.

She just went, in this infuriatingly superior voice, 'I just want people to be able to see the real Mia Thermopolis.'

'No, you don't,' I said. 'You just want one of the networks to pick up on the interview, and pay you lots of money for it.'

'Mia,' Lilly said, sounding wounded. 'How can you even think such a thing?'

She sounded so taken aback that I realized I must have been wrong about that one.

'Well,' I said, 'you could have told me.'

'Would you have agreed to it?' Lilly wanted to know.

'Well,' I said. 'No . . . probably not.'

'There you go,' Lilly said.

I guess I don't come off as quite as much of a big-mouthed idiot in Lilly's interview. I just come off as a whacko who has a thing for cats. I really don't know which is worse.

But the truth is, I'm actually starting not to care. I wonder if this is what happens to celebrities. Like maybe at first, you really care what they say about you in the press, but after a while, you're just like, Whatever.

I do wonder if Michael saw this, and if so, what he thought of my pyjamas. They are quite nice ones.

Thursday, October 29, English

Hank didn't come to school with me today. He called first thing this morning and said he wasn't feeling too well. I am not surprised. Last night Mamaw and Papaw called wanting to know where in Manhattan they could go for a New York strip steak. Since I do not generally frequent restaurants that serve meat, I asked Mr Gianini for a suggestion, and he made a reservation at this semi-famous steak place.

And then, in spite of my mother's strenuous objections, he insisted on taking Mamaw and Papaw and Hank and me out, so he could get to know his future in-laws better.

This was apparently too much for my mother. She actually got out of bed, put mascara and lipstick and a bra on, and went with us. I think it was mostly to guard against Mamaw driving Mr G away with her many references to the number of family cars my mother accidentally rolled over in cornfields while she was learning to drive.

At the restaurant, I am horrified to report, in spite of the increased risk of heart disease and some cancers to which saturated fats and cholesterol have scientifically been linked, my future stepfather, my cousin, and my maternal grand-parents – not to mention Lars, whom I had no idea was so fond of meat, and my mother, who attacked her steak like Rosemary attacked that raw chunk of ground beef in *Rosemary's Baby* (which I've never actually seen, but I heard about it) – ingested what had to have been the equivalent of an entire cow.

This distressed me very much and I wanted to point out to them how unnecessary and unhealthy it is to eat things that were once alive, but, remembering my princess training, I merely concentrated on my entrée of grilled vegetables and said nothing.

Still, I am not at all surprised Hank doesn't feel well. All that red meat is probably sitting, completely undigested, behind those washboard abs even as I write. (I am only assuming Hank has washboard abs, since, thankfully, I have not actually seen them.)

Interestingly, however, that was the one meal my mother has been able to keep down. This baby is no vegetarian, that's for sure.

Anyway, the disappointment Hank's absence has generated here at Albert Einstein is palpable. Miss Molina saw me in the hall and asked, sadly, 'You don't need another guest pass for your cousin today?'

Hank's absence also apparently means that my special dispensation from the mean looks the cheerleaders have been giving me is revoked: this morning Lana reached out and pinged the back of my bra and asked in her snottiest voice, 'What are you wearing a bra for? You don't need one.'

I long for a place where people treat each other with courtesy and respect. That, unfortunately, is not high school. Maybe in Genovia?

Anyway, the only person who seems happy about Hank's misfortune is Boris Pelkowski. He was waiting for Lilly by the front doors to the school when we arrived this morning, and as soon as he saw us he asked, 'Where is Honk?' (Because of his thick Russian accent, he pronounces Hank's name as if it were Honk.)

'Honk – I mean, Hank – is sick,' I informed him, and it would not be exaggerating to say that the look which spread across Boris's uneven features was beatific. It was actually a little bit touching. Boris's dog-like devotion to Lilly can be annoying, but I know that I really only feel that way about it because I am envious. *I* want a boy I can tell all my deepest secrets to. *I* want a boy who will French kiss me. *I* want a boy who will be jealous if I spend too much time with another guy, even a total bohunk like Hank.

But I guess we don't always get what we want, do we? It looks like all I'm going to get is a baby brother or sister, and a stepfather who is moving in tomorrow with his foozball table and who knows a lot about quadratic formulae.

Oh, and a throne, someday.

Big deal. I'd rather have a boyfriend.

Thursday, October 29, World Civ.

Things to Do Before Mr G Moves in

- Vacuum.

- Clean out catbox.

- Drop off laundry.

- Take out recycling, esp. any of Mom's magazines that refer to orgasms on the cover – very imp.!!!

- Remove feminine hygiene products from all bathrooms.

- Clear out space in living room for foozball table/pinball machine/large TV.

- Check medicine cabinet. Hide: Nair underarm hair remover, Jolene facial bleach – very imp.!!!

- Remove *Our Bodies, Ourselves* and *Joy of Sex* from Mom's bookshelves.

- Call cable company. Get Classic Sports Network added. Remove Romance Channel.

- Get Mom to stop hanging bras on bedroom doorknob.

- Stop biting off fake fingernails.

- Stop thinking so much about M.M.

- Lock on bathroom door.

- Toilet paper!!!!

Thursday, October 29, G & T

I don't believe this.

They've done it again.

Hank and Lilly have disappeared AGAIN!!!!!!!!!!!

I didn't even know about the Hank part until Lars got a call on his mobile phone from my mother. She was very annoyed, because her mother had called her at the studio, screaming hysterically because Hank was missing from his hotel room. Mom wanted to know if Hank had shown up at school.

Which, to the best of my knowledge, he had not.

Then Lilly didn't show up for lunch.

She wasn't even very subtle about it, either. We were doing the Presidential Fitness exam in PE right before lunch, and just as it was her turn to climb the rope, Lilly started complaining that she had cramps.

Since Lilly complains that she has cramps every single time the Presidential Fitness exam rolls around, I wasn't suspicious. Mrs Potts sent Lilly to the nurses' office, and I figured I'd see her at lunch, miraculously recovered.

But then she didn't show up for lunch. A consultation with the nurse revealed that Lilly's cramps had been of such severity she'd decided to go home for the rest of the day.

Cramps. I am so sure. Lilly doesn't have cramps. What she has is the hots for my cousin!

The real question is, how long can we keep this from Boris? Remembering the Mahler we'd been subjected to yesterday, everyone is being careful not to remark how coincidental it is that Lilly is sick and Hank is missing in action at the same time. Nobody wants to have to resort to the gym mats again. Those things were heavy.

397

As a precaution, Michael is trying to keep Boris busy with a computer game he invented called Decapitate the Backstreet Boy. In it, you get to hurl knives and axes and stuff at members of the Backstreet Boys. The person who cuts the heads off the most Backstreet Boys moves up to another level, where he gets to cut off the heads of the boys in 98 Degrees, then 'N Sync, etc. The player who cuts off the most heads gets to carve his initials on Ricky Martin's naked chest.

I can't believe Michael only got a B on this game in his computer class. The teacher took points off because he felt it wasn't violent enough for today's market.

Mrs Hill is letting us talk today. I know it's because she doesn't want to have to listen to Boris play Mahler, or worse, Wagner. I went up to Mrs Hill after class yesterday and apologized for what I said on TV about her always being in the teachers' lounge, even though it was the truth. She said not to worry about it. I'm pretty sure this is because my dad sent her a DVD player, along with a big bunch of flowers, the day after the interview was broadcast. She's been a lot nicer to me since then.

You know, I find all of this stuff about Lilly and Hank very difficult to process. I mean, *Lilly*, of all people, turning out to be such a slave to lust. Because she can't genuinely be in love with Hank. He's a nice enough guy and all – and very good-looking – but let's face it, his elevator does *not* go all the way up.

Lilly, on the other hand, belongs to Mensa – or at least she could if she didn't think it hopelessly bourgeois. Plus Lilly isn't exactly what you'd call a traditional beauty – I mean, *I* think she's pretty, but according to today's admittedly limited ideal of what attractive is, Lilly doesn't really pass muster. She's much shorter than me, and kind of chunky, and has that sort of squished-in face. Not really the type you'd expect a guy like Hank to fall for.

So what do a girl like Lilly and a guy like Hank have in common, anyway?

Oh, God, don't answer that.

Homework:

Algebra: pg. 123, problems 1–5, 7
English: in your journal, describe one day in your life. Don't forget profound moment.
World Civ.: answer questions at end of chapter 10
Gifted and Talented: bring one dollar on Monday for ear plugs
French: une description d'une personne, trente mots minimum
Biology: Kenny says not to worry, he'll do it for me

Thursday, October 29, 7 p.m.,
Limo back to the loft

Another huge shock. If my life continues along this roller-coaster course, I may have to seek professional counselling.

When I walked in for my princess lesson, there was Mamaw – *Mamaw* – sitting on one of Grandmere's tiny pink couches, sipping tea.

'Oh, she was always like that,' Mamaw was saying. 'Stubborn as a mule.'

I was sure they were talking about me. I threw down my bookbag and went, 'I am *not*!'

Grandmere was sitting on the couch opposite Mamaw, a teacup and saucer poised in her hands. In the background, Vigo was running around like a little wind-up toy, answering the phone and saying things like, 'No, the orange blossoms are for the wedding party, the roses are for the centrepieces,' and 'But *of course* the lamb chops were meant to be appetizers.'

'What kind of way is that to enter a room?' Grandmere barked at me in French. 'A princess never interrupts her elders, and she certainly never throws things. Now come here and greet me properly.'

I went over and gave her a kiss on both cheeks, even though I didn't want to. Then I went over to Mamaw and did the same thing. Mamaw giggled and went, 'How continental!'

Grandmere said, 'Now sit down, and offer your grandmother a madeleine.'

I sat down, to show how unstubborn I can be, and offered Mamaw a madeleine from the plate on the table in front of her, the way Grandmere had shown me.

Mamaw giggled again and took one of the cookies. She kept her pinky in the air as she did so.

'Why, thanks, hon,' she said.

'Now,' Grandmere said, in English. 'Where were we, Shirley?'

Mamaw went, 'Oh, yes. Well, as I was saying, she's always been that way. Just stubborn as the day is long. I'm not surprised she's dug her heels in about this wedding. Not surprised at all.'

Hey, it wasn't me they were talking about after all. It was—

'I mean, I can't tell you we were thrilled when this happened the first time. 'Course, Helen never mentioned he was a prince. If we had known, we'd have encouraged her to marry him.'

'Understandably,' Grandmere murmured.

'But this time,' Mamaw said, 'well, we just couldn't be more thrilled. Frank is a real doll.'

'Then we are agreed,' Grandmere said. 'This wedding must – and will – take place.'

'Oh, definitely,' Mamaw said.

I half expected them to spit in their hands and shake on it, an old Indiana custom I learned from Hank.

But instead they each took a sip of their tea.

I was pretty sure nobody wanted to hear from me, but I cleared my throat anyway.

'Amelia,' Grandmere said, in French. 'Don't even think about it.'

Too late. I said, 'Mom doesn't want—'

'Vigo,' Grandmere called. 'Do you have those shoes? The ones that match the princess's dress?'

Like magic, Vigo appeared, carrying the prettiest pair of pink satin slippers I have ever seen. They had rosettes on the toes that matched the ones on my maid of honour dress.

'Aren't they lovely?' Vigo said, as he showed them to me. 'Don't you want to try them on?'

It was cruel. It was underhanded.

It was Grandmere, all over.

But what could I do? I couldn't resist. The shoes fitted perfectly, and looked, I have to admit, gorgeous on me. They gave my ski-like feet the appearance of being a size smaller – maybe even two sizes! I couldn't wait to wear them, and the dress too. Maybe if the wedding was called off, I could wear it to the prom. If things work out with Jo-C-rox, I mean.

'It would be a shame to have to send them back,' Grandmere said with a sigh, 'because your mother is being so stubborn.'

Then again, maybe not.

'Couldn't I keep them for another occasion?' I asked. Hint, hint.

'Oh, no,' Grandmere said. 'Pink is so inappropriate for anything but a wedding.'

Why me?

When my lesson was over – apparently, today's consisted of sitting there listening to my two grandmothers complain about how their children (and grandchildren) don't appreciate them – Grandmere stood up and said to Mamaw, 'So we understand one another, Shirley?'

And Mamaw said, 'Oh, yes, Your Highness.'

This sounded very ominous to me. In fact, the more I think about it, the more convinced I am that my dad hasn't done a single solitary thing to bail Mom out of what is clearly going to be a very messy situation. According to Grandmere, a limo is going to swing by our place on

402

Saturday to pick up me, Mom, and Mr Gianini. It's going to be pretty obvious to everyone when my mom refuses to get into the car that there isn't going to be any wedding.

I think I am going to have to take matters into my own hands. I know Dad assured me that everything is under control, but we're talking Grandmere. GRANDMERE!!!!!

During the ride downtown I tried pumping Mamaw for information – you know, about what she and Grandmere meant when they said they 'understood' one another.

But she wouldn't tell me a thing . . . except that she and Papaw were too tired, what with all the sightseeing they've been doing – not to mention worrying about Hank, whom they still hadn't heard from – to go out for dinner tonight, and were going to stay in and order room service.

Which is just as well, because I'm pretty sure if I have to hear one more person say the words 'medium rare', I might hurl.

More Thursday, 9 p.m.

Well, Mr Gianini is all moved in. I have already played nine games of foozball. Boy, are my wrists tired.

It's not really weird having him here on a permanent basis, because he was always hanging around before, anyway. The only real difference is the big TV, the pinball machine, the foozball table, and the drum kit in the corner where we normally keep Mom's lifesize metallic gold bust of Elvis.

But the coolest thing is the pinball machine. It's called Motorcycle Gang, and it has all these very realistic drawings of tattooed, leather-wearing Hell's Angels on it. Also, it has pictures of the Hell's Angels' girlfriends, who don't have very much clothing on at all, bending over and sticking out their enormous bosoms. When you sink a ball, the pinball machine makes the noise of a motorcycle engine revving very loudly.

My mother took one look at it and just stood there, shaking her head.

I know it's misogynistic and sexist and all, but it's also really, really neat.

Mr Gianini told me today that he thought it would be all right for me to call him Frank now, considering the fact that we are practically related. But I just can't bring myself to do it. So I just call him Hey. I go, 'Hey, can you pass the parmesan?' and 'Hey, have you seen the remote control?'

See? No names needed. Pretty clever, huh?

Of course, it hasn't exactly been smooth sailing. There's the small fact that on Saturday there's supposedly going to be this huge celebrity wedding that I know has not been cancelled, and that I also know my mother still hasn't the slightest intention of attending.

But when I ask her about it, instead of freaking out, my mom just smiles all secretively and says, 'Don't worry about it, Mia.'

But how can I help worrying about it? The only thing that is definitely off is my mom and Mr G's trip to the courthouse. I asked if they still wanted me to come dressed as the Empire State Building, thinking I should probably start working on my costume and all, but my mom just got this furtive look in her eye and said, Why don't we just hold off on that.

I could kind of tell she didn't want to talk about it, so I clammed up and went and called Lilly. I figured it was about time she gave me some explanation as to just what was going on between her and Hank.

But when I called her, the line was busy. Which meant there was a good chance Lilly or Michael – or both of them – were on-line. I took a gamble, and instant messaged Lilly. She wrote back right away.

```
FtLouie: Lilly, just where did you and Hank
disappear to today? And don't lie and say you
weren't together.
>
WmnRule: I fail to see what business it is of
yours.
>
FtLouie: Well, let's just say that if you want
to hang onto your boyfriend, you better come up
with a good explanation.
>
WmnRule: I have a very good explanation. But I
```

am not likely to share it with you. You'll
just blab it to Beverly Bellerieve. Oh, and
twenty-two million viewers.
>
FtLouie: That is so totally unfair. Look,
Lilly, I'm worried about you. It isn't like you
to skip school. What about your book on high
school society? You may have missed out on some
valuable material for it.
>
WmnRule: Oh, really? Did something happen today
worth recording?
>
FtLouie: Well, some of the seniors snuck into
the teachers' lounge and put a foetal pig in
the mini-fridge.
>
WmnRule: Gosh, I'm so sorry I missed that.
Is there anything else, Mia? Because I am
trying to research something on the Web right
now.

Yes, there was something else. Didn't she know how wrong
it was to be seeing two boys at the same time? Especially
when some of us don't even have *one* boy? Couldn't she see
how selfish and mean-spirited that was?

But I didn't write that. Instead, I wrote:

FtLouie: Well, Boris was pretty upset, Lilly. I
mean, he totally suspects something.
>
WmnRule: Boris has got to learn that in a
loving relationship it is important to

406

```
establish bonds of trust. That is something you
might keep in mind yourself, Mia.
```

I realize, of course, that Lilly is talking about *our* relationship
– hers and mine. But if you think about it, it applies to more
than just Lilly and Boris, and Lilly and me. It applies to me
and my dad too. And me and my mom. And me and . . .
well, just about everybody.

Was this, I wondered, a profound moment? Should I get
out my English journal?

It was right after this that it happened: I got instant messaged by someone else. By Jo-C-rox himself!

```
JoCrox: So am I going to see you at Rocky
Horror?
```

Oh my God. Oh my GOD. OH MY GOD!!!!!!!!!
Jo-C-rox is going to *Rocky Horror* on Saturday.
And so is Michael.
Really, there is only one logical explanation that can be
drawn from this:
Jo-C-rox is Michael. Michael is Jo-C-rox.
He HAS to be. He just HAS to be.
Right????????????
I didn't know what to do. I wanted to jump up from my
computer and run around my room and scream and laugh
at the same time.

Instead – and I don't know where I got the presence of
mind to do this, I wrote back:

```
FtLouie:     I hope so.
```

I can't believe it. I really can't believe it. Michael is Jo-C-
rox.

Right?
What am I going to do? What am I going to do???????

Friday, October 30, Algebra

Michael, for instance, didn't catch a ride with us this morning. Lilly says that is because he had last minute problems printing out a paper that is due today.

But I wonder if it is really because he is too scared to face me after admitting that he is Jo-C-rox.

Well, not that he actually admitted it. But he sort of did. Didn't he??????

Mr Howell is three times as old as Gilligan. The difference in their ages is 48. How old are Mr Howell and Gilligan?

T=Gilligan
3T=Mr Howell

3T-T=48
2T=48
T=24

OK.

I will never underestimate Lilly Moscovitz again. Nor will I suspect her of having anything but the most altruistic motives. This I hereby solemnly swear in writing.

It was at lunch when it happened.

We were all sitting there – me, my bodyguard, Tina Hakim Baba and her bodyguard, Lilly, Boris, Shameeka, and Ling Su. Michael, of course, sits over with the rest of the Computer Club, so he wasn't there, but everybody else who mattered was.

Shameeka was reading aloud to us from some of the brochures her father had got from girls' schools in New Hampshire. Each one filled Shameeka with more terror, and me with more shame for ever having opened my big mouth in the first place.

Suddenly, a shadow fell over our little table.

We looked up.

And there stood an apparition of such god-like stature that, for a minute, I think even Lilly believed the chosen people's long-lost Messiah had finally shown up.

It turned out it was only Hank.

But Hank looking as I had certainly never seen him before. He had on a black cashmere sweater beneath a clinging black leather coat, and black jeans that seemed to go on and on over his long, lean legs. His golden hair had been expertly styled and cut, and I swear, he looked so much like Keanu Reeves from *The Matrix* that I actually might have believed he had wandered in off the set if it hadn't been for the fact that on his feet, he wore cowboy boots. Black, expensive-looking ones, but cowboy boots, just the same.

I don't think it was my imagination that the entire crowd

inside the cafeteria seemed to gasp as Hank slid into a chair at our table – the reject table, I have frequently heard it called.

'Hello, Mia,' Hank said.

I stared at him. It wasn't just the clothes. There was something . . . different about him. His voice seemed deeper, somehow. And he smelled . . . well, good.

'So,' Lilly said to him, as she scooped a glob of creamy filling out of her Ring Ding. 'How'd it go?'

'Well,' Hank said, in that same deep voice. 'You're looking at Calvin Klein's newest underwear model.'

Lilly sucked the filling off her finger. 'Hmmm,' she said, with her mouth full. 'Good for you.'

'I owe it all to you, Lilly,' Hank said. 'If it weren't for you, they never would have signed me.'

And then it hit me. The reason Hank seemed so different was that his Indiana drawl was gone!

'Now, Hank,' Lilly said. 'We discussed this. It's your natural ability that got you where you are. I just gave you a few pointers.'

When Hank turned his gaze towards me, I saw that his sky-blue eyes were damp.

'Your friend Lilly,' he said to me, 'has done something no one's ever done for me in my life.'

I threw an accusing gaze at Lilly.

I knew it. I *knew* they'd had sex. It was just like Lilly to lose her virginity and not even tell me about it.

But then Hank went, 'She believed in me, Mia. Believed in me enough to help me pursue my dream . . . a dream I've had since I was a very young boy. A lot of people – including my own Mamaw and Pa – I mean, my grandparents – told me it was a pipe dream. They told me to give it up, that it would never happen. But when I told my dream to Lilly, she held out her hand—' Hank held out his hand to illustrate this, and all of us – me, Lars, Tina, Tina's bodyguard Wahim, Shameeka and Ling Su – looked at that hand, the nails of which had been perfectly manicured ' – and said, "Come with me, Hank. I will help you achieve your dream."'

Hank put his hand down. 'And do you know what?'

All of us – except Lilly, who went right on eating – were so astonished, we could only stare.

Hank did not wait for us to reply, however. He said, 'It happened. Today, it happened. My dream came true. I was signed by Elite Modelling Agency. I am their newest male supermodel.'

We all blinked at him.

'And I owe it all,' Hank said, 'to this woman here.'

Then something really shocking happened. Hank got up out of his chair, walked over to where Lilly was sitting, innocently finishing her Ring Ding, not suspecting a thing, and pulled her to a standing position.

Then as everyone in the entire cafeteria looked on – including, I noticed, Lana Weinberger and all her cronies over at the cheerleaders' table – my cousin Hank laid such a kiss on Lilly Moscovitz, I thought he just might suck that Ring Ding right back up again.

When he was done kissing her, Hank let go. And Lilly, looking as if someone had just poked her with an electric prod, sank slowly back down to her seat. Hank adjusted the lapels of his leather coat and turned to me.

'Mia,' he said. 'Tell Mamaw and Papaw they're going to have to find somebody to cover my shift at the hardware store. I ain't – I mean, I'm *not* – going back to Versailles. Ever.'

412

And with that, he strode from our cafeteria like a cowboy striding away from a gunfight he'd just won.

Or I suppose I should say he *started* to stride from the cafeteria. Unfortunately for Hank, he didn't make it out quite fast enough.

Because one of the people who had observed that searing kiss he'd laid on Lilly was none other than Boris Pelkowski.

And it was Boris Pelkowski – Boris Pelkowski, with his brace and his sweater tucked into his trousers – who stood up and said, 'Not so fast, hot shot.'

I'm not sure if Boris had just seen the movie *Top Gun* or what, but that *hot shot* came out sounding pretty menacing, considering Boris's accent and all.

Hank kept going. I don't know if he hadn't heard Boris, or if he wasn't about to let some little violin-playing genius mess up his great exit.

Then Boris did something completely reckless. He reached out and grabbed Hank by the arm as he went by and said, 'That's *my* girl you had your lips all over, pretty boy.'

I am not even joking. Those were his exact words. Oh, how my heart thrilled to hear them! If only some guy (OK, Michael) would say something like that about me. Not the Josiest girl he'd ever met, but *his* girl. Boris had actually referred to Lilly as *his* girl! No boy has ever referred to me as *his* girl. Oh, I know all about feminism and how women aren't property and it's sexist to go around claiming them as such. But, oh! If only somebody (OK, Michael) would say I was *his* girl!

Anyway, Hank just went, 'Huh?'

And then, from out of nowhere, Boris's fist went sailing into Hank's face. *Pow!*

Only it didn't really sound like pow. It sounded more like a thud. There was a sickening crunch of bones splintering.

413

All of us girls gasped, thinking that Boris had marred Hank's perfect cover guy face.

But we needn't have worried: it was Boris's hand that made the crunching sound, not Hank's face. Hank escaped completely unscathed. Boris is the one who has to have his knuckles splinted.

And you know what that means:

No more Mahler.

Whoopee!!!

It's unprincess-like of me, however, to gloat over another's misfortune.

Friday, October 30, French

I borrowed Lars's mobile phone and called the SoHo Grand between lunch and fifth period. I mean, I figured someone should let Mamaw and Papaw know that Hank was all right. Well, an Elite model who would soon be posing in nothing but a pair of tighty-whities on a giant billboard for all of Times Square to see, but all right, just the same.

Mamaw must have been sitting by the phone, since she picked up on the first ring.

'Clarisse?' she said.

Which is weird. Because Clarisse is Grandmere's name.

'Mamaw?' I said. 'It's me, Mia.'

'Oh, *Mia*.' Mamaw laughed a little. 'I'm sorry, honey. I thought you were the princess. I mean, the dowager princess. Your other grandma.'

I went, 'Uh, yeah. Well, it's not. It's me. And I'm just calling to tell you that I heard from Hank.'

Mamaw shrieked so loud, I had to hold the phone away from my ear.

'WHERE IS HE????' she yelled. 'YOU TELL HIM FROM ME THAT WHEN I GET MY HANDS ON HIM HE'S—'

'Mamaw,' I cried. It was kind of embarrassing, because all sorts of people in the hallway heard her yelling and were looking at me. I tried to make myself inconspicuous by hunching behind Lars.

'Mamaw,' I said, 'he got a contract with Elite Modelling Agency. He's the next Calvin Klein underwear model. He's going to be a big celebrity, like—'

'UNDERWEAR????' Mamaw yelled. 'Mia, you tell that boy to call me RIGHT NOW.'

415

'Well, I can't really do that, Mamaw,' I said. 'On account of the fact that—'

'RIGHT NOW,' Mamaw repeated, 'or he's in BIG TROUBLE.'

'Um,' I said. The bell was ringing anyway. 'OK, Mamaw. Is, um, the, uh, wedding still on tomorrow?'

'The WHAT?'

'The wedding,' I said, wishing I could, just for once, be a normal girl who did not have to go around asking people if the royal marriage of her pregnant mother and her Algebra teacher was still on.

'Well, of course it's still on,' Mamaw said. 'What do you think?'

'Oh,' I said. 'You, um, talked to my mom?'

'Of course I did,' Mamaw said. 'Everything is all set.'

'Really?' I was immensely surprised. I could not picture my mother going along with this thing. Not in a million years. 'And she said she'd be there?'

'Well, of course she'll be there,' Mamaw said. 'It's her wedding, isn't it?'

Well . . . sort of, I guess. I didn't say that to Mamaw though. I said, 'Sure.' And then I hung up, feeling crushed.

For entirely selfish reasons too, I confess. I was a little bit sad for my mom, I guess, since she really had tried to put up a resistance against Grandmere. I mean, she really had tried. It wasn't her fault, of course, that she'd been going up against such a inexorable force.

But mostly I felt sad for myself. I would NEVER escape in time for *Rocky Horror*. Never, never, *never*. I mean, I know the movie doesn't even start until midnight, but wedding receptions last way longer than that.

And who knows if Michael will ever ask me out again? I mean, not once today has he acknowledged that he is, in fact, Jo-C-rox, nor has he mentioned *Rocky Horror*. Not once. Not even so much as a reference to the cartoon network.

And we talked at length during G & T. AT LENGTH. That is on account of how some of us who saw last year's groundbreaking episode of *Lilly Tells It Like It Is* entitled, *Yes, You as an Individual Can Bring Down the Sexist, Racist, Ageist, and Sizeist Modelling Industry* (by 'criticizing ads that demean women and limit our ideas of beauty', and 'finding ways to make your protest known to the companies advertised', and 'letting the media know you want to see more varied and realistic images of women'. Also, Lilly urged us to 'challenge men who judge, choose, and discard women on the basis of appearance') were understandably confused by Lilly's helping Hank to realize his dream of supermodel stardom.

The following exchange took place last period during Gifted and Talented (Mrs Hill has returned to the teachers' lounge – permanently, one can only hope) and included Michael Moscovitz, who, as you will see, did NOT ONCE mention Jo-C-rox or *Rocky Horror*.

Me: Lilly, I thought you found the modelling industry as a whole sexist and racist and belittling to the human race.

Lilly: So? What's your point?

Me: Well, according to Hank, you helped him realize his dream of becoming a you know-what. A model.

Lilly: Mia, when I recognize a human soul crying out for self-actualization, I am powerless to stop myself. I must do what I can to see that that person's dream is realized.

       (Gee, I haven't noticed Lilly doing all that much to

417

help me realize *my* dream of French kissing her brother.

But on the other hand, I have not exactly made that dream known to her.)

Me: Um, Lilly, I hadn't noticed that you had a real foothold in the modelling industry.

Lilly: I don't. I merely taught your cousin how to make the most of his God-given talents. Some simple lessons in elocution and fashion and he was well on his way to landing that contract with Elite.

Me: Well, why did it have to be such a big secret?

Lilly: Do you have any idea how fragile the male ego is?

Here Michael broke in.

Michael: Hey!

Lilly: I'm sorry, but it's true. Hank's self-esteem had already been reduced to nothing thanks to Amber, Corn Queen of Versailles County. I couldn't allow any negative comments to ruin what little self-confidence he had left. You know how fatalistic boys can be.

Michael: Hey!

Lilly: It was vital that Hank be allowed to pursue his dream without the slightest fatalistic influence. Otherwise, I knew, he didn't stand a chance. And so I kept our plan secret even from those I most cared about. Any one of you, without consciously meaning to, might have torpedoed Hank's chances with the most casual of comments.

Me: Come on. We'd have been supportive.

Lilly: Mia, think about it. If Hank had said to you, 'Mia, I want to be a model,' what would you have done? Come on. You would have laughed.

Me: No, I wouldn't have.

Lilly:	Yes, you would have. Because to you, Hank is your whiny, allergy-prone cousin from the Boondocks, who doesn't even know what a bagel is. But I, you see, was able to look beyond that, to the man Hank had the potential to become . . .
Michael:	Yeah, a man who is destined to have his own pin-up calendar.
Lilly:	You, Michael, are just jealous.
Michael:	Oh, yeah. I've always wanted a big picture of myself in my underwear hanging up in Times Square.
	(Actually, I think that is something I would really enjoy seeing, but Michael was, of course, being sarcastic.)
Michael:	You know, Lil, I highly doubt Mom and Dad are going to be so impressed by your tremendous act of charity that they're going to overlook the fact that you skipped school to do it. Especially when they find out you've got detention next week because of it.
Lilly:	(looking long-suffering) The most eleemosynary are often martyred.

And that was it. That's all he said to me, all day. ALL DAY.

Note to self: look up *eleemosynary*

Possible Reasons Michael Won't Admit He is Jo-C-rox

1. He really is too shy to reveal his true emotions for me.
2. He thinks I don't feel the same way about him.
3. He's changed his mind and doesn't like me after all.
4. He doesn't want to have to bear the social stigma of dating a freshman and he is just waiting until I am a sophomore before asking me out. (Except that by then he'll be a freshman in college and won't want to bear the social stigma of dating a high school girl.)
5. He isn't Jo-C-rox at all and it turns out I am obsessing about something written by that guy from the cafeteria who has the thing about corn.

Homework:

Algebra: none (no Mr G!)
English: finish Day in a Life! Plus Profound Moment!
World Civ.: read and analyze one current event from *Sunday Times* (200 wd minimum)
Gifted and Talented: don't forget the dollar!
French: pg. 120, huit phrases (ex A)
Biology: questions at end of chapter 12 – get answers from Kenny!

Saturday, October 31

I woke with the strangest feeling of foreboding. I couldn't figure out why for a few minutes. I lay there in bed, listening to the rain patter against my window. Fat Louie was at the end of my bed, kneading the comforter and purring very loudly.

Then I remembered: today, according to my grandmother, is the day my pregnant mother is supposed to marry my Algebra teacher in a huge ceremony at the Plaza Hotel, with musical accompaniment courtesy of Phil Collins.

I lay there for a minute, wishing my temperature was one hundred and two again, so I wouldn't have to get out of bed and face what was sure to be a day of drama and hurt feelings. WHY ME???

MY ENGLISH JOURNAL

A Day In My Life
by Mia Thermopolis

Saturday, October 31

8:16 a.m. *Awake to find loft ostensibly empty, with exception of bodyguard (Lars). Decide mother probably sleeping in (something she does a lot these days).*

8:18 a.m.–8:45 a.m. *Play foozball with bodyguard. Win 3 out of 12 games. Decide must practise foozball in spare time.*

8:50 a.m. *Curious as to why riotous game of foozball – not to mention incredibly loud pinball machine – have not wakened mother, so knock gently on bedroom door. Stand there hoping door does not open and reveal view of mother actually sharing bed with Algebra teacher.*

8:51 a.m. *Knock louder. Decide perhaps cannot be heard due to intense lovemaking session. Sincerely hope I will not be inadvertent witness to aforementioned lovemaking session.*

8:52 a.m. *After receiving no response to my knock, I go into mother's bedroom. No one is there! Check of mother's bathroom reveals crucial items such as mascara, lipstick, and bottle of folic acid tablets are missing from medicine cabinet! Begin to suspect something is afoot.*

8:55 a.m. *Phone rings. I answer it. It is my father. Following conversation ensues:*

Me: *Dad? Mom's missing. And so is Mr Gianini.*

Father: *You still call him Mr Gianini even though he lives with you?*

Me: *Dad. Where are they?*

Father: *Don't worry about it.*

422

Me: *That woman is carrying my last chance at having a sibling. How can I help but worry about her?*

Father: *Everything is under control.*

Me: *How am I supposed to believe that?*

Father: *Because I said so.*

Me: *Dad, I think you should know, I have some very serious trust issues concerning you.*

Father: *How come?*

Me: *Well, part of it might be the fact that up until about a month ago, you had lied to me for my entire life about who you are and what you do for a living.*

Father: *Oh.*

Me: *So just tell me. WHERE IS MY MOTHER?*

Father: *She left you a letter. You can have it at eight o'clock tonight.*

Me: *Dad, eight o'clock is when the wedding is supposed to start.*

Father: *I am aware of that.*

Me: *Dad, you can't do this to me. What am I supposed to tell—*

Voice: *Philippe, is everything all right?*

Me: *Who is that? Who is that, Dad? Is that Beverly Bellerieve?*

Father: *I have to go now, Mia.*

Me: *No, Dad, wait—*

CLICK

9:00 a.m.–9:15 a.m. *Tear apartment apart, looking for clues as to where mother might have disappeared to. Find none.*

9:20 a.m. *Phone rings. Paternal grandmother on line. Requests to know if mother and I are ready for trip to salon for beauty makeover. Inform her that mother has left already (well, it's the truth, isn't it?). Grandmother suspicious. Inform her that if she has any questions to consult with her son, my father. Grandmother says she* *fully intends to do so. Also says limo will be by at ten o'clock to pick me up.*

10:00 a.m. *Limo pulls up. Bodyguard and I get into it. Inside is paternal grandmother (hereafter known as Grandmere) and maternal grandmother (hereafter known as Mamaw). Mamaw is very excited about upcoming nuptials – though excitement is somewhat dampened by cousin's desertion to become male supermodel. Grandmere, on other hand, is mysteriously calm. Says son (my father) has informed her that bride has decided to make own hair and make-up plans. Remembering missing folic acid tablets, I say nothing.*

10:20 a.m. *Enter Chez Paolo for a marathon day of beauty.*

6:45 p.m. *Emerge from Chez Paolo. Amazed at difference Paolo has made with Mamaw's hair. She no longer resembles mom in John Hughes film, but member of upscale country club.*

7:00 p.m. *Arrive at Plaza. Bride's absence attributed by father as desire to nap before ceremony. When I surreptitiously force Lars to call home on his mobile phone, however, no one answers.*

7:15 p.m. *Begins to rain again. Mamaw observes that rain on a wedding day is bad luck. Grandmere says, No, that's pearls. Mamaw says, No, rain. First sign of division within formerly united ranks of grandmas.*

7:30 p.m. *I am ushered into little chamber just off the White and Gold Room, where I sit with the other bridesmaids (supermodels Giselle, Karmen Kass and Amber Valetta, whom Grandmere has hired due to fact that my mother refused to supply her with list of her own bridesmaids). I have changed into my beautiful pink dress and matching shoes.*

7:40 p.m. *None of the other bridesmaids will talk to me, except to comment about how I look so 'sweet'. All they can talk about is a party they went to last night, where someone threw up on Claudia Schiffer's shoes.*

7:45 p.m. *Guests begin to arrive. I fail to recognize my maternal grandfather without his baseball cap. He looks quite spry in his tux. A little like an elderly Matt Damon.*

424

7:47 p.m. *Two people arrive who claim to be parents of the groom. Mr Gianini's parents from Long Island! Mr Gianini Sr. calls Vigo 'Bucko', and slips him a twenty in exchange for a seat in the front. Vigo looks delighted.*

7:48 p.m. *Fergie stands near door, chatting with Donald Trump about Manhattan real estate. She is looking for a four-bedroom for under ten grand a month. Donald wishes her luck.*

7:50 p.m. *Sting is growing his hair out. Almost don't recognize him. Looks faintly babe-like. Queen of Sweden asks him if he is friend of bride or groom. Says groom, for some inexplicable reason, though I happen to know from having looked through Mr Gianini's CDs that he owns nothing but the Grateful Dead.*

7:55 p.m. *Everyone goes quiet as Phil Collins sits down at baby grand. Pray that my mother is in different hemisphere and cannot see or hear this.*

8:00 p.m. *Everyone waiting expectantly. I demand that my father, who has joined me and the supermodels, give me letter from my mother. Dad surrenders letter.*

8:01 p.m. *I read letter.*

8:02 p.m. *I have to sit down.*

8:05 p.m. *Grandmere and Vigo in deep consultation. They seem to have realized that neither the bride nor the groom have shown up yet.*

8:07 p.m. *Amber Valetta whispers that if we don't get a move on, she's going to be late for a dinner engagement with Hugh Grant.*

8:10 p.m. *A hush falls over the guests as my father, looking excessively princely in his tux, in spite of his bald head, strides to the front of the White and Gold Room. Phil Collins stops playing.*

8:11 p.m. *My father makes the following announcement:*

> **Father:** I want to thank all of you for taking the time out of your
> busy schedules to come here tonight. Unfortunately, the
> wedding between Helen Thermopolis and Frank Gianini
> will not take place . . . at least, this evening. The happy
> couple have given us the slip, and this morning they flew

to Cancun, where I understand they plan to be married by a justice of the peace.

8:13 p.m. *A shriek is heard from the far side of the baby grand. It does not appear to have come from Phil Collins, but rather, an elegant old lady with mysteriously dark eyeliner. In other words, Grandmere.*

Father: You are of course urged to join us in the Grand Ballroom for dinner. And thank you again for coming.

8:15 p.m. *Father strides off. Bewildered guests gather their belongings and go in search of cocktails. No sound whatsoever is heard from behind baby grand.*

Me: *(to no one in particular)* Mexico! They must be crazy. If my mother drinks the water, my future brother or sister will be born with flippers for feet!

Amber: Don't worry, my friend Heather got pregnant in Mexico, and she drank the water, and she just gave birth to twins.

Me: And they had dorsal fins coming out of their backs, didn't they?

8:20 p.m. *Phil Collins begins to play 'The Circle of Life' from* The Lion King. *At least until Grandmere barks, 'Oh, shut up!'*

What the letter from my mother said:

Dear Mia,

By the time you read this, Frank and I will be married. I am sorry I couldn't tell you sooner, but when your grandmother asks you if you knew (and she will ask you), I wanted to be sure you could say truthfully that you didn't, so there won't be any ill feeling between the two of you.

Ill feeling between Grandmere and me? Who does she think she's kidding? There's nothing but ill feeling between us!

Well, as far I'm concerned, anyway.

More than anything, Frank and I wanted you to be there for our wedding. So we have decided that when we get back, we're going to have a another ceremony: this one will be kept strictly secret and very private, with just our little family and our friends!

Well, that should certainly be interesting. Most of my mom's friends are militant feminists or performance artists. One of them likes to stand up on a stage and pour chocolate syrup all over her naked body while reciting poetry.

I wonder how they are going to get along with Mr G's friends, who I understand like to watch a lot of sports.

You have been a tower of strength during this crazy time, Mia, and I want you to know how much I — as well as your father and stepfather — appreciate it. You are the best daughter a mother could have, and this new little guy (or girl) is the luckiest baby in the world to have you as a big sister.

Missing you already.

                                                        Mom

Saturday, October 31, 9 p.m.

I am in shock. I really am.

Not because my mom and my Algebra teacher eloped. That's kind of romantic, if you ask me.

No, it's the fact that my dad – *my dad* – helped them to do it. He actually defied his mother. In a BIG way.

In fact, because of all this, I'm starting to think my dad isn't scared of Grandmere at all! I think he just doesn't want to be bothered. I think he just feels it's easier to go along with her than to fight her, because fighting her is so messy and exhausting.

But not this time. This time he put his foot down.

And you can bet he's going to pay for it too.

I may never get over this. I am going to have to re-adjust everything I ever thought about him. Kind of like when Luke Skywalker finds out his dad is really Darth Vader. Only the opposite.

Anyway, while Grandmere was having a synaptic breakdown behind the baby grand, I went up to Dad and threw my arms around him and was like, 'You did it!'

He looked at me curiously. 'Why do you sound surprised?'

Oops. I said, totally embarrassed, 'Oh, well, because, you know.'

'No, I don't know.'

'Well,' I said. WHY??? WHY do I have such a big mouth???

I thought about lying. But I think my dad must have realized what I was thinking, since he went, in this warning voice, *'Mia . . .'*

'Oh, OK,' I said, grudgingly, letting him go. 'It's just that sometimes you give the appearance – just the appearance, mind you – of being a little bit scared of Grandmere.'

My dad reached out and wrapped an arm around my neck. He did this right in front of Hillary Clinton, who was getting up to follow everyone into the Grand Ballroom! She smiled at us as if she thought it was sweet though.

'Mia,' my dad said. 'I am not scared of my mother. She really isn't as bad as you think. She just needs proper handling.'

This was news to me.

'Besides,' my dad said, 'do you really think I would ever let you down? Or your mother? I will always be there for you two.'

This was so nice, I actually got tears in my eyes for a minute. But it might have been the smoke from all the cigarettes. There were a lot of Europeans at this party.

'Mia, I haven't done so badly by you, have I?' my dad asked, all of a sudden.

I was surprised by the question. 'No, Dad, of course not. You guys have always been OK parents.'

My dad nodded. 'I see.'

I could see I hadn't been complimentary enough, so I added, 'No, I mean it. I really couldn't ask for better . . . ' I couldn't help adding, 'I could probably live without the princess thing though.'

He looked as if he probably would have reached out and ruffled my hair if it hadn't been so full of mousse his hand would have stuck to it.

'Sorry about that,' he said. 'But do you really think you'd be happy, Mia, being Nancy Normal Teenager?'

Um. Yes.

Except I wouldn't want my name to be Nancy.

We might have gone on to have a really profound moment I could have written about in my English journal if Vigo hadn't come hurrying up just then. He looked frazzled.

429

And why not? His wedding was turning out to be a disaster! First the bride and groom had neglected to show up, and now the hostess, the Dowager Princess, had locked herself into her hotel suite and would not come out.

'What do you mean, she won't come out?' my father demanded.

'Just what I said, Your Highness.' Vigo looked like he was about to start crying. 'I have never seen her so angry! She says she has been betrayed by her own family, and she will never be able to show her face in public again, the shame is so great.'

My dad looked heavenward. 'Let's go,' he said.

When we got to the door to the penthouse suite, my dad signalled for Vigo and me to be quiet. Then he knocked on the door.

'Mother,' he called. 'Mother, it's Philippe. May I come in?'

No response. But I could tell she was in there. I could hear Rommel moaning softly.

'Mother,' my dad said. He tried turning the door handle, and found it locked. This caused him to sigh very deeply.

Well, you could see why. He had already spent the better part of the day thwarting all of her well-laid plans. That had to have been exhausting. And now *this*?

'Mother,' he said. 'I want you to open this door.'

Still no response.

'Mother,' my father said. 'You are being ridiculous. I want you to open the door this instant. If you don't, I shall fetch the housekeeper and have her open it for me. Are you trying to force me to resort to this? Is that it?'

I knew Grandmere would sooner let us see her without her make-up than let a member of the hotel staff be privy

430

to one of our family squabbles, so I laid a hand on my dad's arm and whispered, 'Dad, let me try.'

My father shrugged and, with a sort of if-you-want-to look, stepped aside.

I called through the door, 'Grandmere? Grandmere, it's me, Mia.'

I don't know what I'd expected. Certainly not for her to open the door. I mean, if she wouldn't do it for Vigo, whom she seemed to adore, or for her own son, who, if she didn't adore, was at least her only child, why would she do it for me?

But I was greeted with only silence from behind that door. Well, except for Rommel's whining.

I refused to be daunted, however. I raised my voice and called, 'I'm really sorry about my mom and Mr Gianini, Grandmere. But you have to admit it, I warned you that she didn't want this wedding. Remember? I told you she wanted something small. You might have realized that by the fact that there isn't a single person here who was actually invited by my mother. These are all *your* friends. Well, except for Mamaw and Papaw. And Mr G's parents. But I mean, come on. My mom does not know Imelda Marcos, OK? And Barbara Bush? I'm sure she's a very nice lady, but not one of my mom's closest buddies.'

Still no response.

'Grandmere,' I called through the door. 'Look, I am really surprised at you. I thought you were always teaching me that a princess has to be strong. I thought you said that a princess, no matter what kind of adversity she is facing, has to put on a brave face and not hide behind her wealth and privilege. Well, isn't that exactly what you're doing right now? Shouldn't you be down there, pretending this was exactly the way you planned things to go, and raising a glass to the happy couple in absentia?'

I jumped back as the doorknob to my grandmother's suite slowly turned. A second later, Grandmere came out, a vision in purple velvet and a diamond tiara.

She said, with a great deal of dignity, 'I had every intention of returning to the party. I merely came up here to freshen my lipstick.'

My dad and I exchanged glances.

'Sure, Grandmere,' I said. 'Whatever you say.'

'A princess,' Grandmere said, closing the door to her suite behind her, 'never leaves her guests unattended.'

'OK,' I said.

'So what are you two doing here?' Grandmere glared at my dad and me.

'We were, um, just checking on you,' I explained.

'I see.' Then Grandmere did a surprising thing. She slipped her hand through the crook of my elbow. Then, without looking at my dad, she said, 'Come along.'

I saw my dad roll his eyes at this blatent dis.

But he didn't look scared, the way *I* would have been.

'Hold on, Grandmere,' I said.

Then I slipped my hand through the crook of my dad's elbow, so the three of us were standing in the hallway, linked by . . . well, by me.

Grandmere just sniffed and didn't say anything. But my dad smiled.

And you know what? I'm not sure, but I think it might have been a profound moment for all of us.

Well, all right. At least for *me*, anyway.

Sunday, November 1, 2 p.m.

The evening wasn't a total bust.

Quite a few people seemed to have a very good time. Hank, for one. Surprisingly, he actually showed up just in time for dinner – he'd always been good at that – looking totally gorgeous in an Armani tux.

Mamaw and Papaw were delighted to see him. Mrs Gianini, Mr Gianini's mom, took quite a shine to him too. It must have been his clean-cut good manners. He hadn't forgotten any of Lilly's elocution lessons, and only mentioned his affection for 'muddin' on the weekends once. And later, when the dancing started, he asked Grandmere for the second waltz – Dad got the first – for ever cementing him in her mind as the ideal royal consort for me.

Thank God it's illegal in Genovia for first cousins to marry each other.

But the happiest people I talked to all evening weren't actually at the party. At around ten o'clock Lars handed me his mobile phone and, when I said, 'Hello?' wondering who it could be, my mom's voice, sounding very far away and crackly, went, 'Mia?'

I didn't want to say the word 'Mom' too loudly, since I knew Grandmere was hovering nearby. And I don't think it likely that Grandmere is going to forgive my parents anytime soon for the fast one they'd pulled. I ducked behind a pillar and whispered, 'Hey, Mom! Mr Gianini make an honest woman out of you yet?'

Well, he had. The deed was done (a little late, if you ask me, but, hey, at least the kid wouldn't be born harbouring the stigma of illegitimacy like I've had to, all my life). It was only like six o'clock where they were, and they were on a beach somewhere sipping (virgin) pina coladas. I made my mom promise not to have any more, because you can't trust the ice at those places.

'Parasites can exist in ice, Mom,' I informed her. 'There are these worms that live in the glaciers in Antarctica, you know. We studied them in Bio. They've been around for thousands of years. So even if the water's frozen, you can still get sick from it. You definitely only want to get ice made from bottled water – here, why don't you put Mr Gianini on the phone, and I'll tell him exactly what he has to do—'

My mom interrupted me.

'Mia,' she said. 'How are—' She cleared her throat. 'How's my mother taking it?'

'Mamaw?' I looked in Mamaw's direction. The truth was, Mamaw was having the time of her life. She was thoroughly enjoying her gig as mother of the bride. So far, she'd gotten to dance with Prince Albert, who was there representing the royal family of Monaco, as well as Michael Douglas – twice.

'Um,' I said. 'Mamaw's . . . Mamaw's really mad at you.'

It was a lie, of course, but it was a lie I knew would make my mother happy. One of her favourite things to do is make her parents mad. I guess you could say it was my wedding gift to her.

'Really, Mia?' she asked, breathlessly.

'Uh-huh,' I said, watching as Papaw twirled Mamaw around practically into the champagne fountain. 'They'll probably never speak to you again.'

'Oh,' Mom said, happily. 'Isn't that too bad?'

Sometimes my natural ability to lie actually comes in handy.

Unfortunately, right then our connection broke up. Well, at least Mom had heard my warning about the ice worms before we'd lost contact.

As for me, well, I can't say I had the time of my life – I

mean, the only person even close to my age was Hank, and he was way too busy dancing with Giselle to talk to me.

Thankfully, around eleven my dad was like, 'Uh, Mia, isn't it Halloween?'

I went, 'Yeah, Dad.'

'Don't you have someplace you'd rather be?'

You know, I hadn't forgotten the whole *Rocky Horror* thing, but I figured Grandmere needed me. Sometimes family things are more important than friend things – even romance things.

But as soon as I heard that, I was like, 'Um, yes.'

The movie started at midnight down at the Village Cinema – about fifty blocks away. If I hurried, I could make it. Well, Lars and I could make it.

There was only one problem. We had no costumes: and on Halloween, they don't let you into the theatre if you come in street clothes.

'What do you mean, you don't have a costume?' Fergie had overheard our conversation.

I held out the skirt of my dress. 'Well,' I said, dubiously. 'I guess I could pass for Glinda the Good Witch. Only I don't have a wand. No crown, either.'

I had no idea Fergie was so good at crafts – but she is, as Catherine Zeta Jones-Douglas pointed out to me, a woman of many talents. In any case, next thing I knew, she was whipping me up a wand from a bunch of crystal drink stir-rers that she tied together with some ivy from the centre-piece. Then she fashioned this big crown for me out of some menus and a glue gun she had in her bag.

And you know what? It looked good, just like the one in *Wizard of Oz*! (She turned the writing so it was on the inside of the crown.)

'There,' Fergie said, when she was through. 'Glinda the

Good Witch.' She looked at Lars. 'And you're easy. You're James Bond.'

Lars seemed pleased. You could tell he'd always fantasized about being a secret agent.

No one was more pleased than me, however. My fantasy of Michael seeing me in this gorgeous dress was about to be realized. What's more, the outfit was going to give me the confidence I needed to confront him about Jo-C-rox.

So, with my father's blessing – I would have stopped to say goodbye to Grandmere, only she and Gerald Ford were doing the tango out on the dance floor (no, I am not kidding) – I was out of there like a shot—

And stumbled right into a thorny patch of reporters.

'Princess Mia!' they yelled. 'Princess Mia, what are your feelings about your mother's elopement?'

I was about to let Lars hustle me into the limo without saying anything to the reporters. But then I had an idea. I grabbed the nearest microphone and went, 'I just want to say to anyone who is watching that Albert Einstein High School is the best school in Manhattan, maybe even North America, and that we have the most excellent faculty and the best student population in the world, and anyone who doesn't recognize that is just kidding himself, Mr Taylor.'

(Mr Taylor is Shameeka's dad.)

Then I shoved the microphone back at its owner and hopped into the limo.

We almost didn't make it. First of all, because of the parade, the traffic downtown was criminal. Secondly, there was a line to get in to the Village Cinema that wound all the way around the block! I had the limo driver cruise the length of it, while Lars and I scanned the assorted hordes. It was pretty hard to recognize my friends, because everyone was wearing costumes.

But then I saw this group of really weird looking people dressed in WWII Army fatigues. They were all covered in fake blood, and some of them had missing limbs. They were holding a big sign that said, *Looking for Private Ryan*. Standing next to them was a girl wearing a black lacy slip and a fake beard. And standing next to her was a boy dressed as a Mafioso type, holding a violin case.

The violin case was what did it.

'Stop the car,' I shrieked.

The limo pulled over, and Lars and I got out. The girl in the nightie went, 'Oh, my God! You came! You came!'

It was Lilly. And standing next to her, a big pile of bloody intestines coming out of his Army jacket, was her brother, Michael.

'Quick,' he said, to Lars and me. 'Get in line. I got two extra tickets just in case you ended up making it after all.'

There was some grumbling from the people behind us as Lars and I cut in, but all he had to do was turn so that his shoulder holster showed, and they got quiet pretty quick. Lars's Glock, being real and all, was pretty scary looking.

'Where's Hank?' Lilly wanted to know.

'He couldn't make it,' I said. I didn't want to tell her why. You know, that last time I'd seen him, he'd been dancing with Giselle. I didn't want Lilly to think Hank preferred supermodels to, you know, us.

'He cannot come. Good,' Boris said, firmly.

Lilly shot him a warning look then, pointing at me, demanded, 'What are you supposed to be?'

'Duh,' I said. 'I'm Glinda the Good Witch.'

'I knew that,' Michael said. 'You look really . . . You look really . . . '

He seemed unable to go on. I must, I realized, with a sinking heart, look really stupid.

'You are way too glam for Halloween,' Lilly declared.

Glam? Well, glam was better than stupid, I guess. But why couldn't Michael have said so?

I eyed her. 'Um,' I said. 'What, exactly, are you?'

She fingered the straps to her slip, then fluffed out her fake beard.

'Hello,' she said, in a very sarcastic voice. 'I'm a Freudian slip.'

Boris indicated his violin case. 'And I am Al Capone,' he said. 'Chicago gangster.'

'Good for you, Boris,' I said, noticing he was wearing a sweater, and yes, it was tucked into his trousers. He can't help being totally foreign, I guess.

Someone tugged on my skirt. I looked around, and there was Kenny, my Bio. partner. He was in Army fatigues too, and missing an arm.

'You made it!' he cried.

'I did,' I said. The excitement in the air was contagious.

Then the line started moving. Michael and Kenny's friends from the Computer Club, who made up the rest of his bloody platoon, started marching and going, 'Hut two three four. Hut two three four.'

Well, they can't help it, either. They're in the computer club, after all.

It wasn't until the movie started that I began to realize something weird was going on. I very cleverly manoeuvered myself in the aisle so that I would end up sitting next to Michael. Lars was supposed to be on my other side.

But somehow Lars got pushed out, and Kenny ended up on my other side.

Not that it mattered . . . then. Lars just sat behind me. I hardly noticed Kenny, even though he kept trying to talk to me. I answered him, but all I could think about was

Michael. Did he really think I looked stupid? When should I mention that I happen to know that he is Jo-C-rox? I had this little speech all rehearsed. I was going to be like, Hey, seen any good cartoons lately?

Lame, I know, but how else was I supposed to bring it up?

I could hardly wait for the movie to be over so I could spring my offensive.

Rocky Horror, even if you can't wait for it to end, is pretty fun. Everybody just acts like a lunatic. People were throwing bread at the screen, and putting up umbrellas when it rained in the movie, and dancing the Pelvic Thrust. It really is one of the best movies of all time. It almost beats *Dirty Dancing* as my favourite, except, of course, there's no Patrick Swayze.

But you know, I'd forgotten there aren't really any scary parts. So I didn't actually get a chance to pretend to be scared so Michael could put his arm round me, or anything.

Which kind of sucks, if you think about it.

But, hey, I got to sit by him, didn't I? For like two hours. In the dark. That's something, isn't it? And he kept laughing and looking at me to see whether or not I was laughing too. That counts, right? I mean, when someone keeps checking to see whether you think the same things are funny that he does? That totally counts for something.

The only problem was, I couldn't help noticing that Kenny was doing the same thing. You know, laughing and then looking at me to see if I was laughing too.

That should have been my next clue.

After the movie, we all went out to breakfast at Round the Clock. And this is where things got even more weird.

I had been to Round the Clock before, of course – where else in Manhattan can you get pancakes for two dollars? – but never quite this late, and never with a bodyguard. Poor Lars was looking a little worse for wear by that time. He kept ordering cup after cup of coffee. I was jammed in at this table between Michael and Kenny – funny how that kept happening – with Lilly and Boris and the entire Computer Club all around us. Everyone was talking really loud and at the same time, and I was having a really hard time figuring out how I was ever going to bring up the cartoon thing, when all of a sudden Kenny went, right in my ear, 'Had any interesting mail lately?'

I am sorry to say that it was only then that the truth dawned.

I should have known, of course.

It hadn't been Michael. *Michael wasn't Jo-C-rox.*

I think a part of me must have known that all along. I mean, it really isn't like Michael to do anything anonymously. He just isn't the type not to sign his name to something. I guess I'd been suffering from a bad case of wishful thinking, or something.

A REALLY bad case of wishful thinking.

Because of course Jo-C-rox wasn't Michael. Of course it turned out to be Kenny.

Not that there's anything wrong with Kenny. There totally isn't. He is a really, really nice guy. I mean, I really like Kenny Showalter. Really, I do.

But he's not Michael Moscovitz.

I looked up at Kenny after he'd made that comment about having any interesting mail lately, and I tried to smile. I really did.

I said, 'Oh, Kenny. Are you Jo-C-rox?'

Kenny grinned.

'Yes,' Kenny said. 'Didn't you figure it out?'

No. Because I am a complete idiot.

'Uh-huh,' I said, forcing another smile. 'Finally.'

'Good.' Kenny looked pleased. 'Because you really do

remind me of Josie, you know. Of *Josie and the Pussycats*, I mean. See, she's lead singer in a rock group, and she solves mysteries on the side. She's cool. Like you.'

Oh, my God. *Kenny*. My Bio. partner, *Kenny*. Six foot tall, totally gawky Kenny, who always gives me the answers in Bio. I'd forgotten he's like this huge Japanese anime fan. I mean, he'd only told me he was dedicating his life towards promoting it . . . once he'd found a cure for cancer. Of course he watches the Cartoon Network. He's practically addicted to it. *Batman* is like his favourite thing of all time.

Oh, someone shoot me. Someone please shoot me.

I smiled. I'm afraid my smile was very weak.

But Kenny didn't care.

'And, you know, in later episodes,' Kenny said, encouraged by my smile, 'Josie and the Pussycats go up into space. So she's also a pioneer into space exploration.'

Oh, God, make this be a bad dream. Please make this be a bad dream, and let me wake up and have it not be true!

All I could do was thank my lucky stars that I hadn't said anything to Michael. Could you imagine if I'd gone up to him and said what I'd planned to? He'd have thought I'd forgotten to take my medication, or something.

'Anyway,' Kenny said. 'You want to go out sometime, Mia? With me, I mean?'

Oh, God. I hate that. I really hate that. You know, when people go, 'Do you want to go out with me sometime?' instead of 'Do you want to go out with me next Tuesday?' Because that way you can make up an excuse. Because then you can always go, 'Oh, no, on Tuesday I have this thing.'

But you can't go, 'No, I don't want to go out with you EVER.'

Because that would be too mean.

441

And I can't be mean to Kenny. I like Kenny. I really do. He's very funny and sweet and everything.

But do I want his tongue in my mouth?

Not so much.

What could I say? 'No, Kenny? No, Kenny, I don't want to go out with you ever, because I happen to be in love with my best friend's brother?'

You can't say that.

Well, maybe some girls can.

But not me.

'Sure, Kenny,' I said.

After all, how bad could a date with Kenny be? What doesn't kill us makes us stronger. That's what Grandmere says, anyway. Usually she's referring to slow waiters, but you get the drift.

After that, I had no choice but to let Kenny put his arm round me – the only one he had, the other being tightly secured beneath his costume to give him the appearance of having been severely injured in a land mine explosion.

But we were all jammed in so closely at that table that Kenny's arm, as it went round my shoulders, jostled Michael, and he looked over at us . . .

And then he looked over at Lars, really fast. Almost like he – I don't know . . .

Saw what was going on, and wanted Lars to put a stop to it?

No. No, of course not. It couldn't be that.

But it is true that when Lars, who was busy pouring sugar into like his fifth cup of coffee that night, didn't look up, Michael stood and said, 'Well, I'm beat. What do you say we call it a night?'

Everyone looked at him like he was crazy. I mean, some people were still finishing their food and all. Lilly even went,

442

'What's with you, Michael? Gotta catch up on your beauty sleep?'

But Michael totally took out his wallet and started counting out how much he owed.

So then I stood up really fast and said, 'I'm tired too. Lars, could you call the car?'

Lars, delighted finally to be leaving, whipped out his mobile phone and dialled. Kenny, beside me, started saying stuff like, 'It's a shame you have to go so early,' and 'So, Mia, can I call you?'

This last question caused Lilly to look from me to Kenny and then back again. Then she looked at Michael. Then she stood up too.

'Come on, Al,' she said, giving Boris a rap on the head. 'Let's blow this juke joint.'

Only of course Boris didn't understand. 'What is a juke joint?' he asked. 'And why are we blowing it?'

Everyone started digging around for money to pay the bill . . . which was when I remembered that I didn't have any. Money, I mean. I didn't even have a purse to put money in. That was one part of my wedding ensemble Grandmere had forgotten.

I elbowed Lars and whispered, 'Have you got any cash? I'm a little low at the moment.'

Lars nodded and reached for his wallet. That's when Kenny, who noticed this, went, 'Oh, no, Mia. Your pancakes are on me.'

This, of course, completely freaked me out. I didn't want Kenny to pay for my pancakes. Or Lars's five cups of coffee, either. I mean, I am a feminist. I don't let boys pay for me.

Also, I didn't want Kenny to think this had been a date, or anything.

'Oh, no,' I said. 'That isn't necessary.'

Which didn't have at all the desired effect, since Kenny said, all stiffly, 'I insist,' and started throwing dollar bills down on the table.

Remembering that, while I'm a feminist, I'm also a princess and supposed to be gracious, and all, I said, 'Well, thank you very much, Kenny.'

Which was when Lars handed Michael a twenty and said, 'For the movie tickets.'

Only then Michael wouldn't take my money – OK, it was Lars's money, but my dad would totally have paid him back – either. He looked really embarrassed, and went, 'Oh, no. My treat,' even after I strenuously insisted.

So then I had to say, 'Well, thank you very much, Michael,' when all I really wanted to say was, 'Get me out of here!'

Because with two different guys paying for me, it was like I'd been out on a date with both of them at once!

Which I guess, in a way, I had.

You would think I would be very excited about this. I mean, considering I'd never been out even with *one* guy before, let alone *two* at the same time.

Except that it was totally and completely *not* fun. Because, for one thing, I didn't actually want to be going out with one of them at all.

And for another, that was the one who'd actually confessed to liking me . . . even if it had been anonymously.

The whole thing was excruciating, and all I wanted to do was go home and get in bed and pull the covers up over my head and pretend it hadn't happened.

Only I couldn't even do that because, what with my mom and Mr G being in Cancun, I have to stay up at the Plaza with Grandmere and my dad until they get back.

But just when I thought things had sunk to an all-time

low, as everyone was piling into the limo (well, a few people asked for rides home, and how could I say no? It was on the way, and besides, it wasn't like we didn't have the room), Michael, who ended up standing beside me, waiting for his turn to get into the car, went, 'What I meant to say before, Mia, was that you look . . . you look really . . . '

I blinked up at him in the pink and blue light from the neon Round the Clock sign in the window behind us. It's amazing, but even bathed in pink and blue neon, with fake intestines hanging out of his shirt, Michael still looked totally—

'You look really nice in that dress,' he said, all in a rush.

I smiled up at him, feeling just like Cinderella all of a sudden – you know, at the end of the Disney movie, when Prince Charming finally finds her and puts the slipper on her foot and her rags change back into the ballgown and all the mice come out and start singing?

That's how I felt, just for a second.

Then this voice right beside us said, 'Are you guys coming, or what?' and we looked over and there was Kenny sticking his head and his one unsevered arm out of the sun roof of the limo.

'Um,' I said, feeling totally and utterly embarrassed. 'Yes.'

And I got into the limo like nothing had happened.

And actually, if you think about it, nothing really had.

Except that the whole way back to the Plaza, this little voice inside my brain was going, 'Michael said I looked nice. Michael said *I* looked nice. *Michael* said I looked nice.'

And you know what? Maybe Michael didn't write those notes. And maybe he doesn't think I'm the Josiest girl in school.

But he thought I looked nice in my pink dress. And that's all that matters to me.

And now I am sitting in Grandmere's suite at the hotel, surrounded by piles of wedding and baby presents, with Rommel trembling down at the other end of the couch in a pink cashmere sweater. I am supposed to be writing thank you notes, but of course I am writing in my journal instead.

No one seems to have noticed, though, I guess because Mamaw and Papaw are here. They stopped by to say good-bye on their way to the airport before they fly back to Indiana. Right now, my two grandmothers are making lists of baby names, and talking about who to invite to the christening (oh, no. Not again) while my dad and Papaw are discussing crop rotation, as this is an important topic both to Indiana farmers as well as Genovian olive growers.

Even though, of course, Papaw owns a hardware store, and Dad is a prince. But whatever. At least they're *talking.*

Hank is here too, to say goodbye and to try to convince his grandparents they are not doing the wrong thing, leaving him here in New York – though to tell the truth, he isn't doing such a good job at either, since he hasn't once got off his mobile phone since he arrived. Most of these calls seem to be from last night's bridesmaids.

And I'm thinking that, all in all, things aren't so bad. I mean, I am getting a baby brother or sister, and have also acquired not just a stepfather who is exceptionally good at Algebra, but a foozball table, as well.

And my dad proved that there is at least one person on this planet who is not afraid of Grandmere . . . and even Grandmere seems a bit more mellow than usual, in spite of never having made it to Baden-Baden.

Though she still isn't talking to my dad, except when she absolutely has to.

And yes, it is true that later today I have to meet Kenny

back at the Village Cinema for a Japanese anime marathon, since I said I would, and all.

But after that I am going down to Lilly's, and we are going to work on next week's show, which is about repressed memories. We are going to try to hypnotize one another and see if we can remember any of our past lives. Lilly is convinced, for instance, that in one of her past lives, she was Elizabeth I.

And you know what? I, for one, believe her.

Anyway, after that, I am spending the night at Lilly's, and we are going to rent *Dirty Dancing* and try to make it like *Rocky Horror*. You know, where you yell things in response to the actors' lines, and throw things at the screen?

And there is a very good chance that tomorrow morning, Michael will come to the Moscovitzes' breakfast table wearing pyjama bottoms and a robe, and forget to tie the robe like he did once before.

Which would actually make for a very profound moment, if you ask me.

A *very* profound moment.

MEG CABOT

Ho, ho, ho. Grab your tiara – it's CHRISTMAS!

Christmas is a time for giving. So, with a little help from her beloved friends and family (plus Grandmere), Princess Mia presents the ultimate guide to Christmas. From choosing your boyfriend the perfect gift to releasing your inner party-princess, Mia has the festive period all wrapped up.

Includes 'Mia's Christmas' – the hilarious story of Mia's Christmas trip to Genovia.

MEG CABOT

The tall, flaxen-haired lord brought colour to Victoria's cheeks – not to mention a flutter to her pulse. He was just so handsome. What girl would *not* blush? And he was flirting with her!

Lady Victoria Arbuthnot is used to doing precisely what she wants. So she's not exactly overjoyed at the thought of being packed off to England to find a husband. But when she bags drop-dead-gorgeous Lord Malfrey before she's even got off the boat from faraway India, she's delighted. Then a dashing young sea captain starts persistently interfering and spreading stories about her man. Could it be that Vicky's happy-ever-after with Lord M. might not be so happy after all?